CW00517383

REDO ME

again and again

by Malcolm

Copyright © 2022 D.A. Maclean
All rights reserved.

No part of this publication may be reproduced or transmitted in any form or by any means, electronic or mechanical, including photography, recording, or any information storage and retrieval system without the prior written consent from the publisher and author, except in the instance of quotes for reviews. No part of this book may be uploaded without the permission of the publisher and author, nor be otherwise circulated in any form of binding or cover other than that in which it is originally published.

This is a work of fiction and any resemblance to persons, living or dead, or places, actual events or locales is purely coincidental. The characters and names are products of the authors imagination and used fictitiously.

The publisher and author acknowledge the trademark status and trademark ownership of all trademarks, service marks and word marks mentioned in this book.

Formatting: Polgarus Studio, Tasmania, Australia
Cover design: Altitude Design Studio, Kerikeri, New Zealand

'In the depths of winter, I finally learned
that within me there lay an invincible summer.'

Camus

Me

In this life I am known as Malcolm.

My spirit has lived many lives over aeons.

I tell of some lives but not all. They are memories from my spirit.

'REDO ME again and again' was written during 2000 to 2005.

I refer to these years as the time of 'the writing'.

I wanted to share The Knowledge, and inspire hope.

REDO ME again and again

by Malcolm

Aeons ago

Glimpses

Finding Purpose

The present and the future

Epilogue

Dawn of Humanity

She is waking up. She is bringing warmth.
The light of her sleep is still visible at half its full size.
She is bringing life. The plants will grow; her animals will feed.

I take the Giver's girl-child from my body by the hand
and show her all that we see in all places.
Birth of the dark and the light.
Birth of the waters from the sky and the soil.
Birth of plants; birth of birds; birth of animals; birth of my kind.

I arrange stones in a circle around us
and the rest of the group enter.
We celebrate the goddess as she starts her new day.
All we see, hear and taste is her gift.
Everything is a part of her.
My child, what other way can there be?

Aeons ago

1: Return to Earth

My spirit is to return to Earth, yet again, into one of countless lives that will take it through hundreds of thousands of years.

Once again I am moving, across distances well understood for longer than human imagination. I pass the lights of great clusters at infinite distance, until I see the light of the universe which holds the spiral galaxy called the Milky Way. My speed must slow if my journey will take me back to the tiny yellow star called the Sun, with its pretty blue planet, the Earth. I am to be born again.

The ocean is wild this morning, and the wind sweeps into our cave over waves higher than the largest of our group. We are hungry; it is hard to gather food. I look upon the one who gave me birth, and see that she has left the child she was feeding at the last sun light. Her milk has all gone. I think it is not long before she will be food for the animal kind. Those that look like me are lucky to last for as many cold periods as there are fingers and toes on my body.

Hair covers our body and we move mostly on all fours, sometimes standing on our rear quarters to gain advantage over rival or beast. I have seen as many cold times as almost all fingers. I now gather food with the strongest of my group.

I fear, as strong one has pushed the one born before me out into the cold to gather food from the shore or forest, and he is looking my way. We can perish if we go in small numbers or alone while the animals are hungry.

It has happened, and I am in the forest trying to see where the ones before me have gone. I hear noises and look to see the worst of my fears. It strikes swiftly and the pain soon ends.

My kind stands now and we have less hair on our bodies. The sun is always hot, and we try and stay in the water for periods of time each day. Hair covers only parts of our body.

This has been a good life, as our dominant male has given us a large area to hunt and gather. He struck a dominant male in the next group with the bone of a beast. We have the best food and more females. Our offspring will be more common. The one with the first weapon will have the most children at hearth.

It is probable I shall see the seasons change for the fingers on the hands of two creatures and the toes of one.

The great ice stretches from the mountains to the north. The furs are thick on my body and I am straight and tall. I carry a sharp stone and the leg bone of a large beast. Beside me walks my mate and others of my body and group. We stay in a large group and fear animals less than other creatures, apart from the large cats, bears and mammoth.

In our group we are fortunate to have a female who carries the memories of the herbs of healing. Our spirit man also has great knowledge of healing, as well as the ancient memories of our ancestors. It is not a wise thing to be part of a group without these mysteries.

2: The Ancients

It is 250,000 years before I started 'the writing' and my spirit has been reborn many times over a great time span. I am now born into a civilization that will later be known as 'the Ancients'.

My people have long inhabited all parts of Earth. During the later period of our global spread the Earth was warm, and our preferred homelands were in far north and south latitudes. This was a disaster for us at the close of our time.

We have science, art and music. Above all we have long ago, and still from time to time, gained knowledge from high entities that have had life in our world. For more than 350,000 years we have known the basic laws of the Spirit and we have obeyed these laws.

The most important law of the Spirit that we follow is to live in harmony with all nature. We must live a life that uses only those resources that we can replace. Our people retain the population suitable to the environment, and teach their children to use nature at a rate it can sustain. We sometimes control animal species if they in turn use more than nature can provide.

We spread out across the Earth in family groups, with community centres that are globally connected. We have for thousands of years used the powers of nature to comfort our lives: the sun, tides, wind and running water. We also have science that is capable of moving swiftly, lifting great weights, and cutting solid materials with great accuracy.

Ours was the most spiritual, knowledgeable and physically responsible development of humankind to happen on this planet. However, in the end, even our great science did not protect us from the power of the universe.

3: Joala, an Ancient

I open my eyes to my old world again. It is a time of greatness. I am to grow and learn all the lessons of life. As I grow the elders teach me of the spiritual importance of my place on Earth, and how to gain the most joy and contribution that the physical existence can provide. I, as always, know nothing of my previous lives. However, what I am and will be is partly affected by previous existence. The most powerful influence will be the people around me and the environment in which I live. The spirit guide will travel with my life, as with all life of a higher order.

I am from a land south of the equator called Golanner. The land is rich and green in the winter and golden in the summer. We grow food in plenty for ourselves, and a little extra for when the crops of some other region on the Earth fail due to flood, drought or disease. Life is good. Our diet consists mainly of vegetarian content with small amounts of meat which we source mainly from wild game, as this is the way of nature. We take care not to over-harvest any family of the animal kingdom, only holding them in enclosures if their numbers are threatened.

Tonight is the start of the first of the gatherings. From ancient times at the end of harvest, our people have travelled to express a joy for life and to share the gifts from learning. It is also a time when participants get to explore the joy of sex and find partners, sometimes for life. Our life can be for a long time, as we have the capacity to replace the ageing processes and can reach ages of hundreds of years.

However I am twenty-seven years old, and this year I hope to have time with a woman from the river country of the people of great music. Our elders select, in co-operation with those from around the Earth, those who offer benefit from learning of environmental and cultural developments. This knowledge is used to keep balance on our planet. Selection also helps with new partners for genetic diversity.

There are close to five hundred people who will travel at first light to the land called Eden. The Earth is named by area names, but not divided into countries with borders to argue over. No people own the land, but recognition is given naturally to the rights of a people who look after any area they occupy, and this sometimes passes from generation to generation. Our population is kept at such a level that disputes can be easily solved, and wealth and quality of life shared.

I rise from my bed and gather few possessions required for the journey. Our dwellings are never large but blend with a diverse beauty into the surrounds. My house is made of earth with thatching for a roof. It has power from individual sun catchers and community wind and water generators. I can do basic cooking but, as with this morning, I eat in the central eating house.

We then gather together to board the tube, a part of a global network of transport that can move a great number of people around the Earth to almost any location, with the minimum use of resources, at the maximum speed with great safety. It is moved with both electric power and the use of the magnetic poles.

The journey is fast and the countryside blurs as we reach maximum speed, then we stop very rapidly for people in various places. We journey over much ocean. Eventually we change when we reach the parallel of the direction we are to take, which is east-west. There is much ocean this time, and then we travel over desert and mountains to a location only 187 kilometres from Eden, and 289 kilometres from the gathering. Small flyers will take us the rest of the way at a much slower rate, so we arrive at our destination just before dark.

I raise the tent, a simple elegant device, not too far from the facilities provided by our hosts. Many of us move off to the community eating area. Tonight will be early to bed, and tomorrow who knows! I know the river country people are attractive. The young women stand tall and proud. Their skin is lightly tanned and their breasts full and bodies curved. The average height of all people on Earth is over two metres but there is a tendency for those in the hot climates to be slightly taller and leaner.

I retire to my tent, saying goodnight to friends as I go. We are glad it is a season of good weather. Our beds are warm and closed to beast and weather. I will dream long and easy tonight. Tomorrow will bring the start of the music, dancing, the sharing of spiritual stories, and past knowledge of legend and history. We will also learn of the skills of our hosts. Many areas specialize in one or two fields of science. They then pass the gifts of science to all other areas of the Earth to combine, and return with the gifts of other knowledge.

4

We sit in an amphitheatre and the elders of each people introduce us in groups. I get to see many of the individuals and hope I will soon meet some in particular, either for their interests or their beauty. I feel drawn to one particular young woman who they say sings of the journey of humans and paints pictures with great skill. Her eyes are blue and her hair short and fair. She moves with grace and confidence. I am sure she will attract the attention of many men. Still, my time may come.

My time not only comes but she notices me, comes straight to me at recess, and asks me if she has met me before. I also feel this way, but I know neither one of us is likely to have been in the same location before. Still, the feeling is almost overpowering. We have many similar interests starting to emerge from the beginning. This is most peculiar for, although she is attractive, it does not feel like a normal male female attraction. Her name is Serina. My name for that matter is Joala.

We decide to seek out a spirit woman or man and discover the journeys we may have had in past lives. This is not hard, for such spirit knowledge is common amongst our people. All people feel close to their spiritual past. However, if there is a dark side we may be simply guided away from each other, although it is usual for one to feel distant to a presence that has bad spirit memories. It is not uncommon for people to be born over several lifetimes and those they knew before to be attracted to their lives and activities, often competing strongly and opposing, or the opposite, for reasons they cannot understand themselves.

The first of the meetings, that occur at most harvest and other major gatherings, is to be conducted by the main spirit leaders. It is on the spiritual and written legends of the history of humans on Earth. Serina and myself, like many young people, doubt much of The Word. It is strange that, as people grow older, they seem to accept more of The Word. Many people are over three hundred years old. This is what has been passed on for hundreds of thousands of years:

The human journey has been influenced by evolution.

The human journey has been influenced on purpose by visitors from the stars. It is believed that the first of these visits took place about 15 million years ago and again, we think, 2 million years ago and 600,000 years ago. There are probably occasions in between that are not passed on in our history.

It is said that the visitors that came from the stars were not alive, but as machines in the form of hominids; and that they came with the imprint of their makers, and placed the genetic makeup of this kind into some of the females of our kind.

It is said that these influences came mainly when the populations had been devastated by global disease or geographic disaster.

Serina and I find much of it hard to believe, and I am finding it hard to listen. The longer I spend by her side, the more her chemistry is enfolding my thoughts and thickening my blood. My journey would rather be down to the riverbank and over the geography of her wonderful womanhood. Such will always be the way of all people. The way she looks at me and her body signs are telling me that we will not be able to wait long, and I fear we will miss some of the activities of the gathering today and that, if I am lucky, the night will be long.

She is running ahead of me. The trees part to show a stretch of sand and water beyond. She has brought me upriver to a secluded lagoon. The cloth wrapper falls from her slender body and I wonder at her beauty. For this I am happy to live a thousand lifetimes.

5: Survival

The Earth became warmer over thousands of years and people lived mainly in the far north and south regions of Earth.

For thousands of years we knew of the laws of the Spirit and we had science, culture and global communication. But now this time of greatness has ended abruptly and we were not prepared to survive.

The Earth has been struck by an object from space causing giant waves to roll over much of the land, and volcanoes to explode and earthquakes greater than any we have had in recorded history.

Only occasional groups such as mine lived for short periods near the equator. We were misfits, rebels and tended to be nomadic. Being near the equator has saved our lives for a time.

The sky became dark with ash and dust. Now, in a very short period, mountains of ice have covered much of Earth. The tropical rains have all but dried up. Glaciers have destroyed the tubes and the sun rarely shines. The number of animals is greatly reduced. Vegetation is becoming harder to find in pockets of warm water near volcanic activity and on the edge of windswept mountains. We are returning to primitive life very quickly in order to survive.

Most people died in the first days after the disaster. The survivors have come from the regions of population. They are not many in number. Their stories tell of fires covering all the areas they travelled following the impact and that the land became hot with gasses. The survivors think that, as the sun never shone, the winds cooled rapidly and the water began to freeze. Many of those who survived the impact suffered death by freezing. The cold and destruction drove survivors towards the equator but as conditions deteriorated nearly all perished. Now we are few. We are alone.

The wind is blowing outside and the waves are higher than the leader of our group but today is a good day. The sky has parted and the sun reached the mouth of the cave for the first time. They may let the next child, who is born to nurture at my breast, live. They have killed two children I have birthed and still I lie with them, for my body warmth and the use of my body is their reason to preserve my life. I hope for the sun to shine every day.

Much time has passed and new life is growing on the hills that roll down to the river, which has given us life as it travels to the ocean where we live. New life has grown in my body and entered the world. They have looked away; the child will survive while there is food.

This day is a good day. They say there are more fish in the river and movement has been seen in the ocean. Today they have seen seals in large numbers and penguins and more flocks of birds.

The number of our people, which went from about 700 to 95, has risen to 137. There is talk of sending people off to communicate with others who must have survived. The sky clears often.

The leader has spoken. We have a new name which is to be both our identity and our purpose. We are to be called the Chosen People. It is said that our purpose will be to survive, to remember, and to preserve the laws of the great Spirit. I have seen the leader break most of the laws. Still, we are and others are not.

It has been said this is the land of the Chosen People, and the first story to be handed down for our people of the future will be when the water washed over the Earth, and ice covered and destroyed all the great that we created. It has been said that the story of our survival must not be forgotten. It has been said that the knowledge of the creators from the stars must be a memory preserved.

6: Clan Storyteller

My spirit is born again on what will be known as the North African plains. Our clan is strong. We have many clans now and we cover much country but vast areas of ice still make travel a rare thing. Still, we grow in numbers and the stories are passed on to our children. Each clan has a storyteller and I am to replace our man who tells of history. He is old now and will soon journey to the ice, leaving the stories with me for the future.

I tell of the creation of humans from those who came from the heavens above. I tell of great people who lived long lives and had much knowledge. I tell how they upset the creators and were punished. Water covered the Earth and left only the Chosen People.

We are descendants of the Chosen People whose tribe still lives in the North. I have children at my hearth and the woman Jelana. We feel that we are spirits who have known a long journey. She seems to know my every thought. I also have the stories of the Spirit to tell. These I find very hard to remember and teach. Many of the laws conflict with our laws needed for survival in our extremely cold and harsh climate.

Our everyday needs are simple. We hunt for food and fur. My weapons are as important as the stories I tell. Often the stories at night are of the kill of the day. The women and children gather to learn as we tell how we outwitted the beast and brought home the gift of food and warmth.

We do not move far during our lifetime, only seeking new hunting ground if the game moves on, or the numbers at our campfires grow too large and a new clan is formed at one of the gatherings. The gatherings are important for my stories are told, and it is agreed by other clan storytellers that the memories are safe.

Glimpses

7: Mother of new Northern Knowledge

It is 145,000 years before 'the writing'. My spirit has been reborn into many lives as both male and female, as it is necessary for the integrity of the living journey to look through the eyes of both sexes. These memories are a glimpse of some lives.

The people I have been a part of for several lifetimes are moving across the land that will be known as the Middle East.

This day is warm. It is good to be moving again, following the animal of the hoof. There is good food, and we are travelling up a river valley where the women and men find fish and grain is plenty. I can see much overhang for shelter under the cliffs which follow the valley so I believe our leader will settle here. We are two moons travel from the nearest of our people. It would be good to light the fires and protect ourselves from the cold winds of the coming winter.

I have seen the change of fourteen seasons and my body is ripe for a mate. I look with hunger at the strong bodies of the men of my tribe. My nipples become firm and the blood surges through the centre of my body. If we settle here I will be a part of the fertility rites, when my body will be made available to the men and afterwards I will choose a mate. The women of my tribe are much stronger in position once they have a fire of their own. Each day I gather food; the plants and fish that we need for our evening meal.

Time has passed and we have moved into a large group of caves and overhanging cliffs. It is a land of plenty and great beauty. My furs are still spread with those of the single women who have reached reproductive age.

Tonight there is much excited talk. The hunters have returned and spoken with astonishment at the discovery of the remains of several freshly killed ox cattle. The meat has been cut off the bones and selected bones removed. They were not killed by wolves or the great cats. We are afraid for our people, as our memories state we are the only ones who would be on this land. Tomorrow our hunters will arm themselves and look for this strange tribe. They will probably be a peaceful people.

The days have passed and our hunters have been sighted returning from up the valley. As they get closer we see strangers are amongst them. They are large and wear their furs and clothing differently to us. They are moving towards the ledge of the cave now and I see, to my amazement, that their faces are very different to ours. They have very large foreheads and the young and women have no chins. Their shoulders are broader than ours and they look strong. Their skin is very light in colour. They carry spears and other wooden implements, for what I do not know. The women have bags and other carrying devices.

Our leader, Tondar, stops many paces from our entrance barrier and speaks to the strangers, before he proceeds alone to stand in front of his partner. After brief discussion with her, he addresses us. He tells us they saw the smoke of the strangers' fires and met them over a day ago. They were offered food and lodgings and treated with great respect. After much sign language they are beginning to communicate. "Two old ones, a male and a female who seem to be a type of spirit people, drew a circle in the earth and drew people all over the circle. They then drew many moons and pointed at us. They also drew marks in the earth that had no meaning to us but which they expect us to understand. It is obvious that they wish to live in harmony, so a group has come to bring gifts and learn of our presence."

Tondar returns to the strangers and leads them into our midst. There is much excitement but some reserve. They are led to the main fire and placed in the position guests of our people occupy. The signal is given and we rush to prepare the evening meal, while our people show the guests our skills at making the necessities for our survival. It is hard to understand their expressions but they seem much impressed with the fineness of our stone tools. They also look with great interest as we show them how we use fire to shape and harden our tools such as spears. They seem very quick to understand, but their hands are large and coarse and have trouble cutting the stone fine when shown how. Still, it is a skill even amongst our people.

The food is ready and they eat the evening meal. It is good to share; still it is hard not to stare. Then, to our amazement, one of them brings out a hide of an ox that has been prepared and shows us the circle with the people. They point to themselves and point to the people in the top of the circle. Then they point to us as the people in the bottom of the circle, often speaking quietly in words we cannot understand.

Our storyteller and healer tell us that they are saying we are of the Old Ones and they are of the Old Ones from another place on the Earth. We do not understand the circle. Then one of them takes a piece of ochre from their clothing and draws shapes all around the circle and takes our storyteller and points at the stars, then points at us and themselves. We are amazed once again for these creatures, so different to us, seem to know a little of our most sacred memories; the creation from the stars and the memories of an old people many moons ago.

It is all we can take for one evening. We are a little afraid that our memories are shared with ones so different. They are shown to an adjoining cave where they will sleep and we will see what tomorrow brings. They also have someone to tend the night fires and keep guard against the animals of the night.

That night I dream of living at the bottom of a circle and I am rising into the blue above, when a most astonishing thing happens and my body seems to fly through the sky at great speed. My reaction is fearful and I am instantly wide awake and back on my furs. I do not sleep for a long time. It feels safer to think of my anticipated fertility rites.

The following day it is decided that it would be good if we learnt more about each other and Tondar has decided that Jimbo, a male of fifteen seasons, and I are to learn all we can of their language and peculiar markings. In return we are to teach them all we can of our language. They seem to understand what Tondar wants and, after a brief discussion, a male and a female who look younger than the others, step forward. After what seems to be a polite goodbye, the rest of the strangers move off down the hill and northward.

8

Time passes and slowly their language comes to us. To our astonishment they seem to have a basic capacity to follow our speech after a few days. Regularly we report to the people what we have learnt.

The first thing is that they are affectionate, friendly creatures. It is rapidly becoming obvious that a bond is forming between us. Our discussions are always held in our cave or out front amongst our people. After a short while these pieces of information are both frightening and wonderful to us:

Their memories have been passed down from before the ice covered Earth, from a people of great knowledge and great age.

They believe in the same great Spirit and the laws are almost the same as ours.

They say Earth is round, and the creators came from the stars that are more plentiful than all the grains of dirt in our land, and that the Spirit, which is within us, is from all those places.

More profoundly, they say the Spirit has been in existence since before the creation of many of those stars, including our round Earth. This, like some long lost echo, we find hard to believe.

Perhaps more amazing than all this, is that they say they have passed down symbols which they call *numbers*, and some of the ancient markings they call *writing.* We are starting to recognize these symbols and are much in awe of such mystery.

The blood has moved from my body and the time has arrived for me to discover the mystery of the fertility rites. The women have heated water and bathed my body. They have prepared a separate place for my sleeping furs. Tonight the leader of our clan will come to me, and for the next cycle of the moon I will experience all the men of my choice. If my blood flows again I will remain without a woman's fire until my blood does not flow. Afterwards, I hope the young man I would choose becomes a partner at my fire.

We now know that these people are spread throughout the country to our north, and that they live in both caves and dwellings of hide over wooden frames.

A group of our people is to travel south to arrange a gathering of the elders and leaders of the clans. Some of them, we hope, will then travel north to meet with these strangers, to see if we can dwell side by side in the same regions. We have also found that these strangers do not occupy the region to the east, and that they had not been long in the area when we made contact with them.

They believe in the teachings of the Old Ones, and seem to think they remember them better than us. Jimbo and I have spoken of this and observed the way they remember our language far quicker than we can remember theirs, so quietly we think they are right. The Old Ones say it is wrong to have more people than you can safely support in your area. As the regions of the strangers are covered in ice much of the time and are very harsh, they have kept their populations small. We, on the other hand, have spread out and created new clans as our people have risen in numbers.

Our people, and those of other groups, have returned. Tomorrow the leaders will discuss where our people will expand to, but it is already said that we will, when the time comes, move into the lands to the north-east and only lightly settle in the lands of the new people.

9

The time has passed and my blood has not come. I have welcomed Jimbo to my hearth. Over time I have found my cooking fires are warm for our strange friends who we now speak freely with. They have asked us to travel north with them when they return. Tondar believes we will gain much knowledge and has chosen some other families to go with us. We are to return to the gathering of the clans after one cycle of the seasons. Jimbo and I are eager to go but I see apprehension on the faces of the rest.

Johan, the male of our new hosts, leads us up the valley at first light. His mate Rasha, whose stomach swells with new life as mine shortly will, walks in the group with me. We travel as fast as we can and make camp early in order to build large fires, as we are small in number and vulnerable to beast.

A few days brings us to the crest of a valley, with a stream and a high cliff system on the north-west. Any cave will be well protected from the cold westerly winds. We are soon to suffer another shock as we see the Other Ones gather at the base of the cliff. There are a number of large wolves roaming freely, even playing with the children. At our look of astonishment we are quickly told they help with the hunting of the ox cattle. This, we are told, is the main food of the Other Ones. The Other Ones is our new way of addressing our new group.

They not only have good caves, but there are dwellings by the cliff base surrounded by large log barricades. We are taken to these and shown individual structures and storage places. We then move up a steep track to a ledge and find a number of caves that have furs for our use.

The change of the seasons happened, and we travelled to the gatherings and gave our findings. Then Jimbo and I announced we wish to return with our newborn to the Other Ones, for we are deeply moved by their beliefs and a new knowledge of the position of what they refer to as the *heavenly bodies*. We also find that the knowledge of numbers and the divisions of the seasons into equal times is intriguing.

To our surprise, some of the families are returning and some of the young. My new numbers tell me we are to be twenty-eight strong.

With the approval of the Other Ones we move into overhanging cliffs, a part day north of our first stay. We are a new clan, and we will share the knowledge of our own people with the Other Ones to create a more complete spirituality and secure future. We will be strong. We will grow in numbers. We will be the new people of the north who live in harmony with the Other Ones.

As time goes by our children become many and grow to maturity and bear children of their own. Even with the cold that is not as kind to our dark skinned bodies, we are living longer. It is because of the healing and nurturing plant knowledge of our life-long strange friends. This knowledge is indeed a great gift from a far distant past.

My body is old now and Jimbo has gone. The life force seems to be growing dim. I thank the great Spirit for this wonderful journey. I am to travel to the ice, and in time this will be the way of my people.

I am alone on the new land of my new people and my life is departing. It comes as no surprise, with the knowledge of two peoples, to feel myself departing into light. My spiritual existence is to return to dominance and more physical lives will some day follow.

My life as Black Legs, mother of the new northern knowledge, was to be one of my higher physical journeys.

10: Naeren

It is 130,000 years before the time of 'the writing'.

For twenty-one seasons I have hunted food for my people. I am Naeren and live on the plains west of the mountains where my people have dwelt for many lifetimes. There is grief in my heart, for the woman of my hearth and her child of this season have been killed by a large cat while gathering seed from the wild grain along the river.

I find comfort in the warmth of the woman of the man named Tefan. She was my woman's closest friend and her grief is genuine. Tefan is a hard man, works her without pity and neglects her badly. She is beaten constantly. Regardless of her bruises she is firm breasted and pretty to the eye. This only adds to her problems as Tefan forbids her to be near other men. So we try not to attract his attention. However, as the season passes we are drawn closer together and, when Tefan is away from camp, we try to find time together, away from the eyes of our clan.

Tefan has not beaten her for many days but he has not spoken to her or me. We fear he is holding back his anger and has been told of our times together.

I try to avoid him seeing me watching, but as the sun sinks low in the sky the woman is returning with her collection of plant foods for the day. She carries her young child and a child of five seasons walks by her side. Tefan meets her by the stream and strikes her to the ground. I find myself running towards them as he starts to repeatedly strike her. There is an anger I have never felt before. I reach down and grasp a rock from the bank of the stream and he turns to face me. In an instant I see surprise, anger, and then fear in his expression. He starts to raise the branch he has been striking the woman with when I feel the rock smash into the bones of his skull.

In an instant I know I have broken the most sacred of our laws; the taking of the life of our people. Life as I have known it is over. My punishment is death. The child flees past me towards the camp and I turn to look upon the expression of the woman I have come to love. I see clearly a look of absolute love and gratitude. I see clearly a look of sheer horror. I hear clearly her last words to me. Flee for your life.

11

I am moving across the stream and into the forest and towards the mountains of the east. My clan will not pursue me far for I am alone, and no other tribe will take in a single man without a tribe of his own. So they believe, and so do I, that my life is over.

My heart is heavy and my mind is full of dread. As night falls I climb high into a tree and tie my body with branches into a fork of the tree. I have not had time to prepare for death; tomorrow will be time enough.

As the night grows long my eyes close into slumber, and slowly a dream in my semi-conscious state takes place. There is an old man talking to the one who gave me life, and he speaks of a people as old as time who dwell over the eastern mountains. I feel myself soaring over high ranges and sweeping down over a valley into the plains below. There is a hunting party of men and boys carrying a large deer towards dwellings at the base of a cliff where women are tending fires and children playing.

I open my eyes and the sun is filtering down through the leaves. The dream and strange flight are still clear in my mind. I wonder if that is death. Then I remember my mother telling of a journey my grandfather took when he was a young man, and how he told her he and a friend had seen people in a new land across the hills. My grandfather died the season before my birth.

I do not believe I can survive, but there is a feeling inside me that I am not supposed to die. If the journey goes south, I have heard that the mountains are not so high and the weather is not so cold. I am afraid to travel at night because of the animals that hunt at night, and I am at risk of being seen by other clans if I travel during the day. I must wait until the moon is over half full, and travel during the late afternoon and the early time of the morning.

I must get food and weapons, and to steal these from a strange tribe would be hard as the area of their camps is not known to me. After dark, when the people of my camp are in their deepest sleep, I believe I can return past the guards and recover some possessions and take food off the drying racks from the camp that I know so well.

The guards have not seen me. The hearth of my dead family is in a simple hut of earth and grass roof. I move quietly in and hear no breathing from my old dwelling. I place a change of clothing and extra furs for warmth on my sleeping furs and gather some sharp tools. There is food drying just one hut away and it is quickly retrieved and wrapped into my furs. I use straps to bind the furs to my back and, taking my sling and two spears, I am quickly past the guards and across the terrain I know so well. By morning I am well to the south-east.

Slowly I will move and hunt and eat. It does not seem that my spirit guide has deserted me and may be the only company I will ever have now. When the time feels right, I will try and find trails of the mountain ibex to follow to the east. These high valley goats may guide my way and provide food for my belly and hides for my survival. If I keep busy my mind will have more hope of stability. There is great danger to me on every level.

12

One full moon has passed and I have seen many signs of people and some clan groups in the distance. At times I am forced to travel in the open but mostly keep close to the mountains and the timber of their foothills.

I have followed a grassy valley onto the higher plateau and located tracks which seem to be fresh. This is good for the hunt. Tomorrow it will be time to start to dry and store food. Once in the high passes and the ice and snow sets in, it may be many days without a kill.

It takes a few days to prepare the food before I am ready to go. The fear is so great but if a move is not made I will stay and perish. I see no human prints on the trail but still great care must be taken.

After several days the snow is taking over from the grass and occasional shrubs, and the decision is made to sleep long and rest for a day before pushing for the high pass.

Tonight I caught a small makhor and the evening meal is good. I have seen no sign of human for many days, so use the flint and dry grass I carry to light a small fire for some warmth. Tomorrow the only work will be to forage for wood along the trail from the shrubby outcrops.

It has been many days since my stay on the plateau and I rest fleetingly, as fear of freezing and not waking up is always on my mind. Several times I have had to turn back and try another route. Animal prints are not common now and seem to go in no set direction. I continue to climb, keeping the sun mostly to the offside of my throwing arm. The ground begins to fall away, and I now have to be careful not to slide on the ice or snow and over the edge to certain death.

My spirits lift as, in the distance, I get my first view of the plains beyond.

Then I sleep and wake up stiff but hungry and ready to survive. My last fire is stoked and I rest for a day and start the journey again. Before leaving the higher ground several fires are spotted and I choose the one which seems to have the greatest smoke stream. As it appears from where I stand, it looks more than one day out. I will not reach the camp.

They may have been around me for some time. They do not approach, but allow me to move as if I am prey being hunted at their leisure. Suddenly, over a hill, I find the trail leads directly into a narrow gorge, and on turning I find them armed and several spears land in the ground behind me. The message is clear; I am to proceed into the gorge.

The walls of the gorge are only about three times the height of a man, and it is not long before a barrier of logs appears to block the gorge. On reaching the barrier I look up to see they are along the top in considerable numbers. As I back away from the barrier, stones are thrown behind me. I am at their mercy.

After a long period a rope is lowered and it is obvious I am to get into the loop on the end. My short journey to the top is far from gentle, and upon arrival a club hits me and drives me to the ground. These are my new people. There is little discussion but they do speak and give obvious direction. My hands are bound and then they move off in the direction of the smoke. One of them strikes me on the shoulder and proceeds to ignore me. They obviously have contempt for my position and know I have little choice but to follow them to camp. For the first few days I am left tethered and food is thrown at the foot of the tree I am tied to. The only way to eat is to lie on the earth and eat.

The rope has been removed from my hands and two guards lead me to the river, with a tether still around my neck. I am shown that I am to clean myself. I am then led to the hearth of an older woman and the other women gather round. The older one speaks to the guard, then several women step forward and take the rope and my work is to begin. It is obvious that I am to be enslaved and the work I do will preserve my life, such as it is.

Many days go by with the gathering of wood, the carting of water, the butchering of the hunters' kills and the preparation of hides. As I learn the work and their expectations and a basic understanding of language, my life begins to improve. I have gained some hides to sleep under and time to build a basic shelter. Their dark skinned bodies are strong, lean, and not unlike my own. Hair grows in the same places. Also their foreheads and chins are less pronounced.

As time passes I find these differences are not noticed. Their customs are becoming easier for me to understand. The guards take less notice of me and when the men are out hunting, as they are most days, I sometimes go gathering grain and roots from the plants in the region, always with the women of the camp. One in particular, who is not young but has no man and no children at her hearth, directs me and seems to have more time than the mothers to work me. It seems her body will not bear children. However I notice the men of the tribe mate with her often, especially those whose women of their hearth are large with coming birth. They seem to have little sexual inhibition, and jealousy between the partners is not obvious. I have seen men mate with other women who are not of their hearth and no one takes notice at all.

13

One day, while gathering water for the tribe, the woman who I now know as Ula bids me to remove my skins and signals that I am to wash and clean my furs. This I am pleased to do, as it is rare that I am given time for such a simple pleasure. I notice Ula looks upon my body with interest and comments to another woman, and points at my manhood. My skin is lighter in colour and my face must be strange to them.

The work goes as normal that day and when they seem to be finished with me I move off towards my sleeping area, only to find Ula standing in front of the entrance to my shelter. I stand quietly to see her intentions and, after a time, she bids me remove my furs. It has been a long time since I have been with a woman; still, my body is always tired from the constant work. Her hand goes to my member and it is swift to respond. There are no sensual moves as I have been taught by the women of my people. She simply turns around and kneels with her body presented to me. Apart from desire, I fear that this may not be a good development for me but my body follows its age old instincts and I mate with her, and try and judge her needs as I feel myself coming to orgasm. As I leave her body I kiss her gently, and cover her furs over her private parts as she turns to me. She seems confused but at the same time her face shows pleasure. I think she has known little gentleness from the men who have come to use her as one who cannot birth, so will not have a man and family at her hearth.

As the days go by she finds opportunities that will allow us time together. She is demanding as she discovers I know many ways to please her body. Ula has also become protective of me, and my work is more and more under her control.

My life is rapidly improving. There are changes to the way the tribe is treating me. I am allowed to eat at the same time and sometimes even addressed in conversation. I have found they have a good supply of flint, but their capacity to make a good edge is not done with a complex knowledge of the fault of the stone. I have shown them that, by picking the right stone and hitting it in such a way, it is possible to get a good edge nearly every time. They have a tendency to strike a lot of stone, and when they find a piece that looks correct they try to make an edge. I do not know if they will master the skill, but I see they are using my tools and that some of my own original edges have returned to my sleeping furs.

After several moons I move to Ula's hearth. She has greatly improved my quality of life with the rest of the tribe. She supplies me with warmth; she gives me a lot of physical relief. She now helps with the preparation of food. These people are certainly not faithful. She still satisfies the needs of young single males and those whose needs may not be met at their own hearth. I do not feel jealousy and, since Ula has taken me to her hearth, women from the rest of the tribe sometimes request my attention. I seem to be popular. The men now include me in some of the hunts although my status is, and for a long time will stay, low in the tribe.

Much time passes, and among other things I notice the spirit of my children, while not of my own hearth, is at a number of the other hearths. For whatever reason their spirit man, the shaman, places emphasis on this and I am included in the ceremonies of their beliefs. My beliefs are kept to myself.

I am older now and realize that my life span is greater than that of my new people. The young have grown up. Ula and the people of my first encounter have all gone. Because of time alone I am respected in the tribe. They know little of my strange beginning and do not seem to notice my facial difference, especially as I have many children and they all have some of my appearance or I would not know they were of my essence.

At one of the rare combined tribal gatherings there are other children of mixed race and adults of combined feature. I am not the only one to have been lost to their people. Long after I am gone, new blood will come over the mountains in increasing numbers, and one race will fade into the other.

My eyes have long grown dim and I wonder what people I wish to be amongst, if that is how it is, when I pass into the spirit. This journey is ending and the answer will be known to me in the spirit only, for it may be that each life is a lesson only to be learnt if it starts from a new beginning.

14: Interlude 1

My spirit continues to be born over many thousands of years.

I will be alive and perish during the long winter that follows the volcanic caldera on the island of what will be Sumatra. A large part of the populations of people over vast areas died with me. I never saw or heard the explosion, only felt the sun grow dim, not to come out again.

It would be nearly 50,000 years before I am born into a tribe of very different people on the land that will be known as Uganda. The lives following will journey up the rift valley along the Nile River and eventually into the Middle East, and beyond into the choice lands of Europe.

In less than a thousand years these people will cover more country than any people in two hundred thousand years, and will wipe out and change forever tribes and species that have existed for many thousands of years.

In the most isolated regions, the blood of the Earth's most ancient people will be strongest.

It would be wonderful to say the journey of my spirit in its physical appearances was without its share of evil. But I am not of a high order, and the effect of the earthly existence and brutal environments will give a dark side to the reality of many of the lives to come.

15: The Warrior

It is 28,000 years before 'the writing'.

I open my eyes to the sights and sounds of an aggressive people. We have taken over another tribe and killed many of their men, taken some as slaves and impaled the bodies of the head man and head woman on wooden stakes each side of the camp. The slaves will travel with us and, in a short time, will join our ways or be slaughtered.

Our chief is the most powerful man in the memories of our tribe. We do not attempt to retain territory but conquer and move on. The people show little resistance and do not fight back as we remove their strongest hunters. We are between four hundred and five hundred strong. If we continue to grow at this rate, we will split into two tribes and continue to move north. I am a fighter of these people and the blood of many bodies flows from my weapons. Our fame is spreading and many camps are empty by the time we arrive.

Hepron, our chief, has decided to send scouts forward, as he is concerned that some tribes will unite and attempt to resist. He is also angry that the strong men will live to fight another day. Still we have little to fear, as we are mighty in our ways of battle. I seem to know by instinct that it is best in these times not to attract the attention of Hepron or his main warriors, for it is the brave who are sent out to scout for new people, and are sometimes gone for a full moon or do not return at all. The risk of death is great for those who are first into camps on our constant war. For a mature hunter like me, I pretend to move a little slower and most of the killing is done before my spear enters the invaded bodies. There is then life to live and the women of the new camps to enjoy. Sometimes we take the best of the women to service our needs. Many times, however, we remain in the conquered location, and those allowed to live look after our needs. We move on when we have used up all their reserves. We take the best of what we want and those who have the nature to strengthen our tribe.

For the last few days I have been taking pleasure from a dark haired beauty. She is sullen and will not speak, and if she does not improve I will slaughter her before we move on. I notice a small boy, who must be of her hearth, try to get close when I or one of the other men are not with her. It amuses us to leave a young child like that. Hepron believes it is good to leave people to look after our future needs.

I take hold of the woman's hair and shove her towards the river, throwing the water bag made from a part of the inside of an ox after her. As I watch her shapely hips move, my member begins to thrust at the front of my hides. After she fills the bag I take her once again by the hair and drag her behind the outcrop of rock a little up the river. She has learnt to uncover quickly in order to avoid more beatings. I take my time; it is good to look at her lovely breasts and firm stomach over the opening to her femininity. My body kneels between her legs and I slowly move my shaft up into the wonderful warmth of her. This time she is good, holding me tight with her arms and her legs, so it is not long before I feel the seed begin to burst from my body and I collapse onto her.

There is intense pain as my head seems to split in two, and I roll off her body to look in amazement at the little boy who strikes again with a rock to my face. I am able to grasp the boy's wrist, but it is then that I feel the sharp edge of the flint knife slice swiftly across my throat. My last view in life is of the woman grabbing the small boy and disappearing into the forest.

16: Boy

I am twelve seasons old, and all my tribe and several others are travelling across the river to flee north. We have just learnt that the Invaders have overrun the people to the south. We have heard that there are two large groups travelling up each side of the river, defeating and destroying all they come across. It is hard to leave the land of our memories but we are no match for these people.

I listened at the last fire of our old hearth to an old man of the tribe as he told a story of how he and his mother had escaped the Invaders when he was a small boy. He said that they had killed a warrior and fled into the forest. They travelled for a whole season, day and sometimes night, only coming close to other camps when they were in need of food or clothing. When they eventually stopped at our people's dwellings his mother was close to death. It was the kindness of our medicine woman and shaman that gave them the courage to stop. Upon healing they had gone no further. His mother had passed into the earth and he had grown old. The memories of the Invaders had faded, and he hoped they had gone away or been defeated.

It is only over the last season we have heard of them and our people are in terror. The old man told of the torture of the best of his people, and their leaders being impaled while still alive on stakes each side of the dwellings.

We come around the bend in the river and, to my horror, there is a line of many warriors across our path. They are painted with red and black ochres from the earth and are a fearful sight. I remember the old man's story of fleeing into the forest and move back through my people and rush into the trees.

The spear goes through my body and embeds itself into a tree. The

34

warrior does not even strike me but pulls me forward and off the end of his spear and moves with his recovered spear to thrust it into another young boy. I then see that there are many men in the forest and our people, trying to flee, see our bodies and return towards the riverside. The point of a spear enters my neck and the forest and the pain begin to disappear.

17: Interlude 2

I will be born into part of a clan of people who have moved over the shallow ice age water to the lands that will be England, Ireland and Scotland. They are the tribes that lived in harmony with the Neanderthals for over 100,000 years.

They will remain the dominant tribes of these islands for more than 24,000 years. They will, for a long time, remember the ones they called the Other Ones, and the monuments they leave behind will create an aura of great mystery.

As Druids they will honour the science of astrology and its knowledge of the seasons. When the great ice melts, this memory will become the greatest story of their existence. The change from the winter solstice to the coming of the summer sun will be shown in monuments that will forever give honour to the Earth, Sun and all beyond. This will confuse the memory, and the legend of the flood will mix with stories of the melting ice and the rising seawater.

Their land will go from two parts ice mountains to beautiful gentle seasons and generous soils. The forts and dwellings they build against the edge of the narrow sea will be 100 feet under water. It will also divide them from the land of their enemies for a long period.

Finding Purpose

The life of challenge

18

27,000 years ago.

I am born in what will be England, on the river Avon. My people have come back from the land of our memories. There is much grief, for we have gone to the gathering that we have celebrated with the Other Ones and they were not there. For many of the legends they have been a part of our journey and have, with their superior memories, given us much of our spiritual and greater knowledge.

In the last of the camps we found only the destruction by the ones we have referred to as the Invaders. The Other Ones would not leave the land of their memories and travel with us to the new areas of the west. The Invaders would not stop their gradual removal of hope for life for the Other Ones. Our stories and our friendships tell us of the importance of these people to us. In time the Earth will return to being flat and our knowledge will only be legend. This knowledge was our age-old history of the development of humans on Earth.

The clan chieftan states it will be important for us to use the ways of war we have learnt from our spying and swapping of stories. He says the Invaders will turn their lust for blood from the Other Ones to our lands in the west. It will be that we will build enclosures of logs down the coast of the narrow sea. Our people are not going to go the way of the Other Ones.

The clan chieftan has declared that from now on we must give equal respect to weapons of war as to weapons of knowledge, for he has told us that without both we will not survive. He has stated we must survive to honour both our own ancestors and those of our friends who seem to have gone forever. Our spirit man and our healer have confirmed the importance of his words. Our spearmen and archers will train not only to kill the great bear, deer and wolf. They will train to kill all those who attempt to enter our lands. We are to tell the stories of this loss to retain the fear of terrorist ways, and remain angry from generation to generation.

I am a boy called Garoke and have been alive for eleven seasons. Although I am but a boy, the memories of the Other Ones are being told with great importance. We are taught to know that the memories were born into them and was knowledge without being passed from old to young. The Other Ones have been the teachers for longer than we can imagine. They have preserved our knowledge of numbers, the stars, round Earth and our origins from the time of the water covering the Earth.

We live in groups of about fifty to one hundred people and cover a territory that we are responsible for. Our climate is often bitterly cold. The reindeer and other animals that we hunt supply us with the clothes to keep us warm.

I wake to feel the wind rush into the sleeping place. My father has gathered his spear and bow to hunt early. The sky is still dark. I wish in a part of me that I could go. The other part thanks the spirits for the warmth of the furs and the warm hut that my sister Hellena and my parents also dwell in. Hellena is older than me by two summers, and the time is close for when she will leave for the place of young women. Her quiet breathing tells me she still sleeps. My mother rolls over. There will be no eating for some time to come.

My hand strays to my new bow. Over the last few days I have received my first bow and arrows. The bow is longer than my body and I have ten arrows for the adventures to come.

It is good to be alive in this time before the sun gives us the most warmth. Soon the ice will melt on the great river and we will fish for salmon, and have much smoked fish for the following winter. Fishing, hunting, exploring and travelling. Life is good.

19

Time has passed. Today I have joined my two friends to go out for the morning. We are hoping to get away before we are given work in the dwelling places. We move down river, keeping to the forest edge. I love the strength of the big trees; they seem to rise half way to the moon. They are good shelters for the reindeer in the winter and the deer in the summer. Birds and small animals dwell in the high branches.

I am careful to only shoot an arrow if I can see its journey, as arrows are easily lost in the forest. We hope to see deer today and I will see if I can get my first kill. The other boys have had bows for longer than me and are keen to show me their skills. It has not snowed this morning and, after some misty rain, the sun comes out from behind the dark clouds.

There is much room under the great oaks so we spread out and run. We are going to see the log enclosures where the different tribes send some of their warriors to stand guard against our enemies across the sea. They have raided us many times. Many have died but still they steal our young women and kill our people if given an opportunity. The signal fires burn when a raid happens and we combine to fight. Still, it is hard to be in all places at all times. Soon I will start to learn the ways of war. My friends and I fight and play war games, and are careful as we travel to look for raiders.

We are nearing the edge of the tall trees and the vegetation is changing. I see open country in the distance. We also hear noise. This is a wolf pack on the move, still some distance but closing. We could be caught in the open with nowhere to hide and no trees to climb. The river will guide us to the largest of the warrior compounds in the area, but it will take us a tenth of the sun time to cover the distance. I call to my friends and they come. We discuss the situation. Life is dangerous to us so we are careful when we can be. We decide to listen for a time and see if the noise abates. Some time later the wolf noise has stopped so they must have moved out of range. Still, we will rest for a short time.

We go to the riverbank. The ice is still thick here, but by seeking animal tracks we are able to find water and drink our fill. There is no sound so we move out, skirting a mob of cattle and staying close to the river, moving in single file as the scrubby bushes force us to travel a worn path. The sun is moving higher now and at times appears between the clouds. Hopefully the big cats and wolves are hunting the ponies, cattle or deer of the forest and our way is clear.

Sandstone cliffs are on each side of the river and we pass several dwellings which seem to be making use of the openings in the cliff face. There is evidence of otters in this area and our bows are ready. Perhaps I will be a hunter today.

We are not long now to the stockade of logs. I continue to watch for trouble and fear strikes at me as I see several glimpses of wolves on the cliff face above. We decide to push for the fort while looking also for a safe place to escape; a small cave or high rocks where we could fight back from. There are more wolves now. They will come down at the first break in the cliff face so we must find safety or help.

There is a pile of rocks near a platform against the rock face. We should be able to get up. The first few rocks are easy but it is too high to the platform. I bend over and a boy goes onto my shoulders, then the next one and they are up. Their bows reach down and they help me up just as I see the animals coming back along the river. Perhaps they will not attack if we are in a position of strength. I know the other boys are as frightened as I am. I can hardly breathe but the strength must come to my arm if we are to survive. I do not know if the wolves can jump this high. As they come nearer my mind seems to focus and the arrow is ready. We hold our fire and I ask the spirits to make the platform high enough.

The animals are hesitating, moving back and forward, seeming to assess our danger to them. After the winter they will be hungry for easy kill. A large silver wolf, I think the leader, is coming now and several are close behind. He leaps and just makes the ledge. My arrow and one other strike his throat. Another passes between his legs. The other wolves fail to make the top of the ledge. The noise is very loud. The silver wolf moves forward and hits the boy in the middle. His teeth fail to close on flesh, and another arrow strikes him in the side of the neck. He is down. We move around him and aim our weapons on the other animals. One arrow finds its mark in the side of a beast. We load and shoot again; another animal is hit. They are moving away now. Two wolves are down and another has gone with an arrow in its body.

I feel weak, but my friend Jessa gives a loud howl like the leader of the pack. He cries: "We shall be known as the killer of wolves". All I can think of is I shall be the survivor of death, and my father may kill me yet for being where I should not have been. A boy's bow made me foolish beyond my age. We were lucky this time. We will skin the wolves and move back to camp. I would not admit it but I am still much afraid, although I feel great elation too. Our flint edges remove the hides while one of us stays high to keep guard. Then we move out for the dwellings.

20

It is towards evening light when we arrive. We are unsure of our reception, but the people gather around us when we carry our trophies into the centre place. Our leader moves forward and I, being the oldest but still not many winters, am asked to speak. The story is told. There are many expressions on the faces of all. Boys of our age do not hunt for big game or dangerous creatures. The wolf has a spiritual totem of great importance.

The leader signals for the fathers of us boys and talks quietly. He also talks quietly with our spirit man. Once again I am afraid. He turns to the tribe and announces there will be a ceremony tonight for the spirit of the wolves. He says the boys are to be acknowledged for bravery and survival but it is to be known that they were lucky and have mixed judgement. He says this time we will not be honoured, but at the time of our initiation into manhood our deeds will be remembered. He then turns to the tribe and asks aloud if such foolish ones are alive who wish to be food for baby wolves. At this there is much laughter and joking at our expense and I am relieved. However, I see much respect in the eyes of adults and awe in the eyes of the children.

The night comes and after the evening meal we move to the central fires. I hope one of the other boys will tell the story. I am fearful of speaking in front of the tribe and I know not what they want of us. Jessa is loud and confident. When it is time I will ask him to go forward, or at least talk for us.

The chief calls the shaman to speak briefly with him, then asks us boys to move into the open. He speaks of the foolishness of boys and declares areas we are to stay in, unless we are with elders. Nevertheless, he says the blood of our people is strong when boys with first weapons can survive an attack and slay wolves. He signals us to speak and I push Jessa forward. Honer also moves forward to speak. The story, although much more expansive, is close to the truth. They forget to say I got them to the ledge on my back, but remember to mention they saved my life by pulling me up. However, they do say that Jessa's and my arrow slew the leader and my arrow finished him off. I apparently was the only one in a position to get a second shot as the wolf was viciously attacking the others. So the story went. They did not know whose arrows struck the other two animals but I think the arrows were theirs. I am relieved I did not have to tell the story in front of the whole tribe.

The spirit man comes forward with the hides of the wolves. I hear him say the wolf is a powerful totem and we must free their spirits and help send them on the next part of their journey. He has prepared dried plants and lights them on a shallow stone surface. The women and children are moving away. I am a little apprehensive about the event. The chief and the fathers of us boys have come forward and most of the men remain. It is unusual for boys who are not initiated to be involved.

The spirit man breathes the smoke and steps back. He who speaks loudest, Jessa, moves forward. Now an expression of anxiety has come over his features. Maybe fear. He breathes and his father follows. Next comes Honer and his father. I am in no hurry. Perhaps the fire will go out before I get there. The other boys are coughing and not looking too well at all. It is my turn and I try not to breathe too deeply. To my horror my father takes my hair and pushes my head down again. I step back. My head is spinning, and my father and all else are becoming shadows in a world that seems to be without boundaries.

21

For an instant all is dark, then I see with great clarity a blue starry night with a silvery moon. I am well aware of my own body and that the shaman is with me. All others are gone. I feel my body rising off the ground and fear makes me jerk back to the surface but it starts to rise again. The shaman says I must let go and the fear fades. I glance down and to my amazement see my own body.

Then in a flash I am standing on a cliff looking down on the silvery great river. I can see smoke and the light of what I feel are our fires in the distance. Then my head goes back and I hear myself make the noise of the howl of a wolf. The pack is all about me. I am in the 'body' of the wolf but I am not him. I know he is the silver leader we killed early in the day. I can feel he is distressed and confused. We move forward to a large black wolf and we tear into him. Nothing happens. The other wolves cannot see us. They are running now down through the tree line. We move in beside the largest female of the pack. She makes a point of moving towards the black wolf. We attack again. I can feel fury in the silver wolf. His spirit has not realized it is without body and is resisting the forces that should be moving it from this earthly existence.

We are looking at the pack and I am aware that the wolf has noted two are missing. One is the mother of cubs. The wolves are going to pass her den. She is the one who was wounded. I see she died back on the cliff tops. The lead female is moving the pups from the den and I recognize this valley. They join the pack and we move off. As we go one pup returns. The female starts to return but the black wolf heads her off and the pack moves away. My wolf tries to attack the black one again.

The silver wolf has become aware of my presence. I have been able to think his thoughts and now he appears to become aware of mine. Although wary, he is not afraid. He is inquisitive. We are still running with the leaders. I am trying to tell him that his body is not here and, if he stops his intense connection with his kind, he will depart. I tell him he will, at some stage, be born again. He has more to gain by relaxing now and rejoining life later on. I can feel he understands. A strange thought comes from him. The cub at the den would not leave because the silver wolf was not with the pack. There was a powerful bond with the lead wolf; the cub is his preferred progeny. The wolf seems to understand I will return to my own body but I do not think he realizes I am human. He is letting me know I should try and gather the pup to run with my kind. He is pointing out it will grow to have great qualities. I sense a flicker of anger as he senses I have been his enemy. Then I feel respect and acceptance. With acceptance he vanishes from my presence and I am back in my body.

There is dead quiet as I become aware that all around me are staring at me in awe. I see the spirit man is in trance and chanting in a language not mine. He stops instantly and opens his eyes on me. I know he has seen part of, or my entire, strange journey.

The spirit man calls for the skin of the silver wolf and places it over my head and shoulders. I hear him say I am to be known as Wolfman and will be initiated at the next initiation ceremonies, and from there on at gatherings I will wear the silver hide of the leader of the wolves. He turns to our leader and my father and says he wishes me to learn the ways of his knowledge. This all frightens me. I wish to go back to my mother's tasks and from now on be hunting otters in the very close river. This is not the games for boys. I am being forced to grow too quickly. I can see father is pleased but I would rather he was proud of himself without my benefit.

I retire quickly to our dwelling. I hope I do not dream tonight. My head is sure it has dreamt enough for one day. Sleep comes swiftly.

22

I am awake again and going over the events from the day before. Far from being a part of the wolf during my spirit journey, the wolf seems to be stuck to me, even when he is enjoying the freedom of afterlife. I feel a strange obligation to, and an affinity with, this whole situation.

I also have a nagging awareness of the pup in the den. It will not last long and may follow the scent of the pack. The cats will make short its journey or probably starvation will. Still, the wolf did not, I think, know I was human. We have long known that the Other Ones often had wolves as a domestic part of their lives and, as we are to preserve the ways of the Other Ones, is this another of their ways?

The young people are gathering around us three. I am not sure of the value of this new respect. Still, the other two seem to have grown taller and obviously intend to make their feats of bravery last. I discuss the wolf pup with the young people. When I talk they listen. They seem partly informed of my supposedly good fortune with the spirit of the silver leader. There is great excitement about going and getting the pup. However the reality is they would be afraid the pack might be there. Jessa comes to their rescue by pointing out he would go himself but the chief's new law states it is outside our territory. That is a saving of face, Jessa. I just hope that none of the children come to the conclusion that the new loss of freedom is their new heroes' fault. Good fortune can turn quickly. Then there is much talk about how we would catch and carry the pup. Although it is young, it is large enough to remove plenty of skin from my body. Still, I tell them I am going to discuss the problem with my father.

He treats me differently today and we go to talk with the chief and shaman. It is decided, with some interest, that we will attempt to fetch the pup. However, if it cannot be trained or tamed it will be killed. They say I have one moon. All of a sudden it is my responsibility to tame it. How did I put myself into this situation? Wolfman (boy) is going from bad to worse. Oh for the simple life. It is apparently my spiritual connection with the animal that will tame it.

I wear the skin of the wolf. My father said I was to wear it. I hope they do not intend sending me head first into the den as old silver himself.

We are moving fast as some of the day has gone. At least I believe I know the valley where the den is. It strikes me to tell the men and Jessa a false location and remove some of this hollow feeling of dread from the pit of my stomach. I do not know how Jessa became important enough to be with us. The look on Honer's face was not impressive. He is losing hero status amongst our peers. Such is life in this hard, icy land.

We branch off at a small stream and start upwards. The going is hard. Although we see some beasts, there is no hunting. This is serious work. The sun is over half way so I hope this wolf is easy to catch. The men carry bundles and ropes so they obviously have a plan. I am hoping it does not include me.

23

We are at the den now and the entrance conceals the pup, if it is still there. We move downwind being careful to avoid being seen from the entrance, and get ourselves to a position above the den entrance. My father retrieves a large piece of ox meat and cuts a piece off. Ropes are looped and placed in circles around the entrance to the den. Then the meat is lowered down in the loop furthermost from the entrance after rubbing it in the furs of old silver. I am dubious this will catch him but it is better than shoving me into the den and tying a rope around my feet.

We settle down to wait. I see some of the men have formed a part circle further out, being careful not to get in the slight breeze. I suspect the pup knows we are here. Still, he will be hungry by now. I listen quietly to the birds singing. It is cold when one sits still. It is nearly always cold, especially if the wind blows from the great ice mountain in the north.

There is movement below but no noise. All people are still. The cub sees a shadow move and drops back. It is not long before it reappears. This time the cub goes swiftly to the meat and grabs it, turning to dive for the den. The ropes are pulled but miss all but a back leg. The cub fights hard, dropping the meat and dragging its foot out of the noose before another loop can fall. Escape is successful. The cub will not leave the den for a long time now.

I can see the men becoming uneasy and looking at me and the spirit man for advice. I say out loud, in a voice showing a little too much enthusiasm: "Perhaps another day." The spirit man is looking at me hard. To my horror loud mouth brave Jessa says I can speak to the young wolf and can go into the den and bring it out. Then the skin of the wolf is put over my head and, regardless of my protests that I can see the pup spirit does not like me, I am

49

thrust into the den. I have no choice.

Ahead is semi-darkness and a bend in the rock tunnel. I can, I think, smell the creature or perhaps the silver skin or my own fear, which I am not sure has caused me to wet myself. I move slowly forward, hoping beyond imagination that the den has a back opening either for me to escape or preferably the cub. I look carefully around the rock and come face to face with two gleaming rows of snappy snarling daggers, and a very bad breath and worse attitude. Do they expect me to cuddle that?

I back up but a large foot jams my leg to the rock face and I have a picture of my father's foot. He would not like to lose face. I look over my shoulder and see the end of the rope. The cub must have dragged it in. An idea strikes my terrified mind and I grab the rope with trembling hands. I am back face to face with white daggers. I pull the rope so I have slack and prepare to try to put it over his holder of gleaming, killing teeth. My hand is shaking so hard I can hardly open the noose in the rope. I hold it open with both hands and prepare to throw it. In my mind, if this animal charges I am dead or scarred for life.

Then the cub rushes. I close my eyes and wait for the end. Then the rope tightens in my hand. As it is around my arm it suddenly jerks, yanking my shoulder around and belting my head on the rocks above. I can hear the cub yelping behind me through my dizzy head and realize that I have caught the cub. Now I have no desire to go outside and claim my reluctant prize and be the reluctant victor.

There is much noise outside, and a little later I feel strong hands dragging me backwards. Thanks be they do not have teeth. As I emerge the wolf cub is now caught between three ropes and seems to have given up. The men all look excited and I can see they cast impressive looks upon me. Once again I am reluctant wolf man. Jessa is quick to point out the cub is not very big, and now it is caught it does not look that big to me. Still, I can see some of the men cast glances at Jessa that indicate he would be best fed to pups of this sort. The sun is half way down the sky. Our reluctant new tribe member half walks and is half dragged as we move swiftly back to camp without incident.

The cub is tied to a stake outside my dwelling. I hope we can communicate. Regardless of my troubles there feels like some kind of connection with this creature. My father gives me flap meat of the ox and I get some bones from other camps. The cub does not eat but probably will when all are asleep in the village. I will rise early in the morning to see.

My dreams this night are full of wolf and caves and snapping teeth. They are just dreams. Anyway, I would tell no one in case more responsibility and so-called privileges come my way.

24

The day starts cold as always and my furs are warm, still I move quietly out into the morning light. I put some wood on the coals. A glance tells me the flap meat has been eaten and the bones moved about. This is a start. There is little movement in the camp, so I sit and try to form a bond with the pup while not getting too close. However he (it is a he) looks very sad and not vicious at all, and much smaller than when I was face to teeth with him in a partially dark hole. He is well fed but I will need to find a way of bringing water to him. There is a hole in the rocks so I pour water from a hide bag into this but it quickly soaks away. Still, it has made me aware of my own hunger and thirst so I retire to wait for early movement from my mother or sister.

My father rises and leaves with a glance at me, and he looks pleased that I have been up, if a little surprised. I guess he will check the cub out. I sleep, and wake much later to the smell of food and the sound of water boiling in the water hides. Perhaps today will be good, although I am a little nervous of this new responsibility. Perhaps the spirit man can help me. I will go to him shortly for he may know how the Other Ones taught the wolves to be as one with the tribe.

I eat the flat cake so often eaten made from beaten grains, herbs and dried fish, and drink the drink our people make using thickening plants and vegetables brewed to keep the cold from our stomachs. After a time doing tasks for our dwelling, and helping with the weaving of cloth that we make from forest and marsh plants that we beat into fibre, I move off to the hut of the shaman.

He is with our healing woman which is often the way as they share knowledge. The spirit man uses plants of the healing woman, and the healer uses the shaman for the more complex cures. I sit quietly outside the dwelling, as they are aware of my presence and will allow me to enter when their talk allows. I can see from their expressions that they are often referring to me. I suppose my hairy friend is also a part of their talk. I see the woman who looks after the shaman tending the fire and boiling water for tea or concoctions I dare not think about. Perhaps it is not such a good idea for me to be here after all. The woman beckons me forward.

I only want a brief talk but sit before the two wise people of our tribe and wait for permission to speak, as is our custom. The shaman asks what brings me to them. I tell them I do not know how to tame the cub, and wonder if anyone knows how the Other Ones trained young wolves to be safe and perhaps useful. The shaman tells me that the journey with the wolf was a rare event, and that something in my present and spiritual past may be unusual. He says the three of us are going to enter, if possible, the world of trance and, if we can find knowledge of the Other Ones' ways, they will try and guide me there. The healing woman has placed herbs into the boiling water which is giving off strange scents and already I feel myself drifting. The shaman lights some plants on a stone platform. I see him tell the servant to block the entrance and stay outside herself and stop all from entering.

25

It is a little hard to breathe for a start, then once again I have the feeling of rising away from my physical form. I am aware that both the others are with me, yet I cannot see them. I can feel the power of them moving me.

We are flying high and moving in a direction that must be north. The great ice passes below, and I see for the first time huge animals with woolly hides and long teeth that curl nearly to the ground. We are moving at speeds that I cannot describe. We flash past whole forests in warmer valleys near the narrow sea. We pass along the coast, then there is an expanse of water and our direction changes and we are out over the vast sea. I see huge icebergs and solid ice stretching into the far north.

Eventually we flash towards land and our progress slows, then instantly we are in a dwelling and it is apparent that a village is outside. We are astonished to see that they are the Other Ones, and we are aware that the man in front of us is their shaman. He signals and two men and a woman leave the dwelling. I presume he can only feel our presence for we have no form, but I become aware that thoughts are being exchanged and images very clear of our appearance are forming in all our minds. The shaman is mind speaking now. We feel or hear him think these thoughts. I cannot describe it any more than that.

They believe that they are the last of the Other Ones, at least in this part of the Earth. Their shaman says that their blood has mixed with people and will spread to the north-west, but that their appearance and shared memories unique to them amongst humans will die out. So, he says, he has been aware of Garoke, now known as Wolfman. He says they looked back into the past to find those whose lives would help bring knowledge to the friendly species across the narrow sea. He says all Other Ones have long been aware of these people. He says that I will not be a great shaman but that I will speak clearly of the memories and am easy to transport. He says that he expects me to come often to visit with the help of my own people of knowledge, who will know how to interpret what I see and transfer it for use by my people.

While I am in this form I feel little fear. The Other Ones' shaman says I will see through his eyes and continue to hear his mind. I am not to be afraid (after the wolf I feel no fear of him). I see he has caught my thought and quickly follows the old silver journey. He looks pleased if that is their pleased expression. He says I am to see these first time glimpses back to the birth of their memories.

In an instant I am in his mind and see clearly the images that are not those of his physical eyes, but I can only guess his psychic eyes. He shows me his group of people. He shows me children playing with young and old wolves. Yet they are wolves not pure. He says they select for traits. He shows me the climate with ice and without. He allows me to understand from period to period times were warmer, and that the Other Ones covered vast areas from warm to freezing. Then he shows me how the Other Ones changed to develop for cold climates after several global catastrophes, hundreds of thousands of summers ago.

He tells me that only a few of his people had the ability to remember events from the past lives at the time of the great impact, which he says in our legends is known as the time of the great flood that covered the Earth when the creator was angry. The memories developed as an evolutionary advantage and eventually became common, in fact normal, to his type. These memories are unknown to humans but common to animals and birds, especially migratory creatures who remember for thousands of generations their exact journeys. He says some day humans will wrongly say they are aligned to magnetic fields or call it instinct. However it is, in part, inherited memories from thousands of past lives, and usually accurate far beyond immediate human memory. There is also a far greater awareness of the spiritual soul that is a part of the living Spirit that we all reside within. It is not to be called 'intelligence' but could be aided by intelligence. Much I understand in this non-physical state that I would not comprehend in my body.

I am visiting my own past lives where I touched the Other Ones many times in such lives, until finally I am face to face with a tall dark girl who I know was my consciousness long ago. I see her meet the Other Ones for the first time and learn the beginnings of our main shared legends. I see why I am susceptible to their needs, and suspect this shaman had much to do with the silver journey.

I am journeying back further and see all light has gone from the Earth. We rise above the darkness to see a great explosion of a huge volcano, and awareness of the vast loss of life is in me. Finally I see strange beautiful buildings, and a line with an arrow full of people moving at great speed across the Earth. I see an ancestor, and am aware that two of the people here are both the Other Ones' shaman and me. These people are not like us but much wiser than my people, and with a different but greater physical science than the Other Ones. Here the shaman and I come face to face as lovers, a he and she at the end before the impact, and at the start of the great memories his people developed.

He allows me to see that these people developed over a very long time span, more than ten times as long as the time since the great impact. He allows me to learn of a story that will stay in legend with humans for long after our time has passed. He shows me that a huge rock came down from the sky and almost stopped life on Earth, and that humans started again in three small groups in different regions on what he shows me to be Earth. I can see his mind picture clearly in my mind. I do not know how much my healer and shaman can see, but I am aware that they have not been able to travel with me.

The Other Ones' shaman registers that I have enough to tell for a start and lets me know it is my duty to show what I have seen, as there are those amongst my people wiser than I will become who will know what to do with this knowledge. Then I am instantly in the dwelling I departed from.

For a brief period the others remain in trance, then the spirit man opens his eyes to mine, followed by the medicine woman. There is grave silence. I am a small boy again and afraid of the responsibilities and the journeys I have seen. I had only wanted to avoid being bitten by the wolf cub. However, they simply ask me to talk quietly and remember in any form I am comfortable with, but be as accurate as I can be. This I do, and then there are many questions. When it is over I am told I will regularly do as I have done today.

I think to myself on leaving, how does that help me with two lines of sharp teeth and claws all keen to tear me apart? The thought instantly enters my mind that I should let the cub get hungry and thirsty, and eventually let it know that I am the only one who feeds it. That is all I am to do at this time. I turn to see the healing woman smiling at me with a knowing look. She says she will tell everyone that they are not to feed or water the cub. I am really shocked now, for they are in my head or is it the Other Ones' shaman who is there? Even this thought is not sacred. I hear laughter as I walk away. My poor privacy. Still, perhaps that is better than being torn apart, especially as this wolf youngster grows.

I will be a great wolf man. Still, as fast as this thought enters my head, all the frightening consequences occur to me. Give me a simple life. Let me go back to being a bold hunter of otter amongst my own age group, where it is easy to be respected with no risk and little judgement. I go past 'all teeth'. No food for him for two days and I shall ask my father about water.

That night the gathered people are told they are not to feed or water the cub. Thankfully my part is not mentioned. I am finding I am guarding my thoughts. Still, life goes on and I sleep the tired sleep of youth but earlier to the furs than usual. There is more on my mind regardless of the guarding of thoughts.

26

I rise early and do tasks for my mother. When they are finished I sit for a while with the cub. It occurs to me that I should call him Silver as he is the same colour as his father. I remain just out of reach of the rope and he remains as far away from me as he can. Still, I notice he moves closer as people pass by the other side. Perhaps I will get my friends to move him closer to me as time goes by. It is obvious that a lot of patience will be required.

My friends arrive, and with other children we take our bows and move to the forest. We decide to see if there is game, that which the elders smile upon the taking. The elders say it is wrong to kill if the food is not needed. They tell how the Invaders run large numbers of creatures over a cliff, then skin and eat only a few of them. It is wrong to waste resources, even though there are many more animals than people. All must live in harmony. Still, the elders also know we must develop our skills to survive. So it is that the rabbits are often left for us young to harvest. This we also do in a way that leaves some in every warren. Thankfully there are still burrows in the area of our restrictions.

Keeping upwind and moving quietly we form three groups, finally arriving in a position where all can get a shot at the prey. Honer and I are in trees in the valley furthermost from the dwellings. The hunt will take place when the call of the blackbird is heard once to say all are in position, then twice when all are in agreement that the best time to shoot has arrived. All settle down for the creatures to settle into a secure grazing pattern.

Not long passes when we hear the signal to shoot from the other groups. As we take aim and Honer imitates the sound of the bird, an arrow strikes a rabbit in front of us and another two are imbedded in the trunk of the trees nearby. We do not need to be curious. Both of us flee, screaming to the other children as we bolt for the camps and leaving behind our arrows in the fear of the moment. The rabbits make better use of cover than us and are instantly invisible. As all the children rush towards home, a whoop of laughter goes up behind us, and a quick look tells us we have fallen prey to the humour of the young initiated warriors of our own tribe.

We will be the stories around the main fire tonight. Still, when I get over it the laughter of the clan will perhaps be a relief. Jessa has a look that says he is mortified and it will not be long before he finds reason to turn the blame on Honer and me. Such is life.

27

Several cycles of the moon pass and three things of significance happened. The shaman told me I was to come to him every fourth day to see what was to be achieved. I started to accept the journeys as being a normal part of my life, although they did not all seem to be impressive. Sometimes after I told all that I remembered to the shaman and sometimes the healer, the journeys tended to fade quickly from my mind. That is all but two, which will stay with me probably forever.

Another was that the cub started to eat and drink with confidence and recognize that I was the one to trust. I fed him at the same time each sunrise and sunset. He gradually came closer and grew quickly, much quicker than I was growing. I stayed out of reach of his tether but sometimes put my hand out towards him. He is still inclined to growl but I notice change. It will take time.

Hellena has been called away to the Mother. She has left our clan and gone away to the secret place of women, north-east of our territory. I do not know where it is. It is said she will return to us if she is to be an Earth mother and find a hearth with a man, else she will stay as a Mother priestess of the higher orders, that I will maybe learn something of when my initiation ceremonies arrive which are rapidly drawing near.

The trees are nearly full of leaf now and there is shade under the great oaks. It is warmer by day and the sun seems to rise earlier. I still find much time to play with other youth. In fact Honer's sister, who is like a boy with the use of bows, comes with us. Honer did not want her but I saw Jessa looking at her with interest. She is long of leg, fair of skin and starting to take the shape of female curves.

After the first time I must admit I like having her along. She pays quiet attention to me and teases Jessa when he shoots badly, which he seems to do whenever she is looking. He does not seem to know how to deal with her. I do not know how she controls his mouth but I suspect her method, or whatever it is about her, is not what I want to control Jessa. I am enjoying the first boy girl games I have seen.

She who is called Arose is also having effect on me, but unlike Jessa I seem to shoot my arrows much truer when she is looking. Arose is clever. When the other boys are not looking, she calls me 'he of the wolf'. From her I like it. When I am sitting quietly with the silver cub she will stand in the shade of the next tree and watch me. Others of the clan do also. The animal as captive is new to us.

28

The sun is shining in the opening to the dwelling so I rise, and once again put wood on the fire and push the stones into heat that will boil the water for my mother's drink. My father has not long gone. He is the hunter and, now that the animals can drink in many places along the river and in the forest, it may take longer for him to return with the kill. It is important to dry much meat and fish for the cold times.

After my tasks I take a new rope I have decided to use with the wolf. It seems to me if I have a second rope on the one over his head, I could try and gently coax him to come to me. Silver still frightens me but if I am to save his life I must make progress. The chief has said he will tame or die.

I have an idea of how to get the rope over his head like the older men did when we caught him and put several ropes on the cub. They threw hides over him. It will frighten Silver. Still, perhaps I will have to be strong with him. I notice he does not run away as quickly if he has started to eat his meal, especially if there are people on the other side of the area his tether allows him. I have made a loop in the rope, and when his head is down I hope to throw the rope over his head and pull it tight when he puts his head up.

Silver is confident and comes quickly, two steps from me. The meat goes down and he starts to tear meat off the bone which is a large leg bone of the ox. I have been practising with the rope and swing it quickly in a loop one step wide. It lands over his head and back. His head flies back and he quickly jerks away but not before I pull the loop tight. I have him first time.

I let the rope go and it drags behind the cub. It only bothers him for an instant as he is now used to the other lead. Now I can control him from each side with two people or more, or better still I can tie him so he has to stay in one place between his peg tether and a tree or another peg. The rope is made so it will go tight, so that is a bit of a worry. I watch Silver for a while to see what happens. He seems to be fine so I return to the dwelling to get some food and a drink. With help from some friends, we will see what can be done about the rope. Adult men can help me tie the rope better.

Suddenly there is a loud yelping noise of Silver taking fright. I rush out to see he has caught the rope on his tether peg and it has pulled tight on his throat. I call for help. Women, children and several older men come. They are too slow. The cub is down, still trying to bite the other rope but slowing fast. I remember the hides used by the men, so grab my bedding and rush back out and heave it over him but he seems to be unconscious or dead. I pull his head out of the hides and two of the women and Jessa take hold of the cub. I loosen the rope and I do not know why, but in desperation push hard up and down on the cub's body. He gasps for breath and we are glad he is alive. After quickly asking the people to keep holding him down, the rope is retied in a fixed loop through the loop that is already around Silver's neck. I loosen this loop and retie it as it has become tight from the rapid growth of the cub. The others take the end of the new rope and tie it to a tree, then the covers are removed and we move away from him.

Silver stands but seems very dazed for a short time. As he becomes aware of his new situation I see fear and he begins to fight but not for long, as he has been through this when we brought him in. He seems to know he is beaten. Arose and the other children are all here. I can see Arose is impressed with me and it makes me feel good. Still, my body is shaking and I can feel my chest thumping hard. I think that is the blood pumping in my body.

I can now take the food close to the cub without him moving away. It is much safer, and one can sit close to him and talk to him. The meat is left so he will have time to eat, drink and recover. Then a large part of the day is spent sitting close to the animal; getting Silver used to my presence, the smell of me and the sound of my voice. I stay with him until the sun is over the sky, then I go off to see what the other young are doing.

All the boys of my group are away, so I take my bow and go into the forest. My skills are getting better, still I will not go far without company. It is good to be alone sometimes and I have favourite places, pools and valley that I can enjoy, but the big cats are hungry too so I am soon back in camp.

I feel keen to be close to Silver so I sit near him and offer little pieces of meat and, to my amazement, he takes a piece out of my fingers. Both of us seem surprised, especially me. I extend my hand to him, this time allowing him to smell my hand then take of the meat. Until the sun gets low in the sky I continue to feed him with small pieces of meat. I eventually become aware that many from the tribe have been watching. The cub is left and I return to my own food and dwelling. My parents do not speak of it so I retire to my furs and sleep soundly, too tired to plan ahead.

29

It is another morning when the cold is not so bitter, still I sleep under several hides. This day is one when I am to see the journey people. I know out of respect to go early and sit outside their dwelling until someone tells me they want to see me.

I know there are many hides and woven fabrics covered in diagrams, and the markings that tell words, time and amounts. I have tried to understand these but I am not good at learning such details. I think this is why I am only to be a journey man for the good of others to learn The Knowledge. Many of the markings are circles which I know are the Earth representative. Some others are the position of the sun, moon and stars. A lot of the words I have spoken from the Other Ones' shaman are concerned with this. Sometimes the marks in the circles are to tell the period of all the seasons, cold to hot. One of the circles apparently designates in steps an important measurement - the number of days of the full cycle of the seasons.

The spirit man is without the healing woman today. He has his helper bring me forward and the trance soon starts. I hardly have to breathe the plants now, just clear my mind and repeat the chant the elders have taught me and I am soon away. Most times I find the Other Ones' shaman but increasingly, as today, it looks to me to be repetitive and much of what I see I do not understand. I only observe and repeat when I am back in my body but I enjoy the freedom of the journey.

Today's journey is not long. Still, when I return I feel in a daze. I also find an increasing desire to be alone. These events, although I am not clever like Jessa and many others, are making me grow differently to others of my age. Perhaps the herbs I breathe have effect.

I find the young wolf an increasingly large part of my day. For some days now I have been feeding him the tiny bits of meat. This is now the only way I feed him. When I am not doing this I untie the other rope.

Today Silver took another amazing step. He licked my hand. No animal has done this in the stories of my clan. However, I have seen this and much more on my journeys. I learn from these experiences and know that I must soon try to stroke the animal's body.

I still have fear but we are growing more and more used to each other. Silver is already half as big again as he was when he first came three moons ago. The chief sometimes watches. He says nothing but he must be pleased with what is going on. I think he thinks it is spiritual and will not interfere unless the animal becomes a threat to his people.

Today I have done the same as yesterday but now Silver is licking right up my arm. Many people watch but they are treating me as if I am odd. What do they expect to happen? Arose comes close to watch but her mother quickly takes her away. It enters my mind that these people, or at least many of them, think that the animal and I are forming some sort of dangerous bond. The spirit man and healing woman seem amused. They are powerful friends.

Things are happening fast now. Yesterday I left the rope a little loose and Silver sniffed me all over. Today I intend to try and stroke him. He frightens me less each day, although I am not sure that this is a good risk.

I have started by feeding him as usual with both ropes fairly tight. He sniffs and licks me between receiving pieces of meat. I get the feeling that there is anger that the ropes are tighter than yesterday. The back of my hand touches the side of his head and he instantly takes my wrist in his mouth. I freeze with some fear. There is no pressure. Then he releases and rubs his head on my arm. I am shaking all over now but slowly the back of my hand rubs up the side of his head. He allows this to happen a little, then takes my arm in his mouth again. It occurs to me that Silver is playing but cautioning me at the same time. Slowly the shaking eases and my blood pumps easier. I go to the rope and loosen it, then return and gently stroke his face and the top of his head. Before I know it he jumps, knocking me over, and his teeth are once again on my arm which is raised to protect my throat. I look up to see my father's hunting bow fully extended ready to kill Silver. The young wolf releases me and quickly licks my arm and face then bounds away, and as I get up he bounds back and puts his feet up on me and licks my face.

The look on my father's face is of astonishment. I see several other hunters with bows drawn. I hear the shaman caution them not to shoot, and I realize that he has probably seen the Other Ones in his spirit journeys, as I have, with the animals playing with children and adults.

To my surprise it is not fear I feel but elation. My heart soars and I throw my arms around Silver, and in that instant realize that there is a bond that will probably only be broken by death. I go to one rope and remove it completely, and spend most of the rest of the day playing with my new friend.

I am partly aware that the adults are keeping the young people away but I notice they have not gone hunting today. Many of the men are still about. This is an unusual event in our tribe's story telling or the story telling of any of the clans, except for the Other Ones. I think they cannot believe that Silver does not want to draw blood when he holds me in his mouth. I am not encouraging him to do this, as he is going to get very big and extremely powerful.

As the afternoon wears on I leave meat for Silver as there is no point feeding him small pieces now, and go to the riverbank to wash. Here I find Arose, Honer, Jessa and two others. They are reserved but eventually, with Arose's natural lack of reserve and Jessa's very unusual reserve, they start to ask questions and cannot stop. Although afraid, I can see that they wonder if the wolf will be friendly and safe with them. Realization emerges in my weary consciousness that these young friends are going to grow accustomed to Silver much quicker than the adults. I answer their questions quickly and with a peculiar feeling of gratitude to them that I do not fully understand. Then I am glad to head back to the dwellings. They walk with me but as we enter the outskirts they drop away. I see Honer talking seriously to Arose.

30

I wake the following morning and, although it is not my day with the shaman, I sit outside his dwelling after a brief hello to gentle teeth. The sun is much higher before I go inside. The shaman has been deep in talk with the chief and healing woman. The chief leaves. He does not acknowledge me. Still, this is not unexpected as he is the chief and I am young. I sit and wait for permission to speak, then talk of what has happened over the last days. The shaman agrees that it would be good to journey and hopes that my psychic form knows how to seek the answers on where to go with the wolf.

We are successful and I am with the Other Ones' shaman. I feel the shaman observe my thoughts and can feel his happiness. I am shown the wolves being allowed to roam free in the camp and others either tethered or in enclosures. I am shown how these enclosures are built. I am travelling with the mind of the shaman and I see his people, apparently long ago, taking cubs from the den of more than one wolf. I am led to understand that this happened over a very long time. That gradually the ways of the wolf became suited to their needs, as I had been shown before. Then I am shown how they hunt. We are on an open plain and I see many hunters of the Other Ones below us. They are downwind from a herd of ox that seem aware of the hunters and are moving away. Then I see the wolf dogs being sent at a command that I can hear. Five wolf dogs circle wide and come in from the other side of the ox. They run back in the direction of the hunters and, at a command as they near, they separate one beast from the rest and hold it at bay, attacking from all sides but not touching. The hunters move in and are able to spear the beast while the wolf dogs distract it. The ox is bled and the wolves are given offal as reward.

Then I am back in my own shaman's dwelling and clear of mind. We speak and he tells me what should be done. The next day he is going to talk to the chief and my father and they will decide, with the rest of the older tribesmen, what is to be done with this knowledge. I can see, and he informs me, there is much magic totem involved, and perhaps great possibilities of advantage and prestige for the chief's people. The shaman says the processes that are followed acknowledge the beliefs of other tribes.

After initial talks, a meeting of the tribe is called for the central evening fire. I attend and the story is told, not of my spiritual journey but of what the chief and the hunters have learnt about using wolves to hunt game. Mention is made that we now know how to train beasts. I think to myself there is a way to go yet. I am not even sure that Silver will stay if I undo his rope, let alone bring ox or any other beast to me or anyone else.

Several days go by and I decide I want to take Silver off the stake. I ask my father to learn to touch the growing wolf. I am surprised to see he is reluctant. I tell him it is because I am afraid the wolf will pull the lead out of my hands and disappear. The tribe will then blame me. He looks at me differently, and for the first time it seems to occur to him that a lot of responsibility is on the shoulders of one so young and that his son may, a lot of the time, be afraid of the future and new blame.

Now father sits and talks to me about the whole situation. After a time he says the hunters have been looking for new dens and intend to get about five cubs for the tribe. He says that he will see that I play a very small role in this. I have done my share. The involvement with shaman and Silver is plenty. He will help with Silver until the next stage is reached. He also will learn how to make wolves hunters, then he can teach the other hunters. I feel better, also excited to be involved with my father. My mother looks pleased.

After some food and drink we go out together. Silver is pleased to see me; I am totally relaxed with him now. I connect the other rope and pull it tight. My father takes a piece of meat off me and, while I stroke Silver's head, he slowly holds it out. It is not long before the wolf smells his hand and allows my father to stroke him. They are both a little wary of each other, so we rest for a while and I take the other rope off and sit and talk to father while I play with Silver.

After a time I undo the rope off the stake while my father holds the rope. Silver starts to walk and I travel beside him. He moves to the end of where his rope would allow him to go. At first Silver looks confused and then panics. He rushes off at another angle and fights for a time. I call him but he is leaning on the rope and sulking. We pull him around in a small circle and tie him up again. Tomorrow will be another day. My father leaves me with Silver and we are soon friends again.

The next day is hard on Silver, but the following day he is running and walking happily wherever we go. He is recognizing his name and most times comes when I call him. This will be important. My father comes with me a few times, then I take Silver on the lead on my own but only down to the river and back. He looks with interest at animals and birds and runs to the end of the rope. He is not trying to fight me and the rope, for if he did he would probably get free.

31

The time of one moon has passed and Silver has been set free for periods of short intervals for the last few days, only with my father and me and away from the dwellings. We took him to a part of the river where the cliffs were high on one side, and the fast flowing water on the other side runs to a narrow point against the cliff face. My father held Silver where the river meets the cliffs and I went many steps away. He was released and at my call he came to me. It was wonderful. Even my father was like a boy and played games with him.

I understand my tribe's fear of this creature, even though he is not yet full grown. Our hunters will kill wolves but only if they pose a threat to people. For in all the stories of our memories, and ones that have often been told around the central fire at night, the wolves are the great fear to people who are lost or injured in the forest. They and the big cats are quick to kill. These creatures are not only feared for their danger, but they have a very powerful spiritual taboo amongst the whole of the clan structures. So what may seem simple with Silver is a huge leap for our tribe, and will be to the whole clan. Our forests and ice covered wilderness are frightening expanses. We have long clung together without changing our ways for the feeling of safety it gives. Thus the taboos against change are usually built into our laws, often for good reason.

As the days go by I lead Silver away from the camp each day and we spend more and more time with him off the leash. I have recognized another danger when we came across some hunters returning down the river. Silver was several hundred steps from me and they drew their arrows on him. It was only when they heard my shout and saw the young wolf return to me that they recognized the animal. If he had run up to them I think he would have died. My father has asked the chief to speak to the tribe and later to try and address the new situation to the wider clan. At the night fire our tribe is told that they will all be taught to feel more at ease with the wolf.

The following day the tribe gathers, and the chief tells my father and me to take the wolf slowly around all the people and see if they are at any risk. The wolf seems only a little nervous and sniffs and licks some carefully extended hands. When he comes to Arose he must sense empathy between her and me, or perhaps he has seen her standing watching more than the others. For before we can stop him, he puts his feet on her shoulders and licks her face all over. To my pleasure and surprise she throws her arms around him and hugs him. She is not hurt, the wolf has broken the tension, and the tribe all of a sudden seems to accept the creature.

In the days following Silver becomes a nuisance to almost every dwelling, often running free and exploring where he is not wanted. He has even received a clout with a few sticks and some stones. Still it is good, and lessons to stop him stealing food have been swift.

Another eight moons have passed. Silver is a large well-fed animal now; perhaps even bigger than he would have grown in the wild where there would have been much competition for food. I know he will grow much stronger.

32

There are three main ceremonial times at the changing of the seasons for our clans: the shortest day giving us the coming of warmer weather; the longest day being the time to reflect on the need to plan for survival in the long freezing time to come; and the first day of the fifth moon, the celebration of the fertility of all things, including the spirit in all life as it is given to us by the Mother, our living world around us.

In the middle of summer we have the celebration of our knowledge of the great Spirit, which gives us the sun, moon, Earth and all the stars. Another celebration is of the Mother, our Earthly goddess who, the memories say, has mated with the gods and brought us from the beasts to those who have the knowledge of their tiny part of the great Spirit. I am not sure, but I think it is why all girls, once they reach the flowering of womanhood, are taken to the enclosure of the goddess, where all stay for one full turn of the seasons, and some stay on to become priestesses. It is hoped that from these will come a favourite with the great Spirit. I have heard it rumoured that no woman has been chosen in the time of our living, amongst all of our clans. Still, it is said that across the narrow sea on a great river, there are children of those who were born from the journeying of the god spirit.

At the times of these ceremonies across all the seasons, the priestesses of the Mother are held in the highest honour. Much centres around them, although they are not amongst the people most of the time. The large wooden enclosure that no man enters is visible from the gathering place on the plains near the river. I now know that some of the information that is shown on the hides and cloth is to do with the Mother. They are not only from my journeys but are combined with the memories. I am glad they are not my responsibility, for mostly my memories fade quickly after the journeys.

I am not called to the shaman as often now. I am lucky if I go twice between each full moon. There are two journeys that, unlike the rest, remain in my memory and I wonder what effect they will have on my future, as I am unsettled and not like my friends. Only Arose remains continually more interested in my company. Both of these journeys seem to have been a surprise to even the Other Ones' shaman. They do not seem to have been of the Other Ones' memories, thus they created confusion. In me they created a particular sort of excitement, unsettling to my young confusions.

We were taken by surprise when we were joined in the Other Ones' shaman's dwelling by two people the mind thought were dressed the way of the ancient people from the beginning. They allowed us to see that they had come from far parts of the Earth, where a fragment of Ancients had not lost all of ancient civilization. They are seafaring island and coastal people. Only legend tells them how they survived and arrived at their locations. They have not sought to populate the rest of the world, but retain the Ancients' way of population control and environmental responsibility.

On the first journey they took the Other Ones' shaman and me on the longest journey around the entire Earth, stopping to see ancient stone ruins on mountain plateaus and in desert regions. They say many are beneath the earth and sand. They allow us to see where they are from a great height, so we can see where these stones are in relation to our homelands.

They show how the Other Ones have raised many huge stones in lines, located over the narrow sea, partly in memory of their lost clans and to try to place spiritual awe into the minds of the relentless Invaders. Other reasons are hidden to them but I doubt hidden to the Other Ones' shaman. The fascination with these ancient stone remnants is strong and remains when I am back in my body. I find myself daydreaming and looking into the distance.

On one of the following journeys they appeared again. This time they showed us beautiful and extensive dwelling areas, mostly of mud brick, but with many winged structures that they show us are for the moving of water, grinding of grain and a thing that sends heat through lines to light up the night. They call them windmills. They are made of wood. They show us wooden boats far larger than anything that we have ever seen, and they are in the middle of vast areas of ocean with huge areas of cloth above them. We see their dwellings in an extensive jungle all along the largest river we have ever seen in the southern part of the second largest landmass we have seen on this Earth. We see these dwellings scattered on islands across the great ocean west of my homeland. I get the feeling they have been aware of our various peoples across the old continent but have not wished to be contaminated by many of our ways.

Before they depart they show me a sadness I am surprised to feel. They introduce me to the pain in the body of the Other Ones' shaman, and show my shaman and me that our great Other Ones' shaman is not going to last much longer, and will find it more and more painful to do the journeys with us. They say that they are unlikely to journey with us again, but our new history and knowledge should register that they are on this Earth. I return to my body after this journey and it remains clear in my head and does not fade.

Sometime later I do something that I have not done before. I give to our shaman the diagrams of what I have seen. After several tries I have been able to draw my own images of what I have seen on these two journeys. This I have kept to myself, for our clans treat the markings on hide and cloth as taboo, to be made clear to the people as the shaman, chief and sometimes healer see fit. Already the desire is beginning to surface in my mind that I want to with my own eyes, touch, feel and smell these ancient places. These thoughts would be hard to explain to the members of my tribe.

33

Another winter has passed and soon there will come the ceremonies to mark, amongst other things, the entering and recognition of boys in their twelfth or thirteenth seasons into manhood. Soon to be hunters we are excited by this, even though I spend less time with the boys these days.

Whenever I can I am with Silver but the hunters have taken him over and are using him to help train the cubs which are growing now. Silver has often helped with the hunt and is greatly respected. He is kept with the others in the wooden enclosure built against the side of the cliffs. I think this is a good idea, as I often see him become very restless when he hears sounds of wild creatures of his own kind, and I wonder if he will some day go back to the wild.

Arose often meets me when I am out on my own. I hope this is not noticed as it is frowned upon for a boy not initiated into manhood to be with a young woman before her time of goddess confinement. Still, she has become Silver's and my own close friend. I am afraid and embarrassed when I sometimes look upon her. She has become beautiful in the last six moons. My young manhood thrusts hard in my clothes and I know she has been aware of it at times, to my mortification. I get the feeling she is happy I am drawn to her. I would not like to approach her as it would bring the bad luck of the Mother goddess on me and perhaps my family. Still, I concentrate on other things and I am glad of her company.

I have shown Arose the diagrams I had hidden and told her of the wonders. I could see she was a little afraid but much intrigued. Arose has another six moons to the celebrations that see her depart to the enclosure. I am uneasy but also pleased.

34

I awake to the morning of the celebration of my entry into manhood. Large heaps of wood have been organized with much of the finest fish from ocean and river plus wild game, fruit and grain. This is a feast to end all feasts. Then we boys are to spend a quarter of a moon in isolation, then return to live in the new hunters' abode until we take women of our own and form a new hearth.

There are only the three of us: Jessa, Honer and me, who will go from Garoke to Wolfman although I will still think of myself as Garoke. From tomorrow, the tribe will expect me to hunt with the men and contribute to the food and hides of all. Even my weapons will be different. My father has been working on a new spear. It is often the way. The son will be given one or two of the parent hunter's weapons. I may also get a new bow. These can also come from my mother's people.

My mother lets me off the morning tasks. I tell her I will still help when the hunt does not take me early. She gives me a look that seems to say that men do not spend as much time hunting as they should. Perhaps this will be part of being a man; to understand the ways of women. When I look at Arose, I certainly hope so. Still, a part of me seems to think it understands Arose. We are so comfortable in each other's company.

I can see Jessa and Honer coming for me as we all have the morning free from tasks. The men will not hunt today so I will get Silver and he can hunt rabbits with us. We have to be careful not to shoot him as he runs into the range of the arrows.

We go to the valley with the most burrows. The winter snow has gone and the ground animals are plentiful. We keep Silver on a lead. He can have a chance to hunt if our arrows miss, as then the animals will be underground or out of sight.

We come in from three sides, one above the rock outcrop and one each side from the front. Two of our arrows travel true and we shall contribute to the food of our people. I signal to the boys and release Silver; he has learnt not to maul the animals that are killed or dying. He races off and the animals dodge out of sight before he reaches them. I see him running further down the valley and call him back. It is not unusual for him to not return straight away if he is after prey. This time he does not acknowledge me and is soon out of sight. It suddenly strikes me that we, more especially me, will be blamed if the wolf does not return. I quickly gather the others. The rabbits are stuffed in the crack of a rock with stones put in front of them and we set off after him. We must be back by the time the sun is overhead. It is a day to be informed of what we are to do in our part in the ceremonies.

We follow Silver, calling loudly. All is quiet. By the time the sun is high we still have no sign of him. It has well and truly occurred to me that tonight I am to be called Wolfman and perhaps honoured for my part in the saga. Now I will be recognized as the one to show the least capacity with the wolf.

We are not keen to return but hurry back, hoping the animal has beaten us back and gone to the younger wolves, or at least getting into trouble for his normal bad habits around the dwellings. I have my doubts as he has not done this before. Silver has led the way and arrived back in camp first a few times but this does not feel right.

Our fears are realized. The dwellings seem empty without him, mostly right now because of the consequences. Arose is looking at us (me) as we search. It is obvious she knows what is wrong. I am again struck by the power of the communication between us, without words. There is nothing we can do, so the three of us decide to go together to see the chief.

All the tribe is gathered together in preparation for tonight's celebrations. The men are mostly in the area between the river and the dwellings where we hold part of the festivities. The ground has been cleared and a raised platform of soil covered with flat river stones is in place, with the fires to be near the river and on a high hill. Late at night after the final fire is ablaze, we will see the fires of many other tribes that make up the clan lit on high places all across the land, signaling the solidarity of our people and the power of the great Spirit in our hunters. It is a wonderful sight and reassures us of the strength of not being alone and the warmth of the fires, and what it represents with the arrival of the warm period of the year; the growth of food both plant and animal, and also that we will have the strength to survive when the ice moves back on the river and the sea. All this keeps my mind off the look on the hunters' faces for a few blinks of the eye but unfortunately it is not for long. They are angry.

The chief states not only is it bad for the safety of the tribe if the new way is lost, but he must talk to the shaman to find out the totem significance of the wolf leaving on the day of the celebration of male fertility. More than one uncomfortable, slightly fearful, and significantly angry look is cast my way.

We are glad to take our leave and go back to our own dwellings. The other boys seem to want to separate from me. How quickly blame can go to one person. Is this the way of men?

As the afternoon passes the women have dressed in their finest, and the cooking fires and the cooking pits in the ground are full of the smells of rich aromas.

35

My father and his brother and two of my mother's brothers have gathered with me at one of their dwellings to apply the marks that they all wear. Each man has the design of the clan, and then the mark that designates his own name and place in the clan. Each man tonight will tell a story of his own from the period since the last ceremony. If the chief or shaman or all the men wish it, his marks may be altered to signify an event. Sometimes only the shaman can know how this mark should look. Then the man will wear it at a future celebration until another event may change his appearance again. On rare occasions the clan may change his name.

Regardless of my problems the coming night is bringing great excitement. We move to the cooking fires and the feasting starts. Most of the eating will be finished before darkness falls and the lighting of torches and fires takes place. The food is being taken out of pits and placed on raised platforms. Beast, deer, and parts of ox have been cooked over open fires and moved to join the rest of the food. It looks great. Normally we would eat last but tonight we are led forward first, amongst much joking about boys becoming men. For the moment Silver seems forgotten; still there is a fear in the back of my mind. I keep hoping he will run into the crowd, especially with the smell of all the good meat. I would even part with my food to see his furry face right now.

Our three mothers greet us at the place of the food, as a symbol of their last feeding of us before we are separated from them and their nurturing of the past. The food is placed on flat slabs of wood using tools of both wood and bone, and sharp flint is used to carve the meat off the bone. I will eat well and close my mind to any troubled thoughts as best I can. I see Arose smile at me from the place of young people behind the adults and there is excitement on the faces of all the young. The food is as good as any I have ever eaten. It is not often that it is cooked in the coals under the ground. That makes the best flavours. It is usually cold and the best is gone by the time I get food at these feasts. It is not long before I am full but more is brought to the boys and me.

We are treated well so far. Drink is handed around and there is gaiety in the talk of the women but, as expectations of the sights and stories to come nears, there is a change in the volume of speech as a feeling of awe settles over the feasting. The drink is fermented so gaiety and some intoxication is happening. I feel light in the head.

The shaman is starting to dance and chant. It creates a feeling of importance and, one by one, he lights the torches around the ceremonial platform. The chief is first to tell his story and he holds high the hide of a woolly rhinoceros. It is one of the greatest of creatures and was his proudest hunt. My father is fourth to tell of his tale, and the men are now performing ritual dance to symbolize the animals of the hunt, and also to honour their spirits. The storyteller pretends to hunt the ritual animals of his story and it is great excitement with strong drink, good food, firelight and torches. My father mentions the wolf in the hunt but there is surprisingly little other talk of Silver. The stories are eventually told.

The shaman comes forward again and Honer's father leads him to the front and the weapons to be his are placed on a raised area. Herbs are lit and smoke covers the weapons and the shaman, and then all the tribe ask the great Spirit and Earth Mother goddess to give strength to the new hunter and power to his weapons to protect him in the journey to come. Jessa is next with the same events. Then my father is before me and his weapons, soon to be my weapons, are on the raised platform. The same events occur and I turn to join my friends in the space that has been made for us. My father stops me and I notice the chief has stepped forward. I turn to see the old hide of the silver wolf that I slay held high in the shaman's hands. He is chanting again and there is hush over the tribe. By the spirit I am slightly concerned now. The chief says the people are to join in asking me to contact the spirit of the leader of wolves and to bring back the Silver we have lost. He says it is strong magic that the Silver has left on the day of ceremony of the new hunter, now to be officially known as Wolfman. I had almost forgotten this bit.

The hide is placed over my head and shoulders. The herbs are lit and I well know how to breathe them in. I am slightly intoxicated and, without a clear head, they do not seem to work. I am not leaving my body behind, although at this moment I wish it would sink into the ground. I know what is expected of me and, in a flash, I put on a performance. After a brief period of what I hope is long enough, my eyes open again. I have been searching for the best words to say. About three breaths later the words flow. I say: "Clearly Silver has left to seek strong spirits on this day of the ceremony. He has sought out his father to bring the wolf totem to protect the new hunters and the tribe of the riverbend, makers of stone. Silver does not know yet if he will return, but his leaving was necessary to bring good fortune to the tribe and the greater clan."

The gathering stirs and the hunters look sufficiently afraid of the strong spirits that are particularly keen on looking after Wolfman. My companions look awed. Then I see the look on the face of the shaman and see that he most definitely has not been taken in by all this fine acting. I should have known. He looks hard at me, and then continues to dance and chant around the fire. After, he signals to the chief and we proceed to the high ground for one of the last parts of the ceremony.

36

A long time seems to pass with the sounds of chanting in the background. We are all aware the first fire will be lit to the north, which we may not see, at the areas of the goddess priestess compound, then fires will radiate out from there in a circular motion as each tribe sees the light. This represents the old Earth, giver of ancient knowledge, and all other fires are as the stars in the sky and the spirits of all life on this Earth.

Before long we are aware of many lights in the night. We are many and cover this land, and are strong and unified in our single belief of the great Spirit, and the blessing which has given all life spirit, and that which has visited this Earth and raised up Earth Mother priestesses in the ways of the Earth goddess, giver of life, with the form of the ancient travellers. So it is this that is told around the fires at our gathering of all the clans. I think my thoughts also get mixed up with the shaman's journeys and the Other Ones' ancient knowledge.

After a long silence and then some quiet talk the chief leaves, while signaling the people to disperse at their own leisure. I am still tense but there is also a feeling of fear for what is to come and excitement too, for we have heard rumours of the time of seclusion for a quarter of the moon. It is forbidden for an initiated hunter to tell of events of seclusion to boys of pre-initiation. I still only wear the marks of the clan; no identification marks.

The fathers and some of the uncles are taking us to gather our new weapons. Then we are making our way with the torches of the celebrations up the river to the forbidden caves which are half way up the steep cliff face north of our dwellings, about three of twenty fingers of a day. It is a quiet journey, and all but one of the torches are extinguished until we start to make our way up to the cave entrances.

There are many openings. We break up into three groups and I see the others disappear into openings in the rock face. Then we enter through a small opening which, after a short time, opens up into a large cavern. I am informed that I am not allowed to leave this cavern until one of the clan come for me. No matter what happens. If I break this covenant I am no longer a hunter and have no clan. It would probably mean my death. I am also to speak in whispers only, like all the other men.

Before they leave they light the small fire and show me that there is sufficient wood, if I am careful, to keep it going. They also leave me furs for the cold and my new weapons for my protection. Then they are gone.

37

Fear starts to set in but I take time organizing my furs and use a fire stick to look around the edge of the cavern. I am glad to see there is only one entrance. If I keep an eye out, no bears or other nocturnal creatures should seek to become my companions. I find much dry meat in the furs and there are already water pelts in the cave. It must be a test to see that I behave with the discipline, as well as the bravery, of a full grown hunter. I wish I had some of the drink of the feast to dull my senses because, as I look upon the dark cave opening which I can just barely see and see the shadows made by the fire light, my imagination works overtime. This imagination is going to be very good, especially with my journey experiences to feed it.

I pray to the great Spirit and Earth Mother that I will not need sleep for the whole time but to my horror I am already fighting to keep my eyes open. As much wood as can be spared is put on the fire. Then I put my furs against a large stone so I can sit up and watch the entrance. The night is late and much has happened to exhaust me so my eyes close, and when next they open there is a faint light showing through the tunnel.

I am alive, and all is well with only six nights to go. The fire can be lit again, so I preserve the wood for the long dark night. Time passes into what I think must be the afternoon. Without the sun it is hard to tell time of day. There are many small stones in the cave so I practise striking the stones as toolmakers do, and try and get an edge. I am not sure that this is respectful but no one told me not to and it is making the time pass more swiftly.

I see the light beginning to fade so make the move back from the tunnel entrance where the most light was, and start to strike the pyrite stones to light the tinder for the fire. It takes some time to get the small sticks to light with much blowing but eventually I have a nice little fire. As I look up to see the entrance is safe, I fly to my feet and stumble backwards.

There in the cavern, well inside the entrance area only five steps from my fire, stands a beautiful white robed young Mother goddess priestess. All the parts of her body I can see are painted with many designs. I can even see the outline of her body through the thin, white cloth. She signals me to remain silent. For some time she just observes me without any facial expression. Then she says, in a quiet voice, that I am to obey her wishes and she will show me the way of the Mother, as has been the way of the fully ordained such as her for many memories in the life of the clans. This is like the rumours we boys have heard but I really did not believe. I can feel my chest beating strongly but it is not all fear. I am nervous, but glad I am not alone to go into the long dark night. We are taught that the priestesses are wise and kind. All look up to them.

She is also a beautiful sight. All her decorations are designed to show the beauty of a woman as I have never seen before. I do not know what she wants of me but she slowly starts to touch me on the face and neck. Her hands are like butterflies. Her voice says that all love of this kind varies, for many people's passions and needs are fulfilled in different ways. She will not be the only servant of the Earth goddess to visit me during my time in the sacred retreat. Each will show me different ways to love, so that when I take a woman to my hearth I shall be more a man than a mere hunter or teller of tall tales.

Her hands move over my chest and start to remove coverings. In a short time I am naked and unashamed of the obvious excitement my young body is showing. I am aware of what will happen, as when I have left the company of Arose I have been unable to rid myself of my manhood without finding seclusion and stroking myself to an exquisite relief. My mind returns to Arose for a blink of an eye and I wish she were to be my Mother priestess. Then the thought crosses my mind that she may be with other young initiates. I realize with absolute certainty that I wish to take Arose to my hearth and do not want her to become a Mother priestess. This thought nearly loses my desire for another and, for an instant, I see the look of confusion or interest on the young woman's face.

Then her robe slips from her and her hands are moving again. She is careful not to touch me too much on my shaft, as I guess she knows my young body will come quickly. She is behind me now and, for the first time, I feel the exquisite touch of the soft yet firm contours of a woman's body moving sensually against my back and neck and even my legs. Her hands are all over my body without touching my manhood, which feels as if it is getting harder and larger. I have not been so engorged with desire. She tells me the first time we come together will be short, but then we have the long night ahead.

We are on the furs and her legs have gone around me, and I feel for the first time a woman's hand as it guides me into her. Her mouth finds mine and I feel the most wonderful sensation mixed with the lust. The feel, smell, and sounds of her are more than my body can cope with. The life force in me explodes in her. Then I become aware, although the hunger in me is relaxed and a great feeling of dazed happiness is in my mind and body, that her movements are still insistent. Then it occurs to me that she is not yet satisfied. Now she starts to teach me the ways a man can please a woman, and informs me that next time will not be long away and will last much longer. It is a beautiful classroom and as she leads my hands, fingers, body and mouth over her wonderful body, I can feel and hear her responses. It is not long before my desire grows strong again. This time it does not seem so urgent for me, but as her fingers close on me I can feel there is urgency in her. It is wonderful. I am very quickly back in her womanhood. For some time she is below me and guiding my movements, then she is on top and I am on my back, and her movements above me are noisier and more violent than the silent reverence I was taught about. I do not feel I am in a position to complain. I feel the life force release from me again plus I feel contractions and movements which tell me she has reached a crescendo also. I am awed by my teacher and elated. Then my new happiness explodes.

A large silvery form strikes her, sending her flying to the ground at least four steps away. Screams fill the cavern and the snarling of a wolf. With what diminished strength I have I leap for my spear and turn to thrust it into the beast, but I hear myself call "Silver" as if I am a distant observer. The wolf is off her and has knocked me over and is licking my face. It is my wolf.

The woman scrambles to the other side of the fire, grabbing a burning stick for protection, and I see her throw a vast amount of the stored wood on the fire. I thrust Silver off me and, while holding him around the neck, tell her there is nothing to fear. She is not remotely convinced. Even as she looks at me, I have become as fearful to her as the animal. Apparently she does not know the stories of our clan. In this dark cave, animal and man must appear as demon to her. She gathers a large piece of burning stick and grasps one of my spears. Then before I can blink she has gone. Her white robe is as it lay. I am greatly confused.

38

The great Spirit knows what this creature has done to my initiation into manhood. Probably I will be outside every law my people have ever thought of. I pull wood off the fire to preserve it and store it again. Silver will probably leave and then my nights will be without fire. I have no doubt without women also. It would greatly amaze me if one would return to do their apparent spiritual obligation, for what I am sure they will not see as a wonderful adventuresome development into my manhood. This is no way to treat a woman. This silver demon has a way of turning my life upside down. Perhaps I feel safe and secure when he is with me but I felt really good and very safe before he arrived. He should wonder if I am pleased to swap a beautiful young woman for a smelly furry creature.

He dumps himself down by the fire on my furs and shows much disregard for my feelings, except to look greatly assured that I am privileged to have his company. There is no choice but to lie down on my furs with my second choice and eventually sleep takes me. When my eyes open a large tongue slaps my face and a proud hairy creature drops a well mauled rabbit on my chest. He waits long enough to see me cook it on a very small fire and give him half and then he is off again. No doubt to look for rabbits he does not have to share with me, and female wolves he definitely does not have to look over his shoulder to make sure I am not a risk to his entire future.

The time passes slowly until the light starts to disappear in the entrance tunnel. It is the only way I have of knowing that the day has passed. I hear virtually no sounds. I decide to sleep as much as possible during the day so I will be awake longer at night when I am most afraid. Perhaps the wood will last longer that way.

From a restless sleep I feel a touch on my shoulder and my eyes open to a frightening but very beautiful sight. There are six young women and one we clan people see least of all, the mysterious and highly revered leader of the Earth Mother goddess priestesses (I know it is her but this I cannot explain). I move back to the rear of the cavern. They hold many torches and there is much light showing that all are armed, even the leader, with a spear that has a strange shape and the image of the Mother on top. They are obviously aware that Silver is not here. I am struck dumb and fearful.

The leader says three are to go to the others at the mouth of the cave and prevent wolves or other totem animals or demons I may conjure from entering. The others are obviously to stand guard, for what I am afraid to ask. I am afraid to speak. Some initiation into manhood this is. I would like to go back to being a boy before Wolfman was thought of.

She speaks: "Where is the wolf, can you conjure or call other animals or demons, and explain how this is so and why?" That is a lot for one very frightened half-man. I hear myself say: "The wolf is the only animal and he has been tamed by me since he was young. I was taught by the Other Ones' shaman the ways of using wolves for hunting, and my tribe is now training other wolves for use in the hunt. I do not know where the wolf called Silver is but I am afraid he will be killed." I ask her not to hurt him if he returns, and that if they part he will come to me without touching them (or so I hope). The spirit only knows what they will do this time if he attempts to place one of his slobbering licks on one of them, especially the head priestess. She says: "It is taboo to tame the spirit of the wild creatures." So I tell her of the leader of wolves and the events following.

She watches me for a time then asks: "How is it you have spoken to a shaman of the Other Ones, and how is it the devoted of the Mother have not heard of these events?" I do not know where to begin or how much to tell her. So I describe my first journey to the people we thought were lost to the Invaders. I can see that her face shows astonishment. She asks if this is true, and says: "I can see the wolf proves that you are telling the truth." She says: "It is knowledge that must be shared with the ordained women of the Earth and recorded."

I tell her of the capture of the young cub. It seems easy to talk to her. She says: "That is enough for tonight" and tells me that tomorrow and for as much of my confinement as is needed, they will return with the scribe who will record my story and The Knowledge brought from my spirit journeys. At the meeting of all the clans this will be discussed, and its meaning in conjunction with written memories for the future of the clan. I tell her that I have been told I am not one to know The Knowledge, only the one who can travel; that there are those of my tribe who are more capable of understanding what I have seen. She may be pleased. Her expression is hard to know with the many coloured markings on her face.

I hear noise outside and Silver appears quietly this time. He seems a little cautious of these new people. He probably senses their fear and sees raised weapons. He comes immediately to stand in front of me and issues a low growl. I tell him all is well and wrap my arms around his neck. He licks my face and I feel his tail wag. All is quiet. I walk quietly over and stand just in front of the all high and say: "If I call he will come and you can stroke his head without fear." Within a brief time Silver has worked his magic and has cautiously made himself new friends. The leader says they will be back tomorrow and I am aware that my manhood development is apparently forgotten.

My wolf, my friend, my so-called privilege. Still, I must admit the wolves have made my life more interesting. The night goes quickly with the two of us sleeping close for warmth and comfort, and in my case safety.

39

They arrive not long after light. Things have changed. Food, water and much more wood are brought in. Apparently all thoughts are off for my initiation. I just hope, with the caves being forbidden to the clans and my two friends still stuck in the dark, that all this will not be mentioned among those who are to judge me fit to be hunter, warrior and father.

Silver greets them with interest and inspects all the newly arrived goods. He even manages some food while my hunger is being neglected. They have brought seating for the all high and the scribe. My furs on the stone will do me. I am certainly not bored, afraid or lonely any more. I am a bit concerned with the breaking of traditional ways but, spirit, look who I am breaking the ways with.

They have materials on which to put down what I say, and I can help a little because, even though I do not understand all I have been shown, I have seen the drawings and can repeat some without knowing all about the stars and the relationship of the moon and the sun and the Earth; also the effect on the light, hot periods and the cold, dark winters.

They have me start from the killing of the wolves and the spiritual journeys. They obviously are interested in all detail as the light is fading when they leave; the wolf marching off with them much to my disgust. There is no thought to have a companion teacher for me in exchange for my furry friend. Life seems a bit one-sided sometimes. Still, I have a good guarantee of wood and food supply so I build the fire up and eat well. Tiredness is upon me, so to the furs early with fire to protect me.

I sleep, to awake the next day with Silver beside me. He is a part of me regardless of the faults I find in him. I am pleased to be Wolfman and contribute to the clans, even if it will not make me a great shaman and does get me into trouble for breaking the ways. My newly increased sexual awareness tells me my friends are happy not to be Wolfman and to, I presume, be experiencing the very ordinary initiation at the hands of the friendly priestesses' instructions.

They are back early and, as the journeys are told as best I remember, the diagrams begin to form. Over one in particular they seem to be especially interested: the circle with three hundred and sixty-five steps and the three inner circles, one large outer and two inner smaller circles. I do not know what they signify, except that they are connected with the combined memories of the Other Ones and the clans.

It is day six, and they have come every day with many questions. It crosses my mind that they have not asked me to go into trance and journey for their answers. Perhaps they have enough. The men are meant to come for me tomorrow. I do not know what to expect or what will be the result. I ask the high one to protect me from the things that I fear. She signals that all evidence of the extra activity is to be removed. She looks, as far as I can tell, well pleased with me. They depart once again with Silver now as their regular escort.

I prepare my last fire with more like the wood I should have to use, and take up my position with my back to the rear of the cavern. It is not long before they appear. There are two of them and they carry water hides. I hear the words: "The high priestess has said the smell of you will offend the nose of the wolf. We are to wash you." Muffled laughter comes from the other mouth and I wonder at the reverence of this. They waste no time, and my health and education by the time they leave is at least far greater than I feared it was going to be. The only problem was I was so tired from all the stress and questions that they had to work on me to keep me awake. I sleep in exhaustion.

This time I awake to the sound of men, and when I reach the cave mouth and my eyes adjust to the glare, I see the sun is overhead. The other boys appear and we head for home. I do not need to think on it to realize that I will mention nothing. Not even, or especially, not Silver. Still, I know he will turn up if he has not already been back to the dwellings. The other boys do not mention him so I know he stayed away from them. They are walking tall; I just feel exhausted. I think I am uneasily happy. I do not know if I am any smarter but I am certainly more experienced.

Before we reach the dwellings Silver enters our group and walks along with me for a time. Then, as the dwellings come into view, he runs ahead and it is hard for me not to look pleased. The hunters look pleased too and a little awed, so I gather he has not been back before now. Life may turn out for the best after all.

40

Everybody treats events as normal. We young men move to the dwelling of those without a hearth. I am surprised to hear no loud noises from Jessa and Honer. Perhaps the ceremonies and priestesses have an effect on our character. Still, they look pleased with themselves and, in a way, more confident. With confidence there is less necessity to speak loudly of ones own abilities.

Life settles down. The main thing of note is that Arose and I seem more and more drawn to each other. Every time I am in the home site I look for her, and I am pleased to see her respond to me. It is a worry that she has to go to her own ceremonies, then leave for the period that a young woman must serve the Mother. I worry that she will be taken as a priestess for the Earth Mother as she has become a great beauty. There is no other I can think I would like to form a hearth with. I know all other men want her.

I am compelled to hunt and am learning the ways of the warrior, the latter to protect against the Invaders. Before long I will be expected to spend the period of a moon in the fort of the warriors and patrol the shores of the narrow sea. There is both excitement and fear in these coming events. The men are also called on to build, repair dwellings and, in their spare time, learn the art of weapon making. The privileges of being a man has a lot of work involved, and this is without a woman and children at one's own hearth.

The joy of being at ones own hearth with Arose would be worth all the work. I think a lot this way and, unlike the other young men, do not spend all my spare time trying to earn favours from the few young women who have returned to make a hearth. Most are taken. Sometimes one of the women who has children and has lost her man, or is alone for the period of the warrior moon, will be very generous to young men. It is the way in our clan and sometimes I am very grateful, but still I think only of Arose.

Time has gone by and Arose and I have started to meet away from the clan. We both leave at separate times and join up in a favourite valley in a generous oak forest. We are aware that it is taboo for Arose to mate before her time in the enclosure of the Earth Mother goddess. Now that I am hunter I am not to be alone with her for the reasons that are close to my mind and firm in my body. Still, it has happened that we have explored and become skilled with each other's bodies without, I hope, breaking the final taboo.

We find great joy from each other and I am happier with her and sometimes Silver, than I have ever been. She knows and agrees that I must wait for her to return from the priestesses. She says she will do all in her power to return to me. The time of her leaving is drawing closer. This is making me quieter and sadder. Still, I must be careful not to draw attention to us, as I know I should not be alone with a girl who is not initiated into the ways of the Mother.

It is easy to talk to Arose and she knows all there is to know about me, including the events in the cave which I know I should not have revealed to her. We often talk for a long time about the Ancients, and sometimes of my dream of travelling to the sites I have seen from the spirit, where there are still ancient stones, sometimes in the form of walls of huge dwellings made entirely of large carved rock. This she finds as fascinating as I do.

The sun is getting low in the sky. I lift my face from the valley of softness between her legs. She looks relaxed and beautiful. It gives me a pain in the chest. It is both wonderful and somehow painful to experience her like this. We must move now, so I cover her body and lift her to her feet.

We are soon back on the track and loping along towards the river that will lead us towards the dwellings. Silver has gone ahead as usual. Most times he returns to base, but sometimes he does not. I suppose he has made contact with the wild wolves. The females of the younger wolves of our tribe help hold him. He is to be the proud father of cubs, as one of the females is pregnant.

The pain strikes me in the side of the stomach and the leg. Two arrows are in my body. As I fall I see Arose seized by several men. Pain strikes my head from behind and my world goes dark.

41

I awake in much pain and am aware of noise which, although it is close, seems from a great distance. My eyes open on a hazy view of the roof of a dwelling, and I can hear the shaman chanting and feel the medicine woman moving around me. She is changing dressings on my body and the pain increases.

The world goes dark again. I feel myself leave my body and see clearly the inside of the dwelling. Then a feeling of horror enters my mind as I remember the capture of Arose. Then I am aware of the shaman spirit communicating with my mind. He wishes to know where Arose is. He is indicating I am to journey in the spirit to search for her.

In a flash I have arrived at the scene of the disaster and am drawn swiftly down the river, then north of the warrior enclosure and over the narrow sea. From up high I see the camps of the Invaders, and then a group of long lines of standing stones the Other Ones have raised over many aeons to mark the length of the memories since the impact. I know where they are, and that the Invaders keep away from them because of their apparent magic. I see a large group of about one hundred men and women moving along a river valley. There are women in the centre of this group and I see they walk dejectedly. They are young and Arose is second from the front of about twenty-five women prisoners. I flash down to try and communicate, and for a blink she seems aware of a presence of love and I try and tell her I will come for her. I do not know how but I can tell where she is. I flash down the valley to see many dwelling sites and I see the huge central place of the Invaders. Then I am back in my semi-conscious body and vaguely aware that the wise man and healing woman of my clan are fighting for my life with me.

I do not know the passage of time, but I once more travel and see Arose moving further away and against the great inland sea. I feel myself drifting in and out of my body. I can see at these times great concern with the people of the dwelling. I know I am close to dying. My desire to find Arose makes me fight harder for my life.

Slowly I feel the world take shape and I know I am growing stronger. They have let my furry friend visit. Few others come to see me. The medicine woman feeds me and dresses my wounds.

Eventually the chief and several hunters arrive, my father and Arose's father amongst them. They ask what happened and how it was that I had taken an uninitiated young one so far from camp and apparently so often, as they have learnt. I say: "We were close but respected the taboo of the Earth goddess." They are unimpressed. I say: "As soon as I gain my strength I am going after Arose, and that in the way of my journeys I know a little of where they took her." I see hope on her father's face but still anger.

The chief says: "She will have been enslaved, used, and violated by the Invaders. She will not be able to enter the enclosure of the priestesses so cannot, if rescued, take her place in this tribe or any part of the wider clan." Still, he says: "If you cannot answer us as to why you, a hunter, contributed to the loss of a daughter of the tribe, then when you are strong enough you will be removed from the dwellings for the changing of the seasons. Twelve moons. Thus you will learn the error of your ways."

When they are gone the medicine woman tells me that it was Silver who came for my father and saved my life. Also, she and the shaman had informed the chief that it could bring misfortune on the tribe if I was not treated and was allowed to die, because of my spiritual and physical contribution to all. Then they had been allowed to heal me. This explains why my good friends, and even my mother, have not been to see me.

My strength or enough of it returns, and my weapons and some belongings are brought to the dwelling. The message is that the tribe is to celebrate the Earth Mother ceremonies. I am to leave tomorrow and not attend the ceremonies. I do not know how I feel about this, but I do know that I will leave early in the night as the moon is full, and that I will take my furry friend if he will come with me. That will make me feel better. I am unclear of my feelings, except those concerning Arose, and still far from strong.

The truth is I would be ready to leave for Arose now anyway. Perhaps I would have liked some warriors to travel with me, but in my heart I knew enough of the clan ways to know the captured women are forgotten after a very brief period of time; the end of the following day.

42

I go quietly to the enclosure of the wolves and let Silver out. With a signal he runs ahead as I do not want the guards, if they see me leave, to connect me to the animal. The pack is heavy but perhaps it is all I will have for the rest of my life. If I find Arose and the clan will not take her, we will have each other and hopefully Silver. Then I will try to find another tribe, probably far from my homeland. If the tribe comes after me in search of the wolf they will not follow far into the lands of the Invaders.

First I will need to steal one of the many water conveyances to cross over. At the narrowest point near the fort, it is only five or six stones throw across and then followed by a lot of marsh country. If I cross at night I will wait until daybreak before travelling the marshes. Once out of the marshes, if I or we survive that long, it will be best to travel at night especially while the moon is fuller. It is fortunate that the time towards the end of the warm is still with me, for this climate is far from kind when winter arrives.

Not long out of the dwellings I feel my friend's arrival and we set off for the coast. It is just before light when I reach the place of the fisherman. It is easier to take a small boat from one of the poorer of the villages, but it will not be easy to cross as the moonlight will show the boat and the water is too cold to enter.

There are guards all along the narrow part of the sea. Also the current runs strong. I am in a difficult situation and I do not know what to do. A woman comes out and puts coal from the inside fire into an outside communal cooking place. I then think that I have seen the warriors burn the reeds along the river to remove concealment from those who would attack from cover.

The wind is blowing steadily. If the fire is started upwind from the place I wish to cross, the warriors may go to the fire to check. Plus the smoke may allow me to cross unseen or at least get some protection from arrows. If unseen I will not be pursued. There seems to be no other choice. I quietly remove some burning wood and throw it out into the dryish coastal vegetation. It seems to take forever. Then a gust of wind fans a blaze, and my fire burns so well I am lucky to get to a boat and breathe and see in the smoke to get away. Thank the spirit Silver has been in riverboats before, and we cross in the smoke and early morning light unseen. After depositing the boat out of sight, I move away and leave the shore to wait until the day is light enough.

Tiredness is a part of my being now but I must move through the marshes, hopefully to dry ground with the sun to guide me and keep me out of the bogs. As the sun reaches the high point in the sky we reach a long timbered ridge. Silver has a lead from him to me, as he seems to know how to move through the marshes much better than me. There is no smoke in any direction so I light a small fire and we eat some dried meat. It is too risky to untie Silver as I need his protection for the long night to come. He seems to instinctively understand.

I sleep and wake up in the dark. It is too risky to travel by night and fear of creatures of the marsh, that I can hear all around, makes me put more wood on the fire. My friend will wake me, I hope, if any creature approaches. He may also act as a deterrent.

The next day we are travelling. I have collected eggs from a colony of ibia and both of us have eaten well as we travel. By nightfall the ground is firm and easier going. I know we have to hold this direction until we climb over a ridge of high ground which looks to me like an ancient sea shore. Then we need to travel towards the midday sun for many days, past ancient ruins and the huge stone ceremonial places of the Other Ones and those before them into the mists of time, eventually to arrive at the great inland sea which I have seen from high above in my journeys; all this while avoiding the hunter warriors of this land, where possible.

I will paint my body, both for camouflage and to help me look more like one of the Invaders. I also know a little of what a shaman of these tribes would look like and, if I appear under the wolf skin I carry, they may think me shaman. Then they are more likely to accept me being alone and in the company of an animal. Their superstitions may allow me freedom to travel if sighted, although I imagine I would be watched from a distance, if not killed. If approached I will go into chant as their language will not be mine. This, and their customs, will be part of my many problems. I could be enslaved but they more commonly keep women and boys and kill the hunters.

43

The next four days go smoothly. By day I see the smoke and avoid these places, but when travelling in the moonlight often pass close as they are on the more easily travelled routes. We are not making good distance but it is better to be safe than dead. I have collected rock pigment by day and my body wears, what I hope are, the marks of many a shaman. Even travelling at night I travel under the cover of the wolf skin.

We are living on a diet of eggs, roots, fruit, berries and small animals. The latter, if cooked at all, only require a very small fire which I sometimes light amongst rock outcrops or similar protected places. Silver seems to be almost enjoying the journey. His lead comes off but he does not stray far. It is as if he knows the territory is dangerous, or perhaps he senses my fear and has become protective. Whatever it is, I would not move as easily without him.

On the fifth day I pass the largest stone constructed by man I have seen. It is like a huge spearhead and stands straight up from the ground many times thicker than a man's body and twelve times as high. My senses tell me it has been here from before the tribes arrived here, and may be connected with the stones of time constructed by the Other Ones.

The next night sees us arrive, as morning light appears, at the long lines of huge stones too numerous to count that I have wanted to see. These are the markers of time and special or remarkable events, going back almost to the time of the great impact when ice first covered the northern lands. I know the tribes are afraid of these ancient constructions, and few if any people have entered them since the Other Ones held ceremonies to celebrate their life and memories. Even my people did not come here in the time of our common bond with the Other Ones. I stay two days, and I think I am able to use the stones as cover for fire. It is good to stop where I think there is less danger. Silver hunts and catches food for us both on the second day.

Late the next day I go to high ground to spot the smoke and plan the next part of the journey. On the way down Silver's fur rises and, although I see neither man nor beast, the animal is telling me we have company. I start to chant quietly and move, without looking obviously aware of company (I hope), back to what I think is the protection of the stones.

As dark sets in, the sound of bone flutes and drums gives an even more eerie feeling to the strange stones. I am much afraid. No one advances. We stay put all the next day and I decide to try and move out in the middle of the night. There is some moon left to guide me but I hope dark enough to go unseen. My body is covered in dark earth. I do the same to my friend who acts most offended and attempts to roll on the grass and clean himself. I would laugh if the situation were not dreadful.

We move out and again my animal indicates we are being followed. We travel well past dawn and find some high rocks to climb up on with a wall behind to give some cover. Again I see no one but the wolf remains uneasy. I sleep in exhaustion and then wake. It is still daylight and I can see by the afternoon sun where I want to go. There is smoke in two directions, including the way of my journey.

We move down the rocks and should pass the village soon after dark. Staying just off the tracks in daylight, I begin to run. Then they appear. I turn back to the rocks and they are behind me as well. More and more of them emerge from every bit of cover in two directions. It is definitely time for first contact. Now we will see how the youngest spirit man these tribes have probably seen can perform, with his body shaking greatly.

44

No one is aiming a weapon at us. There must be at least two hundred of them. I pull the wolf skin down over my face and begin to chant. The hunters separate and a very large highly decorated warrior and two shamans, one on each side of him, approach me cautiously. I am not even sure what I am doing but I look directly at no individual, and when they address me I pretend not to hear. I can tell by their faces they are not sure and are perhaps even fearful. My instincts are telling me that there is only one thing that may stop these tribes from killing or damaging; that is fear of a world they do not understand.

They certainly are not touching me. The shamans throw dust and herbs over me as they chant incantations which brings a snarl and a flash of attack from Silver. At a word from me he stops just short of the shamans. They retreat considerably but nobody tries to kill the animal.

I cannot get away from these people so, still ignoring them, I walk without hesitation straight through them, pulling Silver with me. They form a line around us and we travel straight onto the path and down to the dwellings, arriving just before dark. I go near to the central fire but on the opposite side to where I can see the chief holds court. I sit and chant for a brief period and then, with wolf beside me, appear to go into meditation, as still as I can be, which is not so hard for I am almost frozen with fear.

There is silence except for a young baby somewhere. The chief and shamans take positions opposite the fire with several very old men, and an ancient woman is carried out of a dwelling and put by the chief. Their eyes find me. I have positioned myself so I can see them without appearing to look at them. The old woman signals to the chief, and he picks her up and carries her around to just in front of me. This causes some noise and wailing amongst women who are in the background. Then, to my surprise, Silver goes to her so quickly that no one has time to react, then gently sitting by her puts his face on her crippled knee. Still I do not register awareness. Her hand rests on his head and he licks it. The chief looks dumbfounded. She slowly moves her body over to me and raises the wolf skin on my forehead, then feels my face and runs her fingers over my eyes, then my ears. I do not register. She turns and speaks to the chief and is returned to her seat of honour beside the chief. Silver stays with me.

At a signal food starts to appear and a few move off to individual dwellings. A young girl approaches me, obviously afraid, and in her fear I hear her asking the spirits and wolf not to kill her. I realize she is a captive slave, and without moving my lips I say for her ears only: "Do not fear and do not tell of my words or the spirits and wolf taboo will revenge me." I say: "Feed me" and without me moving my face she brings the food to my mouth and I eat. I say: "Food for the wolf." She is gone and soon back with a large slab of meat. All are watching but eating now. Water is brought by another who also speaks in my language. I do not respond and the first girl says nothing. Slaves obviously attend the central fires.

45

The sun has now long gone and the day is at an end. At some apparent word from the chief, warriors form two lines locking us in, with an open end leading into a log enclosure. It is obvious I am to go in that direction. I can only see it from the angle of my eyes as I have still not looked in any direction. The two slave girls are given the task of coming close to me, and the one I spoke to takes my arm fearfully. I allow her to turn me towards the enclosure then walk straight into it without looking around, pulling Silver with me. He seems to have taken all this in his stride. My chest has been pounding so hard for so long, my whole body seems to hurt. There are two small dwellings in the enclosure and, to my surprise, they are clean but almost empty. I am pleased to see that there is wood for fires.

I still have my pack and my bedroll. My weapons, except for arrows, have fallen by the way. Somehow this situation will have to be turned to my favour. We are not dead; there is one who speaks and, with care, perhaps will help or at least help me understand. She may help me with language and then, if I am able to assimilate with the Invaders, it will be easier to find Arose.

Arose has been up to now constantly on my mind and still is, except I will have to survive, hear and learn. Perhaps I will need to gain trust or create fear, as I have so far. I must think it through as carefully as possible. I know Arose is at least as far as the great inland sea to the south-east. It seems, at a guess, she had been travelling more than two moons before I saw her in my last spirit journey, near the edge of the sea. They probably would have moved faster than I could, so whatever I do it will be a long time before I get to her if I ever escape from here.

If possible I must be well prepared. I have some of the herbs that enable my entry into another world. If I can, I will use them to give me a more solid place in the tribe and keep my position of awe. I hope the slave girls continue to bring food. I keep chanting and roll my bed out on the far side of the dwelling furthest from the entrance. I will wait until it is safe to check out the walls of the stockade. It is still half a moon and the sky looks mostly clear. It may be best for these people to make the first moves.

As night deepens I hear the sounds of approach, then four men and the two slave girls arrive. No words are spoken and I drop back into meditation. More food is supplied and fed to me. The men seem glad to stay outside the entrance. The young woman who feeds me tells the other to get wood and light a fire in the hearth. When she is gone the other quietly asks how is it that I survived in the army of the spirits of the giants. She says quickly: "The tribe believes you have great protection, and that all who enter the stones of the Other Ones will never leave." She says: "They are not sure that you and the wolf are not of the spirit world." She does not know if I am or not, but is sure that I am a powerful shaman. "The tribes have not killed you and will probably not harm you because the spirit army of the ancient giants will come down on them. The shamans are in a difficult position, as they have always said that even their power is not sufficient to protect them if they entered the soldiers of the giants."

I know that the circle at the end of the stones represents the Earth, and that the lines of stones mark the passing of time and were put there at the winter solstice to mark a group of seasons. They were able to tell from these stones when the shortest day arrived and celebrate the coming of the warmth. I know a little of the request to the spirit of what they called the Living Earth, to continue to send warmth to the people of these regions through time.

The other girl has been in and out with wood and is staying now. The food is gone so they depart. The one who speaks has given no indication that she has spoken. I must try and organize it so she is a regular presence for this very young, and still frightened, new shaman. It will take time. I must move carefully. There is still great danger. I will just try to live day by day, while endeavouring to become a part of this tribe, without becoming a slave. Being a prisoner is not very different to the life of a slave, although it is hopefully a less permanent position.

46

Several days pass with little change, except the warriors on the fourth day remain outside the enclosure. I am still guarded with speech, as only the one girl must have any idea that I am partly normal. The second slave is heavy with child, while the first is showing signs of a growing stomach. I have found out that Normora, who speaks, has been with this tribe since she was traded, very soon after she was taken. She was only nine seasons old and she was taken with her mother and sister. She does not know how many seasons she has been here but has had a boy child who was taken off her after birth and she presumes he was killed. They only keep girl slaves; apparently they are less trouble. Her mother and sister went with the raiders on to some other tribe.

She says the tribes are not interested in conquering the people from across the marshes, but value the women who they steal to trade over a large area. She says there is surprisingly little fighting between the tribes of the Invaders. There is a meeting of chiefs at the gathering of the longest day, and if any tribe or individual has broken the rules or stolen from another they are dealt with ruthlessly, sometimes even losing their identity as a tribe.

Normora speaks their language completely, as is the learning way of the young. I fear it will be harder for me. The fact is, without language I have less hope of finding Arose and being able to enter the tribe that holds her. I also have little hope of leaving here without the spoken word.

If the quality of the food is anything to go by, they wish to feed the one who has the ear of the army of the giants very well. They bring more than I can eat: fruit, berries, cakes made from grains, small game, birds and large game. I have hardly seen the same food twice.

The moon of falling leaves has passed, and when the fire grows large at night I am pleased. The snow has started to fall and the weather is already very cold. The second slave has stopped coming as she is having her baby, and the guards seem to be less and less interested in me. Normora's belly is swelling noticeable now. Her fear of Silver and me has reduced. She understands I wish to learn the language and takes time, longer each day, to teach me new words. I learn the hand signs used by the hunters and many people around the settlement.

Normora is not attractive to me. The tribe does not seem to value the cleanliness of the slaves. I have asked for water hides and washed my body and hair. She has noticed and her appearance has improved after this.

Another two moons have gone by and, through all this time, Normora has been the only one to come near me. Apparently they will be happy to let me die of old age in here. If I can get through the winter in this way, then I will have learnt enough to make some moves.

47

Time passes quickly and Silver grows very strong and a little fat. He gets restless with the voices of his kind at night especially when the moon is full. Several times late at night he has woken me with his restless movements, and I have seen the light of eyes and shadows of dark bodies moving on the snow beyond the compound wall. I would say that escape over the wall would be possible, but the tribe seems to understand that I may not wish to travel into the depth of the winter at this time. Their lack of interest in me has made it possible to learn, and easier not to have to keep up the deep spiritual act at every moment. Still, I am as careful as I can be.

The people are leaving for a period of time for the shortest day festival, which is to thank Mother Earth for life and ask the sun to return. To my astonishment six slaves are locked in with me. With the settlement all but deserted, except for some old people and what appears to be only two guards, it is necessary for me to return to seclusion. There is much meditation and chanting. The slaves use the other dwelling during the day and I presume will at night. Some food is brought to me, and I think Normora will depart but she makes to roll out an old fur by the fire. I take no notice and continue in a quiet state until dark.

The fire has been built up. Normora keeps me fed, warm, and supplies what I need to keep clean. She has made an effort to make herself cleaner. As the night deepens the cold bites, and I hear her restless movement and am aware that normally, with her lack of furs, she would rely on the warmth of other bodies to keep her warm. I call quietly and instantly feel her body against my back. Her fur parts and the cold nipples and rounded belly press close for warmth. Her body warms and mine hardens. Her hand finds me and I am glad to be guided into the female and our relationship changes. I must admit that I now feel close to her, and when no one is looking she is quick to my side. My mind stays with Arose.

The people return after three days and the slaves are, once again, out of the enclosure. I presume as women, when their work is done, they serve another purpose during the cold, long, winter nights. In a way I miss the constant attention and definite language learning that was occurring during the days past.

Things return to as they were and three more moons pass. The snow melts and the river roars in the valley by the village. There are more bulbs in our diet, and flowers are appearing on the slopes behind the stockade and nearby dwellings. It is time to try and make my move.

The day arrives when I decide to pass a message to the chief and shaman by Normora, but the other slave arrives and for some days I do not see Normora. No speech is possible, so I can only hope she will return. Things are not as I would like. It will not surprise me if Silver does not wish to stay with me when, or if, we leave the enclosure. It has been six moons or more.

Normora appears on the seventh day and I see her body is flat. There is no child with her so I treat her gently and stroke her face and flat belly but ask for no explanation. None is needed and would perhaps only complicate matters.

The next day she is alone again, so the instructions are given. "The winter has passed and the spirits of the soldiers of the Ancients are pleased that the tribe has looked after the one who is favoured. Now I am to be returned to them, to gain wisdom of what is required of me and perhaps the people of the region. They are growing angry that perhaps I have grown fat and lazy with the tribe and forgotten the real purpose for my being called. On the next full moon I am to return to the place where the tribe found me."

I can see this no longer puts as much fear in Normora as I would hope, but she obviously respects the request and I see tears in the corners of her eyes as she leaves to give the message. It is seven days to the full moon. The girl I hope will handle it. She is very obviously depressed by the loss of her child and does not want me to leave.

The following day, when the sun is high, she returns and informs me that the words were too many, so she told the chief's mother that the army of the stones is coming for me on the full moon. By the spirit, that is not as I would have said it. If they do not come for me by the full moon, I know that my strengths will no longer be taken seriously.

48

As evening closes I smell the cooking fires and see the central fire being built up. Soon it is obvious that there is a full gathering. After much chanting, I presume by a shaman, a quiet falls and I hear the gate open. Normora has been and gone earlier.

There are two lines of warriors each side of the gate all the way to a space in front of the chief, with his mother on the left and a shaman on the right. There are six of the largest warriors of all, on one knee in front. The chief's seat and area is raised about one step higher than ground level. We move directly to stand in front of the warriors. Silver is on a short lead.

This time I focus directly on the chief for several blinks of the eye, then turn to his mother and bow my head slightly to her. She may be old but her eyes look sharp and full of interest. I then turn to the shaman. There is only one I see this time. I say to him: "It is necessary for my spirit to talk to the soldiers of the giants. If this does not occur immediately, my spirit will join with yours and become shaman to the Ancients as they march to reclaim the respect that it seems is being denied them." This brings about a look of fear and chanting from the shaman. It is only those close who have heard these words, and weapons are raised but the head man halts them.

Nothing happens for a time, then the head man lifts his mother from the stage and carries her to be placed in front of me once again. She pats Silver and strokes my face. This time I tell her gently: "I am going to burn herbs and speak to those who are in the world of the giants. If all is well, I will ask for the blessing and protection of their warriors and that they help guide me on my way with all I need to protect me in the first part of my journey."

I then turn and approach the fire, pulling the fur of the wolf over my body and face and removing the herbs I have saved for such as this. In a blink they are smoking and, as I move back past the old woman, I hear a sharp intake of breath. I quickly push smoke under the nose of the shaman, then return in the smoke to sit by Silver. I breathe in deeply and, as I hoped, the tribe seems to fade in appearance and once again I am spirit.

To my surprise I am not with the shaman but it is the old woman who is now with me. I know it is her however she is young, tall and slender. I am aware that she is laughing and happy. I receive the mind message that she believes the wolf and I are good and, although strong medicine, should not mean harm to her tribe.

Suddenly I see and feel the presence of my shaman from the Other Ones of the northern lands and he indicates, as we rise above the landscape to view the beautiful, clear, silvery blue scene to all horizons, that the spirits of his ancient people are meeting at the ceremonial place of his people. We view from all sides, as far as the eye can see, groups of Other Ones converging and heading for the thousands of standing stones in a nearby valley. He tells the chief's mother that all will be well with her people if Wolfman is helped to achieve his cause. Then all is gone and we are back in our bodies.

The old woman stares at me and says she is medicine woman. Then she turns to the head man and tells him she has seen the armies of the dead stretching to all horizons, and that we can give thanks that they favour Wolfman, also that we can obtain their protection by looking after the needs of the favoured one. At best I hoped to put on a convincing performance. Thanks to my friends, there was some sort of event far greater than I could have imagined. I do not know who is most in awe, the medicine woman or me. I suspect we have both seen a great amount of the world of beyond.

The chief asks me: "What is your quest?" I can see he is a little concerned. The pretend shaman looks very angry and is perhaps very worried of me. We will both be pleased to see the back of each other. I tell them that my journey takes me to the great inland sea to the south-east, and that I would wonder if the tribes would attempt to obstruct me and perhaps my many warriors. I see the old woman's eyes sparkle at this. The chief talks quietly with her for a small time then looks at the wolf and me without speaking. All is quiet.

Then he rises and raises his arms to enclose the tribe and calls in a loud voice: "Good fortune has come to my people and their borders will be safe and the hunting will be plenty. Each warm season the sun will return from the land of the great Spirit to give life to new children. One who is respected in the world of the ancestors has been amongst us, and is to travel to the great water in the south. If we are to seek favour for the many tribes of our people, he will be looked after on his journey. My son and my brother will take warriors enough to cover two of both hands to make this journey to look to the future of our people."

I can see after this that something is required of me, so when he returns to his seat I put my forehead to the ground in front of him, then turn to the people and say in my broken language: "Your chief is wise and great and will bring good fortune to the future of his people." Then it crosses my mind it might be a good idea to put a word in for the old shaman. So I say: "Your spirit man has spoken wise counsel and the valley of the ancient warriors is as his wisdom tells. No person of all the tribes will go there." I turn and bow slightly to him. I think my Other Ones' shaman would be pleased, as I know the site is sacred to them and I owe them plenty now. The chief looks pleased.

49

At a word from the chief's mother, she is unceremoniously carried to a large dwelling close to the centre and the empty seat is offered to me. I climb up onto it with Silver by my side and hope that the audience will soon end. In my opinion anything else I do or say cannot improve upon my present situation.

Food appears again and a wooden drinking vessel is placed in my hand. The chief signals and drink is poured into three vessels. The one who pours the drink consumes the contents of one cup then is watched carefully for a time before the signal is given for me to drink, which I do in time with the chief. I am in the process of wondering why the other man drinks first when I realize that the headman is not a trusting person. The thought is cut dead as a burning sensation enters the back of my mouth and sears its way down my throat to endeavour to create a hole in the bottom of my stomach. I gasp for air and wish I was close enough to the river to attempt to swallow the lot. A horrified look at the chief shows me a look of sheer pleasure and satisfaction, and I thank the spirit he is busy organizing the other entertainment, not seeing my reaction to the drink I have heard the Invaders call 'spirits'.

Attractive women, near naked with many designs on their bodies, begin to sway, dance and sing as drums and flutes create the accompanied sounds from a group behind them. By the time my host turns to me I have controlled all expressions, and can feel the warmth of the liquid moving through my body. That part is enjoyable. I sip the drink gently and it goes down easier. My host throws his head back and empties the vessel and immediately refills. My situation is topped up also. It is not long before my head starts to spin and I feel an elation that I have not experienced from drink. Control seems to be slipping away from my tongue and I sense danger, so spill some of the liquid when I hope nobody is looking. It is better to pretend to drink than to say the words that may be my undoing. Still, I would like to try this drink amongst my own people. Before long the chief seems to have had enough and signals the end, then without a word moves off with a group in attendance.

They seem to have lost interest in me so I return to the enclosure, closing the gate behind me. My head is spinning. Now there is pain emerging in my forehead with a desire to vomit the contents of my stomach. Water seems to be a help and I lie on the furs but sleep does not come easily.

Time passes and movement raises my head. The old woman is sitting beside my furs with Normora kneeling behind her, seemingly in attendance. She obviously has helped her to my presence. I rise and put wood on the fire and sit quietly while the flames build up, lighting up the weather beaten visage. Then she smiles and says: "It is good that the ancestors of the ones you call the Other Ones are our neighbours and are content." Then she says she has travelled in the land of the dead many times but always only with the ones who were her people's ancestors. However she does not feel that the stones are the soldiers of the giants. Still, if the ghosts of the Other Ones will live in peace with her people, she will preserve the legend in order to protect all parties. She asks: "Why are the stones there?" I tell her the location was at a time when the ice mountains stretched all the way to that place. At a period of many seasons, perhaps ten hands, and on the shortest day, a reminder was put up to mark the passage of time and the angle of the sun at the beginning of the new birth of the sun. It was a part of the celebration of their memories. I explain a little of their memories. She thinks quietly for a time then says her people needed the land for the hunt but I can see that she is saddened, as if there is a loss that she does not quite understand. I tell her of the circle of stones and the Earth they represent. This seems more than she can believe. I show her the herbs I use which she knows, but says she will do some searching with the help of her people. I do not think she will try to make contact again but suspect her influence with her son will not do any harm.

Now I receive my next surprise that I have mixed feelings about. Normora has become special to her and it has pained them both that her last child was removed. She says: "The chief has agreed that you should have a slave to look after your journey. You will leave at the second sunrise and my people will take you only to the great sea then return to their mother, grandmother and their people."

My thoughts turn inwards and I worry that I want to find Arose on my own, and wonder if Normora will not get in the way. The old one signals for the girl and me to take her back, so obviously the decision is made. It is not to be mine. It strikes me that I may have a friend, but wonder about the complexities of one female slave and twenty-two warriors.

50

There is not much to gather so the following day we are quickly on our way. There is fast travel; even the female is hardly slowing us down. Each day we seem to be reaching warmer climates. Several times we stay on the outskirts of villages. The runners who travel ahead seem to clear the way for us. We lose little time hunting and some days are even fed. It comes as a great surprise that those who we have known to be so violent for time into memories have so much co-operation between their own tribes.

The mountain passes would have been a major obstacle for me. There is no sign of mammoth or reindeer now, and I see the clothing designs and jewellery of these people is changing. It is not as fine as the people of the north and has little fringing. They do not have needles as fine as my people, but I see an increase in woven cloth from wool and thin plants that are apparently common to this area.

We have already been travelling half a moon. It feels good to be travelling south of the cold. The new leaves are starting to make appearance on the birch, elm and oak which are a common part of our surroundings. This is a sure sign of warmth to come.

The runners have returned and informed us that they can go no further. They say the people of the last encounter were harder to understand. The language was similar but, as we move south, more words have no meaning to them. They suggest the reception was not threatening but cautious, and it may be better to go around communities when smoke is seen. Our pace may be a bit slower; it is hard to tell. When it is flat of surface or there is track to follow we move easily but this is not always so.

Today the vegetation is changing and from a high rise I see dunes in the distance. We are approaching the sea. We will soon be just two people and a restless wolf. I have a feeling the warriors are becoming uneasy in strange lands with language and customs a noticeable difference. Still, the slave traders obviously travel this route amongst different people.

Just before dusk we make camp in the valley of a dune, with a small fire which we will build up after dark to keep away the large cats that hunt in the night. The woman gathers seeds and kindling as we travel. She keeps me warm at night and is better by far than I am with communication amongst the tribes. I still find I play the silent shaman and it seems to have effect. I doubt these hunters would hesitate to kill some stranger who has no protection of taboo.

The next morning we move up the dunes onto a ridge with exposed high, bare ground. There is smoke in three directions. We choose to travel the remotest direction but still as I would journey. The view is beautiful; pine below and forests of deciduous tree in the valleys where one stream runs between sand dunes. We are approaching a high point where I hope we will be able to get an idea of destination. I part some low scrub and follow the warriors who are now pointing excitedly at something. I come over the top and stop in my tracks.

To see it for the first time is wondrous. I can hardly breathe, for as far as the eye can see is an endless blue green ocean. Below me, waves roll in white stretches onto golden sandy beaches and outcrops of rock in many colours. As the waves break, rainbows of every colour rise in the mist with the sun behind. In the distance to the east lies the entrance to a large river, and on the far bank are many elephant and several mercks rhinoceroses. On this bank is a herd of ox. Alder and ash grow in the valley with new spring leaves. Further this way are stands of ash and aleppo pine, with red deer grazing not far from the frames of what appear to be three deserted oval huts. With the colour of the heather on the slope between the groves of trees, it is the most beautiful sight I have ever seen. Even more so than any I saw in the silver blue twilight world of the journeys. Further north-east behind stands of what I see are of sylvan pine, fir and spruce, are the foothills running towards an endless mountain range.

It seems a long time before I look back to speak to the warriors. They are gone without a word and I do not have to ask to know they will not be back. This world of beauty must have evoked fear into their very being. Even the woman is moving close to me and I can feel her trembling but the look in her eyes holds excitement too. It is great discovery for us both. I know Arose came this way and moved east. From here I will try to locate her from the world of the spirit. We will approach the tribes if we must.

51

Amongst these tribes Silver could quickly be dead, with Normora and me back in slavery to masters probably more fearsome than we have seen. We move out and I plan to go to the huts after dark if there is no sign of people. We will look at the sea and perhaps tomorrow I will hunt for deer or boar to replenish our dried meat. Normora can try the river and seashore, if she recovers from her fear, for fish or the flesh of the shell. There is definitely a great wealth of food here. It will be the territory strongly guarded by a powerful people. If we decide to stay longer than a day we will have to make contact with the tribe. Offence or crime may be judged upon our taking of resources.

The following day before dawn, I put out the fire and tell Normora to stay near cover and keep a look out while she moves about. As the sun rises I am upwind of a watering place, below a spring of fresh water. I do not have long to wait. I hear the sound of boar and their dark shadows move close to me to drink. It is a strong temptation, but I know the deer were close yesterday and will probably water morning and night. The boar moves off and I wait. The mist clears with rays of sun slowly penetrating over the colours of heather, silver bark and new leaves.

Then a set of majestic antlers is outlined against the morning light. My bow is loaded and pointing but I stay perfectly still, keeping my breathing slow and even. He moves to the water and drinks, then looks around. It is some time before he gives an unseen sign that all is safe. Then five more deer move out of the shrouded forest. This is what I have waited for; a fawn that can be butchered and carried easily; one that will feed us well for a quarter of a moon without waste; one that will be easier to butcher then dry. They put heads down to drink and, as my beast turns to leave, it presents a perfect target. The arrow goes deep into the chest just behind the front leg and it is down within three steps. The deer are gone and I quickly cut the throat then slit the stomach cavity to remove the contents, keeping the liver and heart. The carcass can be carried swiftly now on one shoulder. Before any large predators arrive at this water hole I hope to be back in camp, leaving little scent on the trail to follow. There are no events and within a short time I am back near the huts. I gather the woman and Silver, then move into rocks near the pine grove to complete the butchering.

Before the sun is above we have the meat we will eat today separated, and the rest in thin strips for drying tonight. We risk a small fire and eat wild bulbs, roots and small pieces of meat. It is good. We feel relaxed, and the sight of Normora's happy smile and the food in my belly makes me aware of a growing need for the closeness of my companion's body. She quickly comes to me, and the sun is lower in the sky before I release her and rise to my feet.

All is still well. We wait in shelter until evening is close then move our meat to a hut. Silver is tethered and fed at the entrance to the hut. He will guard our meat while we move to the seashore to discover in last light what shellfish are here. A stone quickly frees several rocks, and the smell and taste are not unlike the river mussels from my home river. This will be food for the days to come. In the cover of the hut after the sun has gone to sleep, the fire is lit and meat is placed over framework. Long before dawn we sleep, with food to travel.

52

The next day sees us moving inland along the great river. It is not easy to cross. We will travel inland towards one hill in particular that stands out higher than the rest. I do not know how to get over the river as we have had help this way over the last part of the journey. I speak with Normora and she surprises me by simply saying there will be many rivers to cross. If we move inland away from the coast we will build a reed raft for our packs and swim with Silver to the other side. This we do on the second day without incident. The hill is now to the east and in the direction instinct tells me we must travel.

We travel over many rises, gradually making our way to the high point. There is evidence of large and small game everywhere. Ground marmots are common. Bird life is prevalent in the sky and in the foliage on the earth. It is a cold day but the sky has enough blue to keep away the rain so we travel well. Smoke from inhabited sites is to the north and south. We make camp in a steep gully just below the west of the hilltops. It is cold up here so we gather a fair quantity of wood and brush ready for the fire of the night. I have to risk Silver running, as we must allow him to feed and water himself and live in many ways as those of his kind. There is no water to spare in this high place.

I leave a spear and my bow and head for the summit. Several high country sheep move away from me but with food to carry and only one spear they are safe. As dark closes I feel in harmony with my world. It has gone better than I could have hoped, and it is time to call upon the spirit within me to hopefully find guidance for us. The sky is an expanse of deep red, running from an orange sun moving to violet and green, then deep purple. I have been careful to note my way back but should see from above the fire when it is lit and follow the gully down.

Just before dark I take dry matter and herbs for the journeys from the pack and create the smoke of the shaman. With chanting, it is brief time before I leave and soar once more into the silver blue world. There is no sign of the sunset colours here. I want to see the journey I have come and the way to go.

My spirit soars high above the clouds and I see the ocean take shape and eventually the whole way of my journey. I see the great white sheets of ice that come nearly down to the land of my people. I see the ocean as it runs to the entrance of the enclosed sea that we are camped near. I see huge mountain ranges running to the north and far to the west. Across the sea there is a large land running south. There is the lay of magnificent rivers with the feeling that, in other lives, I have travelled much of this land and many of these rivers. I know this is true. I see there are two ways to the land in the south; one over land like a leg kicking a stone connected to a rope which continues then to the south land, and the other east then south over rivers and between gulf seas towards the land of the greatest of all rivers.

My whole being centres on Arose and I am drawn far to the south-east. I see the direction I travel and, to my horror, see that she has not stopped moving, but must still be with those slave traders who stole her from us. I move down and find a camp with a large fire and some thirty warriors and some five women. They are settling down for the night. The traders have valued the beauty of Arose, and I see her take food and drink to one of the men who seems to be a leader. He roughly takes the drink, motioning the food to be put aside. As Arose starts to move away he commands her to return. She seems to know what is expected of her. She kneels in front of him and his hands travel over the private parts of her body. I see her uncover his manhood and lower her face.

I am back in my body. My heart is tight in my chest and I feel tears flow down my cheeks. Not only has she moved a great distance away, more than three times the distance I have come, but I presume the traders are on their way to another raid or continuing to raid. I also fear for Arose for another reason, for I see her body is swelling with child.

I look back in the direction of my homeland and am aware that I have little to go back to. I have always been strengthened by the thought that where Arose is can be my home and I will be strong with her. Now I have to overcome my doubts and understand her hopeless position, and continue until I find out if she lives or dies and what she wishes to do when I find her.

53

For a long time I sit as if numb, then slowly my thoughts come together. It is late when I come down the hill. I am not alone, and as I leave the summit I hear a noise and before I can raise the spear my wolf is by my side. He has a way of making me feel very vulnerable when he does that. Still, he may be equally good at protecting us, and many times he has warned me of approaching animals and sometimes the approach of man. I hug the animal to me and feel great comfort. Then attaching a lead to him, I find it easier to go to the light of the fire I can see burning dimly in the gully below.

Normora has kept the fire burning and I expect the fear of being alone has kept her awake. I call as we approach to let her know it is us. In her fright she may put an arrow into a body that has had its fair share of pain for one night.

I do not speak to her of the journeys but I will in time. She is not like Arose to me. However her company is important to me and the warmth of her body is now a part of my life. Her appearance has become clean. She is no slave to me. This awareness is apparent since the warriors have left. She speaks her mind more often and is quick to offer opinion.

At sunrise we stoke the fire a little and warm some meat. Then we roll our packs with the few possessions we hold and rope them, leaving Silver tied to them much to his disgust.

Normora and I go to the top of the hill. I tell her as shaman I travelled in the spirit and saw all the land from a great height. I point to where we have come from, and do my best to tell her what lies in the other directions. It is said that I will take a long journey and travel around the sea to the great rivers. It will take a long time and I will risk meeting the tribes from time to time to learn their ways and, if possible, become in part as they are. I say to her that she is welcome to stay with any people she finds good to her, or try to return to her people or travel with Silver and me. She looks happy when I say these things. I say: "You are a free woman." She says she would not be welcomed back to the customs of her people and alone would be food for the great cats. The traders and tribe were not good and slew her children. "Normora belongs, if not to Wolfman, then she belongs with him and the wolf as long as you will have her." I am quietly, greatly relieved, partly because she has an ability to understand language much more quickly than I do.

The coast runs for as far as we can see. It has good food and shelter from the weather. We have seen that the warmer ocean supplies easy food. As time goes by and knowledge increases, I expect there will be more food. If we ever settle only time will tell. All these thoughts have passed through my mind and been spoken openly to Normora.

54

We recover our very sulky and slightly angry friend and the journey begins. We will not look for people but if their dwellings or hunting parties cross our path, we will acknowledge them and attempt to come in peace. After our time with the Invaders my friend is as one with them, and the hide of the lead wolf and the companionship of wolf should place me as a probable shaman regardless of my young age. These past seasons have made me much stronger and I feel old beyond my time as the head of a tribe of three.

By nightfall we are closing on the coast again and camp upwind of water, so hopefully the beasts will not smell our presence. They often hunt the creatures that come to drink. Where possible I camp with a cliff or cave behind me. Here this is so, and we feel some protection with fire in front.

It is three days before we come across smoke which is directly in our path. We find the people first: three warriors, five women and children. The men quickly take up weapons as we approach. When we are in range of their arrows, I lay down my spears and bow on the ground and open my arms in what I hope is a gesture of friendship. I pat Silver to show that the animal is friend and my companion does the same.

There is much talk for a time, then they approach. The men speak first and then, without touching, inspect my weapons. I slowly bend and pick up one of my spears by the sharp end and hand it to one of the warriors for his inspection, using the words: "We travel in peace. We wish to pass through your lands. After rest and, if required, shared food, we will depart. I ask the great Spirit and Earth Mother to bring blessings on your tribe." They speak, and the words for Earth Mother and great Spirit are repeated. I make the sign that I would like to hunt or gather food to share with their people. The warrior returns my spear and signals to the women. They approach a little but I can see they are afraid of Silver so I place him on a lead. Normora pats and ruffles his ears then walks to the women and opens her hands as a sign of friendship. She comes in peace. Then they are all talking and moving away towards the smoke.

Both the men and the women are heavily tattooed on both the face and arms. The women also seem to have a lot of earth ochre marking their features. I hear some words the men speak that are familiar. They, however, use hand signals as the Invaders and similar to mine for the hunt. I see boar and deer at the watering place of the animal kingdom. These look fearsome men but their behaviour is as I would greet a traveller from a friendly tribe.

We move off at a brisk pace, only stopping briefly when we hear the call of a tiger. They point to women going to camp and the tiger call direction, then where we are going. I see that the creature is to be considered but is not an immediate threat. Still, they can come at any time but are a greater threat at night. Before evening my arrow finds a boar. They waited for me to kill. It is as though they are allowing me the courtesy of being a part of their tribe. This is a custom but I am surprised. Perhaps these men are unusually good men.

We move back to the dwelling place by the light of torches, as clouds have covered the moon and stars. I am pleased to see that Normora is helping the women with food and children. She is laughing and singing happily. There is much joy in these people, a tribe of about fifty people. There is obviously much food but it is the good time of the seasons. With the winter behind, all nature is coming to life with all the resources it brings.

The boar is presented to the headman and he laughs, and I can see the welcome in his eyes. The creases on his face speak of wisdom as he looks upon me. He observes the wolf skin and the presence of Silver. There is a great depth of character behind the laughter. This man will know how to be harsh to protect his own, but I sense he will treat us fairly and learn all he can from me about the places I have been to and the ways of the people, and especially all he can of the wolf. I can see as he talks to the warriors that

Silver is the main topic. He asks me a question, which I get the gist of. My answer with words and signs is: "The animal helps me to hunt." I am careful to say: "He can only hunt for me, as he has been with me since a very young age. He is a friend and helps protect me when the fire burns low and during travels in unfamiliar land." The chief obviously only half understands me which does not surprise me, as even the people of the warrior stones had to listen carefully.

A woman is signaled forward and the headman speaks to her. She turns and says she is from a northern tribe and came after a gathering of the clans. I call Normora and ask her to speak for me as the woman will speak for the chief. They talk freely with each other. I also understand them better. Through them the chief hears my words on Silver and learns that a far northern tribe is my home. No mention is made of the lands west of the narrow sea. He asks me if I am of the ways of the shaman. I say I have knowledge. He seems pleased and more relaxed with Silver. None have tried to touch him and I keep him on a short lead. Food is brought and we talk for a long time.

I am very comfortable with this man and his people for they seem to have genuine warmth. There is much laughter and love with their women and children. We are told we can stay until we are strong to continue on our way, and shown a space under a lean-to for our furs. We sleep long with full bellies and feel safer than we have for a long time.

55

A quarter of a moon goes by and their language becomes a little more familiar to me, and very familiar to Normora. She is good for me but I wonder, as I see her amongst the women and children, if she will continue with me. The decision is hers. She may seek love and freedom wherever she wishes, as long as it does not endanger me and my furry friend.

On the seventh night, after learning much from these people and some of the ways of the slave traders, I thank the chief and ask his permission to move on the next day. He motions to one who I now recognize as his favourite wife, who then enters a dwelling and returns with a string of teeth and nuts. He places this around my neck and says this will give me introduction and, as long as I respect the spirit of the hunt and the resources of the tribe, safe travel until I am beyond the twin rivers. He tells me that the slave traders do not raid any tribes this side of the rivers, and usually travel many moons to the land of the south before taking women to trade. Their trade in humans is much in demand: dark skinned women from the south and fair haired women from the north. "The traders are nomads without a single tribe. This also means there is less war between the clans of the south. They sometimes come north looking for their lost people, and have won wars and taken our people in return". I thank him and praise his wisdom in front of many of his tribe.

The next morning I fold my sleeping furs and start to leave without Normora, but she catches up and I see tears in her eyes. Her speech is angry and hurt when she answers me. She softens when I say she may have been safe and happy with those people. "Where I go there is much danger." So I say: "For your safety you may have to return so, as much as you can, you are to remember the land marks. Not the details. One outstanding feature, every few days. The sun, bark and moon will guide you in between. That way the direction will stay with us both."

We move south of the rising sun towards the coast once more. I remember the two fingers of ocean I will have to go north of but that is many moons from now. There is enough dry meat for several days but the new food of the ocean will help if the hunt is not successful.

Some good things are happening to us. The rain that has fallen for the last three days has stopped so the distant mountains should be clear to guide us on our way. I free Silver while we are still in the area of this tribe as he is safer to roam without finding an arrow. Silver is soon back to show us his skill at marmot hunting. His belly is full.

I have heard wolves in the distance while we have been here. I hope his other desires do not get the better of him. I feel some instinct tells him he has no group and this will make him cautious about crashing in on the females of a dangerous pack.

The days pass and we continue to avoid people where possible, mostly because it takes time to follow the customs. I kill only what we can eat or dry to take with us. In the first days one group of warriors approached us. The necklace was recognized and they allowed us to pass along, and assured us there would be recognition of our fires as we pass through their lands.

We still hear the odd tiger but the largest increase is in the number of lions. Our journey has been forced to change directions on many occasions. Silver even stays close while these great beasts are about. We have been lucky no great tiger of the huge curved teeth has been seen on the journey, although many have warned us of this beast. It is the most dangerous and fearsome of all to humans who travel in small numbers. The look on Normora's face tells me she has some after thoughts about returning to the good people. Still, when she lies with me at night her movements are eager and happy and comforting to me.

56

Five moons have passed and, regardless of avoiding people, we have taken on much of their appearance. As we have moved in and out of tribes, exchanges of clothing and stories have taken place. At first Normora, who is a wonder with strangers, allowed herself to be painted amongst the women with the many coloured ochres. However we are still separated by the colour of our hair, as ours is lighter. The skin of these tribes grows gradually darker, with some members being totally black. I presume they are the children of slaves. There is some fair hair but most have black hair. There are now fewer tattoos on the bodies we see. When the meaning of the teeth necklace faded we were given a new totem to travel with.

The worst problem we had was a headman who drove us out of a village after enclosing Silver in a blockade, not without a struggle, and two warriors will wear scars on many parts of body for many moons. We travelled until dark and then I returned, but before reaching the village was knocked flat by a creature that had an expression accusing me of blatant disloyalty. At times I think this animal is more human than almost all the people I have met in my travels.

I am beginning to realize that, except for the slaves, I have travelled more than any of my clan. I suspect what has happened to Arose and how she has gone so far away is most unusual. It would have been better for her if she had not been so attractive to men. I pray to the Earth Mother and great Spirit that she will be all right, and also that I will find her and know what to do when I get there. I will not be able to trade with the dealers in human beings.

We moved inland and passed a great finger of water to the south, and now are approaching the first of the twin rivers. It has been a little colder again and a lot of rain has fallen. Hunting has been good and when we were in areas of tribal recognition Silver ran free, often helping in the hunt. Some tribes have observed this, and I think there will be cubs taken from wolf dens in the future over some of the area we have touched. Many rivers are not easy to cross. The snow and ice of winter is travelling to the sea at a rapid rate. The rafts we have become skilled at making even carry Silver several times.

57

We have come over the cliff top with the river below. It is wide and swift. Then we see it; the huge body with fewer stripes than a normal tiger but nearly twice as big. It is in rocks moving towards a water hole with auroch drinking. As we see it, the great head snaps around and sees us. We are upwind and it caught our scent immediately.

We pull back quickly, running as fast as we can towards a thicket of trees and rocks while out of sight of the creature. We are nearly at the thicket of trees when the tiger tops the cliff. With all the speed total terror can produce, we enter the trees and instantly seek cover. There is hope in holes under rocks. I grab Silver and slide under a large ledge just wide enough for our bodies. The woman comes next but, to my horror, it is not deep. The entrance at the rear is too small to leave by. I jam Silver as far back as I can and drag Normora in as far as possible. I thrust the rocks forward, making more room for her and giving some hiding space. I do not have room to use a weapon properly. Still, I thrust the spear out the entrance and it snaps like tinder and is swiped from my hands.

The worst has arrived. The great head thrusts forward and the large curved teeth are no more than an arm's length from Normora's legs. Some smaller stones are behind me. I pull these forward, telling her to push them between herself and the beast. Its hot breath is filling the space, and the terrifying noise coming out of the depths of the creature drowns out the girl's screams and probably mine. The wolf is struggling behind me to escape. A great paw appears and swipes two of the stones and one pack clear of the entrance. It attacks again as I desperately remove more rocks, making space to move back, when a scream of agony fills the air. I thrust the stones forward and finally drag Normora out of reach, I hope. There is blood and her leg covering is torn clear off her body in a bloody mess. I now have room to pull her under me, and I grab the other pack and pull it towards us. We are out of reach of the tiger but it is not giving up. I have never felt such fear. My hands find her wound and I am glad to find the wound is flesh and not into the bone. Her screams go on. The surface is stone above and below, so the creature can only come as far as it can fit. I frantically remove more debris and shove it towards the beast. Now I have room to perhaps draw the bow. Normora must have gone into shock as the screams have stopped.

The beast is going from side to side, alternating its head and its great claws as it desperately tries to get three very easy meals. It crosses my mind to let Silver try and pass and draw the tiger away. I do not think he would live to get out. My best hope is the bow. I cannot use the other spear as it is too long and would be splintered before it could reach its target. The bow is moved into position and an arrow fitted. I cannot aim but it will not matter as long as I can draw far enough. The claws rip the arrow out of the bow nearly taking the bow with it. I try again, pushing the bow as far back as possible and placing the arrow further from the entrance, then moving the bow forward to draw the string. I can see Normora has registered as to what I am doing and is lying dead still to help. Even the wolf seems to realize something and stills. I take the shot but the speed the beast moves avoids it. Another shot is set up. The beast is quieter now, concentrating on how to reach us; angry but aware that we are not going to be an immediate feed. The auroch and other animals will be well gone by now. We are food or go hungry for the immediate future.

I cannot be sure where its body is so I must wait for its head to move in front of the arrow. There is little room to direct the aim. The pain in holding the bow open in an unnatural position is acute. The arrow hits but moves sideways off the top of his head, not damaging him at all. If possible it has made him more furious. I rest for a time then pull the bow again, but he is gone for the moment and walks a little way off. Terrifying screams exit from his mouth. He is giving voice to his fury, letting us and the rest of the animal kingdom know he is king, or queen for that matter, of beast and earth which very definitely means woman, man and wolf.

He is back and the mouth snaps open. The arrow leaves, burying deep in the open mouth and apparently pinning the tang to the animal. It is gone with hardly a noise, except for the struggle to remove the arrow. The noise is moving away. Then the realization of what has just happened enters my mind. My body shakes uncontrollably and then I collapse. I am not sure if the sound of sobbing is from me or Normora. The fear and trauma in me is too great for me to register relief at this stage. How debilitating the wound is to the tiger I cannot be sure.

Slowly I become aware of the woman's attempts to deal with the wounded leg and the pain it is causing her. There is little to help her until I find out what is going on outside. I ease my body forward to look carefully from under the ledge, ready to flee back at the first movement. There is blood and fur on the rock but no sign of beast. No sound can be heard from bird or animal. It is as if all have stopped to listen as the attack is completed. Now all are confused. The beast should have been feasting, leaving the rest of the animal kingdom to continue the journey of life. I wait a time. Perhaps it is on the ledge above, waiting to leap as I emerge. I do not think so. There is blood in the direction of the river from where we came.

We cannot stay under the rock. If possible, I must clean and bind the wound. I put an arrow to the bow and ease my spear out, then quickly follow and stand up. With fear in every step, and my back to the rocks where possible, I move through the trees on the trail of blood and into the clearing on the cliff top. There is no sign of it. I see from the blood it has moved north along the high country of the river. The problems facing this creature will prevent its return.

With Normora leaning on me and quiet in her pain, I follow Silver down the slope to the river. It is hard on her but thank the spirit the blood is not flowing freely. She is brave or still in shock for her body is, at times, shaking violently. Mine is not much better, and the wolf seems to have lost much of his normal free-ranging adventurous nature. With our brave guardian on hand I gather moss and clean the wound, then bind it with clean moss and strips of hide.

After washing the blood from Normora's torn clothes we move back towards the small cavern. It will be a safer place to light a fire and sleep. I think all creatures will steer clear of the area for the immediate future.

The sun is low by the time I get the fire going. I arrange the furs in the cavern and make Normora warm and as comfortable as possible, then take her food. Normora eats then collapses into sleep. It is good to know I care deeply about her. After gathering wood I move in beside her with the wolf at her feet. Eventually sleep comes but the dreams are full of nightmares.

58

With first light I stoke the fire. I do not think we will travel today. I do not even know how I can travel Normora over a long distance for help from a local tribe, if it can be found. After checking on her I move to the cliff top and scan the landscape to the far horizon for smoke or sign of human occupation. There is a lot of smoke to the south-east and north-west. They are river people and it does not surprise me, for this must be one of the richest places of all my travels. Contact is within easy reach for me but will be a long and difficult journey for Normora.

Looking at the countryside there is no sign of game. The land is full of grassland and forest, both deciduous and conifer, and a tree called cedar that is of this land and not mine. I wonder at the lack of animals. It does not seem likely that one or even two large cats would cause this exodus. There will probably be wolf, hyena and a family of lion in river land such as this. The animals that graze know that predators are a part of existence. I am confused as to why even elephants are not visible somewhere in the distance.

I decide to take water from the river and dress the wound then stay for two days or longer if needed. See if the wound heals. Without knowledge of the healing herbs I am fearful that the leg may become poisonous. Then death follows. This much I know without being a medicine man. It is also necessary to replace the spear shaft and replenish the arrows.

After dressing the wound I leave Silver and my spear with Normora, and follow the river to a marshy area with tall thin growth of what turns out to be a hard light timber. It does not take long to find material for both spears and arrows. I have also seen good flint for my needs, so the days will be busy while hopefully Normora heals. I return with the wood and then go for the flint. It is not long with a good small fire burning before the wood takes shape and hardens in the smoke and flame.

Normora sleeps a restless sleep until the day is late. With waking comes the pain. I bring her out into the fresh air and decide that, if we are to stay here, it would be good to extend the cavern with some supports and rushes to keep out the weather. After talk we decide the spear first, then the dwelling tomorrow. Silver and I try to keep her happy but, although she is brave, I can see she is in pain. A low growl comes from Silver and he suddenly moves away from the fire. The hair is up on his neck and he is turning now in all directions. Whatever it is, it is not alone.

59

Then they are there; on the stones, in the trees and vacant areas all around us. Their bodies painted. I lay down my spear and bow and move to bring the wolf to Normora's side. There are too many to count. They are in every vacant spot and beyond. They are silent. Several who are obviously headmen step forward. One speaks, and I recognize the words for "the tiger that kills men", but no more understanding do I have. I look to Normora, and she says they asked if I am the one who looked into the mouth of the man killing tiger and put the death blow to the creature. She confirms this and I presume explains something of what happened.

They speak back and forth for a little time. Then she tells me they ask why it is that I speak through the mouth of a woman? I say: "Tell them I am shaman and that I come from far to the north where little of their language is spoken." The chief signals and several of their men leave, and very quickly the sound of drumming fills the air. They speak, and I am told that the tiger killed people from all the tribes in the area of the twin rivers. He killed with such cunning and ferocity that the tribes believed the Earth goddess protected him. The hunters of six tribes came together to drive the beast into a corner not far from here and destroy it. This they had done, for no single tribe was a match for one of the saber tooth such as this, the most fearsome predator of all. Even a pride of lions runs from the fury of the terrible leader of cats.

One says: "You are young to be shaman. Is it the way of your people?" I place my hand on Silver and say through Normora: "I am known as Wolfman and, at a very young age, slew a leader of wolves and the father of my friend. My spirit then ran with the wolves and has journeyed far into the world of the spirit since, bringing much ancient knowledge to the leaders of my people and the servants of the Earth Mother."

More people try and move into the confined area. The crowd parts and two more headmen step forward. Much conversation is exchanged. We are asked what we are doing in the country of the tribes of the twin rivers. I say: "I have journeyed with the spirit to see great achievements from time beyond our legends, a time before the legend of the great impact. I am travelling in the body to see with my own eyes some ruins that may have survived." There is talk, and they say they have heard of such things in the southern lands. They say they are forbidden, even to the tribes of such regions. They are known to be the possessions of the gods of the Ancients. They have heard this from the only ones who travel south of the rivers; the slave traders and some of the dark skinned women that are traded on their return. I will ask of this later.

I say to Normora, whose pain is obvious to all: "Tell the one who does most of the talking, I seek help from the best medicine woman and do not know how to get there on the leg of an injured woman." It is said that we will be taken in the morning to the central dwelling settlement of this area, and honoured for delivering death to the one who has placed fear in the hearts of all the women and children on the rivers. There will be a gathering to celebrate with the hunters of the six tribes. We will be welcome amongst the river tribes for as long as we want. This is good to hear but if I had to go through what we have been through to get this result, I am sure that I would rather have fought the tribes. The look on Normora's face is just pain and exhaustion. One of the chiefs looks at the spear I am working on and steps forward, extending his own spear for me to take. I take it and say: "I have nothing worthy to exchange for such a powerful weapon." When this is repeated to the crowd, a loud cry goes up from the hunters and the chief looks well pleased.

A word from the chiefs and the crowd moves away. The main speaker says they camp by the river but wood and food will be brought with water to bathe the wound. "Sentries will keep watch over you, as well as the river area. Sleep well for tomorrow you travel far."

By the time the food arrives the fire is roaring. A small water bag is handed to me with a finger pointed at Normora. I understand the words "spirit water". I sip and the liquid burns its way down my neck, making my eyes water.

We are alone again. I get the girl to sit up and sip a number of times, after initially gasping. The pain seems to be relieved and she looks a bit like one who is not right in the head. Some of the liquid is saved for her pain on the journey. How they are to move her is a mystery to me. If they carry her on their backs it will be great pain over the distance.

60

Next morning Normora vomits and says the pain has moved partly from her leg to her head. This is the other world drink. Water is given to her and some of the flat bread to put food back in her belly. She drinks deeply but hardly eats and asks for more strong drink. I tell her to wait until we are ready to leave. She looks at me as if she would like to transfer more than a little of her pain to me but does not argue.

Two of the chiefs arrive and some ten hunters. They have two poles about three paces long which they lash the hide of some large animal to, and lay it on the ground beside Normora. The headman speaks to her and, with his help, she moves onto the hide and is covered by furs. I think to myself he has been too long away from his wives for his hands are quick to feel the firmness of her breasts when he arranges the furs. I look away. Four warriors lift her gently off the ground and both of us are greatly impressed. Our packs are taken by two of the others and, for a moment, I wonder if they are about to carry me too. Great hunter that I supposedly am, I would have to act greatly offended. They move off and I fall in beside Normora.

There are many hundreds of men, all hardened warriors. These tribes are a force to be reckoned with. We move along the river south and I see that we are not going to the smoke of the closest dwellings. For a time the headman moves beside Normora, opposite me. He talks quietly to her, then moves off at a run towards the head of the column. She tells me he said their land of the twin rivers is rich with animal, fish and grain. It is necessary to keep an army of men to protect these lands and people from the tribes of the south land. Because they are strong, no slaver dares to raid his people. He states they rarely trade the slaves of the south. This the tribes know, and war is less likely. Still, they tolerate the slavers and trade furs, weapons and other items, especially some of the exotic furs from the south. She says a medicine woman will meet the hunters before the sun is overhead.

I give Normora a little of the strong drink. For a time she looks very happy and, with slurred voice, talks with animated speech. To look at her I would think she was the most revered one of the tribe. Still, behind the bravado there is a look of fear in her eyes. I presume she knows that if poison sets in, her life is still in danger.

When the sun is high and we are closer to smoke just to the east of us, a woman of many seasons is presented to us and the hunters rest. There have been no kills that I can see and it is obvious that so many men on the move is the reason all animals in the region have fled. My friend is awake and speaking to the medicine woman who is showing her herbs. The leg is uncovered and I see that already the leg is growing red around the wound. Strong drink is consumed and the cleaning takes place. Then a poultice of herbs and moss is bound to the leg.

More than one glance is cast my way to see if, as shaman, I will chant the evil spirits away or cast spells for her protection. This is certainly not my knowledge. I would fear the consequences of one such as me calling upon good or bad spirits for Normora. So I say to her in our own language: "Call Silver to you and let him lick you over. Then they can see you have the protection of the strong wolf totem." I will wear the hide of the wolf when we arrive at the settlement. If possible though, the part of shaman will be slight, as I wish to be as much like these people as I can become. This will be the best way to travel.

Over the last season my facial hair has developed and is more prominent than the beards of these men and lighter in colour. Tomorrow I will cut it off and colour my face with ochres of earth these people use. First though I will endeavour to observe what initiation markings are worn, in case I cross over their customs. I seem safe, but new people bring a need for careful approach, as this world is not easy even for one with his own tribe. My life has been proof of this.

The stop is soon over and we set off at a slow rhythmic run. Before long an easy chanting melody rises from the hunters and I realize they are matching their steps to the rhythm of the song. The chant seems to dull the senses and relax the breathing so, to my surprise, we arrive in what seems like no time at all, at a place of many dwellings.

61

When glancing back I cannot see the smoke from the area we came from, so we have travelled a long way and no one seems tired at all. This is good knowledge and not of our people's ways. We are taken straight to a hut near the centre, near two of the largest dwellings I have seen.

Several people move in to attend to Normora who has only just woken up, such was the drink and perhaps the effect of the chanting during the journey. She vomits again. This is not a good first impression but she is to be respected for her part in the story of the cave tiger. She seems beyond caring. I cannot help so don the wolf skin and, holding Silver and weapons, move out of camp to make sure I am not captive and to find some time alone.

The sun is low in the sky. I return as the red orb finally sinks below the horizon. After tying Silver on a short lead outside the hut, I make my way to the front of what I think will be the headman's dwelling. There are poles standing five steps high across the front of both large structures, six in front of this dwelling and four in front of the other. The two centre poles have a carving of the symbol of a man on one and the symbol of a woman on the other. Animals and birds are on all the others at both dwellings. They are skillfully done in a manner I have not seen before.

Several women come out from one dwelling and indicate I am to follow. The interior is lit with torches along each side and hanging from the roof. Then the greatest wonder of all. The walls are lined with a material that looks like smooth clay; pure white but with the most beautiful drawings I have ever seen, all of animals and birds, with some trees and, in one place, even the stars. There are some fifty people in the room which measures about five steps wide, three steps high and about thirty-five steps long. The people hardly intrude upon the space. They are seated on mats woven from grasses of many colours. At the far end is a raised platform with six beautifully carved wooden seats with back and arm rests that are inlaid with ivory. Elephant tusks curl in great arches behind each of the seats along the walls. Shells are in line around the top of the walls.

This is man-made beauty the likes of which I have not seen with the eyes of the flesh. The paintings are what astound me the most. They are shape and colour so real that the animals almost appear to move around the walls. These paintings rival, if not better, those I saw from the spirit of the great Ancients from the beginning of man's journey. All of a sudden I realize that I have been staring at my surroundings with open mouth, and have not even acknowledged the chiefs or people who are, I now see, silent and observing my reaction. I presume these paintings have great power for the hunt and prestige for the people of the tribe.

I move to the front of the seated people and open my arms to the seated chiefs and a shaman, and bow slightly to each in turn. I hope that will do, and am pleased to see a look of pleasure on the warrior-like faces of the chiefs. I turn to each wall and again open my arms with an expression on my face of open admiration which I do not have to pretend. Then I turn and say: "I have travelled over many chieftains and have met or seen no people with the power or greatness to produce such wonders." There is confusion on the faces before me, when suddenly again my words are translated from the mouth of another. This time the wizened, crinkly old face of shaman uses his voice to much excited conversation amongst all. Apparently what I said was well received.

I am motioned to take a seat on an empty mat in the centre at the front of those seated on the floor. The conversation continues, with me understanding a number of words but not the full meaning. My gaze returns to the paintings. They have moved something deep inside me. I do not know if I wish to cry out in joy, awe, or from some peculiar feeling of sadness. They have created such a mixture of emotion in my chest and head.

Apparently this meeting of what I suspect is the elite of the tribes has ended, for the chiefs rise and leave while we remain seated. It is indicated that I should follow, so I go outside to find each chief seated in front of one of the poles except for the one with the woman symbol on the top which is occupied by, I suspect, a woman who represents some sort of priestess to their version of the Earth Mother goddess.

62

I am again seated in the centre surrounded by warriors. There is a circle of fires around which hundreds upon hundreds of people are gathered. When all are seated, singing by the women breaks out with bodies moving in time to the music. With naked breasts it is a sight to match any gathering of the clans back home. There is a break in the singing and all is quiet, then the shaman appears after a cloud of iridescent smoke rises simultaneously from each of the fires. He chants and dances, sprinkling dust in the direction of the crowd on all sides. I do not understand the words and am relieved that Normora has been left in good health and, I hope, will recover. Strong drink and water are passed around. I take the water and pretend to sip the spirit drink. Then meat and assorted fruits and vegetables move around on large wooden benches carried by six women. I take and eat. Hygiene is not big at this event. Perhaps the spirit drink will make the food more hygienic. I take a larger drink.

As this settles down the central chief speaks, and about thirty warriors move into the area between the fires and begin to pantomime, with some as hunters and some as women digging bulbs and collecting seeds. From out of the dark on the far side three figures emerge covered in the skin of the saber toothed tiger. They fall upon the play actors who flee, leaving some dead on the ground. Their bodies are removed after the tiger drags one off into the dark. Then the hunters return to the singing of the women. They fan out and disappear as if they were stalking a predator. Then three more appear, one covered in a wolf hide. Then the tiger appears and, as it attacks one and tears at its leg, the other aims a pretend arrow and shoots it into the tiger's open mouth. A great roar of appreciation goes up from the crowd and more singing breaks out. This time even the headmen join in the celebration. The hunters return and find the dead tiger. They seek out the three on the other side of the fire, and one is lifted onto a carrier and all disappear into the dark. The tiger is skinned in pantomime and the shaman appears beside me. The hide of the tiger is brought and laid in front of me, and I see by its freshness it is the terror of our journey.

Even now, and with some strong drink, I feel the tremor run through my body. I look to the shaman and he sprinkles me and the hide with small flowers and herbs then says that the tribe has honoured me as I have honoured them, and it is obvious I am to take the hide. I can hardly lift it. So I stand and lift one side of the hide and show it to the shaman, then the chief, then on the other side show it to the people. Then I raise my hands and bow to all around with open arms in the gesture of peace, appreciation and thanks. I then say out loud: "The chief, shaman and people have honoured us greatly", then thank them for their medicine and receiving us at the fires of a great people. The shaman has repeated my words. I stand behind my mat and he indicates I should sit. The singing and dancing continues with the drinking and eating. A thought crosses my mind that I am grateful they did not want me to see this terror into the after life. To take the journey in its body may have brought about my permanent residence in the twilight realm.

I am totally exhausted now, and eventually I cannot stay awake so return to the hut. My eyes close, then open next day with the sun well into the dwelling. Silver is asleep at the entrance, still on the lead I left him on the night before.

63

Several days go by and it is obvious that this is going to be a long stay. There will be questions with the woman if she heals. I do not think it is right to take her into more danger when she will find a place with freedom amongst these tribes. If their medicines are good she will heal quickly. The wound, although deep, was of the flesh. It is only the poison that turns the body red then black that kills.

As days pass I spend time learning the ways of these people and their language. The climate is much warmer and the winters rarely freeze. The ground can be dug. It is not frozen under the surface as in the land of my birth. The shaman is a reserved person but he speaks to me a little more each day as he is the best one to answer my questions. They are many because there are astounding things with these people I have never seen before.

They have a large community enclosure made of fallen saplings. It encloses an area of maybe three hundred by five hundred steps running from the river, along the river, then back to the water. There are tame sheep and goats under the care of the whole tribe. They have captive meat, and from their wool and hides come much of their clothing. They also weave cloth from local plants on looms.

As I look they seem to have areas of plants where they have taken out all but the plants that are of use to people. They grow thicker and more plentiful that way. Inside the sheep enclosure is a smaller enclosure in which are some fifteen pigs. It has astonished me that, in a land of such resources, people should have gone to such trouble. The land is plentiful with game and all else a body can require. My people would grow fat in this land.

Normora spends her time on her furs. She is well tended and, in her way of cheerful spirit, is making friends with the women who tend to her. I think she is quite a hero, and probably the only person to survive the attack of a great tiger in the tribal stories. She may be talked about in the future around the fires for the changing of the seasons.

64

Today I will see the shaman and ask him questions. I stand outside the shaman's dwelling and he comes almost immediately. I feel comfortable with this man. I say to him I would like to hunt, to contribute food to the people in the manner that is my way. I ask him if I am allowed to hunt the land of the river, or can I join with the hunters in the normal way of things. I say that I also have much admiration for the ways of the tribe and would like to learn while this is my place of residence.

He says I am to join him at his hearth when the sun goes to sleep, then indicates for me to wait, then moves off between the huts. It is not long before he is back with five men who are ready for the hunt. Their hand signals say they are to fish and if deer are available they will hunt. I think to myself these people have too much food and are not used to preserving for the cold times. Then I realize it is already winter and we are not trapped in our lodges by the ice and blizzard-like winds. This world is not as desperate as the one I have always known. That is why there are perhaps five hundred people living here. We travel well and fall into the chanting jog. There is another surprise in store for me. They have nets and fish traps that they pull up as we travel.

As the sun is lowering in the sky we are nearly back to base when three of the men take the fish, now strung on poles over their shoulders, and continue on their journey. We head away from the river and follow a stream, and by dark my arrow has killed a spotted deer. All seem to think that is enough and we quickly move it across country to the dwellings, arriving in time for me to help with the butchering and take a quarter of the beast and the hide. It is a beautiful fur, a woman's adornment. The meat is delivered to our hearth and hung in a woven bag out of reach of beast, then I take my body to the river to bathe.

The sun is well down when I return. The lovely body of a young woman bathing at the water's edge has made me aware that, at the moment, I have no comfort in my furs. She had a strong athletic build and firm breasts. These are a darker people. I do not know what they think of my pale skin but she was not bashful in her observations. I grab some dried food and eat, then say good night to the girl and wolf and move off to the shaman's dwelling.

65

The entrance to the shaman's dwelling is open, as is mostly the way of people until they sleep. The shaman quickly ushers me in and I lower myself onto a wooden bench with a comfortable backrest.

A woman is looking after his food and serves us both on platters made out of the bone of a large creature, possibly elephant by the size of the large flat area of bone. The food is good and we eat. The woman sits quietly and eats with us. There is only light conversation about the hunt, plus the skill of the fishermen with their nets. I tell him we also use nets but catch only what we cast our nets over each time we throw them. As he is shaman I am not eager to ask him how he speaks words of people from far to the north-west. He simply says when he was eighteen seasons he travelled with a brother to the great ice in the far north. He saw such wonders as the woolly elephants and rhinoceroses; also the great deer that stand as high as an elephant's back. He was not shaman then and wonders at the words "I am shaman" when they are spoken by one so young.

I tell him of my times with the shaman and the journeys. I am careful not to mention the Other Ones' shaman. Our people know of much slaughter of many things by the Invaders. Still, I have seen how the aggression of the tribes varies. We talk of the animals they hold captive and the way of my wolf. There seem to be similarities of how some of their ways started. They have held animals for many generations. Then I learn that the painting skills are handed down, as in the ways of the medicine and the spirit.

I decide to confide in him that I was not going to be shaman, but my ability to travel in the spirit and see the past with all the vast lands was valued by the learned of my people. "It was to be that I would not be shaman but experiences have made me, without choice, knowledgeable in the ways." I say: "I would greatly like to know more of the painting." He says he will speak to the master of artists, whom he says has much of the ways of the taboos and is considered to have power by all the people. I say: "I can see the power with my own eyes, and that it must bring great favour with the animal world to the lands of the tribes of the twin rivers."

He signals the woman to leave, with caution that no one is to observe us until Wolfman leaves. Then his gaze becomes more intense and I can see I am under great scrutiny. He says that the shamans of his people are skilled in the things that I have called 'the journey'. Then he brings out herbs, some of which are familiar to me, so I presume what is to happen next. My instincts tell me not to be afraid of this man. It seems to mainly be the frauds that are a danger to a traveller like me.

We breathe in the smoke and go into the beginning of the chant. I can feel his presence as we soar into the sky and the fires of the village become more distant. There is a silvery light on the river close to the dwellings. I rise further and see two fingers of water running to a sea that is separate to the one I know as the inland sea. I can feel the shaman's presence, and his thought words tell me that he is quietly seeking to know what he can learn of the origins of me. I sense Arose and am surprised to see she is close. My consciousness centres on a spot between the top of the south-east strip of water and the north-east bend of the river.

I feel the shaman moving with me as I zoom in on Arose. The camp of the traders is virtually deserted; only a small fire burns and two warriors stand guard, one on a cliff above camp and one eating by the fire. Some fifteen women are roped together and sitting in a line back from the fire. Arose is with them but not roped. She looks filthy, and I can see with the one fur on her skinny body she is no longer pregnant or attractive. She looks exhausted and I can feel her pain.

Our journey starts to rise again and we move suddenly to view an attack on some thirty people. The slavers are seeking people close to the twin rivers. I feel the shaman's anger and realize they are of the twin rivers tribes and not usually attacked by slavers. We rise again moving away and the oceans open up below. I can feel the shaman questioning my mind. He is very powerful. Suddenly I see glimpses of my journeys to the Other Ones, and flashes of the lives I led that have lost knowledge imprinted on them. Then we are back in our bodies.

We sit quietly for a while, then the shaman sends for the woman and hot brew is made. He says: "You may not be shaman but there are many things I, and perhaps my people, will want to discuss with you." He asks about Arose and I tell him. He says: "The traders are returning from the south land. After what we have witnessed, they will try to pass around our lands undetected. I must now speak with the chief." I rise and leave.

Normora is asleep but Silver greets me as I return to my furs. My head is full of Arose and what will happen in the morning. My heart is full of several emotions. I still feel great love for her and, although my fear is great, there is hope. I sleep.

66

At first light I am up and not surprised to see many strangers have arrived, and more arriving as I look. I move close to the shaman and tell him I am afraid that if an all out attack on the slavers occurs I will lose Arose. He says the tribes are going to try and recover the stolen women of their own people and that I may run with the warriors, but leave the decisions to the headmen and take my chances with the others. Once again there are several chiefs talking together. They call over some twenty men and, after quick discussion and a hand signal for scout, they leave. I see the warriors forming into lines so I join them. It is all I can do and more than I could have hoped for.

The shaman is chanting now and throwing more of the magic into the fire to create the iridescent smoke. It is not long before the number of men arriving dwindles, and we set off once more in the singing chant. This time the sound of the song is much more sinister. There is a sound of anger in the chanting, singing verse.

I am surprised to see we are heading due east when I feel the events I saw were south-east. It occurs to me that they may know the route the slavers are likely to take. I start to move forward and pass warriors when several strong arms reach out and pull me back. Then I realize these hunters have been assigned to travel with me, either to protect me or see that I operate by the ways of these warriors.

The sound and steady beat of the feet seem to form a rhythm as we run, and after a time it is as if the whole army of warriors is of the one mind, and I can feel courage and strength in the vibration and rhythm as it flows through me. When the sun is overhead we stop for drink but rest is not for long. All men have dried food and some appears for me. I am grateful as it is the first food today. We camp that night and still it is made clear that I am to hold my place, so I lie as all do on the ground and sleep.

Long before morning light all men quietly rise to a position on one knee; those with bows holding the bow in the right hand and those with spears the same position. It is becoming very clear indeed that they are a well disciplined army. I also realize that I seem to be the only one with both bow and spear; the spear on back strap and the bow in hand. They give me a small feeling of confidence.

The sun rises above the horizon and some food is eaten at a sign I do not see. Then still holding the same rest position, all wait. I wonder why we are not moving. Then I see about ten men come over a rise to travel to the chiefs and drop into rest. Two of them collapse from this position to the ground. All are given water then food. I presume our decision makers are about to learn the lie of the land and, I hope, the position of the traders.

The sun is half way up the sky before we leave. I do not understand but just before we leave two more runners arrive. Then we travel east again through deciduous forest, grassland and groves of cedars. I am dimly aware of the area but my mind is caught up in the rhythm. There is also a background tension at having come so close after such distance and time.

At sun up we water again. This time there is no stop, and the ground gets rougher moving into foothills, with some evergreens mostly in ancient dried up watercourses.

It is probable, even to me, that the traders are travelling as far as possible towards the ocean inlet in order to avoid the river tribes.

67

At night there is still no contact and I am none the wiser. We lie down and sleep again. This time I am woken long before light. The half moon is up and we move out. I can only see the men front and back, for we are about four wide and travelling at no more than a fast walk. Even at that pace I stumble more than once. Still, there must be some sort of track or it would be hard to travel with so many men. As the sky lightens we drink at a stream, then break into the rhythm again down a broad valley with still good forest but areas of scrub land as well. I see scouts appear ahead. We rest.

This time the travel is silent. The valley with a growing stream narrows through a pass. The men, at signals only partly familiar to me, begin to break up; some heading for high cliffs each side of the pass, and archers into the woods in the region of the entrance to the pass. The spearmen are dropping back into the forest, well away from the pass entrance. I am with the archers in the woods.

There is now no sound and no sign of people except those close to us. Communication must rely on signals or calls not known to me. Once again I have to rely on these people but I yearn to stand and look down the valley. All remain out of sight of the valley.

Eventually I see the sun at its high position then it goes down well below the trees. Time passes and two of the chiefs appear. One stops and talks to the warriors and me. I fail to understand all but get the idea. The traders used the slave women as human shields when they moved on through the pass so were allowed to travel through, but were under surveillance. I hear the words 'night stop' so presume we will perhaps take them at night.

As dark approaches warriors appear and we move out, not the full force but still about one hundred and twenty men. It seems forever before we stop at a drink rest. I see men from each area gather centrally and, by the light of the moon, discussing diagrams drawn in the earth. Now we move off in groups of about ten, leaving a space of time in between each.

Eventually I see a fire in the distance. Then we veer off and skirt wide of the fire through the forest, eventually passing other groups and arriving at the far side of the faint glow of the fire. There is no noise apart from the wind which is now blowing fairly strongly. We move silently inwards. I get a glimpse of men spreading out in a line and have the feeling each warrior will be in touch with the next by view.

Without any signal I see all stop and are dead still. Before long I see a figure rise on a rock outcrop not thirty steps from us and, after looking in all directions, start to sink down again. I hear the faint thong of a bowstring and see numerous arrows strike. He is dead without a sound. Several warriors move forward, then the rest of us advance. The fire is close now and figures begin to take shape. The line is tight with figures left and right of me, no more than three steps. Every bow is fitted with an arrow, including mine.

Then I see the slaves tethered in a line close to the river. Several are moving amongst the men. We rise as one and move swiftly. There is hardly a noise. Arrows fly including mine and figures fall. I grab my spear and am amongst them. Suddenly a man starts to rise at my feet. My spear thrusts down and through his back between his shoulders. I hear his cry and that of an unseen woman as well. Then it is over. I put my foot on the man and heave my spear out. Men are moving swiftly about me. I move to the women some twenty-five in number. I quickly discover Arose is not there.

Then it dawns on me. I do not want to think. In a horror of darkness I swoop on the dead man to find Arose being taken limply from under his body. She is naked, and I see the blood from the wound on the inside of her shoulder where my spear entered. Once again strong arms hold me. It feels like my mind has died. I do not seem able to register properly. I see her laid out on the ground; then I see two other girls beside her.

68

My eyes do not leave Arose. She does not move. They are working on her; feeling for the flow of blood then bandaging her shoulder. The stretchers appear again and she is raised and moving out. Now I start to fight. I can hear my voice for the first time and I strike out with fists and feet. Then everything goes dark.

When I awake with great pain in the side of my head, I discover we are beside the river in the steep valley. I do not know what time of day it is. After rolling to my feet I see my spear and arrows are not with me. It crosses my mind to pursue those who have taken Arose. Then I realize that if I try to strike west it could be days after these people arrive at the destination. I am still at their mercy. At least they were treating Arose well. It is I who has perhaps dealt her the mortal blow.

A terrible depth of despair is upon me. I move to the brush to relieve myself and see no movement from the sleeping men. Apparently it is not considered likely that I will run off. In fact I am having trouble even walking. The side of my head feels very swollen. These people are not always gentle. I sit by the fire but the pain soon forces me to lie down.

Dawn comes and the sky begins to shine with a deep glow running from vermilion to gold, and the mist blends with the silver of the birch trunks. It is a setting that should have been the beginning of hope. In my stomach the scene is like one from the worst of the dead, shrouded in a mist of dread and deep foreboding. Then I am surprised by the arrival of a stretcher and none too gentle hands virtually throw me onto the contraption. I have learnt that I am outnumbered and must obey.

Water and food are consumed. I drink. The chanting song begins and the procession moves out. It seems to be the full body of men and about seven young women in good health and no longer roped. They travel well forward near the headmen. The day passes and then we stop again. I sleep fitfully but sleep full of ghosts does arrive.

The following night sees about one-third of the full force arriving back at the settlement. Groups of warriors departed in different directions throughout the second part of the day. Today the stretcher thankfully was not needed. If the pain still exists it is clouded by the despair in my heart.

Arose is not in my hut. I free Silver; perhaps he will find her. I go straight to the dwelling of the shaman. He is not there and my thoughts take me to the meeting house. He and some fifteen men are in discussion. They see me and fall silent. The words are spoken. "My spear entered the body of my woman through the body of my enemy. I did not see her or know any woman was there. Where is she and does she live?" Then I am told her body and that of one other wounded woman were taken to medicine people in the nearest village of the river people. "You are to wait here and her body, dead or alive, will be returned in the right time." I cannot speak for the words will not come. I back out. My mind and body are finally numb.

Silver joins me and I go into the forest. Exhaustion takes me and I lie down with the creature beside me and sleep finally comes. Sometime towards morning I am awakened by Silver's soft growl. My hand tells me the hair is up on the back of his neck and I remember I am still without weapons, so move swiftly back towards the dwellings. As we move the wolf's attention travels in a circle and finally loses interest. Whatever it was is not pursuing us or is moving away.

The dwelling is empty. Normora's furs do not appear to have been slept in. This surprises me but my body is still numb with exhaustion, so I lie down leaving my friend free of leash and sleep again. Next time when my eyes open, the sun is shining through the entrance from high in the sky. The pain and numbness of mind and chest are still with me. Normora is not, but I feel only vague concern for her safety. These people seem, as all people seem to be, very fond of her. Only fleeting jealousy crosses my mind that someone in particular is very fond of her. Jealousy is not a big thing amongst the tribes until the bond of hearth, family or close feelings, such as I think Arose has for me and I know I have for her.

This time I sit and eat in front of the hut. I see people back away from the wolf who now is a very large creature even for one of his kind. I know he must show trust with the children to break the tension of these people. Perhaps it will depend upon the taboo. It is difficult to think at the moment. It is as if a dense fog has enveloped the total of all that I am. The thought is clear that Arose's body will arrive, alive or dead, soon. No offer is made to take me to her. I know not where to go and somewhere in the midst of my mind is the knowledge that I will have to confront the fact that it was my spear that entered her.

Several days pass. I am aware that Normora has been moved to the enclosure of the women of the chief. She came to me, I think once, and tried to help me eat more. I could feel her gentle care and warmed to her presence but was hardly aware when she returned to where she came from. My thoughts have partially closed down.

69

I do not know how many days had passed when Silver, who was sitting beside me, came suddenly and alertly to his feet and emitted several excited howls. He moved quickly away. On following his direction, I see a stretcher with two carriers and a warrior trying to pull an over-excited wolf off the occupant. My strength returns and I call out to wolf and man, and run to the stretcher in time to save the animal from a perhaps fatal blow.

Arose is pale and still, but the eyes that are open are not dead. But the eyes that are open do not seem to register Silver or me. I touch her face and speak. "It is Garoke. It is Silver. We have been looking for you over all this time and distance. You have never left our hearts." There is no sign upon her face, or in her eyes, of recognition. The stretcher is taken with a growing number of people to the headman and shaman who are sitting in front of the meeting place. They speak with the bearers and the shaman says to me: "She is recovering in body. The poison is departing. Our medicine people will treat her in your dwelling. Her spirit has fled to a safe place and it is hoped will return as her body recovers. She has taken food and drink but has not spoken to, or shown recognition of, anyone as yet." My mind is coming alive. She will recover. There is strong hope and a heavy burden is being lifted off me. All is not lost.

Her body is moved to my dwelling place, and I put Normora's furs on top of mine to soften the resting place. Arose's face, pale and still, registers no pain as she is gently moved from the stretcher to the sleeping furs. The medicine woman comes in and the clothes are drawn back to remove the dressing. There is some redness and swelling but the wound is absent of the smell of death. I look away as it is cleaned and dressed with the ingredients only a medicine one understands.

The face that I knew so well is still there, thin and pale but, with the absence of the spirit, a face of calm, and for a small time I am pleased that she feels no pain. Then I look past the beautiful full lips and above the finely pointed nose, to the eyes that still have all the wonder of colour and depth, from violet purple through to light blue. The pupils are so dark that I can see into a fathomless depth that seems to take me, in an instant, to the place that holds all the emotion that is in my being.

Then, as I gaze down into such depth, another image begins to reflect off the surface of the stillness that is her. For an instant I see the face that is searching for her soul. The ochres of the ways of strangers cover all but my eyes, and hair thicker and darker than she knew covers my lower face. The hair on my head is not free but twisted into locks. This is the face of a different man to the one she knew just emerging from boyhood and before. Then realization dawns that my speech has also changed in tone and full of words that are not those of Garoke. Tonight she will rest after I have arranged sustenance for her. Then tonight I shall endeavour to try to uncover the one who left our far-flung home, so she is greeted once more with familiar sights.

I sit with Arose until the light fades. I am aware when the medicine woman leaves who fed her broth to give her food and drink without choking. I am aware of Silver leaving as dusk settled, then torches being lit as Normora briefly enters then leaves. Finally I see Arose's eyes close and hear the gentle sleep rhythm of her breath.

Rising from my vigil, I dig for my clothing from the north and the now tattered wolf hide, then depart quietly for the river, passing the shaman sitting facing my way outside his dwelling. I can see from the slight movement of his lips that he is in a semi trance, so I bow slightly in universal respect and pass on.

The sand scours and clears my skin, and then that of my indignant wolf. Then slowly the hair begins to unravel and takes on the fineness of northern youth. Lastly I take my flint edge and, smoothing my face with tallow, remove the hair. It is too dark to see my reflection but I know that there are only two living here who will be familiar with the one who will greet these people in the morning. I am a stranger in a strange land, but I hope familiar to one whose spirit has, I believe, gone briefly to an infinitely stranger land. I return and lie down on my furs, with the fire to my back and Arose to my front. Sleep arrives to eventually be replaced by a new day.

70

Arose has rolled over during the night, so I rise without disturbing her to feed Silver and myself, then place stones in the fire to use to boil water to make broth to bring warmth and strength to two bodies. Wood is brought and a good fire soon warms the interior of the dwelling. The hot stones are moved by tongs made of deer antler into the water bag of ox hide. It quickly boils and herbs and other ingredients are added.

If Arose hears my movement or smells the broth she shows no awareness. I sit quietly in front of her and gently touch her shoulder. Her eyes flick open and for a blink I see fear register. Then a mist seems to pervade her countenance and the consciousness withdraws. She does not seem interested in registering me at all.

The brew is poured into bowls, and I gently lift her head and pour a tiny amount of warm liquid into her mouth. She sits and takes the bowl and drinks, then lies back on her side staring at something that is far outside the walls of this abode. My voice, or that which I hope is my correct voice, is careful to use original language and says: "I am Garoke who became Wolfman from the tribe of the riverbend in the land of your people from over the narrow sea. I have come to take care of you and you are with me, among safe people. You have time to recover." I turn her face and say: "Arose, forgive me for losing you. Look into my soul and know where you belong and return to the warmth of a good hearth."

For a time her eyes clear, and I see the colours open up as if looking into another realm, then slow wonder as they register on my appearance, and it is as if I can see deep within her pupils a far light coming towards me. Her mouth moves into a gentle curve and the fingers of her hand rise to my lips.

Then she glances beyond me and fear strikes her features and she is in an instant gone. At the same time a cry escapes her, of sorrow, like a ghost in some distant valley doomed to a lonely eternity.

All the day I stay with her. Silver comes and goes. I am dimly aware that, with Normora's help, he is breaking down the tribe's reserve towards him. Normora is warm to me and with the medicine woman gives help. She seems to have formed an alliance elsewhere. If the night is empty without her, my body is unaware. All awareness, except for the one who holds my being, is without clarity. The wound looks clean. I sleep soundly, as tiredness eventually overcomes any despair.

71

The following day there is still no recovery but Arose sits for a time propped up by soft coverings against the wall, and takes broth with some food brought by Normora when the sun is high. She says she will sit with Arose and speak the language of our people. I hear her words: "Go and clean yourself, and take Silver and hunt or collect fuel. It will be good for Arose if you contribute to these people and keep yourself healthy." My heart does not want to leave but I am grateful that my journey found a friend as complex as Normora. She also still has pain and walks slowly. Her spirit is strong.

With recovered bow, spear and trusty friend I move to the river to bathe, then on into the forest. The deciduous alder drop branches and dry wood is easier to find this close to the settlement in the winter, so I soon have a load of wood strapped to my back and some to drag. After depositing this in the central wood heap, I return for more. Regardless of my feelings it is good to work, and I can see by the looks I am receiving that people are both startled by the change in my appearance and pleased that I am being a part of the community. Even in this milder climate it seems only the sick and elderly are allowed to be idle. Their expressions say why would a young warrior choose to remove the appearance of manhood in order to take on the look of a boy again?

Then I move away towards a not too distant valley, shooting at some ground creatures and one brush buzzard as I go but to no avail, as my aim does not seem good. Silver gives chase and his body disappears in pursuit of a very rapid hare. This still concerns me in the land of strangers but I cannot stop him from being alive. Time passes and he has picked up the scent of my trail and returned. There is sign on his face that he has eaten well. He looks pleased with life and bounds ahead, destroying my chances of success.

I change direction, still with my knowledge of the lowering sun, and move slowly back towards the dwellings in order to arrive before dark. The home of the lions, even this close to humans, is no place for a single hunter at night. As I come back along the river, still within the edge of the forest, some pheasant going to roost are spotted. With quiet movement and no wolf, my shot is close and accurate. A marmot soon follows. Although I am no great hunter (the marmot is good for winter food only), I am one who has brought four stomachs to these people even if, as I suspect, the body of one has become a comfort to the night furs of the chief. This thought brings not jealousy nor a smile or arousal in my slightly numb body. I return to the home stretch of river, with wolf once more by my side, to dress the creatures. I am keen to return to Arose but pleased that life has active continuity.

Arose is now alone. I speak and show her the food. She remains absent and silent. Her face looks a little fuller even if life is still absent. Health is returning. I am tired but I have Arose and I have hope. For now that will do. I touch her cheek, eyes and hair, and try once again to find a spark of recognition by talking to her quietly of good times in the homeland. I look deep into those lovely now vacant pupils but no spark of light returns. After placing wood on the fire I kill the flame in the torches and lie down to sleep, at first holding Arose gently in my arms then rolling over to sleep.

72

The next day I see the shaman and ask for enquiry to be made as to if the chief will see me. I also say that I will try to find Arose's spirit through the journeys. He gives no opinion but we go to see the chief. This time he is at his own dwelling and, after a brief wait, we are taken inside. This structure is also large and is full of ivory and carved wood, with the addition of several more large paintings. Normora is here and, by her flushed complexion which I recognize, is very much a part of this household. Her fair hair and pale skin plus wonderful nature must make her an exotic and delightful companion amongst this darker skinned race.

We sit and food is brought to us. I ask Normora to talk for me. The questions are fairly straightforward. Firstly, I thank the chief for all he has done for me and those that I care for. He asks why I have changed my appearance. I say: "The spirit of the woman I came for has departed her body. From where we came from, both in the body and the spirit, this is the appearance she would best recognize." I ask him for permission to stay with his people for at least the time of the woman's healing. Then I say: "What is required of me according to your customs for us to remain (meaning Arose and myself) amongst the tribes of the twin rivers?"

The chief says: "By your service of presenting the great beast, killer of my people, for its delivery into the spirit world, you have earned the right to remain as guest of the twin rivers." He also says: "If you remain longer than the healing, you must vacate the lodge you are in and build your own on the outskirts of the village or at a place of common agreement. One seeks community because there is sometimes a common enemy to the south. You may hunt as is the custom, with respect to the resources of the hunting grounds. It has been noted that you bring wood for the warmth of the hearth."

I say to the chief: "Your ways of keeping animals are different. It will be good to learn from your people and, if I may, I will teach the way of the wolf." I point to the paintings and say: "Also the culture which brings the spirit of the hunting into your lodges is greater than I have seen in the long journey. This makes me feel I am amongst strong people with deep respect for taboo, and this one must honour." As I take my leave Normora looks very happy so I presume the headman is pleased. I still have only a growing ability to understand a portion of their conversation.

It comes to me that I should leave Arose's spirit in peace so she can put all her strength into physical recovery. Perhaps it is nature's way. Half a moon passes and her wound closes over.

The settlement seems to have accepted her silence. She is clean and her colour and gentle beauty have returned.

The children seem to have adopted her and, as she moves quietly around the dwellings, they sometimes run and take her by the hand, leading her to toilet and waiting to return her, then rushing off to play their games in the way of children. When she goes for wood she only carries a piece at a time, so they have made a game of who can carry the most for her, but still they do not register with her. Something tells me that the empathy of a child can sense much of the inner ways of those that differ in suffering.

My Arose will return. She is forever taking me by surprise. Within the confines of the dwelling she can dress herself, fetch wood, and even water and feed herself. She does things so quietly and at unexpected times that I will turn and find her gone, or turn to find her sleeping, or find her sitting fully dressed. She even seems to put wood on the fire without noise. Every day I speak to her of youth, journey and the hunting. Sometimes even of the way of these tribes.

Time passes and we live like brother and sister. I cannot bring myself to take her body, as it would be without her consent and possibly be without her knowledge.

73

Much time has passed and Arose's shoulder is only a smooth scar. It seems to cause no pain, but I have not seen her register pain even when the dressings were changed on the fresh wound.

This night finds me with the spirit man. Now I will ask his help in a quest to find the reason for Arose's continued silence. After discussion of tribal matters, and an expression of interest in building my own dwelling, the herbs are delivered and the chanting meditation begins. It is quick and the shaman's presence is still with me. We move to Arose who seems to glow with a silver aura in the light of the half realm of the afterworld. She is calm and Silver sits with her. He rises and looks about, as if he is aware of presence. Arose senses no presence and I try to merge with her consciousness. I cannot, for there is some sort of barrier.

There is a feeling like an astral wind and we are drawn high where land blurs into silver blue. The shaman is still with me. I know we have travelled over time and space. There is a tiny tribe and the sky has a dark colour to it. The tribe is in the mouth of a very large cave. These people are ancient, with sloping foreheads and smaller chins but large well-proportioned bodies. We are aware they are survivors of a great disaster. As we watch a leader says: "We are to be called the Chosen People and our purpose will be to survive, to remember, and to preserve the laws of the great Spirit. The first story to be handed down to our people of the future will be when the water washed over the Earth and ice covered and destroyed all the great that we created. It has been said that the knowledge of the creators from the stars must be a memory preserved." I see a young woman with baby in arms and we are aware that she is me.

Once again we are back in body and dwelling, and the eyes of the shaman are watching me intently. He says: "Do you know who and what these people were?" I say: "They are the ancestors of all of us. The words we heard were, for a long time, passed down to all the tribes as they spread south and north across the Earth. They were one of a few groups to survive from the greatest disaster ever to strike any form of people. Only the ones we called the Other Ones, a people who developed a shared memory almost as old as this time, were capable of accurate legend. They passed this knowledge through me at the close of their time, to try and preserve the memory of the spiritual journey of all life, and give respect for the spiritual life of the Earth and the great Spirit. I, Garoke, a man of small intellect and limited intelligence, was able to bring these memories to my people. In the time to come, before we depart on a journey I know not where, these memories, or ones as close as I can reproduce, are yours. My memory is not good. That is why, amongst my own people, I was not to be shaman."

We speak a little more, but as always after these events I am drained of strength and wish to retire to Arose and my furs for sleep. This I do, and the sun comes up on many more days in which I rapidly, with the help of new friends, build a dwelling along the river on the outskirts of the settlement. It is a vulnerable position, but with wolf to pre-warn us and these people behind us, I feel safer and more settled than I have for about two seasons.

As time allows I sit with the shaman and speak of all things. I hear some similarities of legend. Diagrams are sketched. They seem particularly drawn to the aspect of the Chosen People. Shaman believes he is aware of the original location of these ancient people and it is not far from the lands of the twin rivers. The chief has taken to using the term 'descendents of the Chosen People' in his address to his people. It is said that they are going to travel in search of the ancient cave by a river, when the growing season turns to the hot season and the festival of the longest day has passed. This is the day they pay homage to the god who brings the sun to warm our lodges. There has now been quiet debate as to whether this god may actually be the Ancients' great Spirit. This message is not spoken freely amongst the people.

74

Silver is now fully accepted, especially as he has been seen to take Arose by the hand and lovingly nip at her without harming her. She ignores him but he is undeterred.

Several days after we moved into our new abode there occurred an event, at first disturbing, and then a great commotion. Until this time, on any occasion Silver and I approached the enclosure of the sheep and pigs, I placed him on a lead. I had been interested in this enclosure that is at the other end of the settlement but those I sought the company of were the hunters. Hunting, Arose, shaman and building our dwelling had taken all my time.

On this day though I am tired and do not think to place Silver on the lead. We approach the enclosure and, before I can stop him, my wolf is over the wall and circling the sheep. A shout from the animal minders goes up and bows are drawn. I call to them to lower their weapons and I call to Silver to come to me. The training of our way of the hunt is too strong in him, and he brings all the adults and some of the young and holds them against the fence in front of me. Then he kills a lamb. I reach him and drag him off just as two arrows strike the ground nearby. The men are angry. Thankfully I can now understand much more of the anger. I hear the wolf must go or be destroyed.

Then one older than the others, who seems devoid of anger and is somewhat thoughtful, asks me: "How is it that the beast brought the sheep to you and can be controlled?" I then tell the herders of the way of hunting with wolves; how they corner and hold an animal until men can move in for the kill. They are used to all animals being wild. I think and say: "It may be that a wolf can be taught to herd sheep and perhaps pigs, and obey a command not to kill, and to stop on command and perhaps other movements, like sit."

This information is treated with astonishment then the elder speaks, followed by much animated talk among the five herders and a growing group of villagers. Then I remember something I learnt from the Other Ones' shaman. So I say: "I have heard of people who find wolves more suited to one thing than another. It may be that, if young wolves were caught as you catch the young of the sheep, you can teach them to be as one with yourselves. A certain young wolf may be taught to keep company with sheep, as Silver has been taught to keep company with men, women and children."

I lose much of the rest of the day as plans are discussed to raid a den, and information is swapped about the ways of keeping animals. All talk of killing the wolf is gone, but talk of how to keep him away from the vulnerable creatures is discussed. I see the lamb quietly dressed for some evening meal.

Then another astonishing thought occurs. Could a wolf protect a sheep from another wolf or even warn against big cats or hyena? After thought I say: "A wolf will, to some extent, protect man." Then I think and say: "If the animal is so inclined and is in that vicinity. In our case Silver warns of the presence of predators or any danger before we are aware of the movement of any living thing in the vicinity."

I move out of the village to hunt in the evening light. There is rarely large game this close in, so I seek smaller ground dwellers or those of limb or wing, and soon have two partridge. When I arrive back I find Arose at the fire of one of the new dwellings. I am pleased they have taken to her. Their talk goes on around her as if she is a part of the story but her expression rarely changes, if at all.

The dwelling, like ours, has low walls with a steep roof made of coarse grass, and it is the way they have lined the inside of the walls with a smooth surface of lime and straw that gives the dwelling a beautiful smooth interior. It is this surface that they paint on, and many of the dwellings have simple landscapes with animals, or occasionally birds. Never people. I have learnt, as is the way amongst most people, that to make image of a creature is to capture its spirit, or a part of that spirit. So it is taboo to take the spirit of a person. I am not a believer of this, although there is always some doubt in my mind.

75

Each day I go about life and routine has set in. They seem to have forgotten about wolves for the sheep. This is an easy country and there is plenty of food at this time. Their ways are clever. Still, one day they will come across a den of pups and the opportunity may be taken up.

One morning, while visiting the shaman, he tells me he is to go with the master painter to perform ritual on the paintings just completed in the dwelling of the headman. He says: "You are welcome and will meet the one you wish to know the ways of. The painter travels to all the dwelling places of the tribes of the rivers so is only here for a part of his life."

We go to the dwelling and the paintings, like all, are beautiful. It immediately strikes me that the faces and eyes are not painted. All other detail is completed. When we arrive there are about twenty of the leading people including women. Normora is not present. The shaman places a half circle of skulls full of animal fat and bees wax. The skulls, which are those of the beasts in the new paintings, have hemp wicks which are lit. Then circles of small fires are lit and I smell lavender and burning hemp. I join the group in a half circle five steps back from the ceremonies and the shaman chants.

Then the painter enters with pots of ochre in skulls and proceeds to paint each face. The fierce countenance of the largest of cats appears as if by magic. The shaman calls to the spirit of the tiger to dwell in peace with the river people and dine well in the hunting grounds of the outer world. He calls: "Look in favour upon the river people", and we repeat: "Look in favour upon us." Then he says: "May your spirit respect the power of the river people who can capture the spirit of the greatest of beasts." A similar event then occurs with the face of a huge cave bear, almost filling the entrance to a magical looking cave. This time we ask that our hunters have the strength of the greatest of bears and warn him that, although we respect him, we have the power to destroy the spirit that we have captured. We vow to honour him if the bear spirit remains in peace with the tribe. Then the faces of deer, antelope, and other game of the hoof are painted and we call to them to be of use to the tribes of the rivers and their friends, the saber-toothed tiger and cave bear. Then it is over.

I notice a slight heady feeling from the hemp but it is the paintings, which for reasons I do not understand, that give me the highest feeling. I sit on the ground outside, facing the entrance near the carved poles. If I can I will speak with the master. A young man and woman enter, and come out with several beautiful furs and pots of ochre. They move off to the hut Arose and I had occupied. Eventually the headman, shaman and master painter come outside. I stand and extend courtesy. Shaman says: "This is a traveller in body from the far northern lands; a traveller in spirit over great time and distance." The master painter says he has been told of my experiences and seen the simple diagrams. He says: "It is the wish of the people that a wall be prepared, and the diagrams be presented in order that we have a greater understanding of how this is a part of the creativity and power of the Earth Mother goddess and our god." How this concept of the great Spirit fits in is, according to the shaman, of great importance as to where we came from and where we are going.

The next five days see the construction of a new structure, on a rise over the outer side of the village away from the river. It is well positioned with the front opening facing away from the prevailing winds but giving a view of the river and the settlement. Its walls are higher than a man is, and it is about three times the size of a normal dwelling. The three walls are now a beautiful white surface. It has been good to work with the men on construction. I have learnt much. At the same time I have spoken often with Jonthon, the name of the painter, and he has sent me out with his two young assistants to prepare the ochres for painting. They are mostly from stones ground to powder but plants and flowers are also used to get greens and blues.

Shaman and I are to work with Jonthon on the paintings, so he has been talking and sketching details of discussions. The cave of the ancient Chosen People is to be a part, as well as the circle showing the Earth and the stars. There are no people but there are markings symbolizing people, in the regions they survived in and spread out from. Then, of course, the sun and the moon and how the days of the full cycle between the shortest day to the shortest day exist. Much of this these people already know. Also their main ceremonies: for the female who are considered in some way daughters of the moon cycle; ceremonies on the shortest day emphasizing the coming of the new sun, and the ceremonies on the longest day for the men. I am not yet familiar with their spiritual beliefs.

Shaman performs a ritual with Jonthon and me, then I am allowed to learn the techniques of mixing and applying the paint with brushes made from the coarse hairs of creatures. As I work this way, and beauty and design begin to form on the walls, an immense satisfaction enters me such as not felt before. Also, a feeling of awe I can only describe as close to reverence.

Jonthon has a great knowledge of what he calls composition and aesthetics. I seem quick to grasp this. It soon becomes apparent that I have a better capacity to paint than I have of grasping the meaning of many of the symbolic markings I have transferred from my journeys to their diagrams.

76

Normora and many others care and look after Arose. Normora, who now wears a small circular blue tattoo on her forehead as a mark of one of the chief's wives, is showing signs of a growing baby. The tattoo I find disturbing, as it is the common mark worn by the priestesses over a large area. This time she seems very happy and I am pleased for her.

There is only one person who touches my desire. Several times I have tried to awaken Arose by arousing her body but she has no response to me. To take her would be like an act of force. So I live without a woman, and when the heat becomes too much I relieve the pressure of my body with my hand and thoughts of her beauty in private times gone past. I do not know why my love for her continues to grow. Perhaps it is the inner sense of her spirit that attracts other people to her, as well as me. She, without showing any expression apart from her gentle beauty, touches those around her in a way I cannot describe. It is, however, sometimes disturbing to see how hunters turn and look, including the chief, when she passes. Still, no one has attempted to invade her person and I cannot stay with her at all times.

The interior of the dwelling, of what they now call the Chosen People, has taken the appearance of a cave, and the diagrams are as if they are on the walls of a cave. There are some creatures but mostly the symbols and circles that I only partly understand.

I have learnt a lot, and am now painting on the walls of my own dwelling. The spiritual reason for painting does not seem so important to me, so the leaving out of the face and eyes until shaman performs ritual is frustrating to me. Because of my journeys through time, I am not convinced the paintings can capture a spirit. My experiences tell me that this is also probably not so. Still, there is safety and respect by living in harmony with others.

My companion has become aware that the painting is happening. Sometimes the paint is moved about. If she knows I am coming, the paints will be in front of where I was last working. While I am in the dwelling she touches nothing.

I still talk to Arose of all things, sometimes trying to surprise her. Once I even tried pushing the edge of a sharp flint into her skin, hoping it would make her cry out. She did not stir, but when I turned to get cloth to clean the small wound then turned back, she had placed a fur upon the wound to stop the bleeding. She is aware and preserves her bodily functions but is not really participating in life.

77

Time passes and I become, in most senses, a part of the tribe. My appearance slowly returns closer to theirs, even painting some ochre of the tribal women on Arose. Jonthon has moved on to paint amongst the other tribes. My walls are becoming more and more complicated. Sometimes I paint over what I have done before. My technique improves and I can paint landscape and beast, not as well as Jonthon but I think I am better than the two young he is training.

Many come to view my work. I wish the warriors would not, as I think they sometimes come out of curiosity about Arose and to perhaps view her. I believe shaman has let it be known that it is dangerous taboo to pleasure with one such as she, whose spirit is visiting the land of the ancestors. It may, they now think, create anger.

The summer festival passes, and the leaves turn to a forest of colour then turn brown and fall to form ground cover to mark the coming of the cold. Once again I am struck by what a gentle climate these people live in, where snow is hardly ever seen, and the ice that sometimes appears on the water in the morning is gone by the time the sun is overhead. There are fish all the time and the animals hardly appear to migrate looking for warmer pastures.

So I settle down. Jonthon and the leaders have given me permission to paint on other dwellings. So my work goes onto the walls of some of the hunters, to improve their standing in the animal kingdom. This, they believe, guarantees they will always be fed and clothed.

Shaman seems to have learnt all he can from me, and spends more time discussing the meaning of the story told in the dwelling of the Chosen People with neighbouring shaman and those of high respect amongst the twin rivers.

With the passage of time many of the tribes' songs have been learnt, and I take Arose to join in when they gather at the central fires to fill the night with harmony, telling the stories and memories of their people. Songs are a good way to pass on knowledge for, when learnt by the young, the story is more likely to be accurate to the words of the song.

I am happy as I can be without being able to take Arose to my body and create a hearth with children. Normora has a child now and is one of these people. My dwelling is extended, not because I need the space but to find a new surface to paint on.

Before I know it four summers have passed and still my love has remained silent. The only glimmer of light is she is still with me.

Silver is still strong. Eventually cubs were found, and I was able to make it simpler for the herders to raise them and helped them with the training.

Silver also took an interest in their training and is now father and leader of a pack of wolves. One seemed better with sheep so was taught to herd but most remained killers of beasts which the hunters learnt to use to their advantage.

I have a strong place in the tribe now. Yet still there is a reserve, and often if I am not with Arose I hunt alone or with only Silver.

78

In early autumn my new world had an awakening. I had painted over a part of the wall with white pigment to make way for new work. After placing wood on the fire I see Arose is comfortable and lie down on my own furs, now often separated from hers, and sleep soundly until dawn. On rising, I stoke the fire and bring water to boil for morning broth. I prepare for both Arose and me as I know that she will take it when she wants, usually while it is still warm. Then taking my brushes I raise my eyes to begin work on the new surface.

The broth and brushes fall from my hands and I stumble back, nearly falling over Arose now calmly drinking her brew. Then I look again with astonishment. I am staring into my own face, and beside that the very definite face of Arose also smiling back at me, as she has not done for the passing of six summers. I sit down and stare. The upper part of the body is also painted. The appearance is as we were six seasons ago.

Only one living creature could have done this. I swing and take her in my arms and hold her in front of the paintings. She has dropped her brew and attempts to recover it. Apart from that, for all I know she is aware of nothing. I let out a cry of agony. All the pain of lonely seasons seems to rip from me. I look into her eyes and call out to her but still, as so often, can see only a fathomless depth with no awareness. How? The paintings are done with skill. Some part of her has watched every stroke of paint I have put on the wall. Some part of her is so aware that she has painted equal to me with no practise at all. Either that, or a demon is painting on the wall separate or through her. Is it my subconscious spirit?

Then through the shock fear strikes me. If these paintings are seen they will bring at least suspicion down on our dwelling, at worst banishment or perhaps death for me, as no one will believe that she is the artist, and if they did the results may be just as bad. I cannot bring myself to remove the work immediately. Arose may be on the brink of some sort of recovery. There is only one thing I have big enough to cover the area. So I hang the skin of the great tiger on ropes from a rafter and tie it down securely bottom and sides. My hands are shaking. My mind tells me I should have painted over the figures. There is danger still, and the superstitious part of me is not sure of the power of the images. How they have been done is frightening, even if I do not think like the others on the power of images to trap a person's spirit. We look and, as far as I can tell, feel no different. I paint over a separate area for fear of what she will do next and work the rest of the day in the dwelling.

Arose goes outside and the children come to her. Later I find her once again with the women in the central place. I will wait two days and, if there is no change in her condition, I will remove the paintings. I also decide to be on the safe side and remove the ochres to a hiding place under some nearby rocks. This I do as night falls, then look for Arose who I now find with a much larger amount of wood than she used to carry. Some things are gradually changing. As always my chest tightens at the thought of her.

The night is as usual: eating, cleaning and talking before sleep. This time, when I lie down, I move against her and put my arms around her. She does not stir but the smell of her femininity and soft skin of her body soon inflame my passion. I roll on my back and the seed is quick to burst from my body. My arms go back around her and I fall asleep.

The movement of her body wakes me as she stands and moves to the fire. She takes a small piece of bark and lights the tallow lamp, then moves to the wall. I do not stir. At first she stands still and looks at the rug of the tiger. Then she moves around the hut looking for brushes she finds and paint she does not find. So she returns and sits in front of the tiger skin. I watch for a while but there is no movement. After a long wait I quietly move to her side and look at her face.

There is no expression, but her cheeks have a dark stain where tears have been flowing. I sit in front of her and take her hands. Her eyes remain on the skin where our faces are located, so I quietly undo the top and one side, allowing the skin to uncover the paintings. There is still no expression or movement. I ask her if she wants to finish the painting. No answer. I leave, and return with the colours that can produce flesh tones. She has returned to her furs after extinguishing the lamp and is breathing in peaceful sleep. The skin goes back, and I hold her in peaceful sleep until the sun brings life to the morning.

79

The next two nights Arose sleeps without moving. I leave Silver with her and hunt with tribe members. It is towards sundown and we are intending to take game at a hillside spring when they come to water. Then we see them. They are slavers. There are about forty of them, with fair skin and some fair hair of a northern tribe. The decision is made to follow from a distance, at least until they make camp. One of our party goes forward so there is less chance of our party being seen in the pursuit. Then we keep him in sight and are guided by his signals. It is well after dark before the slavers stop in the foothills and well away from the river. When their fire is lit our man rejoins us, and we take a guide from the stars and head back to the village, which is now much further than we would normally be without staying overnight. When we are well clear of them torches are lit, and our pace increases so to arrive at what feels like halfway through the night.

Arose and Silver are not in the dwelling. A torch is lit and her furs are empty. Then the shock hits me again. The tiger skin is on the floor, and the images with the upper half of the bodies completed are staring out at me with a life-like smile. I suppress panic and quickly cover the paintings.

With a sinking feeling I head for the centre of the settlement, where I can see what I hope are the hunters reporting the slavers to the heads of the village. They are not all there but shaman and chief are, and I am directed into the meeting house that has many torches lit and Arose sitting quietly in front of the seats facing our way. I do not need to be told that the paintings have been discovered. The chief and shaman are seated and then shaman speaks: "When you did not return two women went to look for Arose. They found her sitting in front of the images. You will take part in a ritual cleansing of the work tonight."

Within a short time, skulls of people are placed in our dwelling. The herbs are lit and a chant to call back and free Arose's spirit is heard. Then the pigments of the faces of Arose and me are washed away and painted blank. Some of our possessions are removed and all move outside. Then the dwelling is burnt to the ground.

I am stunned but aware that to protest would be pointless. The chief turns to me and says: "It is normal to condemn someone who breaks the taboo in the ways of the afterlife. None, to our knowledge, has ever done what you have done." I move to flee, but as I reach for the cover of darkness pain strikes my head and conscious thought recedes.

80

I awake to find I am tied to a carved pole in front of the meeting house. No people are present and the first rays of light have not appeared. Time travels slowly. Then I feel the rope cut from my wrists and feet. Normora hands me the cut rope and my pack and bow and arrows. She says: "Leave all and flee. You can reach neither wolf nor woman. They will kill you at first light as they ask for the blessing of the Earth Mother with the help of the rising sun."

I move away from the river in the direction of the cave of the Chosen People. My mind still in a haze works desperately, and I remember spears and tools as decoration in the Chosen dwelling. I grab sleeping furs off the floor and wall, two spears, more arrows and several good cutting edges, and I am away. The howl of Silver rings out and I pray it will not be a warning.

For a time I move along the river running to high country that follows the course of the river heading north. I hope the matter of the slavers will be more important than me, but my head tells me they will watch the slavers move through their region, and send a party to capture the one who must be killed, to remove the risk of more paintings to trap spirits from being done. It crosses my mind that they will probably have formed the opinion that it was me who stole Arose's spirit away in times gone by. More proof of the need to rid this Earth of Wolfman.

I trot till light then run, using hard ground until my lungs can breathe no more. After rest, I take up the singing chant I know they will use to overtake me and run until dark. The direction is changed, and fear of lions makes me seek protection in small fissures in cliff faces where I hope animals will not reach me. Exhaustion brings restless sleep. For several days I move, until I finally enter a forest of mainly cedar. At last I believe I am beyond them finding me.

Hunger makes me stop to gain food, drink and sleep. Then, seeking a high place, I take a clear view of fires and establish a camp each night in one of three different places far from the nearest smoke. There are no herbs but attempt is made to seek Arose, but I cannot reach a state of mind to release me to the journey.

My whole body, finishing with my mind, is aching with despair and overpowering tension. I know that I must wait until they do not expect me before returning for Arose and, if possible, Silver. For Arose I am well prepared to die to recover her. For my closest friend I will risk all but my love for Arose.

81

One full moon has passed and arrived again. I have spent half a moon hunting as I must and remaking my pack for travelling, with furs enough for Arose as well. Then I moved back towards the river, aiming for a high point of cliffs I have known. Here I stayed for two days observing some hunters and travellers, then moved down into a nearby forest with a good fresh water stream. Eventually I reached a position where only a part of a night would see me in the dwellings.

I store my pack and now, with the full moon to rise, arrive above the dwellings late in the day just before dusk removes my vision. My luck holds and Arose and Normora fill water bags and return to the chief's dwelling. Arose is a part of the head man's women. I cannot think what this means, except that it is the most central structure with more people to confuse the issue. I know Silver is in the new enclosure of wolves I helped build.

The night passes slowly. I see figures move out half way through the night to replace guards and, of course, know where they are positioned. They will be looking outwards, not to where I am already, beside the cave of the Chosen People, and waiting until another part of the night passes. Strangely, I am not afraid. The reasons I am here are more important than any one thing that I have to fear.

I move. My body is darkened with pigment and I travel from shadow to shadow, stopping several times before reaching the dark side of the structure I seek. Here I stop and listen. A baby cries and I hear Normora's voice very close to me soothe the infant. Time passes before the lack of noise tells me she has fed the infant, put it down, and returned to her furs.

After more time I enter the dwelling, staying away from the light of several wick lamps. I look to where I have seen the head man's furs lie and there stands Arose who immediately, without looking at me, moves towards the entrance. She has a fur tightly wrapped and it is as if she knew I had arrived for her. A glance at the chief's furs shows me where she had been lying. He grunts, and I see him reach out for her place and feel for her. I am moving through the shadows as he turns, starting to sit up. My spear strikes him in the throat and my foot pins him to the ground as his hands reach for his wounds. The weapon strikes again, this time to the heart and he dies with barely a sound.

Arose is already outside and moving towards Silver. I lift her onto my shoulder, and in swift movement am back in shadow heading towards the animals. I know the herdsmen stand guard but they concentrate on the outer part of the fence away from the village. I cannot call or look for the wolf, so I loosen the gate holder and swing the gate slightly and move on. If the wolf smells our scents he will, I hope, seek the entrance and gain his freedom.

82

Things have gone as well as I could hope but now I feel the beating of my heart and fear. Once again I could lose all that I want in this life. The woody valley is found and I move back onto the moonlit path that I know well. Putting Arose on her feet, we start to climb. There is still no noise of discovery or pursuit. Taking Arose by the hand I move her forward until she breaks into a run. She has not moved fast for a long time and is slow. It dawns on me that they will easily catch us in the morning if we head north in the direction they think we will go. They will know that we will not cross the river and head into the depths of the tribes of the twin rivers. They know that I have nothing but knowledge of danger amongst the tribes of the south-east. A brave fool would push into the great south land. We have one hope.

A quick recovery of pack sees us then push south. Once they discover they are wrong we will have distance, and their desire to follow without the full power of the war gathering will be less. To avenge a chief's death they may do so, but first there will be a combined gathering to bury him and a new chief will take command. If they do not get us in two days, it will be five at least before the full force sets off after us.

We have a good chance, but I feel it may have been better if I had not killed the headman of all these tribes. A part of me understands his position, and he had allowed us a life amongst his people until that was made impossible. Four shadows pass close and I reach for my bow, even though I know they are wolf.

By the time the light comes up we are well south. The search will be on by now. Runners will be on the way to a wide range of tribes to inform of our existence on the run. We keep the sun away from the weapon arm and stick to rocky ground where possible. The clouds are dark with the coming winter. Rain will be welcome to cover our tracks, and by the time the sun is half way up the sky it is pelting down with the wind behind us. If they have not found track by now they will continue to go north. Luck is with us.

Arose can only run for small periods of time. I have tried carrying her but for only a short time. We are fronted by a long slope of wooded country with alder and ash, and many deciduous trees just losing their leaves. Beyond the base of the slope is a flat of open area to a small river, then some open wood running to heavy forest for as far as the eye can see to the east and the west. There is risk in the open country if they come over the high country behind us, but once in the forest we will be hard to find and can stay in the cover for many days travel. If Silver finds our tracks good, but he is not my main concern regardless of all that he means to me.

We move as quickly as we can down the slope, keeping to the trees where possible, and watching all the time for man and beast. I have seen lion, rhinoceros and elephant in the river valley, so head slightly south of the lion group. Then I stop in my tracks. Several men have come out of the forest where it is closest to the water and are heading for the water's edge. I see quite a number at the edge of the forest. They are the slavers.

We must move and try to reach the forest. There is some ground cover and a brief wait sees the bare ground vacant of man. Keeping low from cover to cover, we move south-west until the sun is almost overhead. I think it is safe to cross the bare ground as the distance has put a bend in the river between them and us. The direction we have taken has also brought us closer to smoke down the river. We cross quickly without incident and are at last in the forest with high conifers and occasional areas of deciduous trees.

There are predators so our journey will remain dangerous. I am going to keep in a south-west direction, as this will take us away from the northern men and allow us to pass by the smoke to the west. This will also lead us deep into the vast forest.

83

Now that the first slight feeling of easiness has come to me I begin to miss the wolf and wonder, with the heavy rain we had, if the scent would have disappeared. He also is the head of a small pack with family of his own whose roots are in this river valley system. Perhaps this time the call of the wild will finally be too strong. I see some tree dwellers and glimpses of deer but take no interest in hunting. Distance and a safe camp spot are the main aims.

There is the smell of smoke at one time, so we change direction slightly to the south and journey long. Arose does not travel fast but shows little sign of being weary, however she alters her own pace and will no longer attempt to run.

The nights are getting colder and our belongings are wet so, if possible, we will risk a fire. The only shelter available is a group of large rocks against an earthen embankment. There is no wind in the trees and the rain has stopped for a time. Still, winter is coming. We gather dry material in the creepers and blackberries against the embankment. The fire may be able to be seen from one direction but the main risk is if it is smelt. The smoke will run south once it climbs above the treetops, so it is travelling away from the three directions people can come from that I know of.

We eat the dry meat I have in the pack and Arose, although not showing tiredness, goes early to the furs. They are damp but the fire is drying them and keeping her warm on one side. A circle of sticks makes racks for drying and helps hide the fire from the open direction. I sit for some time, aware of the distant sounds of lion, wolf and hyena. The fire will have to guard us from the sounds of the forest that are much closer, for exhaustion is going to put me to sleep. My strength, and what clear mind I have, must be retained. So sleep takes me, and the shadows that move in on us are unknown to me.

My dreams are troubled as the future has become very uncertain. It is far from safe. I have my back to the largest of the boulders and, as I hold Arose towards the warmth of the fire, my dream takes me over much of the journey of my life. One part of the dream seems to recur over and over, so on waking my mind stays focused on the idea; a light frame of sticks with light hides made waterproof with sap, wax and fat mixed together, all to fit snugly over the frame for an easy to carry, and easy to assemble, weather safe dwelling. I have seen similar amongst the tribes and on my journeys of the spirit. The idea is more important to me now, as it seems that our journey will be long and I hope we are out of the south land as quickly as possible. We need to be in the north with people whose ways, language and customs are close to ours. Hopefully I will then find a place for Arose and me.

All these thoughts cross my mind as the light from an already risen sun finds its way down through a fog enshrouded forest with dew dripping off branches nearby. As my eyes adjust to the new light, my movement for a blink freezes, then warmth floods my heart and all of a sudden my life feels more complete and safer. A quick glance shows me this infamous friend of ours has brought his family. There are furry shapes dotted here and there around us. I am not sure how this will work out. The wolves cannot all be kept on leash, so they must run their own lives as a pack. If they return to us we must be a pack for each others advantage. This I hope can happen. Wolves like Silver, in numbers I suspect about seven, can be strong protection if friends to man and, in this case, an overprotective and often possessive friend to the most important of women.

I wake Arose who is immediately taken over by wolf which, even in these circumstances, brings laughter to my heart. I roll the hides and kill the fire, being careful to bury the ashes, then with drink and food in belly move out. Silver looks disgusted. I guess he has been up with family all night and thinks it a fitting idea to sleep.

We move south-east, again on the sun, and the animals stay for a part of the light then move out again to do their own hunting. I hope they return but realize that now it will be a very different beast and man relationship.

84

No people find us in half the time of a cycle of the moon. Most mornings the animals are back with us and sometimes a lot of the night. At the end of this period we are out of food so move to hunt. Still in the forest we find a spring which is an obvious animal watering hole. Three days sees us with meat for animal and human plus seven decent hides of deer: five red and two sable deer. The wolves seemed to like me hunting for them but once or twice interfered. They do not usually share the hunt with me as they outdistance me greatly and definitely, or usually, do not bring the meat back for us. Silver has, on occasion, but not since he has been dividing amongst the others of his pack.

In a day I have the tent poles cut and another sees the hides roughly cleaned. The next day sees them bound together with rawhide strips and, although not a perfect fit, they cover two-thirds of the enclosure, so I use an old hide to finish. We must travel on for the journey is long.

I remember from my spirit journey, while looking for Arose, the lay of the land and how we must pass south of a huge river delta, then cross the largest of rivers on this south land. Then moving north-west we will follow the coast of the inland sea until it takes us across the thin strip of land and up the land of the leg, to once again travel to perhaps the land of our people, if we go that far or manage to survive that long.

We have travelled two full moons and I am confident that the twin rivers tribes will not be still pursuing us. The wolf pack is often travelling with us for up to half a day before breaking off to venture on their own. Twice now they have warned us of attack from big cats, and are constantly warning us of predators and man in the vicinity. They have accepted us as a part of the pack, even sleeping close at night and giving and taking body warmth when we do not raise the tent.

The cold time is well advanced and the days shorter but the weather is not noticeably colder. We are still moving south into a warmer climate. Still, the nights freeze the surface of ponds and slow water.

There has been one major change in Arose that delighted, confused, then gave me a mixture of emotions. As our journey slowed and we lay rested in our now waterproof tent, our bodies joined. It was not me that instigated sex. After all this time of no response to my gentle advances, she quite boldly sought out my body and was aggressive in an almost urgent necessity for fulfillment. I can only presume it was the head man's demands, without consideration of her sensitivities, that awoke her needs. After the surprise I am grateful, but still tears spring to my eyes when she has finished and returns to her vacant state. Perhaps aggression will snap her out of it. Still, I presume it was partly aggression that caused her to withdraw into herself. I can only do what I know, and it is not in my nature to beat her into coming back to what might be called reality. I have almost forgotten the sound of Arose's voice.

85

We have struck an ocean by going too far south and again moved north-west to enter the great southern land. Another moon has passed, and we are exposed in open grasslands with more of the grain plants than I have ever seen before. There are huge herds of grazing beasts which I have no name for. There are many predators, mainly lion, which seem less interested in us, possibly because game is so abundant.

The pack has become skilled at avoiding all that they do not seek, which now includes humans. They are one less in number, so I presume man has killed and they have become wary of strangers. We have watched these tribes pass and hunt on various occasions. They are tall, very black people.

We arrive at the great river and the grasslands have given way to a forest of cypress, cedar, olives and some palms. There are many people living on the river. We avoid smoke and only light fire for the time of the cooking, but sometimes avoid fire to eat fish, fruit and grains raw. I do not know if the wolves will cross on reed raft or boat if we borrow one, as there are many boats on the river. From cover I have seen some boats holding many people. This is a richer warmer land, and their cold times are far warmer than our hot periods in the north.

On the third day by the river flowing north, we noticed something that made me extremely uneasy. Game and predators were in great abundance, but no sign of human occupation for one day, and only smoke to the north now fading to the far distance. Why do people avoid this area? What is the great danger? We eat well on waterfowl and ducks. The predators do not seem to be a great risk as they have food in well rounded stomachs. We have even passed quite close to lion without trouble.

I decide to camp and work on a way to cross the river. Over time the skill of reed boats has become mine but it will take four or five days to build one, then with Silver's help teach our pack to travel on water. The current is strong but manageable.

Eventually I come up with a boat some four steps long and one wide with a paddle that moves me, if not easily, at least successfully in a down current direction across the river, at this point some one hundred steps wide.

Three days have passed and the wolves are jumping freely in and out of the boat, always with Silver and sometimes too many trying to get in. I have been tipped into the river many times. They behave as if it is a game. Still tomorrow, three at a time, we will cross.

Three trips take all day but we are across, and have found good camp half way up the cliffs near the water. I feel good, if still uneasy. This has been a major obstacle to overcome. There has been no sign of people. There is always a reason. We will camp and rest while I scout the surrounding area.

86

I start to move off in the morning but have gone no more than fifty steps when my whole pack, including woman, fall in with me. We risk leaving the tent with supplies inside and continue. Soon we reach a high bank of red cliffs overlooking the river and plains. Then I see something unusual; an image from my spirit journey but different. Although some distance away, I see the upper part of a great stone lion partly buried, but even from this distance it appears to be larger than many elephants put together. There are also signs of great stone blocks and walls laid out in one direction all the way to the river, finishing in a still partly-there large wall of blocks, right into the river. It makes the hair stand up on the back of my neck. As always the spiritual knowledge to me is as in a mist, and the physical experience is exciting and baffling. These carved stones are from the dawn of human time. The river people would, I am sure, put them back to the Chosen People. Those who dwell in the surrounding areas obviously hold them as the work of gods or those of an evil underworld. We will be safe from man, as long as they do not know we have entered this place of, I presume, vast taboo.

After initial unease, my memories tell me this has been, long ago, work of a people of great peace and harmony with what they called the universe and especially this Earth as a living spiritual entity, encompassing the total spirituality of all life on Earth. Then I realize that Arose and I have arrived by accident at one of the ancient sites that we long ago spoke of travelling to see. Proof if you like that, at least in part, the ancient knowledge is truth. For a long time I stand and stare. Slowly awareness returns, and a quick look around the horizon tells me we are the only people. We return to gather our packs and move out to explore the new discoveries.

The sun is still high overhead when we arrive so, selecting a grove of trees for cover, I set up the tent and gather wood for a fire in the night. Then, with Arose in company and wolves hunting for their own keep, we move to the giant lion. Although partly buried and worn from aeons of rain and wind, it is the largest man-made sculpture of stone I have seen with my eyes. The features and mane of the lion may have been carved in detail long ago but now are rounded and flattened. It still towers above me. It is not possible to climb up on. It has gone quietly through time when most other objects of long ago have disappeared.

We wander the main causeway, and a picture from my journeys with the Other Ones' shaman shows this as the central gathering point and a place of celebration and entertainment. I see a misty image from the journeys; of crowds of people and many beautiful and huge boats with cloth-like small clouds over their decks, some with hundreds of people and some with goods from up and down the vast waterway. This river was not only a trade route but also an area of recreation and leisure transport.

There is no feeling of sadness at this loss of the past, only wonder and a quiet appreciation of what humans can achieve. Something inside me tells me that extraordinary things could once again come to this area on the great river of an ancient land and perhaps birthplace of many of our ancestors.

We return to our camp area. Arose switches into her quiet motions and, while I light the fire and heat water in the bags for broth, she prepares food. Her movements are slow and accurate and have slightly improved over time but her spirit remains in a safe place. Still now, on more than one occasion, I wonder if it could not be a fright or a shock that will, or may, bring her back.

I take my broth and sit in front of the trees where I can watch for danger. Most of all I watch the silhouette of the stone monolith against a beautiful golden sunset, and dream of the possibility of a great age of people past and perhaps to come. As the sun disappears I see the outline of a large, very much alive cat move past the fading light and hear the death cry of a boar, so move to build the fire and look forward to the return of our pack. Those wonders are, at times like this, such welcome protection.

The morning sees us with a new problem, as one of the females has been injured in the hunt and has a long gash over her hindquarters. I see no reason why a wolf should not be treated as a human. The wound is bathed and I attempt to put a solution of what I hope will be helpful herbs on the wound. At the risk of having my arm bitten off, I wrap hide strips around her. She is slow and stays with the people of her pack as the others move around. We feed her with us but can see she is in pain when she moves.

Three days see her moving better, so we have a last look at this beautiful deserted place that still, to me, seems to ring with ancient laughter and the smiles of happy, celebrating faces.

87

We set off for the ocean that I know the river must travel to but in a north-westerly direction. One day out of the river site, we come across a row of human and animal skulls on a row of sticks. The smoke of human habitation runs north and south of us, and it crosses my mind that we are back in the land of the most dangerous of all two legged predators. They have certainly been the cause of much disaster for me, and more especially Arose. I call the wolves and put Silver on a lead to try and hold all our family of animals close. If they run I will let Silver travel with them. I would prefer to lose him than see the pack run and not return. The other five now magnificent wolves stay close.

The countryside is open woodland. The grass is easy to move through, being heavily grazed here. At the sight of us, the animals of the hoof move away. Regardless of our strength we still give the more fearsome creatures a wide berth. They are wary of us but do not run. We have seen no great tiger which runs from no creature when its hunger demands satisfaction. Even with this great creature, the pack would offer a diversion or warning, giving us time to seek cover.

We are not long out of the forbidden area when I become aware that the wolves are uneasy. Then, from time to time, I see a glimpse of man, well back and meant to be hidden from us but there all the time. It is probable that, at least from the time of the skulls, we have been under constant surveillance. I think we have been lucky to have travelled so far without incident. Now, with tightness in my throat, I put my old security hide on, the now tattered silver hide of the leader, with the wolf face over my forehead.

I have been with Arose for long enough to know that she has been aware in detail as to what is going on. As always she registers nothing. I think if she was to take an arrow, she would not cry out. I pray to the Earth Mother and the great Spirit that we do not find out. The wolves are staying close to Silver who is their leader. He is held to be higher than me, even though I hold his lead short.

There is no change until the sun is overhead. A beautiful valley now surrounds us with grasslands running for as far as the eye can see. There are only elephant in the far distance and no creature of the hoof, so it is likely that we are far from safe in the country we are entering.

Some time passes and we enter a narrow region with high cliffs on each side. If they wish we will die here, for in country like this and without a good head start, I cannot lose a tribe. The drums start from somewhere in the hills south of the valley.

Then they are there. Many warriors all around for hundreds of steps line the cliffs each side. A harmonious, peculiar chanting song rises into the air, to be accompanied by the beating of their spears against a round shield they all seem to carry. Then on a rise just to the south, and about one hundred steps ahead, is the headman and, I would guess, shaman and seven immense naked, black warriors. I stop short of them by fifty steps. It seems to me to march up to them with our pack would be to invite certain death. We must look a strange sight as it is.

I lay down my weapons and open my arms in a gesture of peace. The headman raises his arms and the chant and drums cease. Then two of the huge warriors come forward carrying no arms, only fur bundles. They stop short and, to my astonishment, drop to their knees and place their foreheads on the ground. Rising, they unroll the furs to reveal two objects. There is a woven cloth dyed with many colours and covered with shells and beautiful stones. This is placed in front of Arose who completely ignores them. I can see they are now beginning to look on her with awe and fear. Then there is a necklace of round stone-like objects that shine with an almost transparent luminous quality. It is all white to cream, except for six objects that are black and present the centrepiece of the jewellery, which is the teeth of the saber tooth tiger that are separated by two black pearls and two on each side of each of the two great teeth. I presume, at a glance, both pieces are valuable and more. To my knowledge, they are certainly non-existent in any of the journey we have covered.

The two return to the chief who raises his own spear and crashes it onto his shield, to be followed by the same motion by all. He and company are then back to the rhythm over the rise and then the noise ceases. I look up and all are gone. I am none the wiser but alive. The cloth is draped over Arose and the necklace goes on me. I presume this land will have eyes for time to come. It is not hard to grasp that these people think that, in the least, we are blessed by spirits or something of a similar nature.

88

We continue to avoid the inhabited areas but remain aware that we are constantly under surveillance, sometimes going for three or four days at a time without a glimpse. Then a group or single warrior will appear on a rise, never closer than four or five hundred steps. Several times we have found game already butchered and the hides cleaned on our route and at an appropriate campsite. I no longer try to camouflage campfires or worry about wind direction. It is a strange feeling. One does not know if they are protectors or, in the long-term, dangerous to us.

Five moons pass and the weather is hotter than I have ever known with deep blue skies for several days as the heat builds up and the air starts to feel wet. Then dark clouds of great magnitude rush in and deposit rain as I have never seen before. Gullies flood; then two days later are dry again. Animals I have never seen are everywhere: tall creatures with necks as long as their already tall bodies. Twice more we are met by a group of warriors and are presented with body decoration. The wolves once again run free and we have lost none of their numbers.

Our direction, which followed the coast for many moons, has turned north for the last seven days. I can see, from a high ridge we are on, that the sea is coming in from both sides to form a narrow strip of land that I believe runs from the south land to the northern place of my fair skinned people.

We have a lot of company now. For the first time since the two cliffs there is a large crowd of many hundreds of warriors. They are passing us and moving ahead. We come over a rise, and in the valley before us is a causeway only two hundred steps wide. Women and men have lined up in many rows forming a corridor some one hundred steps long. The wolves have gathered to us, and I can see by their looks they would rather turn and go the other direction. I place Silver on the lead again and begin to move through the avenue of humanity. The strange chanting drumming keeps us company. Arose, in splendid dignity, ignores the whole performance. At least these days she carries a small pack. It has helped.

When we pass through the corridor of people, they form up behind us in several lines, forming a half circle with us in the middle. I turn, and once again lay my weapons down and open my arms in peace. Arose carries on ignoring the surroundings as usual. I get the feeling these people are bidding us goodbye and symbolically showing us the exit gate from what may be a unity of tribes. I will probably never know, but I have the feeling that we have passed through an entire nation of tribes. We have done this without speaking a single word or raising a weapon to defend ourselves. Whatever the connection in these people's minds with the site of the Ancients, it has had powerful effect.

This night we make camp, aware that we are probably now perhaps only observed by animals. I take care again with the placing of the fire. The pack has stayed close, so we share what food we have left and sleep amongst our furry bodyguards.

89

The cold months are finishing as we head north. This helps. We have made contact with one tribe after avoiding all for half a moon's travel. Once again they are lighter skinned people, but still dark of hair and not so heavy with facial hair. The encounter was not a success. They seemed very uneasy about the wolves, so that night we did not camp at all but used the cover of darkness to change direction, and hopefully lose any who may have decided to follow. For the next two days I light no fires and move on.

The country has broadened out, so I use the sun and continue north-east, at times losing sight of the ocean. It has become apparent that the tribes are mainly near the ocean, so use the smoke as direction.

Several full moons pass and it is pleasing to find the days have grown long. Once again, with the help of the pack we avoid tribes, and as time passes a large mountain range looms to the east of our journey.

Arose is now pregnant, with no change to her physical ability either during the travel or in the furs. Although my body is often tired, she seems to feel little effect from the long journeys. I am trying to reach the friendly tribe that Normora and I encountered after we first saw the great inland sea when we were following the ocean.

We are travelling beside a mountain range that is familiar. The creatures of the hunt are now a mixture from the south land and the warmer land of the tribes I once thought of as the Invaders. The past seasons have broadened my impression of these tribes who cover such a vast area. They, like us, are capable of great aggression and occasional human kindness.

There are definitely laws that are similar to the land of my birth and the tribes of the twin rivers.

The weather has been holding warm as we move into the long days, although we travel towards the bleak north. It is still far away, perhaps one full change of the season of uninterrupted travel to the great ice.

90

For days now flocks of birds and many animals have been going south. It is strange but I think perhaps natural for this land. Then I see a great dark cloud to the north, slowly building up to cover the entire sky. Then huge flocks of birds fill the sky, more than I have seen before. They are all flying south, many varieties mixed together. This is definitely wrong. Even animals are moving south in ever increasing numbers and showing little fear or interest in man or wolf.

The wolves are uneasy. There are many cliffs east of our journey, so I lead Silver and am lucky to find cover with many cave openings into the sandstone. The wolves seem keen to seek shelter as I will not let them head south. The sky is growing darker. Four arrows easily find game and I have food in abundance for man and beast: one auroch and three red deer. I bleed and gut all, and drag one red deer into a cave entrance. Arose is gathering wood which is plentiful, as the forest follows the cliff face. It is a lucky site.

Then the cold strikes. Winds streak down, forcing me to move the fire further back from the entrance. The cold, like I have not felt since the northern winters, descends. I quickly put as many furs as possible on both of us, and put up the tent as windbreak and cover, leaving the front open to fire. The animals and birds have made this blizzard strike fear deep in my being. Even Arose seems to register the fearsome difference. With what little light that is left, I quickly drag as much wood as possible into the cave and build the fire high. The wolves' normal fear of fire disappears and they huddle together close to tent and flame. Other predators move past, including the great tiger. They seem not to see us and show no interest in the fresh kills of beast near the entrance to the cave. A last look tells me that, to my astonishment, meat that should still be flexible and internally warm is freezing over. I am, like my pack, afraid.

My world has not, to my knowledge, had a storm such as this, even in the north. For a time the wind howls. Then it stops dead and there is total quiet. No sound of creature or nature. This is a strange twilight world, like moonlight but not the same. I bring Silver into the tent and place him on the outside of Arose then, with almost painfully cold movements, bring another of the red deer into the cave. It is frozen stiff, and already I have to break it free from an icy surface covering the ground.

The fire is as large as I can make it in this confined space. The cave is about two steps high, six deep and three wide. I am sure without it we would probably be dead. I move back into the furs and close Arose tightly between the wolf and myself.

Time passes and eventually darkness of real night descends, leaving us in firelight. The cold would keep me awake if I tried to sleep but sleep is not an option. I rise each time the fire burns down and put more wood on. My hands move on Arose, not seeking the company of her body but keeping the flesh of her body warmer and flexible. The sound of her normal rhythmic breathing that tells me she sleeps does not occur. As my hands massage her stomach, the life in her body moves more aggressively than I have felt before. Even the unborn life seems aware that all nature that is designed to nurture life has ceased to continue in its age-old cycle. Something somewhere has happened to my beloved Earth to strike cold and fear and, I suspect, death into the being of much of the living.

Eventually a light appears outside. It is a little brighter than the previous day, so I wrap myself in furs and go outside. There are icicles on branches that yesterday were heavy with spring leaf but today are bare. Even the needles of the conifers seem sparse. I doubt this south land, of what I think is the foot of the leg, has ever seen snow and ice, apart from the mountain peaks. The auroch and the other deer are frozen under snow. I spend time clearing them, being careful not to sweat as my frozen sweat might cause grievous damage to this body. Eventually I am able to pull the frozen deer into the cave. There is no chance of meat spoiling, as even in the interior it is preserved as an icy lump.

I am able to hack off two legs and a piece of the body from a deer, and get food cooking for Arose and me and thawed for the wolves. Thank the spirit that I shot all these creatures, as the only movement outside is an occasional branch breaking under an unaccustomed load of ice and snow. Each time I feel rested and as warm as possible another trip for wood occurs. By the end of the day the cave is half full of branches, and a large pile now half covered in snow and ice is at the entrance doubling as a wind break. Still, the wind has remained calm and does so for the next two days. By the end of the third day the light has returned to normal but it remains unnaturally cold.

There is still no animal or bird life to be seen, but the wolves have gone outside for short spells allowing me to clean the cave a little, although it is too cold for smell to become a big problem. It is cold to wash.

I lose track of time, but I suspect after about twelve days the biting cold begins to recede. The sky, still grey, has clouds that are now moving with a steady breeze.

Several more days pass and the snow is nearly gone. I venture up onto the cliff top to look for a sign of life. The mountains are pure white, stretching for as far to the north as vision allows. The lowlands have patches of green and I see to my astonishment reindeer, which must have come a great distance from the regions that were previously home to them.

The wolves move off to hunt which pleases me, as I wonder at the supply of food in the not too distant future. The deer are nearly all gone. The auroch is beginning to thaw, so I will dry as much as I can carry in the next day or so. Then with care I will follow the coast north, using the shell food and fish of sea and river where available. When people appear I will endeavour to find out what damage has been done. It still seems to be a good idea to get Arose to the tribe of friendly people, hopefully before she has the baby.

Two more days and I am ready. We set off into the rising sun. The pack, having eaten their fill of the auroch remains, seem happy to travel with us.

It is more than half a moon before we see anything larger than groups of hunters. We continue to avoid them, as I have become aware that in this hungry environment the wolf will be killed for meat, fur, or simply to remove competition for food.

91

A great distance is behind us when a lot of smoke speaks of a large gathering. I skirt higher into the hills and make camp for Arose. After tethering one of the females with great fuss, I move toward the dwellings. Travelling by good moonlight, I arrive while most are still gathered at central fires. There would appear to be at least one hundred men, women and children.

Their dwellings are close to ocean and river with a large cave in the rear, the mouth of which is almost covered by a hide covered structure. This would have been a good place to survive, unlike a number of sites where I saw no evidence of life. I did not inspect too closely but the wolves did on several occasions, returning with full bellies. It is best not to think about the probability of their inspection. I expect they are not working hard for their meals.

I sit quietly until most have retired to various locations, then with only five people near a fire I move into the shadow of a nearby hut and can hear the conversation. The language is totally strange to me so it can be presumed that, at this time, we would gain little from human contact. I quietly withdraw and move rapidly back to my pack.

As the moons pass by, the climate seems to have returned to something more normal and trees take on leaves again. There are still less of the creatures I would expect to see in this region. No sign of large predators, elephant or deer. I get the feeling the reindeer are returning north faster than we can travel, so we are relying on food of the shell and fish.

Long distances pass most days. We are only staying put if the rain is too brutal. The days stretch into a tedious repetition and I think five moons have passed. Arose is so pregnant that I expect her to have the child on any given day. I am afraid for her, even though she has been through it before.

Then several familiar landmarks appear and I know I am only days away from the friendly tribe. First we come across the spot where Normora and I made contact. After camping the night, we move down to a close location. There is smoke and a few people, so we approach with animals close and on a lead, then lay weapons down and stand quietly and wait. They approach cautiously until recognition comes. I think they know Silver and then me, and happy shouts of welcome result.

It is a joy to hear a human voice with warmth and words I understand again. My body seems to relax tension for the first time in many moons. After a quick look at Arose, it is noted by the women and children that her belly is full. This brings happy laughter and questions as to when the child will come. She as usual ignores them, so I say her body is healthy and the baby will arrive any time. I also say that she has suffered greatly and has for several seasons lost the gift of speech. I also say Normora is well and we both have fine memories of this tribe. I say to the men: "I feared you might not have survived the cold." They tell me they lost nine people and their hunting grounds are poor. "You are welcome to stay and your skills will be of value in the preservation of the tribe."

I pick up our weapons and move to a site on the outskirts of the dwellings. Much commotion is created when I set up my tent and leash the wolves, most having not been on the leash since leaving twin rivers. The wolves are not pleased but they do not know these children. I will free Silver soon and take the others to hunt during the day. It worries me a little that they will eat the meat of these good people's hunting grounds, so we will hunt together to contribute.

We share food and broth and talk of the great blizzard. Then they tell me the ice mountains are now further south and cover the grounds of many northern tribes. They know large numbers of northern people died and some have moved south joining tribes such as theirs. Six have become new members of this tribe. This news makes me think of the suffering my own childhood people must have endured. I think of my birth mother and those I knew well. For the first time in several seasons I feel a pain in my chest for lost connections and a desire to return to the ways of my origins.

Arose, with no effort and some help from Silver, breaks down any slight reserve and soon is a part of the women's camp. They seem to be constantly feeling her belly. Then one evening she cannot be found, and on inquiry the women laugh at me and say she is being cared for by women wise in the ways of the Mother and the great Spirit. I sit by the fire until late but eventually sleep becomes impossible to avoid.

There is still no sign of Arose in the morning but inspection shows me she sits quietly in the women's camp. They open her furs to show a bundle of fur with a soon to be revealed little girl sucking quietly on a nipple. Although Arose handles the baby with care, she shows no outside acknowledgment of her to others. When they take her from Arose to show me, there is no sign of protest or awareness.

For the next three nights she does not return to my camp. Then one morning I see Arose gathering wood for me, and inspection reveals the baby tucked in warmly inside her furs.

92

As time passes birds return, followed shortly by many animals. We are accepted as part of this tribe. I teach them to hunt with the wolves and an enclosure is built. The baby is growing and is healthy, and I feel happy to be amongst friends. A full change in the season passes and, although the winter is severe for these people, it is not unlike the ones of my youth, with the ground staying frozen not far under the surface for long after the cold period has ended. They say some plants they have always known and used in healing and food no longer grow in these hunting grounds. There is some hardship on an ongoing basis for these people.

I am glad to share knowledge and, with care, change I have brought from the tribes of the twin rivers. I would like to paint, but I am afraid that a repeat of some of the events of the past might put us into trouble with these people and their spiritual beliefs.

In this tribe the child of Arose is growing each day in a safe and loving environment. She likes to climb all over her mother and I notice that she, like most creatures apart from some men, is gentle with her. I presume the women have taught Arose how to clean and change the soft skins for the baby's needs, as it is rare that I have had to do this. Usually there is no smell or when smell arrives, seemingly without me noticing, the acts occur to take care of such.

Arose is often taken with child to fetch roots and seeds with the other women. They have begun with guidance to spread seed from wheat and rye and I have been much impressed with the idea of keeping other plants away. The area that is dominated by the grains is growing rapidly. The only problem is they seem so impressed with their efforts that they still seek grain elsewhere, and have so far refused to harvest their own area. This will come in time.

The wolf pack has grown with the arrival of ten pups. For the first time I realize that this is going to be a problem. These animals will grow in number faster than the tribe and eat them out of their resources. The problem is approached with the tribal elders and headman. The number of pups decreases to three. They do not offer to tell me what happened so I close my thoughts for the time being. Then the thought enters that, in the future, the females that are to birth should be sent into the wild to find their own den. They may return but if they perish then that is the way of the great Spirit. It seems to me humans can change nature but should remain in harmony with it, and so in harmony with the living Earth Mother.

There are occasional travellers but these people say that, before the blizzard, travellers from far distance were rare, except for neighbouring tribes who often share ceremonies. So, little knowledge has come of the tribes of the far north. With sadness I think of the last of the Other Ones, whose last refuge would have been totally devastated.

As time goes by I want to know what has happened to the clans, and how much of their land has been lost to the ice mountains. I talk to Omar and tell him of my wishes. He says I have travelled far and am lucky to have survived. "The spirit has been strong with you. Your journeys have been of value to my tribe. If you go you will be welcome to return." As the journey now would take me into the cold time of the north, I make my plans and wait for the cold to pass.

Meanwhile I use the time making improvements to my tent and continuing to work with the grain concept within the tribe. Their axes have been made stronger, and many trees have been ring barked so they will be ready to burn with the next hot time.

93

Two moons after the shortest day of the cold moon, I pack my tent and take my old friend and the female wolf he seems to favour. Then with Arose and child who I carry as she will slow the journey down, we set out for the land of the tribe that brought Normora and me to the great sea so many seasons ago.

I cannot leave Arose for it is perhaps her right to confront the people of her birth. Nothing else has brought back the beloved voice that I have not heard since the arrows entered my body at the devastation of our lives. Another thing that has not been heard of since the blizzard is the slavers. Perhaps they perished in the cold or, if they survived, were far into the south land.

Once again we are helped in our journey by our furry friends, when they warned of a large cat who lay in ambush in a thicket that we were forced to travel through. We took to the trees and waited. Eventually he appeared and took an arrow which disappeared with his being.

The only other problem has been teeth. In both Arose and me our deteriorating mouths have, in my case anyway, started to cause great pain. It is a long and difficult process to work the tooth enough to get it to come out. This must be done, else the body becomes unhealthy. We both now have gaps. In Arose's case I can only tell when she stops eating and the area near the tooth becomes red and swollen. Regardless of this, we are soon in slight contact with the tribes who remember Wolfman and the tattered hide I wear again.

Moons pass, and we find ourselves in the camp of those that border the ancient stones of the Other Ones. Reindeer, mammoth and woolly rhinoceros are now amongst the common creatures hunted. Although of the hot month, it is cold. I am told the great ice barrier is only one day's march north of the stones in the region of the largest of all the stones raised by ancient man.

The tribe is smaller by far than I remember. Instead of some four hundred people, there are just over one hundred and many empty dwellings. When questioned, these people seemed stunned by the memories and have the spirit of the cold time to blame. They seem to have elevated this spirit to a position of awe, and made it separate to the collective spiritual belief.

They ask nothing of Normora who was, I suppose, only a slave. They seem to think a woman who does not speak is the result of some spell that I, as shaman, have placed on her. The medicine woman and false shaman are both dead. I do not feel comfortable here, so the following morning bid the headman well and move out towards the coast, as there is little point in travelling towards the ice.

94

Many days pass, and we arrive at the place of the north sea. There is no ocean to be seen anywhere. The ocean level has lowered. The forts to protect from the Invaders are empty, so we move out towards our birthplace. I glance at Arose and, to my astonishment, I see her face has expression. She looks alert and fearful. When I speak to her and ask her if she recognizes that we are home, she stares at me. Something that has been long dormant is moving inside her. I feel a nervous surge of hope. I take Arose gently by the hand and lead her and the child on to the forest track that will take us to what once was home, and is perhaps still there. Many of the trees that needed some warmth are leafless and dying or dead, but new growth of a different sort is leaping into life.

Many emotions sweep through me and the wolves rush ahead. I wonder if even Silver feels he is going home. I recognize the valley that leads to the den where I found him so long ago. We top the rise and there is smoke in the dwellings of our home.

The arrows enter my chest and leg and I hear Arose scream. I hear, from the depth of the being I have loved since my youth, the call of my name.

I am on my back and her arms are around me, and the words flow freely from her mouth. Through the pain and fear I feel a surge of joy that this person is back in the body. Then I see her head yanked back and hear a gruff voice demand: "Who is the tattooed woman of the Invaders and the man who wears the cloth and marks of our enemies who have denied us room to live after the ice has invaded the land of most of the clans? How dare you offend our lost people." Then Arose yanks free and I hear: "You have wounded Wolfman Garoke, the man beyond all men, who has travelled to the end of the Earth's inhabited place to bring back me, Arose, daughter of the clans."

The gruff warrior remains arrogant, but another from the now forming group steps forward and drops to his knees beside me and the weeping figure of Arose who is once again clinging to me. He looks up and I recognize the boy Honer who has now hardened into manhood. He says: "Jessa, make way for those who will get Garoke, our brother, back to our healer and make haste."

I can see my world is blurring. I am not sure if it is the herbs the healer has given me, or the time of the spirit has arrived for me. I hear Arose say: "You will not leave me." The taste this time in my mouth is blood. I know the arrow has passed into the wrong part of my body.

I see my mother holding the child of Arose. Her tears flow freely. I say to her: "I have come home with all that I have loved in life and she is as one with body and spirit." I ask that Arose be strong in the memory of my love, and safe in the hearth of my people. Honer kneels and says: "We did not know you. It grieves us to see you so. Arose is as one with us. This I promise."

I ask how is it that the clans have survived in the face of such a climate disaster. They say the priestesses of the Earth Mother goddess saw the birds migrate and the animals depart eight days before the great blizzard. They sent runners to all places they could reach, and great fires were built in many of the sacred caves. Many survived but now they have no land and have been rejected in the lands of the Invaders. "Now great hunger and anger exists, so you took an arrow."

The world is fading. Even the sound of my beloved Arose is growing distant, but I can still feel her gentle breath against my face. Then another face appears and gently licks my face. As the world fades my last glimpse is of the silver wolf, resting his head on the forehead at the centre of the life that is leaving me.

The light is becoming familiar while growing larger and closer. I feel an ancient yearning and great peace, not as one who is dying but one who is returning.

The life of difference

95

I am born again sixteen years later. I am five years old when my story begins.

I look up at the face of the woman with the smooth skin who provides the food, and looks after the young of our dwelling who number less than the fingers of one hand. She also lives with the tall man and the woman who has many lines on her face and the blue circle on her forehead. It is this woman who, although not the food provider, makes sure we are warm, and it is the soft lines and gentle movements she makes that gives me a safe feeling.

Food provider has the angry face now, and her hand strikes me and pushes me towards the opening to the cold outside. I have been out with the other young but as usual they did not want my company. I can see by the way the branches of the many dead trees lie on the ground that the wind is strong outside.

Blue circle is by my side and, as often happens, she takes my hand and we move down the river, that for a brief time is not covered in ice. Blue circle reminds me of the birds in the sky, not because she can fly but because she seems sure of her movements. She also makes the feelings of my chest and head seem to fly like a bird when I hold her hand and walk with her to our favourite places. She seems to have beauty that comes from inside her and a shimmer of light around her being.

Blue circle carries a bow and arrow. All people who go in small groups or alone are prepared with a weapon. Only women and children in groups that are protected go unarmed. We move off to a valley away from the river, following a small flow of water up over pretty little waterfalls and pass rock pools now surrounded by flowers of many colours. One is placed in my hair, so I take one and place it in blue circle's hair. This makes her face crinkle and her mouth wide as her eyes shine. I know that this is her happy look, and she swings me high so I feel like the bird and feel the air rush out of me in the happy way.

Soon we are at the place where the water falls the greatest distance. There we have good seats on stones with backrests against the cliff. Blue circle and I can see animal or people while they are still a great distance away. Here blue circle likes to take a stick and draw pictures in the sand. She is very good and I often understand.

Today, as always, she starts by clapping her hands together, first on one side of my head then on the other. I always feel the little breeze that her hands coming together make, but the look on her face after this for a very small time is the sad face. I know she expects me to do more than feel the little wind.

I know this is what makes me different and what makes the other children ignore me. I have seen people go near others and clap their hands to make the other person jump and have the frightened face. So I moved carefully up behind blue circle and clapped. She jumped, then looked surprised and hugged me. So I thought it was a good game and tried it with the other children. At first they laughed, then grew angry with me and punched me. Then they moved away.

The stick is moving in the sand again and I watch for a while as animals and people take shape. Then something happens that will stay with my mind. Blue circle draws a person and holds up a finger. Then more and still more until she has all fingers held up. She then draws a marking under each person and again holds up a group of fingers. She points and looks at me. When I do not move she lifts my hand and holds up my fingers all on one hand. I understand. She points again and I hold up the number of fingers as she did. Then she gets groups of stones and puts them in different lots under each figure. Soon I understand. Soon I can draw the symbol and understand it is magic for how many stones or people. She points at what I now know are three birds and raises her fingers, so I point at five birds in the sky and raise the fingers of one hand. She hands me the stick and I draw the symbol for one hand.

For some reason this gives her the excited face, and something deep inside me tells me I am on a new and enlightened journey. We laugh and are happy this day, and even the sky turns blue for a little while and makes me happier. The blue sky is warm, like the warmth of the circle on blue circle's face. She is my world, as she is the only one who gives me a blue sky.

The tall man of our dwelling used to hold me and swing me high and I even remember once travelling on his shoulders. Then his expressions began to change. He made many mouth movements at me so that I smelt the breath from his body. He had the confused look but then became angry and he soon turned away.

Lately tall man has taken food from me and given it to the other young of our dwelling. So, except for blue circle, my sky is always full of cold dark clouds. At night I always have company, for us children sleep tight together for warmth. I always have the outside near the wall but this time of the longer days I am able to sleep mostly warm.

96

Today is the day that the hunters gather at the central dwelling place of the one who they look to most. The provider and some of the women, including blue circle, are there also. This seems unusual to me. The other children are at the river, and I see some of the women look with the interested face at the central dwelling. A group comes out from there and activity around the dwelling has turned to look my way. There is much facial movement, and anger is on the face of blue circle and the one they all look to. Now blue circle is showing anger at provider and tall man who signals to provider. Then provider comes and takes me by the hand. She is unusually gentle and her face, for an instant, has the sad look. Then I am led briskly to the gathering.

Tall man claps his hands near my head as all watch me. Then I see blue circle moving her mouth and I follow her fingers to the sky where I see a number of birds. I understand and hold up seven fingers. She reaches down and picks up three stones. I hold up three fingers, then pick up a stick and draw the magic symbol in the ground. I can see a few mouths moving. Blue circle is making most of the mouth changes. I can see she is pleased with me, so I pick up the stick again and quickly draw four figures and the symbol for four. When I look up all has changed. No mouths are moving, but the one who wears the reindeer as clothing looks intently at my simple drawing. Then he begins to make the same mouth over and over again.

Blue circle takes my hand and leads me to our dwelling. All others disperse. All have the face of the frightened except blue circle who only looks worried. Reindeer antler returns to my drawings where he continues the mouth movements and makes smoke while throwing dirt in my direction.

After a time he removes my drawings. I think the clouds are dark and the rain soon to fall would have done the same.

The sun has passed over the high place when reindeer and he who is looked to come for me. The shaman takes me by the skin on my shoulder and leads me up the river towards the great ice. My last look at my people is of blue circle with the water on her face, kneeling in front of he who is looked to.

We travel fast and I stumble a lot but am lifted to my feet. Reindeer never looks at me or lets me go. My chest is tight and I struggle to breathe. I know I have the fear face; the ugly one. Nothing is clear, only fear. All around me seems to become a blur. My eyes are wet. We cross over several streams using stones but he does not care if I get wet. Finally we stop.

There are cliffs on each side and caves opening over the river. My eyes have gone dry. The breathing is still hard but something inside seems to have accepted that my life is in great danger. There seems to be no one to come to my aid and, whatever I have done, it certainly was not in my favour. I stand still and stare at him. He does the repeat mouth again and covers me in ash which sticks to my skin. I realize I have the water on my skin. Then he is gone.

97

I look to follow but the shaman has gone up and over rocks I cannot climb and has now vanished. The sun is low and the cold is moving in. Even without the night I will die. I cannot light fire or see smoke from fire anywhere. Then my instincts take over and the ancient call of the cave comes to me. I must find a way to cross to the caves.

With the ice melted I cannot enter the near freezing water, so shivering with cold I move up the river. I glimpse the movement of beast in the distance and another vague fear enters my tiny world. I want to relieve the water from the crack between my legs but am afraid even to uncover to do that, and I cannot get my furs wet or they will freeze on me. Now I can see openings in the face of the rock my side of the river. It does little to comfort me. I am too cold and tired to run.

Suddenly I see movement and turn to see a wolf loping towards me. Panic takes over and I run into the water and make it to a rock which I climb up onto. Instantly severe pain, then numbness follows. The creature stops on the bank and, to my horror, I see it can easily reach me by other rocks up the river. It sits and its head goes back and a call erupts that can only be a signal for the pack to feed. My legs will not move. I will die anyway. The world begins to fade and with it the horror my little body feels.

Then I feel the grip of the wolf's mouth and feel myself lifted off the rock. Now it is as if I am looking on from above but can still feel my body. Then another sensation I have never had before. The side of my face registers a new thing and I look down the river to see where it is coming from. There is my beloved blue circle running towards the wolf that is travelling quickly to meet her, with me in its mouth partly dragging as I am becoming too heavy for the beast. I am in her arms and she is running for the opening in the rock face. I see and register what her mouth movements are saying without understanding. I feel like I am half in my body and half out.

They have me in the cave. She glances at my legs, now blue. She hugs the wolf for a fraction of time, then raises a sharp stone over its beautiful head and strikes it dead. Without hesitation the lower stomach of the beast is split open and my legs are thrust into the hot interior of the wolf. Her furs and a pack she carries are wrapped around me. Then she scrambles for a fallen bush at the mouth of the rock opening. A fire is quick to catch. Slowly I feel an attachment returning to my body. I register the warmth of beast and fur. I hear. I hear my voice cry out in pain.

Then in a flash I am back in my body. My silent body and the pain of my legs are with me, but so too are the loving arms of blue circle. I struggle to open my eyes. The battle is lost and I sink back; this time not towards death but into unconscious exhaustion. My eyes open for a short time to find I am being carried, still wrapped deep in furs against her body. I touch her and feel the reassuring stroke of her hand. Then darkness returns. This happens several more times.

On awakening I find a fire burning and some type of padding for a sleeping place under my tiny frame. There is a roof and a feeling of safety, so I sleep again with only small feeling of pain in my lower limbs. When I wake again blue circle is soon there to give me broth. Also the gentle smiling faces of other women are present. All around me I see and feel the gentle mouth and soft-eyed face. The food is good and I sleep again. From time to time I wake to feel hands massaging my body, mainly my legs. I eat. I do not know how much time passes before I finally stay awake and watch as faces come and go.

The mind still feels heavy with tiredness and the pictures of reindeer and the cold river, and the gentle wolf that terrified me so much then had its life taken for the rescue of my life. There is a mixture of horror, wonder, and perhaps an inability to accept the events. My body still grows damp and

Finding Purpose

cold then shakes violently. The gentle women are always near to dry me, warm me and give liquid for a seemingly endless thirst.

In time they carry me out and slowly I start to stand then walk again. My body, that has always been small for my age, has started to grow fuller and stronger. I now receive all the food I want; a lot of fish and some flesh, often of game left by hunters. They seem to help supply the women's needs but only come to a certain place in this settlement.

98

Here I live with only women and three other children. One day I saw reindeer, tall man, the one they look to and several other men. I was sent inside, but looked out and saw blue circle and five other women make many arm movements. Finally the men left meat then went away. When the women came to my dwelling they ruffled my hair and had the happy face.

Time passes without event. Then one morning I am dressed before the sky becomes light and taken outside. Fires are burning on the hills. Blue circle puts my hand on her girdle and we follow other women with torches through the pre-morning darkness. Suddenly I am aware that there are people everywhere I look. We seem to have arrived at a high area and the sky is just starting to show light. I hold tight to blue circle's clothing and my eyes search all around. The torches have all been extinguished.

Gradually a circle of white robed figures begins to take shape. Then the sun breaks the horizon and I see each figure is standing in front of a standing stone, and in the middle of the circle is a large pillar of wood. As the sun rises, the shadow from the wooden pillar emerges and descends onto the figure of one of what I can now see are all women. Her cloak falls and she stands naked in the shade until the rays reach her form. She then moves as all the figures do around the circle, each figure stopping and disrobing, to be bathed by the sun as it emerges from behind the pillar until all are naked and once again facing the pillar, now bathed in sunlight. As the sun rises higher, the figures move the other way and, one by one, the robes go back on. I understand nothing of this, but can now see the men who dress in reindeer and other animal headdress are dancing and swaying to their repeated mouth movements.

When the sun is fully up the white figures leave for a wooden enclosure near our dwellings, and I see that on the distant plain are many cooking fires now starting up and many temporary dwellings. I am returned to my sleeping place and do not leave until the sun rises the following day. My silent world is full of mysteries.

My world is my eyes, my touch, and now my great joy my taste, so that I seem to spend much more time than other people sitting and watching, rather than taking part in events that surround me. Since I have arrived in this place of women my life is full of the smiling happy face. Even my own face, I now know, is often open with the look of happiness and sometimes that of wonder or inquiry. These women are patient and I have not been struck once. Sometimes I am turned around and sent with a slight tap on my rear to my dwelling. This is their way of telling me right from wrong.

I observe the days grow shorter since the morning of the sunrise ceremony. From the top of the hill I can now easily walk to, I can see the great ice wall and feel the coming freezing winds as the days grow shorter. The skies are often full of dark clouds. I help with the gathering of wood, and watch with fascination as blue circle's arrow sometimes finds a bird. As the days continue to shrink and snow falls onto the now frozen surface of the river, my small thoughts wonder how we will survive the coming cold.

Then one morning furs are rolled up, and hunters approach and are given loads to carry. Before the sun is over the high place we are moving in the direction the river flows. We soon come to the junction of another waterway and follow the larger one. As the day grows shorter the cliffs rise and the openings of many caves appear.

There are huge piles of wood heaped at the mouth of the caves facing a ledge looking out over the river. The men deposit their burdens and speak with one of the more lined of the women. They show her what appears to be a peculiar dwelling made of blocks of ice and opening from the side by removing blocks of ice. It is now so cold that the ice will not melt in the shorter daylight hours.

The men depart and we go into one of the caves to find hides over frames built to close off the wind at the cave entrance and fires already burning. It is dry in the cave, like a fire has been burning for some time.

99

Everywhere there is a forest of dead trees, now partly submerged in snow and ice but still clearer on the upper slopes. The winter sets in and it is many moons before the fires slow down. The cold is intense but the cave stays lit for the whole winter as the dry wood is everywhere. The women hardly go outside; only to remove waste and bring food that is stored in the ice dwelling.

I have not been out of the cave for many moons. It is strange, but in a way I feel more like the women because for long periods of time the mouth movements are hardly at all. Activity is little, apart from cooking and stoking the fires. Some work is done on the shaping of stones, hides for clothing, and wood and antler for other objects.

Blue circle returns to teaching me by drawing on the cave floor, but it rapidly becomes of interest and other children and adults are a part of each lesson. The way of counting now goes up to ten times the number of fingers on my hands. I have also been taught symbols for creatures, dwellings, rivers, fire, and many other objects that are common in our lives. I am learning how to make signs with my hands, in some cases to ask for things or about things. My world is opening up.

Other diagrams are drawn on the earth, and some are brought out that are already on a prepared surface. These I cannot understand but I am surprised to see people represented in some of the drawings. There are mouth movements with some of these diagrams and the mood is solemn. The other children seem to understand. I have a dim memory of my out of body experience and the ways of the mouth movements for communication. So I partly understand why my life is different and harder. I still do not understand why I was taken to perish in the cold. I shake when I think about this and feel a sadness and loss. I do not understand when I think of the wolf that found me and then died to give me back life in this body.

I have a thought that, although my world with the restriction of communication makes it hard for me to know much, it also has made me more observant. A vast number of images stay in my head, to be played over in my mind whenever I need them. The others seem surprised when I draw simple things on the ground that perhaps were not remembered by people. I also have symbols for smiles and other faces.

At times blue circle and the other children are the only ones with me. The other women, who number fourteen, put on their white robes and, I presume, go to a near cave as they would freeze if they went out in the light cloths. At these times it seems a long time when they are gone. They have the still face when they return and always look with the expression that is without fear and happy in the still way.

At long last the summer arrives and people are sighted in the valley. Then we move back to the outside dwellings and some hunting occurs. I learn that the hunting is mainly done by the men of the southern clans and delivered north. I think that there are few people this close to the ice mountains and few creatures. I know it is something to do with the fact that our group is only women. I am aware that their role is preserving memories and ceremonies like those I have come to know as the longest day and the shortest day.

100

Life settles into a routine and I grow. One of the children, the only boy, leaves one day with the men and, as the moon passes, I know he will not return. I become upset, and when they finally understand I fear they took him to stand alone for the cold night and death, they are able to reassure me he went to grow to be a hunter.

One day I realize that blue circle has slowed down. Six winters have passed. Her face is deeply lined and her teeth long gone. Her hair, long white, has become thin. Even the blue mark seems to be fading into the skin.

Now it is me who looks after her and makes the broth and loves her, with a growing feeling that she will leave me for a place where I cannot follow. Last winter the woman who we all looked to most did not rise one morning and her body, after ceremony, was taken away. Blue circle was able to show me that she had woken in another world and that she also would go there, and that in turn I also would wake to that world.

One day, in the seventh season with the women tribe, it happens. The beloved eyes of my blue circle close on an evening for the last time and, regardless of me putting her close to the fire in many furs, her body grows cold. I try and wake her for broth but her stiffening form has no movement.

There is a feeling in my head and chest that is so painful I can hardly breathe. No one comes near us, but in time I become aware that they are trying to feed me. Then an expression I feel of the grief face comes to me, bending me in half. My head lies against blue circle's cold feet, and the pain starts to drain from me as I feel the water wet the sides of my face.

A diagram is made for me of the other world and they take her body away from me. As they lift her an ancient fur slips from her clothing and I pick it up. It is what is left of an old wolf hide, and I know it is a symbol of binding comfort and connection for both of us.

As the days go by the sadness dulls, and eventually I take food again and move with the women to the cave of winter.

At the end of the eighth winter we do not return north but go south to the place I recognize as the dwellings of my childhood. These are now no longer occupied and become the dwellings of those who serve. Regardless of the dead forests, the easy to get wood is now far off. Hunters still come from the south and bring wood as well as meat. We still catch many fish in the summer river which flows for a little over one moon.

The ceremony of the long day is conducted and becomes the first one at the new location, with old tree trunks formed in a circle. I now realize that the women also have a ceremony of equal importance at the first light of the shortest day.

At the end of my ninth winter in the caves we return to find the hunters have raised a circle of stones as was at the northern place.

Although my body is small in stature I have now formed the shape of a woman and blood flows from the woman's part of my body. The women do not include me in the ceremonies even though I seem to be old enough, and at times in the winter I am left on my own.

A strange event happens in the tenth winter. Although we are confined to the cave for about seven moons, at the end of the cold time the stomach of one of the two who were children when I arrived begins to swell and her blood stops flowing. I can tell by the faces of great awe that the women believe an event of tremendous importance has happened and another is to take place, I presume with the birth of the baby.

Diagrams are brought out one day and shown to me and I recognize them from old. For the first time they are able to make me understand that people are represented as coming from the sky, and that they believe that this child to be born has come from the sky, as with the old drawings. I am much puzzled by this.

The women perform many rituals and the young woman is given great care. Even I can tell that there is an entirely different air of excitement as we leave for our summer dwellings.

The child is born on the second day of the fifth moon after the shortest day ceremonies. As the sun rises on the third day, mother and child are bathed in the new rays as they emerge from the shadow in the circle of stones.

More people have arrived than I have seen before in my life. There are a vast number of the excited, still face. A great event has obviously occurred and the excitement is catching.

101

The seasons pass and I am happy with these women. I learn to prepare the material to do the diagrams. I learn what is taboo amongst these people of greater knowledge. The women grow older and no newcomers arrive. I know that, as the old forests disappear, not only wood is growing scarce but insects, and all the creatures that depend on them have departed.

The people who I was born into have slowly integrated into tribes in a land that was once forbidden to us. Those who serve the spirit of the Living Earth, the Earth Mother priestesses, are possibly the only ones who remain in the old land which is now in the grip of a great ice invasion. These people only survive with the help of warriors from many tribes.

Two more have passed over to the other world leaving thirteen women and one boy, who is now seven winters. He is a quiet, attractive child, much loved by all around him. He is very attentive to me and has learnt many signs to reach into my world. He has a way of bringing out the laughing face on me, which in turn makes him laugh. However with and without the women's help, already at seven seasons he has studied many scrolls of very old diagrams. He spends a lot of time looking at them and I have even seen him make changes which, when the women noted the changes, they were much impressed. He is good with the sick, and seems to instinctively understand the use of many plants which now have to be brought in by the tribes. Still, the woman with the disease that eats her body fades and dies. She seemed happy that he was present at her departure. Her eyes at the end of this life were alive with joy and she had a kind of rapture face.

The warriors and many others now come in increasing numbers. On the days of the two major ceremonies there are far more than I can count.

At the last ceremony, the boy created a disturbance by entering the circle as the sun appeared and, before the women could act, it was his shadow that went from one woman to the other as the sun rose.

For days to follow the tribes remained, and many sat in his presence and watched as he communicated with his mouth movements. As I watched I felt devastated that I seemed to be the only one who could not understand him. When I was feeling at the lowest point, he turned in the crowd and his eyes found mine. Then for the time that he spoke while he looked at me, which seemed like a time separate to my body, I understood all the mouth movements which came with a knowledge that I knew was far beyond the wisdom of his youth and our Knowledge. In that time I learnt of creation, continuity, pain and physical joy. I learnt of the place of the Spirit and its connection to the conscious awareness of the living world. He transformed my life, as I presume he at such an age was already achieving transformation amongst the tribes.

When the boy was at ten seasons and the summer festival was over, he took the Earth mothers away from their sacred grounds with all their treasures, and travelled with us for two moons to a land where, once again, the forests were growing alive and tall and where creatures abounded.

Wherever we went the tribes came and seemed to know in advance that he was the one to be looked to. At all times he treats his mother with love, and her as one with the other women. A place is prepared for the Mother's ceremonies and us. We have dwellings and caves that are apart from the tribes. The treasures are safely stored.

He stays with us for the winter which is much milder although cold. Then in the coming warmth he calls the eleven of us that remain together and I can see that they are saddened. Then he turns to me, and again I understand his mouth and know that he is to take The Knowledge and the seed of his body to many tribes.

From the blue dye that is common for the markings of the tribe, he draws a blue circle on my forehead and I know his words when he says: "This woman wears the symbol of the living world and she is to be a part of the celebrations of life on Earth." Then he smiles and departs.

Our lives return to a simple but easier pattern in this better climate. The boy returns only once for the long day ceremony in what would be his fifteenth season. That is the last time I see him but a new ceremony takes place on as close as we can get to the day of his birth.

I am shown how to make many scrolls in connection with his life, and eventually learn that the mothers have celebrated the memories of past arrivals such as his in times long gone, and try to be open for these events to occur in times to come.

New young women have joined us from the tribes and, as we grow old, the Earth mothers' Knowledge and old ways and memories of those they call the Other Ones are kept.

Then one day after a change of the seasons, when it seems I have only lived in my silence and a gathering fog, my mind seems to become that of a clear and healthy young life, and I look upon the face of an old woman who reminds me, for a blink, of my beloved blue circle. Then I can see the spirit has departed her body, and I feel the call and the promise of all that is to come, as the being that is me returns once again to its wondrous universe.

Dawn of the Sun

We join hands and pray that the Sun of the great Spirit will rise again, and bring Mother Earth and her daughter, Moon, the cycle of warmth.

We join hands and pray the Sun will bring life to the Earth Mother, so trees will grow leaves and flowers will bring seeds and the bulbs of the earth.

We join hands and pray that the animals and birds will rejoice, as the Sun warms our land and brings forth the young of the Mother goddess.

We join hands and pray the Sun will give life to the Giver's insects, so fish will live in the rivers that flow again.

As the orange ball of living warmth reaches its lowest level on the horizon, it once again enters the realm of the spirits who shine forth in the night sky.

We return to the fires of our hearths and feel secure that, once again, our circle of stones has told us the time to give praise to the Sun of the Father, that nurtures the Earth Mother goddess and her daughter, the Moon.

The life of discovery

102

Malcolm: I am not born again on Earth for 375 years, then there are two ordinary lives. Then about 8,000 years later I am born again in what will be Portugal. I then live and die through seven uneventful lives. Two die in infantile deaths, one dies as a child of nine seasons and one is killed by an auroch in the fourteenth year. The other three grow and have children and die natural deaths. Apart from the normal ceremonies of the tribes, there are no spiritual events of consequence. Then I am to open my eyes around 18,000 years before the time of writing, as a man at the start of his sixteenth warm season.

A flock of gulls wheels close overhead bringing my face up to view the clouds. It is a reflex action, as I am behind the headland only two hundred steps from the beach. The net fans out again and I watch as it arcs its way to the bottom. Then once again I bring a catch of bream to the surface, this time one fish worth keeping and two for the coming season. The bottom of the boat is almost one hand deep with the evidence of a good morning's work. The weather is moving in so I tell my young brother, Dimon, to push the nose of the boat around and we will head for shore. Dimon has made a big difference, and his constant moving of the boat is largely responsible for the better than usual catch. He is eleven seasons now and keen to make his own boat.

Mine, which is almost four steps long and one step wide without rigger for stability, took me two winters to carve from the trunk of an elm tree. It is not the largest of the solid vessels in the village but makes me valuable as a food provider in the eyes of my people. Still, I sometimes go with the men and young women in the tribal vessels, which are half as long again and three times as wide. These vessels are made of a wooden frame with the hides of a large animal stretched over them, then made watertight with resins mixed with wax and lard.

As we make shore a woman's voice calls out "Hon". She is the mother of my son and the keeper of my hearth. She appears with her younger sister and mother to help string the catch for drying and preserving for the winter. Sometimes we trade for the goods of the travellers who trade freely up and down the coast. New stone and flint edges come in from greater distances than in my father's day, including reindeer horn of all shapes and sizes.

Mara gives a squeal of delight and leaps onto my body, squeezing me hard to her groin with her legs. I can feel her firm full breasts through her lighter summer furs. Her young beauty gives me pleasure and it pleases me to see the eyes of hunters follow her, as long as she is in my dwelling when the sun goes to sleep.

The women start a happy song in praise of the fish of the sea, so Dimon and I join in. Mara's eyes tell me I will be well rewarded for the catch. I look at Dimon and see his eyes on her, and notice the flirtatious look she throws his way. He had better seek his reward elsewhere or he will go down with the net as bait for the fish. The mother notices the sex play and quietly goes up behind Dimon, reaching for his groin while telling him he will gain special appreciation for being such a fisherman amongst men. The women roar with laughter and the young sister gives him a female hug. He goes red and then sees the grin on my face and we all roar with laughter.

103

Life is good as the time of the long day and the celebration of the gift of the traveller to the Earth Mother comes near. This season of the longer days has seen many blue skies and less wind, so there is much food in the tribes and little argument or invasion of the hunting grounds amongst the clans.

All afternoon we gut and string the fish over the smoke fire with the stone chimneys. The singing goes on. Dimon talks to me of his need to find a tree for his boat. I know he is young to have his own boat but he is a good fisherman. In two seasons he will be recognized as a full hunter, and able to take a woman to his hearth if he can demonstrate trade to her father and mother.

I tell him, as tomorrow we can have time free from the fishing, we will travel up the waterways and find the tree that loses its leaves and does not rot in the water. I hope we can find it within our own hunting grounds as it will be easier to inform our own people of our need than have to trade with another tribe. Any tree would be suitable, but one made by the great Spirit to carry fishermen to feed the tribe is one that must be respected, revered and spoken of before it is fallen. Then it will be ours until such time as we can shape it for transport by the waterways to the village. Then the shamans will call for protection for those who place their trust in the tree: the boat builder and seafarer.

The journey is uneventful. There are no predators or big game; some deer but too far for a good shot. Most of the best trees in a direct line from the village have long gone and are on the water. If we want a good one it will have to come from a slope, probably at least two hundred steps or more from the water. The other alternative would be in another clan territory far up the waterway. There, though, we would have to stay for longer periods of time, as the boat would need to be finished in order to transport it to our home territory. Shallow water would need winter snow to melt for transport. Still, there are many good trees up river as few inland tribes build boats.

By mid afternoon we find a beautiful tree but will seek at least one more, as sometimes they have rot in them or a hollow in the wrong place. It is a good grove of elm and we find several that are suitable, although four hundred steps from the water. The slope is steep. We mark three trees and now will return quickly as dark approaches. There will be moon tonight so our way will be visible but the beasts will look upon us as a meal.

As we approach, the fires show light and singing is heard. We know we have made good time and are well pleased with ourselves. Dimon walks like a hunter who has already built his boat and caught a great white shark for the village. It makes me smile, so I slap him on the back and say: "Go easy on the girls. A man such as you can cause damage to such gentle beauty." He laughs and struts even taller.

I go to my hearth and am pleased to find Mara, with my son being fed on her ample breast. I quietly watch and then eat that which has been prepared for me. I lie down to wait for her but the day has been long so sleep comes first. The night is long also and, as cold sets in, her body seeks warmth and rouses me from sleep. Mara then gives me that which I value above all else I experience in my life.

The next day we secure the rights to the trees. Then the days following see a return to fishing for me. By the time I return to the tree site, Dimon and his friends have felled the tree and are working on removing the top. A pang of envy strikes me as I realize his boat will be even bigger than mine. He also seems to be getting far more help. I remember the endless time I spent on my own making my boat. Still, he should not be this far back from the home site on his own. Even with boys of his own age to stand guard, it is dangerous. The big cats own this part of the forest, if they choose.

I spend the next two days there and by then we are nearly half way through the log. His helpers come and go, as their desire to follow the hunt is a part of the forest journey.

The new moon has turned and it is the run up to the festival of the longest day. We will arrive in the region of the event seven days or so before the long day. Then is the time to see distant relatives. It is also the time to learn of conditions of the season and hunting in many places, and those who have a particular interest such as flint maker or artist can learn from the coming together. There is also the pleasure of new faces, especially for the young who feast on the opportunity to develop their skills with the other sex. At my hearth Mara has taken up with the medicine woman, and not only do they learn from other medicine women, but get the supply of herbs from far off places that are necessary for the survival of individuals within the tribe.

By the end of the half moon we are ready to leave. Those who are to stay and look after the very old and the sick are selected. It is an honour as they hold the security of possessions in their trust. They walk tall in our eyes and their strength shows out but I can see in their eyes the honour is one they can do without.

104

Three days pass before we reach the gathering ground, and by then other tribes have joined us and our number has grown from about one hundred and forty to between two and three hundred people. There is already much excitement, and both Mara and I have cast more than one glance at each other to see if some new or old acquaintance has captured the attention of either one of us. I am uncomfortable to note that her full body not only attracts attention but she enjoys it and smiles over generously, even as she squeezes my arm to offer some comfort. I hope she is quick to find the company of medicine women. I may ask one of them for a potion to keep her mind on the wonders that are good for other people's bodies. Not hers.

We arrive and set up the timber frames that are soon covered in hides of all shapes and sizes. These mobile dwellings already cover the plain spreading out from the river. I see the huge circular house of mystery that is the domain of the Earth Mother people, who are the keepers of The Knowledge that has come to us from the travellers and other ancient word.

I do not know much of this as I am a fisherman and the ocean is my interest in life, apart from trying to keep Mara out of the hearths of eager warriors from near and far. Still, we as a people are not in general overly possessive of our hearth partners. It is just jealousy on my behalf, and a little too strong. I do not doubt her love for me and if ever one of us wanders, as will probably happen in the coming days, our hearth commitment and the care of the newborn will continue as before. We also have the added knowledge that we are strong enough to resist anything that will make our lives tedious or too restricted. On the whole we are a generous people, and give great reverence to the gift of fertility and pleasure that has come with the guidance of the great Spirit and The Knowledge of the Earth mothers from the travellers.

The day is not gone but the setting up of stones for fire and the boiling of water takes time; then the unpacking of goods I hope to trade takes the rest. The meal is dried meats and grain made into flat cakes. Tomorrow all will fish, hunt or gather. Then the social life begins; the young in pursuit of anything that smiles twice at them and the not so young the same with some discretion. The old will tell tales of past glory.

It is good to come to the gathering, even if I am not one of those who think deeply of spiritual matters but all are aware of such things. We form a fire with several tribes who are from our coastal region and some quiet singing takes place, not too loud as there are many neighbours. We know a lot of people from within these tribes and some are kinfolk.

There is light rain as the sun sinks, and I glance up to see the tall wooden totem poles that will play a part in the ceremonies outlined against the red glow of the evening night sky. Many of the tribal people have come to believe that the return of the long days and the gentle warmth is connected now to the ceremonies of the long day and the short day. We rarely travel here for the short day. The winters here are too bleak for tribes to gather, but young women spend some time in the presence of the priestesses before they form their own hearth. It is these that represent each tribe at the winter ceremony. Some stay to become part of a long-term commitment to the sacred ways that have become knowledge to a few through the aeons of the seasons. It is at the winter celebrations that the fires are seen in all directions on high hilltops.

I take my woman and child and return to the sleeping furs. Tonight I take special care to satisfy my beautiful partner who seems well pleased but, as I drift off to sleep completely satisfied and exhausted, I get the feeling she is capable of infinitely more love play than I am. My head is not sure if this is a blessing from the Mother or just something to cause me endless confusion.

The hunting was good, with the men forming a circle around a small herd of horses which were then held up against the water. With so much game to choose from, runners were sent to fetch women and children to help prepare, wrap and carry food to last for several days at least, for all of the tribes. This takes the next day.

The heads of various tribes claim and distribute the hides. Still, I suspect many will be used to gain comfort for the Earth Mother priestesses. Mara is happy and busy. This night all retire after some singing. We sleep well.

I rise early and seek out Dimon and we move up water to a beautiful sunrise with mist rising through the early light. There is great beauty in this region. The forest gives way to open grasslands with slopes covered with coloured gorse, and higher up the conifers and other evergreens dominate.

We do not seek food immediately but it is good to get away from the people and explore new lands, especially inland from the sea closer to the high country. Some deer move off into the mist. We do not shoot. It is wrong to waste game, although the hides with the fur turned out would be good for summer clothes. As the sun clears the mist we see birds unlike our coastal creatures, and attempt to fell two with beautiful green plumage but are unsuccessful.

Dimon talks of his prowess with young girls. I think he exaggerates but am pleased to hear him happy. In time we come across an area of stone good for tool making and I break off several pieces to work and we return to camp.

It is no special event, still when we arrive there is great activity. At nearly every tribal area are wares from directions near and far; some things in shell, and antler from creatures I have never seen in the wild.

105

As the days pass Mara grows lovelier, and more than once is absent for extended periods of time. My own life becomes more rewarding and I also feel happy to see the glow of pleasure that surrounds Mara's being.

Trade is good, and the produce from the sea is replaced with cloth and hide from mountain and plain. The flint produced good edge and point. Soon most of that also passed to new owners. Then I feel able to leave an offering at the place near the enclosure of the priestesses. The long day ceremony is tomorrow. The people grow quiet and the singing does not take place this night.

All people rise early without the lighting of fires and move with the crowd towards the circle on the hill. A huge half circle forms without guidance from hillcrest to hillcrest, keeping respectful distance from the ceremonial centre. An occasional whisper can be heard; a mother to child but no more. Even with all these people, the sound of the gentle breeze can be heard in the leaves of the forest behind us.

As the light of pre-dawn stretches across the horizon, the sound of many female voices can be heard chanting what to me has no meaning. They slowly become visible in white robes. The surface of the sun appears on the horizon, sending a shaft of light between the two tallest of the monuments, to expose the naked body of who, I presume, is the head priestess.

As the sun's rays completely envelope her and the light spreads over the other priestesses, the robes from centre out slowly fall to the ground until all are bathed in sunlight as an offering to the messengers of the travellers. The story goes that they have brought ancient knowledge and human development through time.

Once the sun is in full circle the women re-robe and, in triple file, move down the hill.

As they come the people form an avenue, and I see that the faces of the women are painted with red lips and white powder. The eyes are outlined in red and flowers adorn their hair. They move to a central place where fires are now lit to supply the morning's needs. On this day the Earth mothers will dine and move with their people, and briefly reunite with their family and friends. Much of this is beyond me but I feel it is good and, perhaps if the great Spirit is pleased with the tribes, the sun will shine with greater strength as the legend says it once did. This is what the tribe is, in its own way, saying a silent prayer for.

The day soon passes and singing goes on into the night. I see Mara move off to join several female friends. I take one more drink of the strong liquor that is drunk by the warriors on this night. I feel the effect and fire burns quietly in my body. Although my thoughts are not clear, I see a woman move to the opening of my tent so I follow, as the warmth of the drink has given me desire to be with a woman.

When I enter the tent her back is to me, and I see her putting stones into the skins for hot water. I hear the cry of the child and she moves to soothe the boy. So I disrobe and wait, with my member full and my body on fire from the strong liquor. I notice she has a cloth over her head as she turns to me and kneels without looking up. I feel the warmth of her mouth cover me and reach for her hair. She looks up with a stranger's face and says: "It is the wish of Mara, and I who go by the name of Rebeca, to lie with the other's partner on this night of the mothers." Each has desired the other's man. She looks lovely and I am in need of her and, with the joy she brings, all thoughts of my hearth mate's doings are put into the back of my mind. It is a long time before I am able to lie back and sink into sleep.

When I awake Mara is beside me, with the boy gently suckling at her beautiful breast. All is well. The Earth Mother has been good to all her people, perhaps even to Dimon, although I still have my doubts that his member is as capable of manly growth as his mouth is.

With a head slightly sore from strong drink I break camp, and by sun half way to the top we are, tribe and all, on the way home. Dimon seems to have grown, so perhaps who knows. He smiles a lot. I do not think a man can look that pleased without the help of a woman. I think I am pleased to see my brother grow strong for, next to Mara, he is closest to me of all my clan.

We seem to make better time on the way home and it is good when the ocean finally comes into view. My home is where I can hear the waves breaking on the rocks.

106

I return to fishing as do many of the tribe. When the sea is up we go in the larger hide boats but the fishing is not so good. However it is easier to reach areas where the birds live who show us the swarms of large ocean fish. These dry better and hold off longer the hunger that can come in the winter.

Dimon and his friends return to the boat, with help from me on some days when the sea is rough. By the winter it is taking shape but still heavy to move. There is talk on how to get it to the coast; either wait until the middle of the winter then move it on sledge over snow and ice or, if good rains arrive early, bring it down the high water, or else it will have to wait until the winter thaw makes the water high and strong.

The rains do not come before the cold sets in, and we are confined to the inside of dwellings once more. We often gather with larger families both day and night to keep body warmth in enclosure, and save the wood for the large fires that are needed for warmth. Days and nights are long and we are used to them growing tedious.

It is two moons into the winter when we decide to go for the developing boat. Dimon, four of our friends and I follow the now solidly frozen waterway to the location. We spend as little time as is needed to force the log from snow and ice. We then use ropes to bind the two wooden skids to the front end then attach the low ropes, four in all. We attempt to move it towards the river, but sense tells us that it will be necessary to wait for the strength of many, in order to not only move it but to control downward movements both to and down the river.

Three days later forty-one men move up the river. All are cold but glad also to find excuse to escape the now smelly interiors of the clans. We divide into four groups and, once the sledge is moving, two groups operate as brakes and two to steer and keep it moving. Also by operating this way we are able to stay out of the log's path on a very slippery surface. Once out of the forest and onto the waterway, we are able to move almost without effort and are back at home base without event.

Dimon has been honoured before his time. Still, the tribe treats all boats as value and survival, so it is really an event that will take place for vessel not person, regardless of whether the person is young or old.

The winter slowly passes and Mara's stomach swells. It is good timing, for the child will come after the first sign of leaves in the forest.

As the days slowly lengthen we increase our hunting and gather more food from the rock pools along the coast. Some tubular plants appear through the snow. With fresh food and outside living increasing, life and our happiness begins to improve.

The boys go back to work on the boat and I hear plans for vessels for the other boys. They will have the right to fish in Dimon's boat for the work they have put in. That in turn will be good for the fishing. The snow melts and eventually the ice melts and I return to my summer ways.

My Mara left me for the company of women early in the leaf, then to return with a tiny girl on her breast. I feel that my hearth has good fortune. It is good to have our bodies clean, our dwellings clean, and our hearth to ourselves again. We can still gather for the singing and flute playing at the central fire whenever we want. Our tribe feels good. There are new children to replace the three old people and one other who died during the cold time. We honoured their memories, and feel comfort to know that they have gone to another place.

The boat is finished and is noticeably larger than mine. The whole tribe was pleased with it as we all gave it the blessing of the tree, and many people made it possible for it to exist. The boys have been trying it in the waterways of the land. It will also be blessed with the help of shaman, but to Dimon's obvious displeasure this has to wait until we return from the gatherings.

Eventually we are home again but with much sadness, for our baby girl stopped feeding during the time of the ceremonies and Mara's sadness, as the child became weaker, removed her interest in other people. The child died on the way home, and the shaman and the tribe stopped to give time for the spirit to depart, with our love, for its world.

My woman is content to be with me but seems to have lost interest in the needs of my body. For the time her laughter has gone. Her friend the medicine woman, who she spends an increasing amount of time with, tells me that time will fade her memories and her laughter will return.

We gather to bless the boat and cover it with flowers as it is launched to the sea, and then escorted out amongst the large and small vessels of the tribe. We form a circle as Dimon casts his first net, and a great cheer goes up when he holds up the first fish. Then all returns to normal. Women and children go back to shore. Men go hunting or to sea.

We hold close to Dimon for a few days until we see that he and his companions are as good as can be expected with the boat. Then we concentrate on our own endeavours.

107

My mind is full of my Mara and her lack of interest in me. Still, she continues to lavish attention on the boy who walks now and grows strong. He has had his naming ceremony and gives me pride. With Mara it is as if she connects me with the death of her baby daughter. I am becoming impatient as I think by now she should be getting over it.

As winter comes on I am hard at work getting wood and hunting for land animals for more winter furs. Dimon seems to spend less time with me now. I presume he finds company with his own age group. The approaching winter often keeps us off the sea and many of the boats are back amongst the trees.

Then one day my hunt takes me into the lovely valley, not far from the village, where young lovers sometimes come. I hear the sound of a couple's passion as I round some rocks, and quickly turn to walk away to give them privacy. Then, to my surprise, the sound that only I could recognize so well of my woman's coming to orgasm crashes into my mind. I turn and stride back to see Dimon thrusting his own climax deep into the body I love, and see the look of passionate joy on the face of my Mara as she combines with him.

Anger and pain combine and my brain explodes. I grasp him by the hair and wrench him off her. I see his seed, still exploding from his body, burst onto her naked stomach and breast. I hear her scream as I bring my fist into his face again and again. I see him collapse, and turn my back and walk away.

I pass through the village and the people's strange looks. I take my boat and launch it through the waves that are too large to be safe. I paddle out to sea. My mind is numb.

108

Unable to take note that the sea is up, I pass the headland and turn the boat in the direction the wind blows and the waves travel. The boat is still going out. I am unable to register fear, danger, or even an awareness of the strength of the ocean. I just had to escape the anger and what I recognize as a confused and dawning shame. I know I am hurt.

Slowly, after too long a period, it dawns on me that the sun will sleep before too long and I must return to land. As I attempt to turn the boat, the size and strength of the wind and waves registers. With shock I realize it is impossible to put the nose of the boat into the waves as they would swamp me if I tried. I could not make progress towards the land and would quickly tire if the attempt was made. Without going anywhere, my mind tells me I am going to die. A part of me seems to feel that maybe this is the best outcome.

Something stronger in my character will not give in. The ocean is taking me very fast, and a quick look from the top of a wave shows me that the land is already out of sight. From this far out in calmer seas than this, no fisherman to my knowledge has ever returned to his people. My mind takes stock of what I have. There are fishing lines; the net wrapped in hides in the front of the boat; a spare paddle, and the baler which remains attached to the hull. Only the Spirit knows what it will be like in the dark and I thank it that, at least, it is full moon. At the moment there is too much cloud cover.

The sky grows darker and I risk moving forward and get the hides to wrap myself in, for the cold of the night will kill me if the ocean does not. My knife splits a hole for my head, and part of the net makes the hide tight for another layer of protection. In between keeping the boat straight, for I am not paddling, I bail out what seawater is in the bottom. It will help to keep it dry. Travelling with the waves, so far I am staying on top of the water and dry. Porpoises break the surface and travel beside me for a short time. I am greatly afraid now and feel the tremor of my body as fear sets in.

The waves are different out here to what I have known. They are now much further apart, ten or fifteen times as far apart as near the land but much higher. I can only keep the boat straight with them and see where it takes me. I pray to the Spirit the wind will drop then turn, so the waves will take me back towards land. I have no idea how the current will affect things.

Food and water cross my mind, but as dark sets in I close my mind to all else but staying alive until the new day dawns. As the night progresses tiredness becomes another enemy, and I keep my limbs moving to stop the stiffness of cold setting in. It becomes necessary to paddle, even though I do not want to, in order to keep the warmth of the body.

Thoughts of Mara and Dimon drift in and out of my mind. Now the anger seems to have receded, and in part been replaced by a regret that it is almost certain I will never have the chance to try and repair the damage to my life and place in the tribe.

There is no way of tracking time, except an occasional glimpse at the moon shows me its changing position. Its place behind the clouds gives a soft and deceptive silver to the surface of the water. A quick look down tells me it is as black as a tomb below the surface. I try not to look down again but keep my eyes on the changing ocean.

Eventually the light of dawn arrives and night changes to an emerging day. The waves with this growing light look even larger than I thought they were in the dark. Still, their crests are flattish with no break, and I realize that the wind must have dropped through the night. I have stayed dry except for an occasional splash from a careless paddle stroke.

As the morning progresses hunger causes me to put a fishing line out. The clouds darken and a rain squall approaches. I grab another hide and keep most of the rain off, as there is an increase in the wind then heavy rain, then complete lack of wind when the rain passes. I drink deeply from the water in the bottom of the boat and leave some for later, plus fill the baler to hopefully drink later. Several small fish take the line and I eat one raw, putting the others under the net.

The wind stays away and the waves flatten out but there is a large swell. The boat sits flat so I stop paddling and rest. Then eventually the day begins to darken again. There is a fish on the line so I pull it in, and eat and drink before the dark arrives. There is no sense in going anywhere but with the sea, and asking the Earth Mother and great Spirit to watch over me in life and probably death. I pull the fish line in so I can concentrate only on staying dry, warmish, and blink by blink alive.

Eventually another day dawns and, as the light creeps over the ocean, I lose my battle with tiredness and sleep takes me again. The wind stays on my side, and I survive to wake again to my now strangely numb awareness of my predicament.

No land birds are seen today and there is only an occasional ocean bird like the great albatross that drops down, seemingly without fear, to try and take my small reserve of fish. The paddle shows him safe distance and he flies with me for a short time, then lands in the water and rides the ocean with me for a while, effortlessly keeping up. Eventually he disappears. For some reason I feel loss when he goes, and only a glimmer of sense stops me from offering fish or bait to keep him with me. I reflect briefly and sadly on how easily he could return to my people and warm, if lonely, bed.

I attempt to drink the water in the bottom of the boat, but find it is too salty so I am forced to drink the water from the baler. Then I clean the bottom of the boat, getting it as dry as I can. As night approaches I bring in the largest fish I have caught so far. The knife swiftly cuts slabs of meat off the bony frame and I have food for several days.

I know not why I am fighting so hard to prolong, what must shortly be, certain death. The human spirit, to retain a hold on physical life, can be strong.

109

If the wind has remained in the same direction, I do not know. It picks up in the first part of the night, then drops away completely to find me asleep again, after losing the battle for wakefulness just before dawn. Another heavy shower of rain prolongs my life and I lose track of time, not knowing any more how many days since I left sanity behind.

Then my eyes open again to something so astonishing it takes me a period of time to register movement, or even think. On the ocean, two or three hundred steps away, sits a huge boat. I can only describe it as being as large as twenty elephants joined together. Above it is an even larger white cloud that travels with it for a time and then suddenly moves down a great tree in several pieces to disappear into flat lines. It sits where it is for a time, and I can see the faces of many people, at least five people high above the water. The surface of the boat looks neither wood nor hide and is pure white, with a surface that shines like a pond on a clear day. Then to my continued amazement it moves as if it has life of its own. There are no paddles or long oars like we use in the largest of our hide boats. The people, although some are moving, are mainly standing still along the side of the boat.

Then it comes to me, and I am surprised that I did not realize earlier. I have died during the night, and this strange vessel has come to take me to the other world I have heard spirit people talk of. A slow feeling of relief and sadness enters me. For an instant I am surprised that I still feel total fatigue, hunger and thirst, and also that my boat is still with me. As I know it, only the inner person leaves for the spirit world. I have never known them to take possessions or old bodies.

These thoughts flash in an instant through my mind as this strange craft, staying the distance it is, travels a circle around me. I see for the first time that the people have all covered the lower half of their faces. When the vessel reaches a point that would have been behind me, a smaller version of the large boat, not unlike mine but with a roof over most of it, is lowered to the water, and I see that there are a number of boats along each side of the huge boat.

The boat with the roof has no one that I can see aboard and starts to drift away from the vessel. Then I see a rope is attached and lengthening as the craft moves onwards in a circling direction. Eventually the rope snakes towards me in the water, and I fear it will capsize me so start to paddle away. The main craft turns and moves away from me and I see the small boat is being towed towards me. Then I realize it must be this vessel that is to take me to the world of the dead. Once again I am surprised, as the legends say the spirit can fly faster than the greatest of birds. I still feel fear but, with all that has happened to me, acceptance seems to be the only course available.

The small boat stops near my vessel so, with mixed emotions, I paddle to its side. I have to stand to see inside and realize that what I thought were empty holes are like clear water but hard. My hand touches a surface but cannot reach to the interior I see beyond. I move back towards the rear and feel no such surface, then climb off my own well-loved boat which I believe is the last connection with my life amongst the tribes.

There is movement as I reach the floor of the vessel and curved spears pass over my head. With slow movement, as if in a dream, I reach up and feel the hard, cold surface where there is nothing. Then I realize I can no longer feel the wind or hear the sound of the ocean. However, I can feel movement, and a look outside tells me I am moving faster than any time I have travelled on the ocean, except perhaps when I have ridden ahead of the surf as it tosses me onto the beach.

I look out the front to see the white clouds have risen over the large vessel that I am following to the land of the Spirit. I collapse on a ledge at the side of my new boat, as I am still weak in this body. Then the interior takes shape to my eyes. There are strange vessels, some empty and some with water and food. There are fruits, vegetables and meat plus places that are obviously meant to lie the body on. They are covered, as is the interior of the boat, with fine woven cloth of many colours and of such quality as I have never seen before. Water is moving, captured in what I see is more of the hard surface where there is nothing. One is open at the top, and the others are sealed with a stone-like top piece. I slowly lift the water vessel and am able to drink my fill. Then I eat and lie down in exhaustion, and still marvel that I can feel so much pain and exhaustion on this strange trip to my new world.

Then a new fear strikes me and I think, what if this lesser spiritual journey I am experiencing is because I struck my brother when he was celebrating the joys given men by the Earth Mother, our connection to the greater Spirit of this and all worlds. Or so I think. Darkness comes and I am so tired that dreams seem beyond me.

110

Only this world knows how long it is before I feel the motion of the vessel rising and falling through the waves. I can feel them striking the side of the boat, and hear a sound like water running over stones in a fast flowing stream, but nothing else. It is still dark when my eyes open; then I realize that it is dark outside but a small torch is burning inside giving me a faint light. The light has no flame or stone saucer to hold the fat for fire. It burns with no heat. I look out through the front and see the large boat is like many small suns. In its own area it is daylight. All else is dark.

My new world is beyond my understanding. I eat and drink, and feel less tired and much stronger. I then explore the clear vessel with stone top and find out it will open easily if turned. My new world is full of wonder and a small dawning of hope. Still, a desperate loneliness seems to be in my chest and head. Thoughts of my child, woman and all I held dear to me are still close. Even this surprises me as I thought such would be left behind. Perhaps this is only a part of the way to the other world and I will soon fly the rest and leave these thoughts behind.

As strength returns my mind clears and I become aware of my condition. I am filthy with the waste from my body and the air is warm in this enclosed space. So the removal of dirty clothes is not hard, and soon I use some of the water and the clothes to wash the waste off my body. Leaving aside the inner furs, I am about to put on the cleanest of the others when an awareness that some of the beautiful cloth in a pile on the sleeping place is as covering for the body. It seems still too good to put upon my somewhat dirty frame. I push at the wall all around but can find no way to reach the outside world, which is becoming light as the sun creeps onto the horizon of an endless ocean. So I go back to washing my body.

With the events of the last days has come an increase in the tiny creatures that plague the tribes in the hair of the body. These also I try and kill off as many as possible. If I must take this body to an ever increasingly confusion of a world, then why must lice come with me? They have not died with me. All I know is the shaman and old people, and even the memories, do not seem right somehow. Lice do not seem to be a part of the journey.

There is food enough to get me through the next two days. I have learnt how to wash and put the clothes on but still the interior is not clean. I hope we arrive somewhere soon.

On the following day land appears, first as a long line of low islands on the horizon but, as the vessel nears then passes, they emerge into four large islands with smaller ones in between two. I see a plentiful amount of bird life that dive on the large boat in great profusion, occasionally swooping my way. Just before dark I see land on the horizon again.

I sleep, then awake to relieve the pressure of my bladder. When my face reaches the clear surface, land is clearly outlined and several lights are to be seen which look strange for a fire. It takes a little time for it to register with me that the sound of water passing the hull has changed. I am not moving, and a glance tells me the large boat has disappeared. So I am a prisoner in this situation with no one to take me to the promised land. My body and mind are completely rested but still overwhelmed, and numbness is the best way to describe my condition. It enters my mind to try to smash the walls that hold me, but a nagging feeling still says to be wary of the messengers of this world. There is little else to do but go back to sleep.

After a restless night my eyes finally open to daylight and the gentle rise and fall of the waves, obviously in the lee of the land. There are dwellings on the island where the lights were last night. They have white walls and red roofs. Once again like nothing I have seen before. Time passes slowly as the sun rises to above, then starts its descent. Apart from all the other mixed feelings, I am now hungry as the food has all gone. My spirit is low.

Finally there is movement, and a boat about the size of this one rounds a headland and moves towards me. This one also has no paddles and no clouds above this time. It stops some fifty steps short of me. I see a very large round object lifted from the water, then the rope attached to the object proves to be attached to my vessel. We move slowly towards the beach until eventually I see trees without branches in a straight line growing on the ocean edge.

The boat pulls into the tree line and a group of strangely covered people disembark. Their faces are covered with what I presume is the surface you can see through but not penetrate. My vessel is pulled in beside the tree line, and I see it is a far more elaborate boat dock than the ones we use in rivers. The wood is cut so beautifully that it goes through my mind that it may, after all, be a better world.

A strange rope is attached to the roof of my enclosure, and all of a sudden I am aware of a wind blowing a misty fog into the inner space. I try and see the faces more clearly but the world fades and darkness descends as I feel my body fall. Strange dreams follow and I view many sights I fail to comprehend. At times I can feel sensation and movement on my body and around me.

111

After what seems like a very long sleep, I wake up on a surface softer than I have ever felt. My eyes open to a roof and walls that all curve to a flat floor. All seem lined with a surface like the soft inside of a young deerskin but pure white. I am naked, and with a start I realize I have no body hair. Not on my head, my chest or my groin. A quick look tells me I also, for the first time I can remember, have no lice; only the red bite marks that seem to be fading.

There is a small open space in the area that I can see should be the opening to this strange dwelling, and also a strange round object high up out of reach. I am lying on a raised surface. My hand touches the wall and it is soft to the touch. When pushed I can feel a hard surface behind it. I am a prisoner it seems, not a welcome guest in the afterlife. Perhaps this is a half way place to see where to send or take me.

I stand up and see a seat about half a step high on the far side of the dwelling. Above it is the captured spirit of a man removing waste from his body into what looks like the seat. I touch a small lever on the back of the seat and water rushes into and out of the object. My body is relieved of waste and, once again, I touch the lever and the water comes and the waste goes.

My mind still feels exhausted and there seems nothing to do but lie down. This I do and close my eyes. When they next open there is change. An opening in the round roof shows two captured birds in an enclosure and two small animals about the size of my foot in another. I cannot reach them, only watch as they move aimlessly about.

For the first time I look out the small opening and see only another wall which appears to be about five steps away. No people have I seen. Then it dawns on me that, apart from the water in the seat and the movement of the creatures, there is not a sound to be heard from the outside world. I hope this is not all there is to the afterlife. Yet I know there are people out there somewhere.

Another opening appears beside what I think is the entrance area. Food and drink are there on objects that I have not seen before. When the food, which is delicious, is eaten I put the food objects back in the same opening. The wall quietly closes over again. I see no human hand move it.

112

What seems like seven days pass but I cannot see the sun, and it is only at the wish of the light without flame that darkness comes at a seemingly regular interval. Then the enclosures with the animals and birds disappear and I am aware, for a very brief period, that the air that looks like mist is entering the dwelling. This time I lie down as the darkness approaches, for I cannot stop unconsciousness from descending upon me. When I awake again I find once more I am clean of body hair and all dirt from body.

There is something else now. On the top of a sloping bench is a stack of square objects. They have images on their top so accurate and beautiful that I have no doubt that the spirit of the people and animals they depict are stolen and locked up inside these images. With full return to consciousness, I carefully and fearfully begin to touch these objects. The top part slides forward and falls to the sloping bench. I see it is like the fine hide parchment that the shaman and priestesses use to record the memories and spiritual matters of clans. This is very different. The images are almost alive but the people's expressions are frozen, as if their life force has been captured for time and kept here. I hold the object with great care and slowly turn the individual pieces over. Every image jumps out at me; not only the reality but the images of things I cannot believe. There are people in structures of vast magnificence, and landscapes not in a natural form but designed to form patterns. It is as if the great Spirit has done it personally. Then it dawns on me that I am being shown what the great Spirit has done with the afterlife. I am to look and learn what is in the world. How spirits live. How I will live.

Tension eases out of me and fear dissolves to be replaced by excitement. The world around me disappears. I do not notice the return of the creatures, and it is even a long time before I notice food is there. Object after object with tiny markings that mean nothing to me, but I suspect the priestesses may understand. A strange world opens up to me. I never seem to tire of looking. Day after day passes. The more I look, the more detail I find.

I have lost track of time, but they regularly put me into the deep sleep and the hair is removed. Also my teeth and levels of health and energy seem to be changing. I have seen people look in the small hole in the wall, but rarely.

Then one day I become aware that I have a feeling I have not known before. I am desperately lonely. The objects of the trapped worlds no longer hold my attention enough for me to not ache for the sound of a human voice, the wind in a tree, running water, but most of all the touch of human flesh. What is going on in this world? Is this a punishment for the life I lived? I ask am I really dead, but if I am alive then things I have seen and experienced are not in my world. Am I mad? I am often talking to myself and answering back. I talk more each day to the creatures. The birds occasionally make a noise which is beginning to seem like they are talking to me.

Then comes the day they put me to sleep and I wake up back in the boat, moving over a fairly rough sea behind the large vessel. This time it is without clouds. From the objects, I now suspect the clouds are woven fabrics they use to catch the wind to move the boat in a manner the tribes have not known.

This time I am brought in close to an island, a long way from other land, which can just be seen as a tiny hill on the ocean horizon. Then another small vessel takes me in tow and moves me into the shallows where the surf washes my boat up to the beach. The roof opens. I see nothing but beach.

For a time I sit and do nothing. Nobody comes. Then it seems obvious I am to get out. My body is naked. I grab all the water vessels and food objects and heave them up onto the beach. Then clothing, ropes and other objects are wrapped in the bed coverings and I climb overboard with my load.

113

The instant my feet touch the ground the roof slides shut and the boat is moved back out to sea. Some time passes as I secure my treasures behind rocks well clear of the surf. A quick look tells me the other world beings are leaving me behind. So much for the spirit world. By all my reckoning I still have my body very much alive but healthier, hairless and lice free. I am still hungry and thirsty and so, very much in the body experience, I take care of this first while all the time keeping an eye out for danger in this strange world. Plenty of gulls gather close to inspect my food which is too precious to share with any creature.

I then cover myself with garments, making myself look like a hairless version of the spirit people in the parchment objects. The thought enters my mind that if tribe people live on this island and see me like this they will kill me, flee from me, or pay homage to me. I am not inclined to any of these prospects unless there are females. After all this time, the mere thought of this makes my body rigid with interest.

First, as the sun appears to be setting, I need shelter and fire. The shelter turns out to be easy, as the cliff face is hollowed in many places by wind and water in times gone by. There is evidence that others have used this suitable spot, as benches are set up and some branches left near a hearth that has been used within memory. A quick look at my stores shows me I have firelighters as seen in the parchments. I prepare a fire and secure my treasures high up and put rocks in front of them. Then I take a quick look at my surrounding area.

In two directions are steep cliffs rising straight to heavy rainforest jungle. A gully runs in the centre of these cliffs which tomorrow, or soon, will be my best way for exploring. Most important, there is fresh water coming from a spring somewhere further up the gully. A quick look along the shore shows me oysters on the rocks and crayfish in the pools dropping from the cliff face by my small beach. It is a beautiful and bountiful place, so my great hunger will only remain my loneliness. This I pray the Earth Mother will bring a change of situation as early as tomorrow.

I return to the cave with oysters and quickly have a warm fire, my first for I do not know how long. I look deep into the flames and return to my people and the arms of my Mara. No past event would matter if I could just feel the soft flesh and warm breath of a fellow human being; one who has given me comfort. The pain of other events now seems small and insignificant.

Pictures like those in the parchments seem to dance in the flames, and I am surprised to see that some of the imagined images are clothed and beautiful like the women I had observed from the parchments. This unsettles me, so I unroll the bed coverings and glad that I have a padded base. It is a good home with this comfort. So the fire is stoked and I fall into sleep, slightly restless but in a way pleased to be in a world that I recognize.

The morning comes and there is sufficient food from the boat supplies, so I heat it and eat before this food can spoil. I decide to find a sharp edge. The stone of the cave reveals something close to flint but not as good. It will do with the help of fire to give point to spear and arm me for protection, and help in the pursuit of food both ocean and land.

If it were not for the objects that are on my back and around me, I would begin to think that all I had experienced was a dream or state of spiritual trance from some form of ocean exhausted madness or other state of mind. The objects of clear vessel, bed covering, clothing and all are staying close to me. Whatever these things are, they are greater than objects the tribes had. A hard rock-like vessel with a top to fit is like one I saw heat food and water over fire in the parchments. So I soon have water boiling in a way not seen by my kind before. A crayfish is speared and goes into the boiling water. This feast I cook is as good as any I have known.

I am feeling slightly safer here, and have only seen harmless creatures that travel like small men with long tails in the branches of the trees. They are noisy and warn of change but no threat to me that I can see. I decide to build a bow and be well prepared to travel and explore the island.

It is two days before I find and have success with wood that can take the strain. Arrows are a little harder, but up the gully reeds grow which will do for birds and small animals. The forest is thicker than any I have been in before, and long rope-like branches grow from ground to canopy. It is very hard to move through.

114

After several days I rise early and set off up the gully. The going is slow and, although I am climbing all the time, I cannot get a view because of the undergrowth and thick forest. There are occasional noises from the tree creatures and birds. As I move inland, the sea birds are replaced by the quiet and beautiful birds that I glimpse in the canopy. The water dries up and the stony bottom of the gully divides into two, and both are very steep. I take what looks to be the larger, but go no more than what seems like four hundred steps when it ends in a cliff too steep for easy climbing. The other gully goes up and over several rises, to fall each time into yet another gully. It becomes a worry that I will lose my way back but, after snapping twigs to show where the return journey leads, I arrive safely back at my secure base. I am tired and not much wiser about where I live. There is no sign of humans in the valley.

The next day shows me no easy escape from the cliffs down to the beach. Huge cliffs go straight to the sea with a rough ocean making any entry into the water from these cliffs certain death. Getting to explore the rest of this island is going to be far harder and slower than I had thought. It may be easier to build a boat if I can find a good enough stone to create an edge for an axe. I also would like flint pyrites to create fire. These are not so easy to find. For the time being I keep the fire small and confine it during the day for hot coals at night. That way the firelighters of the parchment people will last longer.

As the days go by I start to make tracks into the forest, both in search of stone for axe and arrow, and perhaps a way over the cliffs. Eventually I find good stone with the added advantage of a hot spark. Then with the help of tree sap and vine, it is attached to a good handle. It is a good tool and would build a boat eventually, though I know none of the trees here. I will build a small vessel to store food, but mainly to check its qualities such as weight, hardness and water resistance.

For a time it is dry with blue skies and less wind than I am used to, although I presume this should be close to the hot period. Then one day huge clouds and oppressive heat begins to build up. Then the rain starts and I realize that maybe I should have stored food, as this rain is different. It falls so hard with strong winds that the water is ankle deep. This becomes the pattern nearly every day: the clouds, wind, then heavy rain.

After one moon of this weather the wind becomes strong for two days, then strikes with a strength that terrifies me. Rain reaches all the way back into the cave, killing the fire and driving all my goods up onto stone ledges. Me also! It is good that I already had most things up high for protection during my wanderings. The force remains for what seems like half a day, then stops completely. I go outside to see what has happened. I am tired and shaken in body.

Great waves are crashing onto the beach and objects I do not recognize are washed up there. I run down to retrieve what I can, and soon have a heap of timber and some parchment objects. With a total and instant ferocity the wind returns, to my surprise from the opposite direction. As I fight for my life to reach the cave, I see my heap disintegrate into the wind. It forces me at an angle but I make it to shelter behind the cliffs. It is coming from a direction pushing away from the cave entrance and the cliff face. I look up to see objects flying over the cliff top and realize there is more danger. My shoulder is struck and pain flashes through me.

Then I am in my home again and this time out of the wind. It is cold and wet and nearly dark. There is no dry material to light a fire so I go through the night without one. Movement attracts my attention and I see the moving forms of the small tree men with long tails, and there is the presence of several birds. I move hard at them but I am unable to chase them out. Terror of the storm makes me the lesser of the two dangers.

Tonight I have company. Then it strikes me I can probably kill all for food, but something in our shared danger stops me from bowing to hunger. They are so frightened that several on the ledge where my bedding is have to be shoved aside.

For a time I sit up high, eventually in total darkness, while the howling gale rages on, seemingly endless. Whatever my circumstances are, this world is full of danger and discomfort at this particular moment in time. Eventually my eyes close; to open once or twice to register the constant wind, and then finally to open on a new day.

The sun has risen and the wind has stopped. I walk to the entrance and look into a continuous torrential downpour of rain. The creatures have left the cave so I check my belongings. Apart from some wetness all have survived, including me. The bedding is spread on several limbs, and I gather what I can in the way of wood from the cave. There is plenty to light a fire but it is best left to dry further, then take me into the night and perhaps feed me while drying the parchment objects.

While it is still raining I take to the beach to find what I can. There is less there this time, as the wind seems to have taken all that was there back to sea with the change in direction. For the rest of the day I gather wood and stay out of the everlasting rain. Some oysters are all that can be found to feed me. Hunting in this weather is impossible. Fishing in a violent sea is even more so. That night the fire eventually catches, and light with warmth chases away some of the depression I feel. The ground dries and I am able to sleep on bedding that is soft.

The next morning I fetch spring water from what is now a torrent of water and, for the first time, I am struck by the changes. The rain stops briefly and before me the forest is bare. The trees and bushes have been stripped of their leaves. Where before I could see nothing from the cliffs, in many places all is open for inspection. Now there is a greater chance of finding my way over the rugged terrain and beyond.

115

The rain continues to fall for three days. Then the sky clears and the sun returns with an intensity I also have not known. Even without rain the air feels as if it has water in its very presence. For the next two days I stock fish and food from the rocks. The openness of the forest makes it easier to collect large amounts of firewood. This I stack up in the entrance of the cave, not only for the fuel but to break the wind as well. Then taking bow and arrows, axe, spear and dried fish wrapped in a sleeping object, I set off early this time, travelling at the base of the cliffs from the ocean side.

No leaves on branches enables me to see far enough ahead to pick the path of least resistance. Good progress is made, regardless of not being sure of what to look for, apart from a way up. By sun overhead I find myself already at the valley I have explored several times already, so I take the easy way back to base and prepare to start again the following day.

This time I leave from the sea cliff on the opposite side. Progress is again fast, with two places that I get to the top of after a dangerous climb. Then once again I come to the second gully that has been explored. Last time the trek was abandoned because I could not see where to go and was afraid I would get lost. This time my axe blazes a clear trail of strikes against trees and I decide to stay out overnight and try again.

By sun half way down the sky, an entry to a steep but what appears to be a safe ascent has been found. I can see with the improved vision a long ridge running, I think, away from the sea. As I climb, the view of the ocean opens up behind me, giving me a feeling of greater optimism.

I come up safely onto a tree-free ridge top. A wide track has opened up, not only taking me across the island but also enabling me to see the first of what appears to be a line of landfalls on the horizon and probably beyond. The wind is strong so progress is careful, for a fall either side would kill. In most places I can walk just to the protected side and travel in a direction away from the base cave.

The sun is lowering and I must find safer sleeping than that on the top of the ridge. As darkness approaches I find a small flat to the quiet side, eat some fish, and settle down and sleep undisturbed until dawn.

The ridge drops into a valley and back up. There are some leaves on the bushes, but this high up the trees are more sparse and the slopes easier going. I reach the top of the next rise before the sun is at its peak and can see the ocean on the other side of the next hill. The hill is lower. The cliffs do not seem as rugged this side of the island.

On reaching the top of the hill I see I am far from alone, for in a cove rounding a beautiful tree lined bay are a number of about thirty dwellings. People are moving about. There is a large square floating structure about one hundred steps from the beach, and what looks like a raft more than a boat on the sand. Boats I see none of. Perhaps they were all destroyed in the storm. It strikes me the dwellings are unlike those of my tribe, as all would have been lost to us in such chaotic weather. The dwellings have white walls and red roofs.

I move out, while seeking cover to approach. Something makes me a very cautious person. The trees here are not so lush and the branches are still bare. The only cover is by travelling in a low valley towards the sinking sun. This I do but stay distant until dusk, then I move in close.

I see the light without fire is in the dwellings, and also several on the track in front of the dwellings. I see no women or children. There are a large number of men, but it is hard to get a count as they are not all in the same place. As I move closer I see that there are special areas with edible plants, or I think that is what they are, as only a few plants for eating have been grown by us. I see men fishing on the rocks by the sea and musical instruments unlike our flutes and drums. I presume these are those I saw in the parchment objects.

As darkness comes I move all the way in, and remain close as people go about their activities. There is some laughter and much talking. Then it strikes me that these are the first human voices to reach my ears since I left the tribe. How long? I can only guess that it is well into the hot time, so five or six moons at least have passed since the sound of my fellow man. Not a word they say means anything to me. In a way this sends a sharp pang of loneliness into my being.

I am unable to leave and return to the aloneness I have known, yet fear still lurks and tells me that they may kill me if I make an entrance now. I move quietly from opening to opening and glimpse these people in their dwellings. I see several disrobe and retire to sleeping platforms. Eventually all are asleep and only the lights on the track out front are still burning.

There are no guards, so I know they are people who have not had enemies, and I expect they also have no predators to fear. There has probably been neither enemy nor predator for a long time.

After an extended wait with a near full moon above, I move cautiously about the camp. I see several objects about the camp from the parchments, and one is a fishing line better than I have known and that is too good to leave. I take it in hand, and with weapons I move down the beach with wind behind me, until I enter high sand dunes that make a soft and hidden bed.

Sleep comes quickly but strange dreams will not depart. The night is so warm that I sleep with only the sleeping object below me.

116

The warmth of sun and the movement and noise of many birds wake me, and I am quick to reach the top of the dunes to see if I am alone. The dwellings are hidden from here by another dune but no one is in sight. My stomach makes me instantly sorry I did not seek food from the settlement. I move away to hunt and try the fishing line. I catch nothing on the line but using the spear and bow I am able to catch fish and crab.

With my stomach full I set off to explore this side of the island and I am soon rewarded with the sound of pig. The dunes eventually turn into higher hills and thicker forest with some cliff face and reasonable shelter. There is no sign that humans have lived or even spent a lot of time travelling in this area. How do these people survive if they do not hunt? Perhaps they live entirely from the sea and the food they grow. No one looks hungry and I saw several people eating well last night. My mind tells me my fire would not be seen or smelt if I moved my possessions here, but first I will return once or twice to try and learn more of their ways.

The sun is low and the journey too far for me to arrive back at the settlement before they are well asleep, so at night I make a fire under an overhang and sleep. Sometime during the night the sound of several passing pigs wakes me and I reach for bow. The forest is too thick and dark to be successful. Still, it is good to know that, if I hunt well, there will be food to dry and fresh meat to eat.

The next day I move further inland and towards the settlement. There are droppings; waste from creatures I do not recognize. The rain falls steadily today but the wind is light and the air warm. There are new buds forming and the start of tiny new leaves on the sunny side of much of the vegetation. It will not be long before there is good cover. My bow remains ready for beast, or man if necessary. Hopefully man will be friendly but if they attempt to raise weapons I will have no choice but to shoot. Still, my spirit cries out for company.

There are trees here that look as if a boat can be built. Perhaps these people will accept me quicker if I have a boat. Then it strikes me that if I approach by sea and they are not friendly, I can escape by sea. They, at this time, have no way I can see of following me.

Several times I see long legged creatures moving but too far away and too swift to follow. Then I come quietly over a rise and there feeding in front of me are three birds that appear to have no wings. They are as tall as a man, with black bodies and blue and red necks. My arrow flies true and the bird falls as the others flee swiftly down the valley, faster than most four legged animals can run. My chest feels good, and the happiness I have not felt much lately crosses my face. The feathers can stay until I reach camp. The head, neck and insides are quickly removed and left behind. They will perhaps feed a beast that will perhaps feed me.

It is close to dark by the time I return. The fire flares and the feathers are quick to depart, with the best kept to show my respect for the spirit of that which gives its life for my survival. I feast on tasty chunks and the rest is cut into strips for drying. Tomorrow I will have to stay until the remaining food is ready for safe storage.

Two days pass before I find the urge to explore again and discover the ways of my fellow islanders. Once again I keep inland, travelling on the island side of the crest of the hills. This enables me to view the gullies and, with a quick look over the top, I can see if any approach is being made. There are many large flightless birds on the island and I become aware that it was their noise, and not that of pig, I heard in the night. Their meat is tasty but as the foliage returns they will be able to vanish quickly. I watch them for their food gathering habits. If I know where they eat and drink it will help to become as one with them for the success of the hunt. There is no sign of man, and once again I am surprised at their lack of presence out hunting for this good food supply.

Before dark I survey the settlement. There are once again no guards. They fear no creatures on this island. They fish and gather food from their gardens. As dark falls the fireless lights come on again and I move in. I see several looking at parchment objects. Close inspection shows me that they keep their hair short, as mine still is, and all are beardless. I understand nothing of their speech. They eat well with some laughter but not singing, and no voices of women and children. Once again my body feels the deep yearning for what this community seems to be also lacking. The sadness brings tiredness to me and, after a quick look at the outskirts of the dwellings, I move back to the dunes to sleep, being too far away to reach either base by nightfall.

The following day the decision is made to check my camp and return close to the settlement with the objects. I think that now I must decide if contact can be made. My future is to learn who or what these people are, and where it is that I am.

The trek back is already more difficult as the leaves are becoming dense enough to make the axe marks harder to see. The trail is blazed again. I may need to escape to this my private cove; it still feels like the only safe place for me to reside. Even the little tree people seem like friends to me, although the arrows have made them wary.

The night is spent in the lovely bay, and with most of my belongings slow progress is made back over the journey, blazing the trail once again. Sign of me may be seen, but something tells me these people will never come back this far to see the evidence of my presence, unless they observe my movements.

I sleep on my high plateau then move down to my new camp. The day is spent and darkness falls. Aside from people, this is a gentle island with an abundance of food, fresh water and shelter. Sleep comes easily with an improved bed.

Next day I wash my coverings and body as I have seen a lot of cleanliness amongst these people and in the parchment objects.

117

Once again I move down to observe, this time arriving when the sun has not long left its high point. The people still fish and attend to their plants. Some work is done on dwellings but not much. Then the white cloud appears on the horizon and quickly finds its way to this bay. The woven clouds disappear and the large vessel moves in until it is against the floating square structure.

There is a group on the beach now and, for the first time, I can get a rough count. There are between fifty and sixty men. Activity takes place and soon there is a stack of objects on the flotation. The boat moves off and the cloud rises. Three men man a raft and pull on a rope and the raft quickly takes them out to the goods. This way, after three trips, the transport is complete. The people and goods disperse in all directions, and things return to normal as dusk arrives.

I move down and inspect the raft when all seems quiet and dark has set in. Then I make a quick journey to some of the dwellings I have not looked at before. The lights go out and sleep seems total. I move back to the raft and board then, swiftly finding the rope, I pull and the raft quickly moves towards the distant construction. The structure is large and hardly moves at all as I move around its form. It is about fifty steps long and twenty wide, with one step high out of the water. There is some timber but the rest of the material is as the walls of their dwellings. It is not known to me. There is little to learn so I turn and move the raft back to the beach. With the moon behind clouds, visibility is less than twenty steps but I can see the waves breaking on the beach as the raft comes to rest.

I step off the raft and wade towards shore as the moon emerges. Seven men stand in a half circle some fifty steps from me. In front of them, some fifteen steps, is what I can only presume is an offering of food and some other goods. My bow comes quickly to hand but I see no weapon so it fails to take aim. The men withdraw with a few words of their language and I move to take the food.

There is a grass carry not unlike that which the tribes use. I taste and pack the food and move away swiftly into the dark. I am still wary but a little easier and more than slightly confused. Somewhere inside me registers relief that contact has been made and aggression was absent.

118

The following day I move to the end of the beach and quietly fish. The people go about their work and do not attempt to approach me. As afternoon moves on the need to look to the camp calls, and the next two days are spent hunting the area near my new dwelling. It slowly enters my mind that perhaps I do not need to seek shelter so far from people and that some locations can be sought so I can reach my bed from late in the day. Part of this day is also spent in one of several local streams washing my body and coverings. These people look to cleanliness every day.

The sun overhead finds me making an approach to the outskirts of the dwellings. Several people come towards me when it seems that is as far as I will go. Once again food, and this time fishing line, are laid down. Then they withdraw and ignore me again. I take the food and look for shelter in the cliffs by the coast. They are low here and it is not good. There is more food than I need now, so I take the best and return to the far camp.

The next day finds me with good shelter close in, and the rest of my supplies are moved to the new location. They will either be safe or I will suffer. Now I am completely vulnerable, as the blindest of them can easily see the evidence of my fire and probably also smell the smoke.

Two days later they approach my camp. Three of them come unarmed, so I lay my spear and bow down in the gesture of friendship and move back to allow them to approach. One of them comes slowly up to me and extends his hand with a pair of beautiful coverings for my feet. I take them and he smiles broadly and speaks. The others laugh and I feel happiness enter for the first time since I was with my people. A smile and answering laugh crosses my face. I go to the best of the dried meat and extend it to the leader. He takes it and not too eagerly tastes it. The others approach and I show them my possessions. Much talk follows, then they leave and I am lonely again but much happier than I have been. I am now without fear, for they seem gentle, good people. Where are their women and children?

The following day sees me in the settlement and every day after that for one moon. Words begin to open up and understanding of many of their meanings grows. In time I will speak their language. It crosses my mind that in time I may not remember my own language.

On the second moon I hunt and start to explore more and more of this island. The trees have returned to normal but I can still find my way along blazed trails. It is impossible to tell how many of the flightless birds exist. As with the ways of the greater clan, I leave those that have young and hunt only single or mature birds. This I think I have explained to my new tribe and they seem happier now, as at first they looked annoyed when I brought game back to them.

I have retained my own space and improved the protection from rain which still comes nearly every day. The heat is slowly easing so the season is changing. Time has been lost to me but I see these people mark the moons on parchment, so it is likely I will accept their time eventually.

At nights I have worked on a small canoe about half a step long and leave it in a rock pool. So far it floats well. After half a moon, if the wood holds as I expect it will, I will work on the mother tree that will make a boat perhaps five steps by nearly one step wide. Once again it is near the stream but I will need help to bring it to the sea.

The old ways feel good to me and I wonder why these people have no boats. Often, when I am sure they understand my questions, they do not seem to exert themselves to give me an answer, sometimes just going off to their plantings or other activities. None offer to hunt with me, though they have enjoyed thoroughly throwing the spear and using the bow.

119

Moons pass and I have long since lost count of them. I can now hold a conversation of sorts and have been told I will get many answers when my knowledge is good enough to understand. They do not want misunderstanding. Still, I suspect that they have been cast out by their people, for even though regular drops occur with food, clothing and healing, no human contact occurs at all.

I have started on the boat and nearly every day I work on it and the log is taking shape. Now the cool time has arrived but the rains have stopped. It is as if the seasons have somehow become upside down.

Some nights I sit with the people and read the words they are teaching me from the parchment objects that I now know are called books. Not only am I learning their language but also what is called the written word. They have shown me that I come from a world far to the east that is forbidden to them. At this time they will not say why. They have shown me that this island is one of several near what they call the centerline of the Earth. Their people occupy islands that exist for a great distance running north. They also trade and travel regularly to another ancient people who occupy a large land far to the west. Knowledge has been preserved and passed down through great disasters and aeons of time. The people have lived and built great civilizations, only to lose them and have them rise again. Their legends tell of the heroes of dim history who have preserved and saved the people and their ways in great times and times of great tragedy. The greatest of all it is said, from the time of legend, was Poseidon. Such are the stories they most value.

The moons continue to pass and my boat is finished. I have told them of it and they seem impressed but not interested in helping me to transport it.

Finally one day they tell me their story. It has long been known of the tribes and vast lands to the east. It has also been known that the ways of the clans are aggressive and warlike and outside the laws of the great Spirit. Regardless, aeons ago the legends and writings tell of contact being made. The result was disastrous for their people. The ships that landed on the great eastern continent were soon afflicted with several deadly diseases that the island people had no immunity against. They set sail for their homelands to seek salvation from the hands of the doctors. In the thirteen days it took to return, seventy-three people perished and only twenty-one who were gravely ill landed. Within days almost every one of some eighty thousand people was ill. They quarantined themselves and no outsider had access. After a long time, contact was made and a group of healers landed. There were fifteen survivors. Since then all contact with the eastern continent is taboo.

My new tribe, some that they call scientists, some healers and others just good people, decided that they could land and identify these diseases, in order to find a cure for them. They had petitioned the leaders with a result that created havoc for their families and themselves. They were shunned by large parts of the population.

Regardless of this they persisted, in the belief that some day their people would be exposed to the probably expanding and slowly developing tribes who were, in fact, their ancient cousins. So they formed together and began to equip a vessel for the expedition.

On discovery they were tried for what were considered acts of terrorism, and banished for life to this place. They are citizens who obey the laws that have been laid down. They will not venture to ever leave this land, however they believe that I was allowed to live for the reason that life is so sacred they cannot kill. They now also think that I have been quarantined under laboratory conditions and examined for any evidence of disease. I was then put ashore in a cove where no person was ever considered to be able to leave, thinking that in time I would have perished, as I probably would have but for the storm which they call hurricane. Still, they did not know of my people's love for building boats.

It has been said to me that it would distress them if I was to attempt to contact their people, although the events that I have described make it improbable that I am still a carrier of disease. They say, however, things can be dormant and in certain weather or physical conditions or sensual contact disease can emerge. So they would attempt to kill me, to their great distress, if I was to attempt escape.

After many moons I convince them that I will not leave, but my boat I alone will use to fish and hunt against the shores of this island. I also make agreement to keep it out of sight of the supply ship. They are unconvinced of this, so continue to resist helping me.

Then the rains come again and, when hunting one day, I am caught in a deluge that lasts for five days. I realize that the runoff is so fierce and abundant that the boat may reach water if I can control it in the raging waterways. It still takes me two days to get it to the main waterway. It would be lost if the entry was made, so the wait takes place until the water level drops to a safer margin. Two days later, with the loss of much skin, my vessel has reached the sea. The high tide is found and I beach it in a hidden cove. The idea is in my head that, if it creates conflict, I will keep it for my personal use from now on.

I still hunger for the sound of women and the laughter of children. I doubt I would survive to reach foreign shores, so my thoughts turn elsewhere. I shall remain with these gentle people until I am assimilated as much as possible. I now know it is more than their ways. My skin is darker and my features very different. Also the way I think seems to be more adventurous than these people are capable of. Still, the books tell that some amongst them adventure to far places on the great western land and the journeys by sea to such are vast, although in boats made for such journeys.

120

My vessel works well, and in the next half moon I travel right around the island taking many of my belongings with me. It is good to be back in my first cave. I stay for several days. The fishing is better here and the shell fish more abundant. Although they have introduced me to metal and such, edges are far better. I still visit my quarry for cutting tools and arrow points. The old ways are still all around me.

From up here I can see down the valley over pools of clear fresh water to a sea so beautiful that, even to one who has lived by it for a life, it takes my breath away. The day is perfectly clear and colourful birds keep up chatter with the tree men I now know as monkeys. They are far more plentiful on this side where the jungle is thicker with high cliffs and high rainfall. The tracks I used after the storm are almost impenetrable with thick re-growth and no view of where access exists. It is easy to believe that my deliverers had placed me in an area I would never escape from; in their thinking not even to the other side of the island. I am going to leave so I will find every aspect of opportunity until I discover the way.

As time passes their speech becomes my speech and their clothing becomes mine. I study the maps of the great western land and the structure of their boats. There are books in abundance to do with this. In time I know what people come from where, and what areas are virtually uninhabited and those rarely visited. There are a few nomadic people but virtually none who have tribal ways such as I know. There are none that have my appearance, and possibly none who will be keen to accept me if it is known I am from the eastern continent. The taboo and fear of disease and aggression is widespread on all islands and the mainland.

The supply boat comes always in the daylight but often leaves after dark. I have discovered by occasional questions that it nearly always takes the same route, and that it returns to one of the large seaports where vessels from all islands and the western land congregate. I settle on a plan and stock the boat with a good strong rope and supplies protected from moisture by cloth of these people.

121

The day finally arrives in the season of the finest weather, and the supply boat approaches just before dark on a soon to be moonless night. As they unload I move into close proximity and, under the cover of a black sky, tie my boat to the rail, staying tight up behind the outside rear of the boat. The gentle hum begins inside the hull and I climb up my rope then peer carefully over the side. The rope to my boat is lengthened as we move towards the ocean. I slip under the covering of what I know to be a life raft. With luck I will not be seen here. If daybreak comes before our destination, I will pull the boat in tight and hope it is not seen. There is some activity as the sails go up. Then all settle down for the night.

The sea is calm, and a quick look tells me that only the rope can be vaguely seen. After all I have gone through this is just another event. At least now there is a sense of opportunity and excitement that almost balances out the fear in my body. My senses stay on alert.

Eventually light appears in the distance that grows into a vast fire without heat. Land appears behind the lights and, before daylight, we enter a harbour with more ships than I dare count. I know from my reading that the largest ships, and those attached to the docks, are the ones that will most probably leave first and travel to the great land of the west.

My boat is quickly drawn in and, before we come to a halt, I climb down the rope and push off in my boat while seeking shadows behind other vessels, for everywhere here there are areas of light. Apart from us most seem quiet. Sleep is still taking place. However, as I approach the dock there is movement of large dark shapes, some moving rapidly and they are noisy. I tie up under the wharf and climb a ladder.

In the half light I hope I do not look too conspicuous, so move with casual direction down the dock towards a group of large buildings. Several men pass together, then one passes on his own. As he passes I call out: "What vessel is leaving for the western land next?" Without hesitation he points and says: "Starline in one arlm is going to Binarda." I have seen that on the map. After he moves away I retrace my steps, and get rope and what food I can carry and move onto the dock.

There is a gangplank onto the vessel but I avoid this. Using shadow near the rear of the ship I suspend food, rope and myself under a huge rope and, hand over hand then foot over foot, move onto the vessel. There are no people here, but their shadows are moving in the centre and front of the vessel. Large areas of the deck have cargo covered by woven cloth, and once again there are the small rescue boats used in case of shipwreck. My food is stored in one and I drop a coil of rope over the rear of the boat, then move back the same way I have come to my own simple part ocean-going vessel. If I am caught or afraid, I may have a way of escape. So I tie it as well concealed as I can close in behind the huge ship. With the overhang I hope it will not be seen.

The sun is rising now and, although the ship is away from the wharf, I had hoped we would have been sailing by now. A retreat is made to the new shelter in a lifeboat and not long after movement is felt.

I think about fifteen days pass and the only change of routine is at night. I find fresh water and eat raw grain, and a little food that is occasionally left on deck. By the time land is in sight I am weak from hunger. The rope trails empty behind, leaving my humble vessel somewhere in the vast ocean.

The dock is reached early in the day and the decks are cleared first. I dare not look but know that there is more cargo of wondrous book objects below deck. I assume that it will take several days to unload, so dark falls and I emerge to a very much quieter harbour. It is impressive, with a wharf of great carved stones; each stone in many cases taller than a man. There is light here too, and a large settlement running back into the hills. Rows of white walls shine from the light on the tracks that I know are called streets, that stretch away from the docks. I see many people eating, drinking and inspecting goods of all kinds in buildings along the streets.

A heavy downfall of rain arrives giving me cover to make my escape. I am too weak to crawl down the rope, so run for the gangplank and arrive on the dock in heavy rain. Without stopping I grab wet food from a stall and run for a dark part of the settlement. Behind me I hear an angry shout but the rain puts them off and there is no pursuit.

122

So I am in a strange land with little food and virtually no covering for my body, no bedding, and no tribe. I hope I speak the language. The one thing I still have is strapped to my back. I have the bow and a quiver full of arrows.

I would like to sleep but will use the dark to learn a little of this settlement, and hopefully steal some necessities for survival. The best idea, I think, is to find a small group in a remote area and tell them I am from the place far south of the landmass, from a tribe rarely seen, so explaining my differences. I hope!

The buildings in this area are large with little lighting. No one seems to live here, so with few people spotted I move towards higher ground, slightly away from the sea. Amongst the buildings it is hard to tell direction, but eventually I come across a wide causeway running towards what appears to be a break between two hills. I turn the other way and can see down over the lighted area and the harbour. I am hungry so I move towards an area of lights in a less lit up region and am soon there.

The smell of food is everywhere. By moving carefully and passing people with my head down I find that larger causeways are lighter, and smaller causeways are almost dark and behind buildings that seem to be both dwellings and eating places.

I move into the dark area between the buildings and follow the noise of voices and the smell of food. An entrance opens, and a woman deposits something that smells like food in an object besides the opening. After a brief time I move in and soon recover everything that I can tell in the darkness is food.

A little further on are many woven objects suitable for wearing and sleeping. I wrap the food and clothing in a large woven sleeping object and move back to the large causeway until I am in a wooded area. With a word to the great Spirit to protect me from wild creatures, both man and beast, I eat my fill and sleep on a slightly improved bed.

123

The sun is rising before my eyes open again and the day is spent keeping out of sight. That night I find it is usual for food to be left behind most of the eating places. It is taken away every day. These people must be rich indeed in resource to leave such treasures, for there are many wonderful tastes to behold in the food.

Several times I am seen but no one gives chase or even seem concerned. I move about at night and grow in confidence, even answering several greetings. The language is very similar although the way it is pronounced sounds different. After several days I find food is being left on eating plates behind one of the buildings I first discovered, the ones I feel safest frequenting.

About the fifth day my body has recovered strength and I have found water to wash cloths and body. I know I should travel but I am finding it hard to leave food and the presence of people. Even the sound of a woman's voice is like the wind in the flutes of my people.

I am approaching the rear of the first eating place and see the entrance is slightly open and a plate of beautiful food shows in the light. As my hand takes the food a voice says: "Do not be afraid." I back away into the darkness and hear her voice say: "You are welcome to the food but please return the plate." Then the door closes and I am left to wonder in the dark. The tastes are fresh and more delicious than most I have known. I eat in the causeway and return the plate. I take more from a container of food for tomorrow and move away.

Once again I move through the quieter places and marvel at some of the things I see on display. It strikes me how far I have come in a change of the seasons or so. As a tribesman I would have been terrified by all I am seeing. But now my mind has had so many shocks and registered so much that is strange, that almost nothing seems to surprise or terrify me any more.

As people pass I am again aware that all are clean and fresh shaven. It also strikes me that not much strong liquor is consumed. There are no drunken men staggering from a communal drink around the evening camp fire when the women and children have retired, then staggering to the dwellings as often happens at our celebrations.

The next day I find implements to scrape the hair off my face and cut the hair on my head. I arrange my clothes to look as close to them as possible. This time the door is open as I approach, and the plate of food is brought slowly out by a woman who looks old. She smiles with a full mouth of teeth and moves easily on a slim, erect body. For the first time in a long time I look directly into the face of a woman and smile. As she sees me clearly for the first time, her face registers surprise and confusion. I also sense fear but she hides all of these emotions and quietly hands me the plate.

I thank her and say: "I come from the far south from an isolated community. I have travelled alone for a long time and am grateful for the food." Another face appears behind her. It is a young boy and she tells him to leave. She asks me where I live and if I have work. I tell her my dwelling is the forest and my work is to hunt, fish, and make clothes, weapons and gather food. This answer, she tells me, is rare in this land. The plate is returned and I start to move away. The woman closes the entrance, and for a long time I watch from the dark and see her drop food in the container which I now know is for waste. Still, it is good food. After recovering more food from other places, I return to my camp site and retrieve my goods from their hiding place.

My dreams that night are full of Mara, and my body tosses and turns until the sun breaks the horizon. I rise still tired and this day go further into the surrounding hills and their jungle. My arrow finds a pig-like creature and it feels good to be preparing food in the way of natural things.

124

It is five or six days before I go back to the eating houses. I have journeyed and found that there are small agricultural groups of dwellings in fertile valleys. All is orderly and beautiful. The dwellings are of wood, mud and some stone. The people have darker skin than those of the islands, especially in the farm settlements where I can see I would not be quite so conspicuous. I am bigger than most of these people and stronger in build.

This time when I return the door is closed but I wait until the rear door opens. Several times the young boy comes out, then the woman comes out. I step out of the dark and greet her. She seems unafraid and asks: "Where have you been?" I tell her of the hunt and she looks at the bow and seems surprised. She says that it is rare amongst people to eat from the wild and that animals are often protected and killed when numbers become a problem. I have read of this but still this surprises me. Then it comes to me that, apart from fish and other seafood, most of the food was vegetables with very little meat.

More food is brought and I eat while talking to her. She asks me if I want work. I ask her what she means and she says: "Work like washing dishes, gardening or working on the boats." In return, she says, I would receive the means to obtain the things I need without having to steal or beg. I have seen a little of this in the books so am not completely confused. I say: "I had intended to go to the country as I would be more like the people there." She looks carefully at me, then laughs gently and says: "I doubt it. You seem to me like a wild creature unlike any I have heard of before." She says: "Where was your home; by sea, in mountains or desert?" I tell her by the sea, and that I was mostly a fisherman who had his own boat. The food is gone so I return the plate, and she closes the door with the words: "We will talk again."

The next night is the same as the last and I approach. This time she asks me to sit at a small table by the back entrance. For some reason my chest feels happiness. I have been lonely, especially for the sound of a woman, or even the boy and the young woman who come and go to another place in the dwelling as the older one cooks. All this brings a slight smile to my face. These people do not seem dangerous to me. When again asked where I come from I give the location as west of Ilopay, a place I chose from the island people's maps. She looks at me as if this may be the truth, and places food in front of me with eating utensils. I choose my fingers and eat with pleasure. I notice the two young people stare each time they turn my way. The woman says the customers are not to enter the kitchen tonight.

I return each night after that, and find my clothing changes under her guidance and ways. I work in the kitchen for my food and after one moon, which they call by a different name, she has found me a bed in a nearby place. Although I now mix with the people, my nature has become more reclusive.

Regardless of the age of the woman she is clean, and her body movements and smells are attractive to me. I see she looks at me as a woman should and, although careful and reserved, touches me from time to time.

One day the woman tells me there is a fishing trading boat that leaves on a regular journey to a group of more isolated islands. She says she has met one of the heads of the family and others have observed me. They are away at sea for up to one and a half moons at a time. If I wish I can do a trip with them and see if the life suits me. Except for my desire for the woman, the journey would be an adventure. I do not know how to tell her, so agree to go.

Under her direction I board the boat. The work is hard but not constant. I enjoy it with the bed, food and washing facilities. There are small harbours and settlements on each of the islands, not unlike what I have come to think of as my own harbour and life. When I return I have a quarter moon before it is time to leave again.

I give what they call my payment to the woman, as I know not what to do with it, although I am rapidly learning how it is used to obtain goods. She says now she will take some for a room in her dwelling and give me what I require for my needs. The rest she will look after for me. I cannot hide the joy I feel and happiness is all over my face. She also looks pleased and laughs a lot as the evening meals are delivered.

That night, as I leave the bathing vessel, she opens the door and quietly enters. My body is fully exposed to her and instantly responds to her presence. Her eyes are intense. She says: "You have a very powerful body and your manhood is large. Who are you?" I do not answer. I want her and am afraid she will be put off by words. She comes to me and puts one hand on my chest and the other on my shaft. I hear a loud moan almost of pain escape my lips. Her hand explores my face and body while she continues to stroke me. I can feel the intensity building up. She swiftly removes her clothes. I see that, although her hair is grey, her body is firm. I reach for her but her hands push my chest and her words say "wait." Both hands are on me now and I know my climax is near. I can hear my moaning as if it is from someone else's body.

She kneels and pulls back the skin exposing the swollen glands and I feel the wonder of her soft lips. Then the seed bursts forth. I hear her moan as she continues to stroke the jerking thrust of my body. Then she stands and takes my shaking body in her arms and kisses me hungrily. She looks and feels beautiful to me and my mind bursts forth with pleasure. She says: "Go to my bed in the next room. I will bathe and come to you." When she comes we are together and then I sleep. Then again, then I sleep.

When I wake she has gone, so I wash and go downstairs. She is singing happily and the young boy looks at me with a big smile. She sits me down and puts food in front of me, touching me as she does so. I feel stirring in my body again. Mostly I feel clean and whole.

When the time comes for me to return to the sea I resist, but she bids me pack my bag and turns me to the harbour. Still, her promise is that she will love me when I return.

125

The journey passes, and many moons and a routine that is now my life sets its course. I hear often of the main islands that are the centre of what they call the civilized world of an ancient people, and see pictures of great statues and slowly learn of their beliefs. The teachings sometimes touch upon my own tribal beliefs.

Over a long time the stories of taboo stay strong. Even with the one I love, my tongue remains still as to my origin. I never again see any of the men who were my first teachers and contact. The memories of my origin fade.

As my woman grows older I turn to the women the sailors frequent near the harbour and am popular amongst them. Even when she is old I lie beside her at night and her hands take pleasure in having their way with me. She teaches me that good food and its healing ways keep people strong and healthy for a longer life. Then one day she does not wake up and, although my heart is sad, I remember with great joy all she has been to me.

Not long after her death I am called to a building of wise men, and told that she has over the years preserved and increased my wealth, so all I need is taken care of. Her son, and her daughter who is now married, have the eating house and home. A happy family lives there so, although I visit often, I do not return to her empty bed.

As I grow too old to work the boats, my time is spent fishing and taking short trips into the forest, sometimes accompanied by youth who I have taught how to make and use the bow and sharp edges from flint. When I hint that they can kill the beast of the forest for food, they laugh merrily at me and show no interest. Still, on more than one occasion, as my eyes grow dimmer I stay by a fire in a cliff overhang and live the ways of my people.

For reasons I expect to do with the science of the island greats, the diseases of my origin never infect me.

Then one day I can feel my time is near and I go to the forest for the last fire. My arm is too weak to send the arrow true, but as my body grows weak my mind clears of all mist, and an extraordinary life is before me, as if it was all within the rising and falling of one moon. Then I feel my spirit leave my body and, as the wondrous Earth recedes away from me, this time I know, I am as the great Spirit created all life.

The life of survival

126

12,900 years ago before I started 'the writing'.

My eyes open to the sounds of the beautiful parrots singing in the trees by the river. I smile at Niomi, my wife. No beauty, never was, but I was not the one the pretty girls chased into the jungle glades. I have been happy to spend a large part of my life with a kindly woman who has birthed and raised my two strong sons and my daughter.

In three days time we will see our daughter and grandchild when we enter the largest of the rivers that flows into the largest of all rivers on the great southern land. It is here where the huge ships of the ancient civilizations of the people that time preserved come. These are the people who have shared many of our memories. They are generous with knowledge that helps us to live in the jungles and preserve our people's ways. They hold the knowledge of soils which is carried by the keeper of the Earth, who travels with us today. He is one of those most highly revered amongst our people in the cities up and down the flood plains of the river and its many tributaries, and on the endless canals built by our people over vast time beyond written memory.

For me it is enough that I have the privilege of moving those amongst us who preserve such knowledge that allows us to exist in vast numbers, on land that otherwise could not produce the substance to allow thousands to exist. I see Niomi take cool fruit juice to the old Earthkeeper. He is courteous to my wife. This I know brings a look of worthiness to the expression on my face.

The turning of the tide does not reach us here and the wind is calm today, so our progress relies on the strong arms of my two sons and the other six oarsmen who rhythmically bend their backs and defeat the flow of the greatest of all known waterways.

For an instant I am surprised when I look forward from Niomi and Earthkeeper to see a large sleek presence coming towards us. I can see the long white robes of the Mother priestesses, so relax. Theirs is the only boat of the river people that has the power to move without noise or oar. I am used to this so take little notice and expect they will pass as usual, without stopping. The oars stop and our people line the rails of our vessel, leaving the place of respect for our Earthkeeper.

Suddenly their vessel veers towards us, and I see the water churn beneath the hull as if many oars are working to stop the boat. Their bow comes around and they silently move alongside us. My people seem confused and fail to show the courtesy of extending ropes. Their ropes land on our deck, and I send my sons to labour while I handle the stern ropes.

When we are tied off, one of the elder women steps forward and I rush to extend the boarding plank. Although the vessel is twice our length, it is river and built low. The leader and two others board us, and I hasten to introduce Earthkeeper, my wife and myself. The leader acknowledges us and then speaks to Earthkeeper in a way that tells me they are familiar.

The message is quick and not hidden, as far as I can tell. They have on the previous night, just seven arlms ago, sighted a pair of objects slowly becoming brighter and they seem to be heading our way from the stars of the bull sign. They do not know what this means but do not believe it is a sign of the coming of the travellers. This I do not fully understand but, given that they are speaking of the legends and the teachings preserved by the mothers, it is not the knowledge of one such as I. Their word is they are going down river to move their sisters and all they contact back up river to shelter and higher ground if possible. Perhaps nothing will happen but they feel they have vague memories of possible catastrophe. Then they leave us, and their vessel goes around the riverbend and they are out of sight.

Another boat presently appears and, feeling a little foolish, I call out that the priestesses have warned all to seek shelter. I see all looking to the sky. Apart from cloud towards the north-west, it is clear. I do not feel great fear. There is no high ground until we turn into the next river, so I speak with Earthkeeper who looks very grave and tell him we can perhaps avoid his stops for the next time period, and press on to my daughter's village which we can reach in seven arlms with a good three-quarter moon reflecting off the slow waters. The grave face remains silent when I talk with him but he nods, and I see him turn often to look to all parts of the sky and horizon.

The men are tiring so I slow the rate of oar stroke and take two at a time to eat and gain brief sleep.

127

The shadows lengthen. The creatures of sky and earth, that increase in activity when dusk comes, bring the welcome music and sound of wind. Nature doing what it has done through all time make all who hear supremely confident. I can see the shadowy figure of our respected elder take several stiff steps to the rail and grasp it with an intense study of the sky. He then swings abruptly to another part of the heavens.

Then I see them; larger than the great star of the north-west we have all learnt the ways of for dark night travel. One is to the west and is three times larger than the largest and brightest of stars. As I watch, to my horror it is as if it is growing before my very eyes. Another one is smaller and much further north; then a third one, smaller but far to the north-west. The largest is to the east and appears the closest.

Earthkeeper turns to me and says: "Make all speed for higher ground. How long to our destination?" We are, I think, still three arlms away at least. Those who are resting are put back on the oars. They are still unconcerned, and I see resentment as they are asked to increase the tempo of stroke. I take the rear high position on the tiller and darkness is broken by the rising moon. The vision is adequate to guide the oarsmen as we make good time up river.

I become aware that another light is growing, and the river appears as I have not experienced it before. Creatures are coming to life again; the sound of bird voices fill the air. Night is becoming day. A new sun with three smaller suns has become a part of our world, but this sun I can now see is putting fear into the faces of my people. A tail is now starting to appear behind the largest two bodies, and it is obvious that they are coming to

Earth some distance from where we are. My woman brings me hot beverage, then stands close. I tell her I must speak with our traveller and leave her.

The question is put as to what it is and what result it is expected to have, as it appears to be some distance away. He turns and quietly says he only has vague legends too far removed to have seemed reality, and now is not the time to tell of such events. I return to Niomi and talk quietly to her, trying to reassure her but she knows there may be danger.

Then the final descent begins. There is a long blue tail behind it. The sky around it becomes too bright to look directly at it. Then it is gone. For a short time the tail of light continues to light the night sky, while the second is becoming brighter. Then a dark cloud rises from where the body disappeared. It seems a long way off and I begin to feel we have escaped danger. A short time later a resonant boom reaches us, telling all that something extraordinary has happened in a distant land. I now fear, not for us but for the world of another people; perhaps the Ancients of the silent cloud ships.

128

Time passes, perhaps half an arlm, and much further away a trail crosses the sky and the body of the second disappears. The sky is darkening but still eerily different. A blue moon shines in a different light. I call to the Earthkeeper and I am surprised to hear a quiver in his voice. I ask: "Can the oarsmen rest? Has the danger passed?" He comes back to my position and says: "If they struck over water, a great wall of ocean will perhaps travel over sea and land, like we have never experienced in memory. Hold fast and keep an eye on the river."

Time passes and I notice that, with the impact, all creatures went quiet. Then I look up to see huge flocks of birds high and low, travelling south-west. Then I am aware that the current of water flow no longer runs against us, and the water is rapidly rising here and far away from the tidal surge. Earthkeeper calls my woman to tie herself to the deck rail. He then wraps a rope around my waist and quickly to the rails, repeating the same for himself. His voice says: "I will help you hold the vessel straight".

We are approaching a bend in the river, after which I know it runs fairly straight west towards the journey. A surge of water is upon us; a wall some three dwellings high moving quietly over jungle and river. Our speed and downward angle are terrifying. The tops of trees are coming quickly. I can hear the Earthkeeper calling and see the gap in the tree tops. I pull the tiller over and we rush through the gap onto the straight of the river now surrounded by an ocean of treetops.

I am vaguely aware of Niomi's screams but must hold the boat straight down the centre of the waterway until the wave passes beneath us, or we will be lost and dropped in the treetops. Now the crest is reached, and I see some oars in place and others missing. I have only the tiller to work with. We are now in a thick mist of spray sweeping along with a new gale force wind. Then the nose of the boat is up and the wall is receding, and I pray the river is beneath us as we can only try to keep the boat straight until we settle. I see treetops emerging close to the left and ease over on the tiller.

We are in the river. As quickly as the river rises, the river falls. Then it is as if countless waterfalls are erupting from the flood plains back to the river with its new flood level. I see my sons starting to reorganize oars, and two each side appear and start to pull us towards the centre of the clearway. I see Niomi start to move but still clinging to the deck rail and near frozen with shock. Several men look injured but all are with us.

I do not know if this is all there is to come. I ask Earthkeeper if he can hold the direction while I seek out our condition. We have taken water and two men are injured from broken oars. I set all who can work to bailing water and return to the high point.

The moon shines yellow again with a poorer light, and we continue to pull up river with the current surging in all directions and whirlpools which we are doing our best to avoid. I know not how the water will be at the junction, but feel there will be a return of the surge of water when the great wall eventually peters out.

It must have been a mountain of water that reached the coast to have endured this far inland. I cannot think of the destruction that has happened. I pray to the holy that my daughter who is on high ground be high enough, and I cling to the tiller and hope the worst has passed.

It is only luck that we have survived. What world we have survived for I dare not think. I just focus on the vessel and look to all directions. I ask Earthkeeper if the worst has passed or if more water will come. He says he does not know for certain but thinks that no more will come from down river but floodwaters will soon start to recede. "If this is true", I say, "it will be better to run with the water until the worst passes." He nods.

129

I can see the junction of the great rivers when I sense the danger, and I know the water will come from two directions as well as sides in this area, so reverse our direction and call to the oarsmen to hold steady to the open water. It is soon upon us and they row to help keep us straight. This time it is no bigger than the tidal surge, but when it has passed the current has the strength of the yearly great flood when few boats venture forth.

Now there is a growing mountain of debris coming down. We pull for the tree line. This I know how to deal with, so must find a clear way or flooding creek to tie up in until the daylight arlms and the worst has passed. In the wet season the water would stay for the moons of the rains, but this should not happen. We must rest and hope no more is to come. I see Earthkeeper vomit over the rails then sit with ashen face, showing a depth of weariness on his features. I sense he is more aware of the damage to our world than I can understand. I am a simple man. River men are their boat and family, no more. We are back beyond the bend and I see a small clearing. The water is a little less turgid on the inside of the bend. We move rapidly in, and tie up front and back to tall trees.

Niomi is still in shock. I set the men to bailing and repairing whatever we can. The vessel looks sound with only small items lost off the deck and two splintered oars. One of the injured is working again but favouring a damaged area. The other has lost blood from a gash in his side. I cut sail and cloth to bind him and stem the flow of blood. Earthkeeper takes over, freeing me to check on the declining water level. I must not be caught on submerged material, so lengthen the ropes and allow the boat to swing to deeper, clearer water. There is less debris in the water here. Debris will travel on the fast side of the river and the outside of bends. We only need to keep the boat moving to the clear water as the level drops. I can now see it is dropping far quicker than normal floods. It seems it will return to its normal level long before dawn.

The next arlms of time see us move the boat three times until we are back in the quietening river. I finally have time to get Niomi dry and comfortable. There is some food to eat but she does not want it. I hear her say quietly: "What of my daughter?" I tell her: We should be able to travel tomorrow. The ground of their village is high. There is good hope." Still her face wears the mask of despair. Our sons offer comfort with little result.

Slowly the light of the moon is replaced by the light of dawn that casts a soft yellow glow through the treetops. I quietly offer thanks to the great Spirit. I ask for the guidance of the Earth Mother goddess, our living world, who uses nature to keep the Earth in harmony and balance. Perhaps this time it was out of her control, or perhaps the Earth has been damaged in some way and she has corrected this oversight. The Ancients of the Atlanta Ocean and the Earth priestesses have been our guides for time beyond memory, and I thought the harmony of Earth and humans had been respected by their laws.

130

We pull out and begin to seek our loved ones and the answers, if they are to be given to simple ones such as me. Three arlms see us at the junction of the rivers. No boats have been sighted. No people. Several small river dwelling places are totally destroyed.

As we approach the largest of the river towns this far up river, I see several larger vessels tied to badly damaged facilities and numerous small boats but nothing like the number there normally is. Thank all creation there are many people seemingly working to clear the damage. Finally we are sighted, and much subdued excitement is evident as we pull into dock.

The crowd is growing quickly. I see the elders and several priestesses in the place of honour. The ropes go out and we secure. When the gangplank falls I wait for Earthkeeper to proceed, then gently pull Niomi across the plank.

Both of us are scanning the many faces for the ones we seek. Niomi gasps and grasps my arm, and I follow the direction of her gaze to see our beloved daughter with babe in arms and husband by her side. Ceremony is put aside and the gap closes quickly with the flowing of tears between mother and child. I look to the husband, and he says they were fortunate the water only took the houses and people of the river dwellings. Still, hundreds of bodies have been found and thousands are missing. More are turning up in the river all the time but many will never be found. He says he has lost his brother plus his brother's wife and their three children. About one in three parts of the town has gone but most of the port structure is still standing, being built to withstand annual floods.

One of my sons takes my arm and guides me back to stand quietly and await the audience of Earthkeeper and perhaps priestesses. Soon they signal and I approach and bow my respect. An elderly priestess moves forward to stand by Earthkeeper, and I am informed that a boat must make haste down river to find survivors, especially those who may have survived from the ancient cultures. It is also needed to bring knowledge of the fate of the Earth temples along the river, and seek out the remains of the large settlements in the delta country. She asks how long before I will be ready to go with four passengers. I tell her I would like a day to check the boat and provisions. She looks at Earthkeeper who shakes his head. I hear the words: "You have half an arlm to inform the mothers of your requirements. They shall be delivered immediately and you leave in one and a half arlms. You will carry the sign of the grail –the sign of the holy Spirit, and that of the Earth goddess – controller of Earth, nature and giver of life. Take only the strongest of your crew, the rest will be supplied." I tell her in a shocked voice: "I will take the eldest of my two sons. The other crew are exhausted and probably in shock. They have family to seek up river and in this place. I will need four more oars and six of the strongest men with experience to use them." Then it strikes me and I say: "Another two of the remaining boats should be provisioned and travel behind us for supplies and men if we need them." I see a look of surprise cross her face, then respect. She says: "It is being taken care of."

Boatman I mostly know appear, and the holds are cleared of all that is not fresh and not needed. With hardly a word from myself, new grain maize and food is loaded, fowl, several llamas and more canvas at my request, and several small repairs are carried out. A five-sided star appears at the front of the boat and an equal sided cross at the rear. I seek out and say goodbye to my daughter's husband. The women by now are long gone.

131

Once again I am on the river, this time with a heavy heart and no desire for adventure. Even my son looks solemn. Still, I see in all the features of the men strong determination. I have spoken to them all individually but cannot inform them as to what we will find.

Nightfall sees us far down river now. Boats with desperate survivors have appeared and quietly moved past us. As the day passed they were nineteen in number. The young priestesses signaled all to pass on and we inquired nothing of them and offered nothing of information in return. This is a solemn time. There is no sound from the rainforest; no movement of animal or bird. The bends of the river come and go with little change, except here and there we see large trees in the tops of other trees. We have passed by bodies of both human and beast. Nothing is to be done for them. No progress would be made if we stopped.

Night falls, and I put a sail up as there is a slight breeze and rest four of the oarsmen. We travel slowly through the night My son relieves me and I sleep in exhaustion but with dreams that are full of fear. Several times I awake but exhaustion drags me back to unconsciousness.

In the early arlms of the new day I am on deck and my son sleeps. The day passes. The priestesses help with the food which we humbly receive. There are some damaged dwellings but there is little change, as the settlements are inland on the canals that travel away from the river. Some of these, but I expect most now, are impassable. Fewer boats pass this day, and as the next day comes and goes we see no life. The crew seems set on a task and their spirits are resolute.

On the fourth day I am told to pull into a canal which leads to the first of the sisters' kind. We travel no more than three hundred steps before trees have to be removed. The site is on a rise but it is soon evident, after proceeding on well-covered trails, that only wreckage and few bodies remain. The now familiar growing smell is much stronger here. They recover little, and we are glad to be back in the centre of the huge waterway. It has become a place of preference, as we now know that little, if any, human life has survived.

The further down river we travel the more complete is the destruction. Where there were houses on stilts, there is no sign of them at all, even on higher ground.

By the twelfth day only a few trees are left standing and I have not seen a green leaf for days. It is as if we are in another world. One of the men has cast a line and caught good fish, so I have encouraged it. At least it is one connection to reality and life, plus fresh food.

On day fourteen we notice another profound change as we near the delta country and the place of largest human occupation. It has virtually gone. The sea level has risen and my old knowledge is struggling. The main channel is now larger than ever.

The heat, even in our tropical world, has been intense for days. I look to the sisters to see their wishes, and together we try to plot a course for their holy site, where the largest of buildings, many in stone, once stood. Night comes and we anchor in a backwater. There is still the stench of death but no other sign that life ever existed, only broken timbers floating on the water and amongst the tangled vegetation. Now sea birds are moving overhead and it strikes me that nature will heal itself.

Day fifteen and we search all day for sign of the temple. Where we think it was is now several steps under water. I can see that all feel there is little reason to remain in this area. We anchor again on a backwater near the main channel and I make plans to return upriver on the next incoming tide.

The men are exhausted but all keen to get far from here. All sleep with hardly a lookout, although I suspect the women sleep least. They are great in their losses, as we all are. I give private thanks that my family's small place has survived and pray to return, to rebuild some reason for being, as all my river trading has ceased to exist.

132

Rough hands shake me to awareness. Excited voices fill my ears and even those of the women are louder. Still, I am slow to rise. My eyes follow the excitement and there on the river are four of the great cloud boats and human life. Then I hear a woman give voice: "Poseidon's people. Thank the Earth Mother and holy Spirit that some have survived to keep knowledge and direction alive amongst humankind." They have a way with words.

My mind clears, and I ask my son to pull our vessel into range of the boats so we can extend courtesy and seek their intended direction. I move behind the privacy section and clean my body and change my clothes. I have seen these boats many times over my lifetime of thirty-nine seasons, but never as a boatman would I have had dealings with them. This was for the more complicated and prestigious of my kind. Here now they are all gone, apart from the prestigious ones I carry. So it is up to me to speak with respect for the sisters.

When we are close alongside I call out to the gathered ancients: "I carry the sisters of the Earth Mother to seek the answers of all that has occurred, and we respectfully await your direction." There is movement far above and an old man speaks amongst his kind. Then a woman comes to the rail and calls: "Greetings river people and our respects to all. You will come alongside and the master of your vessel and the representatives of the Mother will come on board." This we do, and once the ladders are lowered I follow two women to the deck of the huge vessel. Once I would have been overwhelmed by this event but, with all that has occurred, my tired mind seems to take all in its stride.

Introductions are brief and people disperse to work. The old man says:

"We are keen to learn how much damage has been done how far inland. If you please you will address the leaders of what we think are the sole remaining people of Poseidon. As far as we know we are all that remain. We have reached out on the airwaves to find these four vessels, and all else is silent. In time we will return to our islands but know that all life is lost." I see tears rolling silently down the cheeks of one of the women. I thought all tears had been shed.

We are taken to a large room towards the stern of the vessel and shown places at a table large enough to seat some twenty people. There are twelve including us three. The woman who speaks first rises to her feet and says: "I am Isis", and she quickly introduces the names around the table: "Amon, Sephron, Juniper, Neptunas, Viracocha, Tefnuth, Osiris and Venusia. We have been chosen to speak for our people who now number seven hundred and twelve. They are mostly men and only nine children. The survivors were only those who were far from the explosion, mostly workers on three trading vessels and one research vessel. We have been given the gift of nineteen women and the few precious children. First we have found each other and now, through you and others, we must find the native people of the Earth's land masses. With respect to these people we must then attempt to establish our destiny."

She asks us who will address them first. I look to the women. My confidence and skills are not for large group speaking. One priestess rises, and Isis says her people have always known of the representatives of the Earth Mother and The Knowledge, legends and ancient truths they have shared with her people. The Mother's priestesses are on all the lands that surround the Atlantians world. Isis says: "Similar beliefs were preserved by a select group of women who are now presumed lost. The city that once stood here has gone with hardly a trace of the fine temple centre of your worship. We are saddened. How far, can you tell us, have the great waves travelled?" She sits and gives the priestess her attention.

The elder of the women now tells it as I have witnessed. She says of her own covens on this side of the landmass, only two outposts remain. To know of others in other lands will take longer. "If your ships travel the seas, your people will know long before us. Vast numbers of people have died on this coast and far inland."

I am asked to speak and can only ask their intentions, if they have thought that far. They say before they can decide they must find a place to stop and gain strength and supplies. Then they will send at least two ships to explore the options, and observe how long this damaged Earth will take to regain her balance and harmony. They say they have come to the great river, as it was felt the best way to the first safe place of recovery. "So we ask of you river man, and your representatives of Earth Mother, permission to proceed until we have achieved the only goal we can reach at this stage. Our men are strong and we bring travellers' knowledge that can help those who we dwell amongst."

The women look to me and I can only stammer "yes" in a dumbfounded way. For such as these to ask of me is beyond my experience. All river people have always considered it an honour if the cloud boats came in for provision or trade. We have always known that the secrets of the soils that grow our food, the canal systems and the raised agricultural regions, is knowledge passed to us from Poseidon's people. This knowledge, until now, has enabled us to exist on the river with large populations. Without Poseidon's people we would have always been scattered tribes at the mercy of the floods of the very seasonal rainforests. These thoughts cross my mind so, to my surprise, I hear my voice stammer out the river people's beliefs and, at the end, give my opinion that all would consider it vital to receive the ocean Ancients into their communities. This is the end of the meeting and all depart.

I see our Earth women speaking with Isis, so wait respectfully by the rope ladders. The three approach me and Isis says: "If it pleases you, the women will continue on your river vessel." Isis then says: "If it pleases you, we will take your vessels in tow when the conditions favour our vessels to travel faster, so all can stay together." This is new to me but something within me tells me this should work.

The days pass quickly and the smell persists but changing. Nature will clean up and rebuild outside of human control. On the last day before we reach my daughter's settlement, the first sign of life appears with the advent of fishermen. The forest is slowly starting to take back its creatures. It is evident that much more activity has occurred, and there are more boats tied up to a tidy dock.

In order for the great vessels to tie up, all boats have to clear. We drop anchor three hundred steps from the dock and pull in and tie up to the vessel that the nine representatives travel on. The day is late so they ask that we precede them and in the morning they will, with my help, speak to the people of the rivers.

The following day brings a gathering of most inhabitants who would never have seen the fair people of the great oceans. Their appearance, possessions and vessels are different to any seen in these parts of the river in memory.

133

My life returns to a more normal state and the elders, Earthkeeper and the Earth priestesses decide on future co-operation with the Ancients. I am relieved to be able to concentrate on my simple life, but on occasion move some of their people. They have lowered their own small boats for transport.

So time passes. Dwellings rise on the areas that were destroyed, and a land community of the Ancients dwells with us. One season passes and the crops in this region start to return to normal, and the hunger with rationing begins to recede. My family always has fish, for my boat has become half fishing vessel as the endless journeys to and from the river delta no longer occur. The season has been considerably warmer and some loss of life has occurred due to heat, especially amongst the older people.

Then one day I am called to the vessel I originally boarded. It is beautiful now. Much work has been done to it. I am directed to the main cabin. Seated at the table are the original nine, plus Earthkeeper and another of his kind, two of the elders and three priestesses. I sit, and feel humbled to be in such company.

Amon talks first. After a brief telling of events from the last seasons, he announces that two of the vessels are to leave within days taking Isis, Juniper, Tefnuth, Neptunas and himself to the areas of the homelands. If nothing remains, then they will travel onwards to the lands of the west. There they will establish the bases for knowledge, memories and the laws of the holy Spirit, on some part of those lands that they hope will be safest from future disaster. Also that Viracocha and the lady Sephron will send explorers into the mountains of the east, to seek out suitable places for our future there. In time Osiris and Venusia will seek to establish a base in the great northern landmass.

Much discussion takes place. Eventually I am asked if I will take my vessel with one other river vessel, and go with one exploring party, while two other such vessels made by the Ancients will travel as far south as possible on this river. I ask for time, as I am becoming old amongst my people. I am past forty seasons now, and to see fifty seasons is rare amongst our people. I say: "If I do not go, the young and strong will serve you better." There is understanding. As I leave I see tears in the eyes of Isis and she surprises me by taking me in her arms. Amon also hugs me briefly. My chest feels heavy. The events that brought us briefly together, all the great loss of life, are more than a human can bear. Amon says: "We must carry the strength of the great survivor Poseidon, to give strength and direction to this brave living Earth."

My son is outside to escort me back to Niomi and family. I empty my heart and tell him of my refusal to go. I tell him I want to keep my family around me and see their children become part of a new, strong, river people. He listens quietly and leaves me with Niomi. Without food I sleep long into the next day. When I rise my wife is sullen, and it emerges our eldest son is to lead the river men with Viracocha.

Now four boats are to be made ready by the ocean men, to be manned by a large party. They are to leave as soon as preparations are complete. This happens in five moons and, with the passing of the annual floods, they depart. Isis and Amon's parties are long gone with three ships instead of two. Lady Sephron has departed, and Osiris and Venusia will leave within one moon. They take the last ship with them. Viracocha leaves with the river men, and the ocean people are no longer a part of our communities.

134

For me there is emptiness. My other son takes control of my boat and I have moved to another residence and spend much time tending a food plot and sitting on a bench by the river. Some of the older men talk with me but strangely talk of the loss from down river is avoided.

It occurs to me one day, as I watch the settlement grow around me, that it is now the working families, simple people, who are doing all the work and planning. There is not so much a loss of leadership but a loss of knowledge. Most who had The Knowledge are gone. The great minds are not here. The Earthkeeper is older than me. The priestesses who look after healing for the people are few and distracted with the survival of their kind.

Occasionally Earthkeeper sits with me. One day I complain that the earth in my garden used to produce vegetables for two crops and now they hardly grow at all. I ask him what is wrong. He simply says that the earth he managed had a balanced internal life, in harmony with the life of the universe and the life force of the Earth, often known as the Earth Mother goddess, preserved by the priestesses.

A young man is sitting on a bench opposite us carving figures out of a piece of wood. I have observed him doing this often. He is one of the quiet ones, the loners, prone to too much thought and not enough work. In fact, I have at times snapped at him to find something to do or someone to help. This I do now, perhaps in anger or disappointment that Earthkeeper does not have the answer for my garden.

This time he does not slink off but looks at his work and ignores me for a long moment. All is silent, which is not uncommon for Earthkeeper and me. Then the young man looks up and we are shocked to see anger on his normally gentle face. He almost explodes. "How dare you old men, and the so-called women of the goddess, fail us as a people and fail all those who have gone before you, and all those who have perished after so much great achievement for so long." We are stunned. Then I hear Earthkeeper's quiet voice ask this youth: "What is it we are to do?" He answers without hesitation. "You should teach the young your knowledge. Take us who are young and strong to re-open one of the canals to the lost river towns, to learn of and reclaim the living nurturing earth that is the great legacy from those who are lost. This is our future".

There is silence for a time, then the old Earthkeeper turns to me and asks if I have the spirit to take him and his new apprentice and any who are willing, on perhaps one last journey into the lost settlements? Something I have not felt for seasons stirs in my chest. I can hardly speak but manage to nod. I ask the youth if he can find others who would help in such an obscure task. He simply states "stay" and is gone. Earthkeeper and I look at each other and I recognize the presence of hope and purpose that I thought was lost.

Before three-quarters of an arlm passes he is back with other youth, about seventy young women and men, and still they come. Leaders emerge from amongst them and it becomes obvious that they have discussed and planned amongst themselves for a time.

As the days pass what is needed is gathered, then I am back in my boat with Earthkeeper, going up river where I thought I would never go again. Only some of the fishermen of our people have gone up river since the great flood. There are sixteen assorted boats, and they tell me one hundred and seventy-two people. Every vessel is overloaded.

One day brings us to the canal that is sought, and the next quarter moon sees it opened up again. There, displayed where there is little evidence of human presence existing here, is lush growth in the still vibrant and living earth. Before the end of the moon, it is evident these people and their descendants will reclaim much of this vital living part of their heritage.

335

I feel pleased to have been involved and, on my departure from the area, the young man approaches me shyly and hands me a package. He simply states: "This is living earth to give you health in old age."

For two seasons my garden flourishes, but my teeth fail me and my health passes in other ways. Then Niomi dies and I realize how much a part of my life she was and my will for living departs. Then eventually my life leaves this body of forty-seven seasons.

Life from Earth

135

I am moving now, across distances well understood for longer than the rise and fall of billions of universes. The consciousness of our kind has penetrated to beyond the boundaries of human imagination. I pass the lights of great clusters at infinite distance, until I see the light of the universe which holds the spiral galaxy called the Milky Way. My speed must slow if my journey will take me back to the star cluster called Seven Sisters and to the tiny yellow star with its pretty blue planet called Jura.

I am the spirit of the female to be called Hellan Assan. I am, like all spirit of this species and countless others throughout many universes, connected to the laws of the most complex intelligence known, the laws of the Spirit.

So it is that, at the point of conception, I flash into this universe, galaxy, solar system and the womb of my mother, to depart from conscious knowledge of the Spirit and, once again, learn or lose the lessons that the physical birth can bring.

I open my eyes to see, touch, hear and learn, and to be once again part of a species that has dwelt in harmony with the mother planet and its two moons and sister planet Jana. They have nurtured our species for seventeen million years.

Here, with only the teachings of our spirit guides and the wise who dwell amongst us, I will live and die this life-time and many others in the passage of time until, at last, 1,947 years before the time of writing, I am born once again to the planet third from the sun. I am born into a struggling infant species of humanity, into southern Gaul.

The life of change

136

My eyes open to the sound of moving bodies. The alcohol from the night before draws a spear through my temples and I endeavour to rise to gather my appearance in order to make parade with the rest of the legion. Cold water helps. So too perhaps the taunts of my soldier friends who I think look little better than I feel. Perhaps this is to be expected on only the second night in the land they call Britannia.

Two hundred and seventy-five ships traversed the ocean crossing from Gaul. They stretch in an arc up the coast for many leagues, most on anchor but some on the beach. As I watch I can see the sails of more vessels in the distance, and see many making ready to return for more weapons of war and supplies to back up the legions. Although I am no Roman citizen, it gives me a feeling of pride to be a part of the greatest force of men to be moved, perhaps seventeen thousand in all and another thousand or more men, women and wagons arriving within the arlms ahead.

We have formed into lines and are moving to higher ground. For the first time in two days I come face to face with the presence of the Britons. From this position, for miles in two directions, are fields of barley and wheat. Further out are the dwellings; round houses of home and grain food reserves, and fences to hold in stock. Close in are only the charred remains of where dwellings once stood. I can see some evidence of crops that have burnt a little, but the command has timed our arrival so crops would not burn but will, in the weeks ahead, reach the maturity our great mass of people will require. Such are the first spoils of war. People and animals will come later. I suspect they will be preparing to attack us if they dare, in the days or weeks to follow.

Our scouts have long been amongst them and will guide us to the greatest of their kingdoms. Our authority will quickly take hold, as it did in my native Gaul some seventy years previously. Never before has such a power as Rome existed. Still, some of the older veterans say these Celtic Britons fight bravely, and can travel swiftly with chariots and fine war-horses.

I, like my other young friends in the legion, am eager to fight and find out if there are spoils of war in this land; the most important being the women of the tribes. We jokingly say, with some truth I think, that they will need Roman lances at their hearths when we have put their men to our swords. The sooner the better I say. My body is tired of the trollops that follow the legions from campaign to campaign. Still, with wine in my body all women are desirable. The trollops will be arriving with the later ships but it has been weeks since I have felt the thrust of my male lance. So this day I march with eager step towards the spoils of war. They can only retreat so far. We will have our way.

The end of the second day sees us delay for three days in a position by water that gives us strength. The supply wagons, both Roman and Briton, have arrived and our bellies are full. Some fresh meat is arriving, and I presume the plans of the coming conquests are being refined.

I think a major example will be set for all native Britons. The futility of resistance, I think, will be demonstrated by hitting them at their strongest point, either killing regional kings or forcing them to submit, preferably the latter. Then perhaps, as within most parts of the Roman Empire, they shall pay their taxes and evolve on the road to Roman citizenship and strengthen the boundaries of the great.

We are on the move again, going west towards the place of the setting sun and following a strong river on land much traversed by Celtic chariots. The land is beautiful. There are forests of oak and elm, all rich in the leaves of early summer. The days are long, reaching for the summer solstice. These are good days to conquer new land.

This land feels good to me. All that fill the eyes from river to high hill, from flower to trees, fills me with a kind of familiar joy that confuses me. This I would not discuss with Marcus and Amianos. They say only women think like this, and those soldiers who seek the company of young boys in the sight of the trollops.

137

We have excitement. Marcus is talking to Natalinus who is gesturing toward the rear of the column. I am included now in a battalion of some three hundred men moving rapidly towards supply wagons where smoke rises. As we enter the rear supplies, I can see men wounded and dead. Two wagons are burning and I hear several have gone with a group of women. We form up and I thank the goddess Isis that I am three from the front. The company converges on the forest, and I see a rain of arrows and hear the dreaded sound as they strike our upturned shields. Some men fall but I stand firm and close to Marcus and Amianos. When we reach the forest the formation becomes difficult, with still only glimpses of the enemy and all out of reach of spear or sword.

This is no way to fight. The enemy is to be confronted. I hear the command to drop back towards the rear, and on reaching open ground see the legion has converged on the supplies. Then I hear sounds of fighting further out in the forest. Then all is quiet. Several arlms pass before a large column of Romans emerge in formation from the trees. Some are wounded and several Britons captive. The column had moved to the rear of the Britons who have faced their first taste of Roman steel. They are not defeated.

The next day sees the supplies included amongst a more compact column. As the sun reaches its high point, we enter the first sizable Briton settlement. We see stone foundations for the first time on many of the dwellings, and a layout of walkways close to the river. The river is obviously used for trade as there are many facilities for boats which are not much in evidence. The people have gone but the buildings have not been burnt. They are, in general, well made.

The next four days are spent here, and some seven hundred men are put to bringing logs from the forest some two leagues away. A large stockade soon surrounds five sound buildings on the highest of ground south-east of the river. On the fifth day my muscles are in much pain from the carrying of logs.

This day sees us move south-west, leaving behind some three hundred men in the first of Britannia's Roman forts and administration centres. The area is now named Londinium. There are rumours that a large force of Britons is forming at the greatest of the tribal centres some six days march to the south-west.

Woods and fields of grain and animals cover much of the country. Some is damaged in our passing but we have been told to leave all intact where possible. Hunters have had some success in gaining fresh meat but at a loss, as ambush is becoming more prevalent as we progress.

I have a strange and continuing sense of familiarity, especially on about day four when we top a hill to view one of the great places of worship of the people of the Earth goddess. This I know is so, as it is also so in my native Gaul. The rituals have changed now but still are told in legend and treated with great awe. The priestesses, who are now fewer in number than the druids, are still treated with respect in Gaul and I expect in Britannia also. It will not surprise me if they share the memories.

The scene before us stops all that behold. Slowly the soldiers line up and come to rest on the summit of the three hills. Then silence falls. There in the valley lies a great ring of stones with two smaller inner rings. The shadows of the stones fall from the lowering sun, forming a connection to many of the stones. Great avenues lead away to other sites and a huge artificial hill. At this moment, Rome is not the conqueror but the power that fears the spirits of those whose knowledge stretches back into antiquity.

Images flash into my head as clear as if they were living people. I do not understand this place, but it is as if the images in my mind are my people and my ceremonies. I see great walls of ice where there are none. Suddenly I am aware of hands tugging my arms, and voices coming at me as if out of the mist of another world. Then my friends' faces appear again. The words form: "Alban, are you ill?"

We are moving on. Amianos raises his cloak and wipes the sweat from my face, then shoves me roughly and says: "Fear not the spirit of the dead. Our holy men will give sacrifice and our gods will protect us while we ask to honour the creators of these people's ancestors. Our gods will tell of the great honour Rome will bring upon this new Roman land." Still, the faces and images remain bold in my mind. This land feels like my land and the spirits of these ancestors seem as my people. My mind is young for such thoughts, and I can see the contempt of lack of understanding on the faces of my friends Marcus and Amianos.

Dark falls and the tents rise for soldiers for sustenance. My cloak provides my tent and this soil my blanket. When sleep comes so do the figures; the same figures as those that entered my conscious mind. When I wake I am left with only questions and a feeling of strangeness in a land that has become familiar. I will tell no one of these thoughts. A soldier lives as one amongst those that are to live and be victorious. For my conscious mind to dwell amongst what I can only believe are the dead, will place me amongst those that lose the coming battles. My friends and legion will see it the same way, and at the very least drum the living dead out of the legion. In this land that would mean almost certain death to a Roman from Gaul.

The next day we move south down a river valley and camp there for the night. Reports come in from scouts of another stone temple not far to the east. Part of me wants to explore these new sensations, and the other wants to go to war and wenches.

138

The feelings of army are high but things are changing. Scouts dare not leave the main army for none are returning. On every hill-top, horsemen and chariots are a common sight now. We have few horsemen, with about half pulling wagons. Many of the other horses are for generals and officers of the three legions on march.

The Briton arrows fall but are having difficulty in finding the range, as any forest passed is penetrated by a wall of legionaries with others skirting the outside. The Briton warriors are building up but at safe distance.

Our general is obviously aware of our destination and is taking the fight to a specific place. We bivouac another two nights; then word comes down to Natalinus that a highly fortified fiefdom will be reached this day. Our spies have informed us we are to be confronted by a large group of fighters. They will this day attempt to halt the Roman Empire. That must be a feat of courage that would upset sound sleep if I were on their side.

This being my first great battle my stomach is in knots. Gone are the dreams and familiarities. This landscape does not seem familiar. All is replaced with a sense of fear and excitement. From my position well back in the ranks, it is hard to see the landscape ahead. The rain is falling hard now and the wind growing stronger. This is not expected but can happen summer or winter in Britannia. It is depressing, as my feet sink deep into the mud from the many trampling feet of those before me.

Soon it is night and we bivouac, but word quickly spreads that the battle is at hand and a more permanent site seems to be taking place. This does not make sense to me. Some sleep comes, then I am raised to stand guard with many soldiers. Then, with a lull in the rain, the lights of many fires show up on a hill site some leagues away.

I am still on guard as the day dawns on the shape of a massive hill, with company emerging from the mist of rain. Wooden fences circle earthen ramparts all the way around the fortress, with no visible entrance. On the top I see many timbered dwellings. This is a large town by Briton standards. It is mid morning when, after much parading, I retire to rest and hear the gossip.

It appears the armies of the Britons have moved into this fortified town. Even to me it looks a hard battle to cross these formidable barriers. Still nothing happens on this day and for many to come, except conditions improve regardless of the continuing rain, for we are in a tent now and can sleep dry. Morale is also improving somewhat but no one seems to know when the attack will take place. There are Britons in force in the distance, still holding their place.

There is no excitement until on day eleven when the second legion arrives led by Titus Flavius Vespasian. Many catapults take position to accompanying rumours.

139

Still the days pass. The rain stops and the sun shines. We parade and allow no Briton to enter or leave the site. No Roman fires a shot, except into the accompanying bordello women. Some of my Roman pay enters the lifestyle of the women of the night. It is quickly over to the jeers of my accompanying friends and I regret my emptier money pouch. It seems to me the women are the winners of these brief battles, even though they receive my young lance.

Then the wind begins to blow and the day is warm. All soldiers are formed up and I think, at last, the time has come. The wind is fierce by the time the sun passes overhead. The catapults are released and I see a rain of fire rise towards the fortress pinnacle. At the same time I see the heavy mechanical cross bows that shoot a small spear release fire towards the wooden barricades. Then I understand. As fire takes hold, the inferno from the catapults continues to rain hell. The wind turns the town from timber to a fiery red with huge clouds of black smoke. The voices of human suffering can now be heard. In the back of my mind is a dread and sadness. The timber walls of the outer barriers are burning now. This Briton fortress is beginning to look more vulnerable by the arlm. Flaming arrows are falling like red rain on the hilltop.

At last we are moving, but the attack is brief and only the first of the earthen ramparts is breached before we withdraw. As night falls, the camp routine returns. There is more excitement amongst the ranks and a few Roman dead and wounded, but not my friends.

The following day sees much parading and a change in the weather, as dark clouds give way to ferocious rain. I am glad when my time for food and rest arrives, but am barely dry before I am back in formation again. It seems these Britons are to see the might of Rome without further attack. Perhaps they will surrender.

On day four after the attack, the catapults start again. This time there are few fires. There is not much left to burn, only some of the perimeter stockades. Roman arrows are raining down now and I find it hard to believe there will be any place for Britons to escape.

On day six we attack from the south and west, using only about half our force. After several arlms it is clear our attack is not intended to take the fort. We are drawing on the resources of the Britons. The rest of the legion will attempt entry at the main entrance to the east. I am glad I am not there. Romans near me have taken arrow and some spear, but not many. Then resistance seems to stop and we are able to proceed up the ramparts without assault.

I am near the rear and one of the last to cross the remains of the third timber barrier. What I see is nothing like the smell we were aware of from the camp. Here it is putrid. Bodies have been heaped up. I now see fighting is taking place, but the Britons are fully enclosed by ever increasing numbers of Romans. This battle will be over before I use my sword or lance. Good enough for the hero in me. I will live to be a brave man another day. My words can tell of heroic deeds and my body stays in one piece.

The battle finishes. I cannot see, but word comes back that there is no Briton male, young or old, left alive; only women and not many of them. This does not surprise me, for the bodies of mostly men were in the piled up horror behind me. It is not long before I am dispensed from the battle to camp.

There were no spoils for the men of this conquering force, as nearly every dwelling was burnt to the ground. Amianos and Marcus are not harmed but many Romans died in the main assault. I feel curiously low. This, my first battle victory, does not seem overly glamorous.

Two days hence we set forth again. It is said that some of the captives were set free to spread the word of the futility of resistance.

140

In the coming moon we move quickly from Britannia strongholds to a great island in the south. Only the island puts up a fight but even they are quick to capitulate. The killing of Romans is little and even Britons are mostly spared. Many slaves are taken, and by the end of the second moon young women are made available to our section of the legion. I must admit life is good and the promise of Briton's rewards has been passed to my hearing. The crops are being harvested and much meat and fruit is available to us. Apart from all the marching and mostly sleeping in the open, the feeling amongst legionaries is high.

I feel Roman for the conquering but an uneasy part of me, the Gaul, understands the damage to the pagan spirit. Then one day as I sleep, in dream it dawns upon me that I have seen no sight of priest or priestesses; the druids of Gaul and Briton are not evident, nor the women of the covens. On waking it dawns on me that at least one major part of these people is withdrawing as we advance. The Gaul in me is not willing to discuss this, as I have seen enough of the loss of my people's beliefs from my own native land.

Then one night towards the end of the fourth moon in the Roman year 751, strong alcohol loosens my tongue and I mention to Marcus the suspicions that rest with me. I find it hard to describe my feelings when next day, with pats on my back, I am brought to the attention of the command of our section. Before I know it most of my thoughts are pried from me. I am young, and resistance as I face these great powers removes my strength of Gaulish loyalty.

The situation turns from bad to worse as captive slaves are brought in for interrogation. They are three women and two men, and the horror that follows I witness. From the painful deaths of one woman and a man, the story begins to emerge. I am aware of it, as much of the dialect is common to the language of the druids that I understand. This is the information that emerges. All of high coven and every druid have withdrawn north-west and with many warriors and some chieftains. We have conquered the lands but not the bravest of the people of Britannia, and few of those strong in the ancient beliefs that are shared by most of my heritage. I am careful to wear no expressions, except gratitude when command releases me with brief compliment.

Once again I have mixed feelings and much dread, for those dead and tortured were directly my fault. As time goes by these people have not increasingly felt like my enemy. At times of aloneness I wish I was collecting grain with the simple folk of my home village.

The sun is low on the following day when they send for me. I am stunned the great Vespasian and my commander, Quintus Natalinus, are both present. My blood freezes when, after some discussion, Natalinus turns to me and states: "You will transfer to the second legion under Gnaeus. You are to be part of a small command that will disguise as Britons and venture into the unconquered north-west. It is necessary we discover the depth of strength in the withdrawals you have made us aware of." Apart from fear, my first thought is to request the company of my close friends, Marcus and Amianos. Thankfully my mouth is clamped shut to stop the trembling of my upper lip. The friendship would end very quickly.

There is a small change to my tunic, but to my displeasure a bow and quiver of arrows and short sword are my new armours. They are quick to train me with two other transferred men who speak the native language well, and only speak it in my presence. This is another of my new blessings; a third language. Small thanks that it has many similarities to much I know. I learn quickly. It is very obvious what will depend on it, and I do not mean the welfare of the Roman Empire. The torture I have witnessed will be nothing to that given to Roman spies behind enemy lines. I have gone from peaceful nobody in the rear of the legion where I would have stayed for several campaigns and longer if I could have managed, to hero in the commandos of the most dangerous section of the most vulnerable legion. On second thought I do not want the company of Marcus as this was his idea, which he has bragged of extensively while he congratulated me on what he sees as my aspiring fortunes.

To add to the difficulties, I have to be keen and pleased at the opportunities presented to me. I have seen Gnaeus look closely at me, studying the thin veneer for weakness to show its ugly head. On one occasion I saw him turn from me and make comment to his aide, then they both erupted in raucous laughter. I had no doubt I did not want to know the detail of their humour. It is bad enough that I supply the material of mirth. I am filled with resentment for the predicament I am in.

141

Departure day, and the time of leaving is not known to me but the moon is full and high in the sky, so I presume it is close to midnight. There is no wind and no rain. I would prefer there was no moon. We would travel less distance but the multitude of Britons watching for such as us would not see our departure or direction.

To my amazement the light of a new day dawns without my body taking an arrow. Cover is sought in forest not far from water, and the day passes slowly with no movement or sound. The legionaries seem quietly excited by the journey ahead. They have knowledge of the location of various western covens. They intend to violate these women and places; to learn from the least dangerous where the most dangerous are to be found. I have not been told if we are to take on the might of the angriest of the Briton druids and warriors. Perhaps they think I might desert. I think I may die of fright.

I have made it clear that the women they seek will be well guarded and more than capable of sending arrow as a reception to our advance. To this I am informed that they would not kill one of their own, as we are made out to be. So I informed them men do not enter holy ground of the covens uninvited. They are aware of this, and hope to separate one or more of the women in order to learn more of their required duty. The greatest amount of money of all, a Roman talent, would not persuade me that this is a good idea. Still, I have learnt that, if we survive this endeavour, we are to be paid one hundred sestertii each. This amounts to more than the annual pay of a Roman foot legionary. It gives me an extra reason to be careful, and try and avoid the heroics at all costs.

Five days pass and the nights are growing slightly darker. I am glad to hear them say we have located the coven we seek. Five Britons have died in two ambushes to achieve this knowledge. My companions are effective in gaining information from captives and have disposed of all swiftly: two children, two women and one man. The man supplied most of the information to save women and children to no avail. All lie buried in shallow graves.

Not long after first light we have located what we think are all the guards, a considerable number of men and women numbering some one hundred or more all up.

With the fall of night we move in close on the heavily timbered side of a small stream. It is well-guarded but we have managed to move past five guards. As we do so, six of ours stay and train weapons on the direction guards will come if alerted. Luck holds. Two women are bathing and filling water bags in the fading dusk; one fully naked and the other half dressed when we strike. Both fall. They are probably unconscious. They are gagged and placed on a simple platform made ready to move them swiftly out of range. The entrance to the coven is narrow; that was their weakness.

Dark falls and we slowly move well beyond their perimeters. A part of the night, or all of it, will pass before probable pursuit. Even I am feeling relief that our life is still with us. We move well and, after some distance, what is left of the moon rises to speed us to what seems like a safe daytime retreat.

There the interrogation starts. I cannot see the women very clearly and no torch can be lit. Things go gently for a start; persuasion rather than torture. I know that will come later, as will the pleasure these holy women will give before their deaths. For many reasons the Gaul in me is once again uneasy about all this. I have knowledge of what these priestesses represent: the memories, spirituality and the healing knowledge they possess. I can think of no way to help. A wrong word from me and my life will be worth less than the captives. As they hold knowledge that is required, while this information has value they may live.

There seems to be a leader of the two and, after a brief time, she offers some knowledge. I suspect, as it comes too willingly, it will be wrong. She says the covens do not know the ways of war and are not aware of where the main forces are gathered, if indeed, there are main forces. She says if warriors have moved back, they will have spread out amongst the other tribes as the druids have done. This, she says, she is not sure of.

Then the one who speaks has no more to say and is bound and gagged. At her feet the other is spread out on the ground, also gagged. Impatience grows and soon the women are swiftly in use. Whatever the plan was, lust for flesh soon altered that. My stomach is not in this, so I am easily positioned to wait my turn. Soon I can wait no longer and, for fear of life, take my place on top of one. The others are starting again. My body will not respond so I go through the motions and I am glad of the dark. When free I move away far enough and feel the vomit burst from my body. It is unexpected. This is one of the rewards my young warrior mind bragged of achieving with wine and song in many a camp. Now the connection I feel to these people has placed me, and definitely others, in fatal danger. The images of faces and places are back in my head. I can almost hear voices of spirits crying out in my mind. This pressure only adds to the dread.

With lust satisfied one is bound again, and the torture of she who had the least to say starts. Although gagged, it is not hard for the other to observe the pain inflicted while the agony is muffled. I know now, if I could, I would kill all these Roman colleagues to save the lives of these suffering beings that the ghosts in my head say are all too familiar.

142

Within a brief period we have learnt the whereabouts of a force of warriors to the west. The word is discussed, and it is decided that we will scout this force then return to inform the command. The sword is drawn to dispatch the women and, before I can stop myself, my mouth is at it again. "The command will require more knowledge from them, and they still have much pleasure to give and value as slaves." Faces turn to me, some with surprise and the women with a look that I could only call bewilderment; no hope or relief. They are beyond that. Still, it is discussed and eventually, without my input but to my relief, I and one other are left to guard and kill the instant any discovery occurs. The women, still bound, will require little care.

They move off in the early dusk and my companion and I settle in to this duty. The one I now call Blue Circle, because of a mark on her forehead, is chosen by my colleague and his suggestion for me is clear. He is quick to take his pleasure. I lead the other a short distance away but again my heart and body are not in it. I make her as comfortable as possible, and try not to hear the brutish performance of the legionary. Before long he thrusts me aside and it is the turn of the other. This is their fate.

Time passes and he drags her over and deposits her beside Blue Circle. I imagine it is over and suggest we take turns to guard and get some sleep. To this he heaps scorn, and I remember he was one who showed the most amount of suspicion on my reasons for saving the women. Then he begins to torment them; first with words, then by tightening their bonds and inflicting pain for no reason at all.

An anger such as I have never known has been slowly taking the place of the coward in me. Something snaps and my dagger goes deep into his body. Then his throat is cut. The only regret I feel this instant is that he will not suffer long. Then recognition of my position strikes me. No plan at all. I realize if I free the women they will have me killed before I retrace my steps; probably also the rest of the troop before they return with the information.

It is some time before I decide what best to do and take my chances. Well aware that, regardless of what happens my life is in great danger, and in broken language, I am able to get my message across. I tell them: "I care not what happens to the Romans for I am Gaul, and their ways of defiling your memories and beliefs has restored something that is deep inside me. If you give me your consent that you will try and leave me to my own resources, I will free you to warn your people so they can pursue and destroy the Romans when they return to this site. You must drive my dagger into my leg, a wound that is enough to slow me but still give me a chance of survival."

They consent and I free the elder and, with sword held on her stomach, pass her my dagger and tell her to drive the knife into the muscle of the lower leg. She is swift then moves clear of the sword. The dagger frees the other and without a word they disappear into the dark. My fate is in their hands and with the Earth Mother and the great Spirit. I do not like my chances.

The clothes of the dead Roman bind my wound, and I follow the moon towards the legion I have just dishonoured. It would be impossible to explain the dread. No guilt; just fear and now pain. I move off hoping to get some distance, but aware that if the women have chosen to end my life they will send Britons after me.

When light comes I find water, clean the wound and take cover. Soon exhaustion takes over and sleep arrives with all the dread anew in my nightmares. As the afternoon arrives a new stiffness of leg makes me aware that my chances are slimmer still. I drink and eat the last of my food. I am now sorry for the wound, but I could think of no reason why I would have been separated from the legion when they met their fate. If they, or any of them, arrive back it will make no difference if I survive the journey.

As night nears I see I am not alone, so I presume my end has come. As they near, the threat does not emerge. They are one druid and two women. One I see has the same blue circle tattooed on her forehead. I do not draw my bow, as it is obvious they could have had my life by now.

No description can give justice to what followed but I found myself at a small farmstead, cleaned, fed, and wound bound with a small poultice. Three days pass with hardly a word spoken to me and no answers to my questions. Then one morning they were gone and the farmstead deserted. They left some food, water and change of dressing in a bag.

The next day I set off again, still slowly. I lose track of how many days pass. Thanks to the holy people the wound is healing and I am able to avoid people, though they are scarce. This is like a no man's land. Nearing the boundary of the conquered lands, I find all dwellings deserted with only a sighting of two old people at one farm. If I arrive and my colleagues survive, I have a story which hopefully will save my life.

I am moving with the aid of a tree limb cut to shape to support that side of my body. The days pass and I move closer; losing weight and eating poorly now.

The Romans find me before I see them, and before long I am fed and in front of Titus Vespasian, aware that I am the only one to return. I presume they met the fate my confused, but not so young any more, emotions tell me.

I tell that I was wounded when we took prisoners, and it was decided I would slow the operation and was to wait for their return. Seven days passed and they failed to return, so I forced an old couple to give food, shelter and healing herbs for my wound. Then I returned. It is a simple story. I told the command the news the women had given freely about movements of druid, priestess and warriors, adding that a force had gathered.

143

My wound was slow to heal and a small limp remained. It was enough to ruin my career in the Roman legions which I no longer had stomach for. I had become quiet and depressed. In no time I found myself without friends and was soon discharged from the legion. I never saw the promised sestertii but was given a small farm with a slave and enough money and seed to make a start. It was north-west of Verulamium which, in time, became the region known as Catubellauni.

After some years I prospered with the earth knowledge of Gaul and Roman help. Slowly recognition became mine and a simple Briton wife bore two children.

The years passed without great events. Marcus and Amianos called and once again became friends. I could now see Marcus as both a curse and my saviour. Perhaps back then I would not admit it with wine in my belly but the farming life was far more suitable than that of heroic warrior.

The war became difficult, as frontier lands without established governments are often hard to stabilize quickly. The Britons learned to fight on their own terms, and made much of the land to north and west outside of Roman control; the country being wilder and the Briton chariots fast and light. They attack with speed from cover and withdraw to disperse. If the army advances, the people vacate the farms and settlements as they come.

The losses caused by the Roman legions have been so great that the years have been spent introducing the Latin gods, language, and government to a partly accepting people. Basilicas have gone up in seven towns and many fine villas cover the landscape. The Britons have taken much of the refinement of Roman life to heart. The emperor Claudius landed in the early days and his name has become vilified with a temple in Camulodunum. My household has a small shrine to Isis, and it is still the ancient beliefs that are our private journey.

Suetonius is now governor of Britannia; an admirable soldier sent to advance the boundaries of the settled lands. Still, the loss of life of Roman soldier and family near what I have long called 'the no man's land' is not encouraging to settlers. Few families settle, and then mostly Britons with doubtful allegiance to Rome. To survive they will definitely be paying homage to the commando warriors from the outlands.

144

One day, nineteen years after my release from the army in the Roman year 770, and in my thirty-sixth year of living, a runner arrives at our villa. He has come from Verulamium with horse covered in sweat. When he finally speaks slowly, I hear to my astonishment that an army of Britons led by one female queen has sacked the capital and beheaded all citizens. They are marching on Londinium and Verulamium and have been joined by another large force of Britons, also led by one I know as Queen Prasutagus from the lands east of Verulamium.

I ask: "What has caused this uprising from the settled lands and brought so many Britons together?" The answer comes as no surprise. Suetonius has ordered the death of every leader and believer in the old ways, and sent the largest force since the invasion, ten thousand comprising two legions, to the holiest of Britannia sites; the holy island and stronghold of the druids. It is rumoured that hardly a druid survives. The women of the old ways have sent their covens far and wide. This new force has gathered under the rule of high priestess Boudicca and Queen Cartimandua.

I am informed we are to send all able bodied men to fight under the control of Suetonius. With heavy heart I have much concern, as my land is not far off the route from Verulamium to the way the armies would travel to the lands of the holy island. I gather my people but the servants are going nowhere (there are no slaves). The decision is made easy for me. From a vantage point two hills away, I see what looks to be an entire Roman legion heading north-west. Word comes that they are going to meet the two legions now desperately heading south-east, to join forces and rout the Britons. Another legion of five thousand is to link up. I know not where they come from.

I have dispatched two servants by horse to follow the progress and report back. Several of the Briton farmers have come to my villa, probably for safety. We are pleased to have them. Before night I am informed of the worst possible news. The Roman legion has formed in a valley less than one quarter of an arlm away by horse. The Britons have routed the other legion and are moving in on the Roman position.

There is now constant movement of men and some women passing our farm, going to join the uprising. We are lucky so far that they are single-minded and have not stopped to loot or burn Roman style farmsteads. I presume this will happen once their victory is complete, as the numbers seem to tell is likely. Word comes back to me that the legions to the north are still four days away at least. If Suetonius can hold until the legions arrive, he has hope.

The next day at mid morning, the distant sound of human voices comes over the hills. The battle has begun. My comfort and wealth has come from Rome. This day does not bode well. I am glad to be out of it but have all preparing only the bare essentials to make good our withdrawal. I know not where; perhaps to the coast. At the first sign of Rome's defeat, the scouts are to make haste and warn us out of here; at least my wife and children. Even if Rome wins, the retreating Britons will be a danger.

There is an area of deep wood and rocky outcrop just south-east of my farm. I decide that, before the worst happens, it is best to send wife and children plus one old male servant there now. The instructions are, if necessary, to stay put for up to one week then, if we do not come, to make their way to the coast and try and board ship for Gaul. There are many tears on the face of Sasha my wife and my children but I can see much relief that they are going. Well before the sun is overhead they have departed.

The noise of the battle is less now. The cries for blood and victory did not last long. The sounds, though dim, are perhaps more ominous.

I can see my horses with servants now coming at full speed. The look on their faces is worry. Then the words come once I can stop their cries. "We must get out of here. The Romans have won. There were ten Britons to every Roman. They attacked, with the wagons of thousands of women and many children behind their lines. The Romans formed in a formation like many spears. As the Briton army neared, Roman machines let loose spear-like arrows, tearing the shields apart and impaling many Britons. The Roman lines held and then slowly advanced over a carpet of dead. As the Britons fell, the next in line were held in place by those behind. Eventually when all was hopeless the Britons tried to flee, only to be caught up by their women, wagons and children. The mounted Romans swept down upon them and the slaughter of men, women and children is taking place as we speak."

Mounted riders are passing my farm now, some with women and children aboard. We are to stay no more but flee as fast as we can move, for life definitely depends upon flight. All in the path of this retreat will perish or enter slavery. I tell the servants to go to the safe harbour of my family's location, but the look on their faces tells me they will travel far by nightfall. Within moments only one servant and myself are left. We mount the horses left for our escape and depart. As I leave I can see many people fleeing towards the farm. The battle is over but mine is perhaps just beginning. Only the revenge is to come.

Within half an arlm I am with our people. Part of me is relieved that they are alone in this place. It is still two arlms until dark. If we survive until tomorrow, things will look a little better. My body is sweating and my hands are shaking, still I am not a warrior.

Before nightfall, seven more have joined us. They tell us they are from farmlets not far away. They are recognized, which adds to my comfort, so more branches are felled to cover a larger area amongst the rocks. No fires are lit. Cold food, water and fear are, at the moment, all we have left. Blankets are passed around and my wife and children sleep under the cart, huddled together to avoid the cold.

We decide to place guards and, if lone soldiers approach, they will be killed. If worse happens, there will be little the guard can do but warn us of approach. I take my turn first and then again before first light.

145

As the sun rises I can see smoke in several directions. I cannot tell if my villa has gone but I fear the worst. The day passes slowly with the only plan to stay put. That evening the decision is made that two others and I, all heads of farms, will cover the distance to each of our dwellings, allowing us to return here if possible by first light. We sleep, as the others have taken guard in our place.

The first farm is deserted and burnt to the ground. So too appears the second, apart from the granary and, as we slowly inspect the building, a slight noise is heard and a woman and child are dragged from amongst the remaining bags of grain. She is quick to tell us she was lucky to flee the onslaught and is hoping to get away soon, but the leg of her child is injured so movement can only be a little each night. The Romans seem to have stopped the pursuit. I think Suetonius will wait for the two legions to arrive from the north, before they return to Londinium and the other major centres.

We leave the woman to her fate and move on to my place, the closest to where I presume the Romans will have camped. The smoke of many fires warns us that all is not deserted at the house. Leaving the horses in trust with one man, two of us proceed on foot. As I reach the top of the second hill, looking down on the roadway I see the legions have moved south, away from the death of the battlefield. A vast area is covered with a well-established Roman camp. My colleague will come no further but I must see what remains, so we return to horses and separate.

I move quickly in a wide circle to miss the camp and go to the far side of my farm. There I leave my horse and keep low to approach the rise through the forest. In the dark of the trees I do not see them and, as I look down on my home of eighteen years, I hear movement behind me and turn to the command of "yield or die". "I am Alban Ulpius, returned to seek the destiny of my farm and home after leaving to see to the safety of my family."

Within moments I am looking at the much older face of my second commander Gnaeus and, to my astonishment Marcus, my old friend. Both are sitting in the position of privilege at my place of eating. I am quickly identified and questioned on my activities. I tell them my family is travelling to the villa of a relative, and I am told that there is much danger on that road and all roads that the defeated have fled down. Then I am informed that my house is needed by the command for the near future, and I will be given tent accommodation in the field and to await any further questions that may come my way. I suppose I should be grateful to these men that my house is still standing, though I feel an inner anger that little respect is shown me.

Marcus does pat me on the back as he directs me towards the door, but before we depart Gnaeus stops me with the words: "I remember you were the one who first brought the importance of the spiritual bond these people have with the old ways to Roman attention. It has since become one of the main hurdles to the domination and transformation of the Britannia way. I seek your opinion Alban." I am back in front of my table. This time I am offered a chair and wine is placed before me, my wine I do not doubt. I also doubt they eat any food that is not of my property. I am still in some danger but older and harder than the boy who once trembled long ago.

I am told Boudicca and those they most seek seem not to be amongst the dead, so the task is still ahead to round up those who are most sought after. "You have experience of spying from the heart of these people. We intend to send many capable people to infiltrate the tribes, until we find and destroy this woman and the last of her covens, and any druids who may have slipped through our web. If this infiltration takes a year, so be it. If it takes twenty years, so be it. The operation will be ongoing, both here in Roman territories and all other affected lands." I say: "I wish to preserve my property and family rights. How long will I be needed?" To which I am told: "Your property will be tended, your family protected, and you will be required for as long as it is felt to be of benefit."

I have gone a full circle, but older now and still with the limp. This time I at least observe that Marcus has a look of concern, even worry for my predicament. After some discussion when I give no opinion on where Boudicca would go, I am released.

The next morning I am informed that we will, in due course, start for the land of the Iceni. Boudicca may return to the relative safety of her few remaining people. I suspect her people will be slaughtered to the last child and their lands occupied by the families and friends of the legions of Rome. This will be the way.

I ask leave of absence to see to my family after stating I can be back the following day. It is not good news that an escort is to accompany me, for several obvious reasons. Still, I will say family was told to hide there on the way to our relative's villa. At least it appears I will be able to return to some order, though crops are damaged and by the time Rome leaves much of our wealth will be drunk, eaten and stolen. I can only face one problem at a time.

At this stage in life, my allegiance is to myself and now, I feel, perhaps Gaul. If ever there is a return to normality, it is a growing thought that I should leave my Briton property and take what I can back to Gaul. This will not be a stable future, even if the people bow down to defeat at the hands of Rome. I have seen indications that punishment is to be long and painful. Apparently Suetonius, who I have not seen yet, has sworn great and terrible revenge.

The return to my wife, two children and servant goes smoothly. They are deposited in a tent. Within the week I have virtually ceased to see them, as my old direction is once again pursued. This time I show only the attitude of someone who is not keen. I am older now and the legion to go with me, or I with them, show me a lot more respect.

146

With the arrival of another vast army, the march with me included proceeds
to reclaim all lost territories. The destruction I witness on the first part of
this journey is complete. Few settlements are occupied, as word has spread
and people have fled. I fear they will eventually surface and Suetonius will
have an ongoing program of retribution. Perhaps I have been lucky, even if
life as I know it will possibly not return.

When we arrive in the main centres of Verulamium and Londinium, it is
not the Roman that is the destroyer. Death and smell are everywhere and
most houses sacked with little sign of occupation. The fire was not used.
The Britons may have felt they would claim them later for their own. A
large number of dwellings were already in the hands of the indigenous
people.

It is only when we reach Camulodunum, some eight days from the
battle, that total destruction is apparent, from the temple of Claudius to the
simple dwellings nearby. All have been burnt. The absence of bodies in the
streets and buildings is strange, until we become aware that remains are
amassed in the one huge temple that stands. It will surprise me if the centre
of Britannia Rome does not move to Londinium.

Prisoners have been tortured in large numbers, and all have offered an
opinion as to where Boudicca and anyone else they can think of has fled to.
They would be quick to get an opinion from me. If it was not for my family
I would tell them we should pursue them to Gaul. That would get me out
of here, the quicker the better. We have spies in many places now. There are
always those who will talk for Roman coin and other rewards. Still, they are
not sure if Boudicca is to be located, or if she is dead or alive.

It is decided that five of us, including one woman, will attempt to infiltrate the people in the region south-west of the Iceni tribe, before the legions move in on them. Policy is to dictate that tribes will gather into Roman settlements. The new laws are going to be harsh on the remaining Britons, especially in the areas of the chiefs of the uprisings. We are also informed that all spiritual leaders are to be located for later identification, then a death that will be gruesome enough to impress upon these Britons the foolishness of their ancient beliefs.

I am not sure that by killing some people's physical being you can destroy the soul of an entire race. Still, the might of Rome is daunting and will probably survive in one form or another for time beyond many civilizations.

I am too old for this, is the main thought as we move out into the areas designated for us to infiltrate. This time the danger is still immense, but at least we are moving in a region that has probably lost at least half its population in the most deadly battle that has occurred since the Roman arrival. I am frightened, so whatever happens I will keep my head down. If I run, my family and property will be destroyed. Obedience and a good pretence are my only choice at this stage.

Within a day we are amongst a group of Britons recently returned from battle. They are badly demoralized. Grief is everywhere, with children in a state of shock and without parents. Many have gathered supplies and fled to more isolated regions.

The woman, who is now coupling with several warriors, is said to be my daughter, and one of the men, my son. Her willing body soon gets her an invitation to move with a group who plan to avoid the coming legions. She is kind enough to plead for her loving father and brother. So, once more to my dismay, I am travelling into an extended tour of duty. This time no one has even offered me reward. I suppose I am meant to be grateful for the opportunity to serve the emperor.

We travel swiftly and find ourselves amongst a forest tribe who I can tell have little future beyond that of those who will rob all the surrounding settlements, until the tribe runs its course.

After several days it is obvious there is only rumour of Boudicca, but those amongst them who know of the priestesses and some of their locations have been loose with their tongues. At night we move out and, to my disgust, instead of returning with our knowledge, my enthusiastic daughter and I part company with my adopted son, who will return after depositing his knowledge.

We progress further south-west to touch company with stragglers, and on the third day come to a region where none of the inhabitants seem to have been a part of the uprising. They seem unconcerned and I suggest we can learn nothing here. My enthusiastic daughter is soon in the arms of the willing youth, and I suspect that her fondness for the espionage is mostly in the loins of strong, young men.

On the following day, a group arrives that stirs a memory both real and of the visions I thought I had left far in my youth. As the seven people move into the settlement, it is obvious they are treated with great reverence. Food is brought and dwellings offered.

It is afternoon before I come face to face with three of the women and my body feels as if it has gone into shock. The blue tattoo is on the forehead of each of the women. This is as it was for those who both wounded me for life and saved my life so long ago. One of them, older than the other two, seems struck by my presence and I cannot take my eyes off her. It is as if I have known her beyond my life. She moves gracefully to fetch water and brings me a vessel to drink from. She asks me if I am one who was in the battle as they have been told. I cannot lie to this presence. Eventually I state that I was at the location. She says she would like to talk more, and moves to join the discussions taking place with the leaders of these people.

That night two druids and another woman of the blue circle arrive and are quickly lost in the main dwelling. It is obvious by the quiet talk they are of immense importance, but I see some quiet argument amongst the people, as if their presence may bring not only spiritual gain but physical danger.

147

Next morning before dawn I am called into the main dwelling. None of this is of my choosing and I have deep-seated fear in me. The two druids and the woman of the blue circle are present plus several other leaders of these people. I am bidden to sit. The questions begin and I repeat the story well designed for me. The woman, in particular, looks closely at me, and a slow horror comes as awareness dawns that I am looking into the face and eyes of the woman raped and tortured by my legionaries and later freed by me. If she recognizes me she does not say for a time. Slowly I become aware that conversation has stopped, and that all are looking at us as we now quietly observe each other. Then she says: "The scar has healed well but still you limp."

A deeper dread enters my being and I presume my life is over. So I quietly tell her I am Gaul and inform her of the events that have, once again, overrun my life. I finish with the statement that if I had lived I would have left Britannia and returned to my native Gaul. I would go with or without my family, for I have no stomach for the future that now is, in all probability, destructive to human harmony. I do not know who the woman is but she has the aura of great power. Discussion quietly takes place.

My adopted daughter arrives and is questioned. It is quickly apparent that her fate is no different to mine. We are both bound with arms behind our backs and informed that we will be held for more questions. Then we are removed, with no comfort or food to come before the day breaks. I tell her of my misfortune at being recognized and am profoundly abused for my trouble. Little conversation takes place after that. She still seems interested in who the woman is. I have no interest, for as far as I know life is at an end.

When the sun shows first light we remain bound and are placed together on a horse with a group of some ten riders. We depart. Steady rain falls for most of the morning then, when the sun is overhead, we receive water and flat bread from the woman I cannot take my eyes off. It is the first time that I am aware she is with us but it does not surprise me.

For three days we travel and well into the nights. I recognize no places, for I presume we are avoiding settlements. On the fourth morning I am taken separately to a round house on an isolated farmstead. There the three question me on Gaul and where I come from, and how well I know the locations of various sacred areas. Then I am outside again and nothing happens for a while. Then the woman with whom I feel a bond once more brings me water. She states: "If you are knocked down lie as if you are dead." Then she is gone. We move again. During the day we hear one man clearly state we will be at the site by tomorrow and it is a sadness and a great privilege to be able to be at the funeral rites of Boudicca, the greatest of all Britannia's leaders.

Towards dark I can see they are getting ready to make camp. We are once again dragged from horse and separated. I am led a short distance through some bushes and, to my amazement, a container is upended over my face and chest and blood covers the front of my body. I am then struck several times and hurled to the ground. I lie as if I am dead. I hear the woman arrive and hear the horror in her voice, then the struggle as they drag her past me. One laughingly says: "We will get full use of you before you die and if you are worthy of us you may live." Then they are gone.

Before long my Blue Circle says "come" and I am back in camp before the three again. "You will come with us. It is imperative that we depart Britannia and reach a certain location in Gaul. The woman you travelled with has had her escape organized. She will report your death and that of Boudicca. That is all that I, the one known as Boudicca, Queen of the Iceni, can do for your family. You may never return to Britannia, but if you serve us well and the ancient memories that are at such peril, you shall live."

As I turn Blue Circle reaches for my hand and leads me, under the watchful eye of one of Briton's blue warriors, to the stream. There her hands clean me, and her extraordinary eyes open my mind to an awareness that, regardless of what has gone before, my life is now renewed.

Exhaustion, fear, sadness and loss are all present in my being. The overwhelming presence of this woman and the astonishing presence of Boudicca add to the confusion as I am led back to the campsite. Boudicca looks at me and asks: "Is your soul willing to honour the beliefs of your ancestors in order to preserve the physical body it resides in?" In a still dumbfounded voice I utter "yes". I can see amusement in her eyes and hear one of the druids quietly chuckle.

We move quickly, speaking to no one. I am no longer bound. Only the blue warriors seek and find food. On the coast contact is apparently made and I see gold change hands. Then, under the cover of first dark, I find myself and five others manning the oars of a strong boat.

148

Blue Circle only attends me to give occasional food but I feel her presence at all times. The loss from no contact with my family is somehow growing more distant, with only a quiet guilt. My wife's love for me was becoming reserved, and my son who is eighteen years old will relish new command of my property. For my daughter there is a deeper sadness and a hope I will see her again. She will wed and bear children, her beauty likely to go to a legionary.

Small sail is raised as the wind is stronger than I would like and the steady rain soon makes all else, but the survival of the present, to be put out of mind. I hope they know what they are doing for I cannot see a star in the sky. Now and then a half moon appears, to quickly be lost to the clouds and the rain. Every gust of wind seems to push the boat close to taking water. I have only crossed once, and in a vessel vastly larger than this and in smooth seas. Boudicca has started to call time to the rhythm of the oars and soon we find our course smoother, going slightly with the waves instead of being side on to each dark crest.

When daylight comes I can see no land in any direction and am aware that we are hardly rowing at all. Exhaustion has set in to all but the strongest of fighters. Still, Boudicca rises from her position on sleeping furs and, with the weather improving, a man I have not seen before signals all to feather oars then withdraw them. The small sail comes down and a much larger one goes up. I feel the boat jump immediately and lean a little further but riding with the waves.

It is midday when land is sighted. I was still sleeping but, on hearing excited talk, rose to look. With some food and drink, three others and myself join the two who are already rowing, and we speed towards a Roman Gaul that I have not seen for nineteen years.

Dark starts to descend as we near the coast, with the sails being withdrawn upon sighting sail in the direction that must be to the north. The coming dark is a mixed blessing as it will be hard to land safely in the poor vision, and no light can guide us in as that would lead to questions.

Once again the man named Telusus takes charge. It is obvious he is a sailor of many crossings. Eventually land looms up out of the dusk but the cliffs and distant surf look very daunting. A course is set south until the cliffs appear to flatten and a tentative landing is made. A rocky beach makes it hard work but, after much time in the water, all make it to shore with boat intact. The supplies are quickly unloaded and moved to an inlet out of the wind and misty rain.

With guards set I am relieved that I am not a figure of trust, and notice one guard is positioned to watch our borders and me also. Boudicca only needs to observe me looking at Blue Circle to realize I have no intention of running. It is as if I am a young man again enthralled with the movements of the shape of young women. But I am not young and this woman, although beautiful in my eyes, has much grey in her hair and lines on her face that life experiences and the passing years produce. They do not matter. I already, even in my tiredness, crave the touch of her hand and the warmth of her breath, and even the sound of her voice.

149

Sleep comes, and on waking it is decided two others and I will try and establish contact to define location and plan our movements. Within a quarter of an arlm I have spoken to a group of old men taking a cart of fodder to market. I know where we are, so quickly return without, I hope, raising any suspicions, as we were fishermen blown south.

I have been informed that the druid's centre of learning, the place I know as the location of the prophecy of the virgin who will give birth, is the required destination. It is due west of my origins, so memories are stirring from deep within my soul. For the time, fear and family are put aside.

This growing sense of excitement is seemingly mine alone. I see only serious faces and determination on the countenance of my companions. They, unlike me, are perhaps leaving their homelands forever. My curiosity as to why Boudicca is taking this journey gives me another reason to seek answers from, I hope, Blue Circle.

Upon informing that the journey will take at least ten days by foot, I am again sent out; this time with the same company in an attempt to purchase horses. We are now twelve in number: five women all from the covens I think, four druids, two blue Britons and me. All are armed with spears and most with bows except me, who is yet to get even a knife or sword to look after myself in hostile territory.

It takes me two days to buy eight horses, as the Roman villas that have the largest numbers are purposely avoided. This causes more delays in our journey. The villas seem more prevalent than I remember, and the roundhouses and farmlets are further apart. We come across a kalme, a boarding house, on the second morning and I am able to learn something of the layout of the journey ahead.

Now we are fully mounted with me doubling with one warrior, and the one that I think of as my Blue Circle doubling with one of her sisters. This I will work on changing but the seriousness of the journey seems to be more important. Even on horse it still takes us five days to reach our destination, only to find it deserted. We stop to camp in a valley south-east of the learning centre, and as dark falls we are finally approached.

They emerge from the forest on three sides almost as shadows. I am the last to become aware of them. We are on the move again, and before long find ourselves in the shelter of a forest settlement of roundhouses where I presume they will begin to get the answers to their quest.

I ask one of the warriors for knowledge and am told it is for us to serve the holy priestesses and druids. It is not for us to seek knowledge before it is time for such as us to know. Still, I feel part of what is happening is connected here in Gaul to the Roman moves to wipe out spiritual beliefs and ancient legacy that was kept alive by countless priestesses and the now dominant druids.

It is not long before I hear that druids have been warned of a coming attempt to annihilate all such as they in Gaul as well. News of the Britannia events has reached them, causing withdrawals to hidden communities. Runners have been sent to all other centres north and south.

Blue Circle brings food and water to me. For the first time in days the food is warm and fresh. I learn her name. She is Arros and now knows me as Alban Ulpius. We have furs to lie on, but when dark and the dying fires brought an end to the discussions that I am not included in, she came to me and led me by the hand away from the camp.

We arrived at a small spring gushing out of the hillside. My heart seemed to beat so hard I think she must have heard it. She bathed my body and then hers. She is a wondrous woman. Then we returned to the furs and I am grateful for their warmth and the body that moves in my arms, and I feel a completeness I have wanted all my life. Boudicca and the druids will no doubt have observed me, and at least know I will bring no harm to Arros and likely to be incapable of leaving her.

150

In the coming days I am not invited to attend meetings, but join in the hunt for deer and do other chores in this community of some seventy people. There are few children. These are nearly all people whose beliefs are outside of those acceptable to the Empire. Finally Arros tells me a little. The reason Boudicca and the druids were so far from their final destination was that they had become aware of one Joseph of Arimathea, a man from the Far East and of great wealth, who had settled in the region where I came upon them. He brought knowledge of one born without the seed of man; one whose word is spreading throughout all of the Empire. Arros explained:

"The lives of Boudicca and the druids were at tremendous risk in all the regions where Knowledge was under great threat. Yet, in order to keep this Knowledge alive, they could not withdraw to the Picts in the north of Britannia or the islands to the west. After talks with Joseph's followers of the probable death of most of the druids, it was decided that the druids should seek safety in Gaul. The news of the coming purge spread far and wide.

Partly because of the teachings of Joseph, our destination is to the centre of the druid's school that looked after the nearby sanctuary and holy centre housing the prophecy of the coming virgin mother. Many believe that this man crucified in Jerusalem may have been the one of the prophecy.

The teachings of the covens have much in common with the druids, from beyond remote history and deep into legend. The covens are being hunted down and destroyed. Boudicca is amongst the highest of the priestesses who have preserved the reverence of the living planet some know as the Earth Mother, or even the Earth Mother goddess. The blue circle is the symbol of one coven for the living planet.

The Knowledge is endless and is normally preserved and handed down in trust to those who devote their lives to holy ways. Now, with all Knowledge under attack, it is said The Word must spread. This is one reason we seek out the teachings of the one they call Jesus of Nazareth. They may coincide with many of the old reverences for the living planet, and the greater universes incorporating the holy Spirit."

I wish I understood all this but it is mostly beyond me. The world to me is the area occupied by humans; a flat empire with a few natives on the outskirts. I know the spirits are in all living things and I have been taught by my mother that these make up the Earth Mother goddess, who watches over all life. So it is that all life must be treated with reverence. My father was sceptical about this as the only way, and I heard him on many occasions turn to the human gods that seem to be taking over from my mother's old beliefs. Women, through the time they spend with the priestesses, seem to be much closer to ancient belief.

Now there are gods of human fertility, gods of crops, gods of war and gods of love. To my continued questions Arros quietens me, and says: "That is all for now but when the time is right the teachers, either coven or druid will, for perhaps the first time, come together to provide The Knowledge to all people. It is hoped that we will return to the centre of learning and the students who came from near and far will return."

The days pass and a cloud of smoke is the bearer of bad tidings. Upon dark, the messengers went forth and soon returned to say the centre of learning is no more than a few stone foundations here and there, and that the Romans have questioned the village people none too gently as to the whereabouts of the druids.

Horses and things needed are gathered together and we bid farewell to the eleven wise men who cannot bring themselves to leave this most sacred area. The rest of the druids have dispersed in all directions to carry the message of greater threat near and far.

Once again our group, only ten now with one Gaul for guide, is on the move. I have been told we are to travel towards the Germanic tribes for a time until it is safe for the women to try and return to places within the Roman Empire. My private thoughts are that, with their prominent tattoos of several designs, it will be hard for them to blend with the native people without Rome requiring identification.

Several times the druid who remains with us is recognized by locals from whom we seek knowledge or provisions, and I see immediate fear and a wish to see us on our way. Those who do help show by their reactions that they have many of the Earth beliefs. We are forced to flee for our lives from Roman patrols on two occasions, and we lose one of the women on the second occasion. If they take her alive the existence of Boudicca may be revealed. I am sorry to say, but I hope her fall from the horse or a lance may have killed her before she became captive.

We spend several long periods in hiding before it seems safe to move on, and I admit to myself that I have grave fears for the future of this group. It crosses my mind to flee to my own people if any remain, but I cannot leave Arros and I hope she cannot see my fear. I would not put her spiritual obligations to the test by asking her to depart with me.

151

It is as we are crossing the Seine on the border of the Empire that disaster strikes. There is no cover in the river and we are seen by a border patrol. Arrows fly true and three of our number fall: the druid, one Briton and one of the women, and the Gaul is badly wounded. The six of us remaining flee into the forest, with Boudicca carrying the Gaul over the front of her horse. We need him as he is the only one to speak a Germanic dialect. Without being able to speak and identify ourselves, we are in danger here too. These times are dangerous, even for a Roman citizen in the new regions of the Empire.

Luck turns our way after a night of fear in the best cover we could find. The arrowhead had to be removed and boiling water and fire were needed. The second could be supplied but the water could not so, with the Gaul bound and eventually thankfully unconscious, a red hot knife cut the arrow head out and herbs were bound into the wound. Much of this I did not see, as I and one of the three women were left on guard. The Briton still with us was needed to hold the Gaul while he fought his way into unconsciousness. Boudicca and Arros attended the wound.

The next day the Briton and I set carefully about finding the nearest settlement. It is half an arlm before we see smoke and another arlm before we near a clearing of farmland on the bend of an impressive waterway. We have no choice but to ask for help from these people but, with probable difficulty in language, must wait until the Gaul can travel.

The new day sees us arrive on their mercy. The Gaul, travelling in pain, is on arrival able to speak our case. It is soon explained that the women are those who serve what is known across the world as the Mother. Also it is told that the Empire has decided to rid itself of those who will not look to gods who are either Roman or of those who take human form. So it is, for the foreseeable future, that those who serve the Earth Mother and the existence of spirit in all that is known, are to flee or be absorbed with their knowledge into often remote communities. Arros quietly explains to me that this is the message the Gaul has been asked to interpret.

Whatever it is we are welcomed and I find we are given shelter, even if it is with the oxen and goats under the lean-to at the edge of their dwellings. Their buildings are quite substantial. Not round but rectangular in shape, with living for family in loft as well as in the peaked roofs.

We settle down quietly and immediately contribute to the tending of crops and the hunting and preparation of food. Time passes, and some language is learnt mostly from the Gaul, as we are to return to spread The Word. I must admit I am intrigued with the spiritual word I overhear. I am also baffled by the love I feel for Arros, but I know her allegiance is first to what she calls the Living Earth and to me second. She will continue as a priestess.

Again we have heard of the cult started with the virgin birth, with more travellers arriving and teaching this gospel. It has been said that the companion of the Nazarene and his child escaped the laws of Rome. There is great joy amongst them that Mary from Magdalene, first amongst his church, survived with the lifeblood of Jesus and the doctrine of his spoken word.

The cult followers have also left Rome and its central provinces because of persecution. They are travelling outwards to spread the gospel of this man Jesus. My Arros tells me that much of The Word is central to their beliefs, and they have few doubts that he is as of the stories of old and that his father, who art from the heavens, is as the legends have told. There is no gospel that he is a god, but that he has told Jew, Roman and Gentiles from all places that they who seek The Word and live the laws that give love and reverence to both humans and Earth are in the grace of the holy Spirit.

I am slowly learning a greater depth of The Word and it is having effect on me. Now I see that there is not only joy in the physical rewards of everyday life, but joy in giving reverence to the living spiritual world, known as the world of the holy Spirit, that I am coming to realize includes the stars, sun and the moon. I still find this difficult to grasp and, upon questioning Arros, find some of The Knowledge involving stars comes from legend. I think she cannot fully grasp the extent of the stories either.

152

After the month of June passes the decision is made to try and move south before the coming winter. The Briton has mated with a Germanic lady and attached himself to her two children, so he will stay. With good wishes from many new friends, the now five of us depart. I am not pleased as I know that the others will probably be in more danger than me. I am Gaul and will put what I now see as the truth in a position that keeps me alive. If humans want to worship man as god and others show reverence to the Mother (Living) Earth, then my way is to let all be quiet about how they do it and not be killed.

Arros has explained to me that they are not out to change the Roman Empire, only to resist the attempt to kill all who hold Knowledge. She almost becomes angry with me as she explains The Knowledge has been passed down through countless generations from beyond the mists of time. If I leave the group tomorrow I am aware that she will never stop loving me but she will follow the quest to preserve The Knowledge.

We travel with care and make contact with settlements every now and then; even talking to Romans several times and then always being quick to move on. These women have become very much as the people of Gaul under Roman rule. If one does not know the significance of the tattoos, they now are hard to identify. We have stories to tell of our origins and it is becoming safer to travel. However, as we travel south we hear more and more of the destruction of the druids and any covens, and those who preach of the ways of the Nazarene.

We keep our peace and eventually reach the holy site at the well of the

Mother, the place where the ancient standing stones show the site that has great power. It is in legend one of the most ancient sites of first contact with the beginnings of spiritual learning. Now the site is still occupied by the carving of the virgin, perhaps done by the druids probably hundreds of years ago. It has been untouched. Apparently the Romans are, for some reason, not prepared to risk the wrath of whatever power exists here by removing such a sacred relic. I am of the opinion they will take this belief and change it to their own ways, as they have done with Isis and other divinities of Egyptian and Greek origin.

We are soon informed, without bringing attention to ourselves, that the druids that stayed have all been crucified as an example to the population. We make a quiet retreat after staying no longer than necessary and journey to the forest settlement, now occupied by several families. They make us welcome so we stay.

Shortly into our stay, Arros tells me that the druids and covens have been forced to become secret sects or perish. The druids have taken another name. As time passes I become aware that visitors who come, both women and men, are of this secret way. I learn to recognize the signs they give to identify themselves, and learn that this settlement is still a contact point. Then we start to travel.

153

I have become a caretaker for those who live what are now the secret ways; mostly a caretaker for Arros, as is the Gaul for Boudicca.

Eventually I see my brother and distant relatives, and learn through them and others of my family in Britannia. All of us have long gone by different names and have long been considered dead. My family took the ways of the new gods and prospered, with my daughter marrying a Roman estate owner and taking family of her own.

Arros and I are older now and every day is a blessing for both of us. Boudicca, Arros and the other female have become part of an extensive coven whose members extend across Gaul and other parts of the Empire. We have occasional contact with the new brotherhood that is the continuation of the druids. I am informed that it has a certainty to survive. Always there is the fear of discovery, with those who are betrayed dying a dreadful death. Those known as the Nazarenes are more public in their teachings and their numbers are expanding everywhere we go. As I hear the teachings, they are a large part of the old teachings and in many ways impossible to tell apart.

As the years pass my old wound makes travel harder for me, and I sometimes see Boudicca look upon my limp with a special gentleness. We travel less now and the forest settlement is virtually our home. Roman taxes are sought and outward respect for Roman gods is shown, but the truth goes on with its undercover journey. If ever I have regrets I look upon my aging Blue Circle's love and the regrets vanish.

More years pass and I realize one of us must leave the other, and that it is going to be me. My caretaking days are over. The others are careful to show their love for my Arros and ensure me that she will be cared for.

Day by day I feel my life giving in to whatever disease is defeating me. Then finally, with my body in the arms of my beloved Arros, my last awareness of this world fades. Now my spirit departs to continue its journey, as an infinitely small but willing part of the great and wondrous holy Spirit.

The life to preserve

154

The next life that will become a part of the writing begins with the birth of one who will live at the site of the church now known as the one dedicated to Our Lady, in Chartres, France. I am born to a middle class family, the fourth child of a stone mason in the year of Our Lord 1173. I am now twenty-one years old and, as is the way of my people, have been recognized as a fully fledged mason worker of the stones that are the wonderful substance of, what is to me, the greatest trade a working man can have to support his family. With recognition came my initiation into the guild of masons.

Never before has there been such a time to work the stone. I have travelled with my father and the clergy who work in what has become a sacred trust with the stone guild. I have marvelled at the great cathedral almost completed in Paris. A special honour has been bestowed on my elder brother and me. Stone by stone we have removed the wall joining the two sections of the west entrance, and with skill will rebuild the wall on the outside edge of Our Lady's cathedral at Chartres.

My family and our forefathers have dwelt here for many hundreds of years. Apart from our Christian beliefs, there are the ancient connections going back to the pagan druids and beyond. This is often the way of country folk, but our old ways are spoken in hushed tones and told as children's stories. The Church of Rome has long dealt harshly with those who cling to legends. Still, in places with such profound connections, the symbolism is built by all the guilds into the places of reverence that have dwelt here. Such symbolism has brought retribution upon our holy buildings, and three times they have been burnt to the ground by those who believed our Christian faith was tainted by the old ways.

The time we dwell in has brought a quiet awe and a separate code of secrecy to the ones already passed down. These codes have reached into the guild of the masons.

We have knowledge in harmony with the Cistercian order of monks and the knights of the Red Cross, both started they say by Bernard of Clairvaux, and a Briton abbey in connection with the French kings, starting with Godeffroi de Bouillon. It is known by all initiated masons, me included, that our grand masters dwell often in the holy trust of the highest of the Cistercians and the grand masters of the knights of the Cross, often called in conversation the knights of the Temple of Solomon.

It is known that the original founders, a group of nine knights, dwelt in the ruins of the grounds of the palace of Herod for many years. It is known to us that extraordinary secrets have returned to France with these knights, and some of The Word passed to our masonic guild in order to translate into physical reality. This has created much excitement but also a wary code of secrecy, as it is said that much is in the realm of the heretic.

I, like many of my village friends, have a sense of profound curiosity and a wish to know more. My father has been quick to warn us that the only way to the answers to such curiosity is to respect the ways of the guild, and in time progress into the hierarchy of the Masonic. This, as with my fellows, I accept, and work hard at my trade and ask mostly the questions I need to ask in order to achieve each task.

On a night of the new moon, confidence was placed in me and five of my guildsmen including my father and brother that would, in time, increase my curious nature to an unprecedented level.

We were raised from our beds by the knights, and in their company took the woollen contents of many wagons and built a great wall of wool across the inner entrance of the cathedral and over the entrances to the ancient crypts below. I feared we were about to be invaded by foreign legions but exhausted returned to bed before dawn. Thus it was that I was one of the last to rise and see that a great fire was consuming, yet again, the shrine of the virgin at the druids' grotto.

It was my mother's cry of fear that raised me from my bed. I could feel a growing empty feeling in the pit of my stomach. My father quietened my mother and sent my sisters to their room. His quick instructions to us kept his sons from rushing to fight the fire. Then the full impact of their fears strike me. Our activities last night are probably connected and may place blame directly upon us. I feel violently sick and make it out the back door, there to lie vomiting the contents of my stomach upon this earth; failing to understand what has happened but expecting soldiers to break into our lives at any moment.

We do not have long to wait but it does not come as I feared. A well-known monk approaches us and takes father into his confidence. Soon my brother and I are called. The message is simple. We never saw the wagons or left our beds at night. This confidence we are to preserve for life or face the wrath of God. They have no need to speak to me again. I can feel the stake on my back and smell my flesh as it burns from my bones. This I have witnessed before, so my lips are sealed forever. If my brother were to wish to open his mouth I would kill him myself. So profound is my fear that this secret be safe, even my mind is afraid to ask questions or open the normal curiosity as to why. It is buried.

155

Several days pass and we go quietly about our lives. The town is stunned, in a kind of shock, as if the wrath of God has come down upon us all. Then a curious thing happens that causes commotion and a change of mood. It is led by the monks supported by the knights.

Monks thought to have died trying to save the cathedral have emerged from the ruins bringing forth the most valued icon of the Christian world; the cloth used to wrap the Nazarene. This is the very one from the hands of the holiest virgin. A great cry has gone up that God smiles upon Chartres and its inhabitants. This is a sign that a new cathedral will rise with the support of the Holy Spirit and the blessing of the virgin. The fire, it is being said, was to make way for mankind's glory to God on this Earth. Thus it is said, that the great entrance has been saved with its window of the virgin, in order to show the way. I am too frightened to exchange glances with my family, let alone with those who have also risen from their beds. The back of my mind, indeed all of it, knows that the virgin and God had help, but it will stay firmly at the back of my mind. No word is ever spoken again of events.

A miracle almost takes place in the clearing of the site. Awareness of complete plans for the new cathedral becomes reality to the guild. Upon glimpsing them, and hearing my father talk in hushed tones about such, I know this is indeed an extraordinary plan and have little doubt that divine law has been at work, once again, at Chartres.

The work starts and I find that not only my family but the family of the others in the conspiracy trust are given leading responsibility. My father moves up in rank in the Masonics. By the end of the second year our wealth is at a level far higher than to be expected. The girl I have always admired is my wife and carries a child in her body, under a roof that I can hardly believe is our own home.

The strange feeling returns at times when I see a knight quietly observing me. That is the way of these times. It is best to work hard and that is easy, for never has the work been more exciting. I am upset when my lovely wife is summoned to help keep home for two of the knights and sometimes returns late. Then I am pleased when her growing belly sees her replaced with another. I know better than to question and set my mind to progress within the Masonics, for there I will find security, knowledge and protection from abuse by power. Events could have gone very differently in this dangerous world at God's servants' command.

Time passes into years and one child becomes four. My matron is not asked to serve again; thus happiness and good fortune is in the home of my family.

The walls on the ancient hill have risen, bringing honour to our guild across all of France. As finer stonework and flying buttresses the likes of which we have never seen rise, the work slows down. Many experts from Paris now work amongst us. Each day brings new discovery and sense of wonder as the building, like a flower of the stone, begins to lay open a kind of divinity that perhaps has not been achieved before. From all over the known world pilgrims arrive bringing commerce and, at times, the wealth needed to bring this profound marvel to life.

My father dies, followed closely by my mother. My brother moves up and my station in the guild is strengthened.

Fifteen years pass and now two of my sons work in the guild. I have, over the years, mastered the ways of sculpting figures and spend much of my time, with the guidance of the Cistercians, bringing life to what I now see as scripture with subtle legends. My brother contracts the growing disease and dies in the year 1213.

In my thirty-seventh year, I and two others hold office in second place only to the grand master of the Chartres guild, now the largest stone guild to my knowledge in the known world. My wife has died of smallpox and a new maiden has come to my bed. When her services were requested, my displeasure was registered and another took her place.

Such events, although close to my heart, are as nothing compared to the two extraordinary doors that are opening in my world. One is the edifice that seems already closer to the world of the supernatural or divine laws, and the other The Knowledge, that is slowly and with great trust being placed in my care, of the divine laws and sacred geometry governing number, weight and measure, plus that beyond my reach to explain. Britannia and Germanic masters travel far to hear part of The Knowledge being given to the hierarchy of Chartres guild, in order to complete this profound project.

156

In my forty-seventh year, now the father of seven living children and two grandchildren, I become grand master of the Masonics of Chartres. The curiosity of my youth has been replaced by the most profound awe and reverence. A greater part of the history of the journey of humans opens before me. The symbolism and reasons for the rebirth of this house of the virgin are perhaps as clear as they will ever be.

I am given a glimpse of a brotherhood beyond the brotherhood of the knights, beyond the Cistercian order, and know they are now the shadowy power entrusted to hold, amongst other treasures, the documents and artifacts thought to go back to beyond Solomon to Moses and the beginning of the human conscious journey. In time I realize that this shadowy presence is a continuous line from the druids. They also incorporate many of the female ideals lost in the journey of humans, including the ideals lost by the exclusion of all women from positions of office within the Christian empire.

From my position questions can be asked, and this I do one day in the presence of three knights and four Cistercians, including the one who is chief amongst them. To my joy, quiet enquiry gets assent from all present. A monk takes up the journey, explained I think simply for my understanding. These are the words, as close as I can recall that I heard:

Mankind's ancestors reached a high level of spiritual and intellectual development at a time of great antiquity. Physical buildings came and went with the changing of climates and other disasters in various parts of Earth. The dawning of the recognition of a spiritual self, living beyond death into life then back again into physical birth, came we believe first; then, over the aeons, a slow recognition that not only humans had this spiritual presence but all life.

This point following was crucial and one of the two highest points of aeons of developed knowledge: that on the level of spiritual awareness, it was not the spoken word that was conscious understanding, but at this level both human and beast registered recognition at the level of thought. Not only this, but a forest or a field of grass and herbs was recognizable as healthy or lacking in the necessities of life by an aura, not unlike thought, that pervaded all nature.

From this the Ancients came to the conclusion that across the whole of the Earth there was a connection of conscious thought and the Earth was spiritually alive. From this beyond legend, Word had said the Earth was, as the Greeks said, not cylindrical, indeed round, and that this round world was one of many made up of a living consciousness known through carefully preserved knowledge as the holy Spirit and by other names. Some earlier humans called this the spirit of Mother Earth (Earth Mother goddess), and her wider partner in conscious existence was often referred to as the Father.

At many sites on Earth, great reverence was represented by standing stones, often in circles and temples. It was a 'religion', if that is what the correct term is, that ensured all creatures had to endeavour to live, eat, reproduce and die in harmony with the health of the living world.

For a time longer than we know these laws pervaded, until one major event - at first so innocent but with profound result; taking control of the life cycle of plants.

So humans took seed and sowed it in a plot of soil. They stayed by it, cared for it, and removed other plants from its presence. They took control of nature. They took ownership of an area of the Earth. They excluded other human, beast and fowl. They flourished but stepped out of harmony with nature, and their requirements became more.

More children survived and they had more to tend larger areas of land and protect it. The strength of the male became important, not for the hunt (long revered as part of the living Earth), but for the power to own more and protect more. Soon armies to fight others and take land from others became a necessity. The living planet was not in the interests of this development. Metals for killing and agriculture to increase dominance became all important.

The ancient centres of female reverence for Mother Earth of the standing stones were pushed aside. New gods of man over the living spirituality emerged, and mixed with variations of Ancient knowledge. Through the shaman and medicine women and priestess covens, the memories lived on.

In time a great Empire covered most of the known world, which developed its own gods with those of the other civilizations, some with connections going far back to great people of history such as Poseidon and Isis. Now man began to fight over whose gods were right and supreme.

The spiritual message through humans, and prophets who were mediums with a direct sensitivity to the resurrection of the spirit life, did not cease. Cults who believed in combinations of Earth Mother legends and the 'one god above all' persisted, as with the coming re-emergence of high spiritual resurrections such as Buddha, Muhammad and our own Nazarene, and the many Jewish prophets.

The beliefs for the reverence of the new gods of stone and war began to break down and, in the case of Rome, threatened division to an already weakened Empire. Thus it was that about three hundred and fifty years after the perceived death of the Jesus, Constantine decided to embrace the inevitable and take the words of one prophet and adapt them to the Empire's interests, including the creed that man (and especially not woman) were the chosen creatures. The kings over the Earth were now in the form of God the Father, God the Son and God the Holy Spirit.

With this, and other events in the East, those with knowledge were forced further into hidden circles, even though they were sought out and eliminated for hundreds of years and still are.

In the vast Muslim countries of the East, women were delegated a place and, as with all these new religions, were offered the profound promise of paradise as reward for acceptance and devotion.

The Knowledge that we now hold in trust is for a world in the future that will have need of harmony when the Earth has made corrections that will be needed for the survival of the cradle of life.

So it is that churches built in holy places such as Avalon and Chartres have been removed to incorporate shrines to preserve and honour not only the great

Nazarene but his true recognition of the female worth expressed in his companion, Mary Magdalene, and the many hidden scriptures that we now hold for the time when the necessary recognition of the spiritual Earth is the greatest obligation for humankind.

These things I hear, and turn to see Bishop Fulbert has been standing behind and has heard all that has been said. Old concerns rise but quickly depart as he quietly states: "You have been told such things and learnt such knowledge as our trust in you has never been let down. You will hold such knowledge in trust and pass on to successive grand masters of the guild only that necessary for the preservation of those who hold the truth, and the preservation of the proper words of true prophets." Knowledge of greater secrets, if they came to me, were not to be spoken or written in my lifetime.

Chartres unfolded under the watchful eyes of the silent administrators. A pattern emerged in the form of a maze on the arcane floor; part of the female celebration of the virgin, far older than the Christian church or the prophecy of the druids. The well that, like its counterpart at Avalon has part of the remains of the chalice, is far below the floor; built into the wonder of this building that will become an enduring monument to someday emerge from legend into open knowledge for humanity's future.

I am seventy-one years old now and entering through the doors of the building that has been in many ways the hidden journey of my life. It is the year 1244 and I doubt that, on all the Earth, there is a more powerful or beautiful structure put together by the hand of man.

I am frail now and aware that the days left to me are few. I have come, perhaps for this last time, to see three of my sons working on the wonderful stone sculptures that are the final touches after fifty years of construction and learning.

It gives my failing heart great joy to know that no amount of oppression will now, or in the future, prevent humanity from eventually taking their place as caretakers for the gifts of the spirit of Mother Earth, and knowing of the power and the glory of the holy Spirit.

The present and the future

Malcolm

157

Once again I speak from the world of the Spirit. Lives, good and bad, female and male, pass me by.

It comes to pass that I live nine lives as a Buddhist in far parts of the world. It is in these physical bodies that the real message of the resurrection that was taught by the Nazarene and the Ancients before him becomes clearer under the Buddhist doctrine. I understand the resurrection into the world of the Spirit, and then again into the world of the physical; world without end.

Then I am born amongst those who are of the now widespread Islamic belief. None of these lives are out of the ordinary, as has been the journey for most of countless lives over vast aeons. Wars, earthquakes, disease, childbirth and old age end these lives.

☆ ☆ ☆

So lives pass on this planet and others. Humanity's capacity to achieve great things grows in both goodness and evil through discovery and wars. Then, in a tiny town in the south of an ancient continent now called Australia, I am born into the time of the writing.

I am moving now, across distances well understood for longer than the rise and fall of billions of universes. The consciousness of our kind has penetrated beyond the boundaries of human imagination. I pass the lights of great clusters at infinite distance, until I see the light of the universe which holds the spiral galaxy called the Milky Way. My speed must slow if my journey will take me back to the tiny yellow star called the Sun, with its pretty blue planet, the Earth.

I am the spirit of the man to be called Malcolm. I am, like all spirit of humanity and thousands of other spirits of species throughout this galaxy, connected to the laws of the most complex, evolved intelligence, known by some on Earth as Spirit or God or by other names.

As humans struggle on Earth, they are beginning to look into distances and become aware of the probability of higher intelligences. They seek, through their greatest discoveries, for communication with other life. This is the lore of the Spirit: the Spirit is within and has journeyed with humans for over a million years to beyond death, to understanding.

So it is at the point of conception I flash into this universe, galaxy, solar system and the womb of my mother, to depart from conscious knowledge of the Spirit, and once again learn or lose the lessons only the physical birth can give. I am human without knowing my alien spirit soul. All people have this ancient, subconscious identity.

I open my eyes to hear, touch, see and learn. This is a happy beginning, to grow up on a farm in Australia 1,950 years after Jesus who was born to show humanity a glimpse of the Spirit. I learn to laugh, fall, get up, climb and fall again. I learn greed and sometimes to share. My earliest memories are without event: periods of celebration, grief, birth, Christmas and birthdays, my first day at school, collecting bird nests and riding horses for miles every weekend.

I also remember, during one of our marvellous holidays by the sea, being afraid to be alone in a room at night. Most children experience this. I am only about five years old. It is partly dark and my eyes are open wide. I have absolute certainty that, although I can see all of the room, I am not alone. My parents console, and partly convince me that there is nothing there but my imagination. I obviously have a good one because, regardless of settling down, and at times being less aware and sometimes going for years without thinking about it, the identity and very real presence stays with me all of my life. Eventually it becomes a source of knowledge to me, but the knowledge is not necessarily wisdom.

The most profound event in memory is to occur one night, at about the age of fourteen years. I am wide awake on my bed in my home. My body feels like it is being dragged down the bed. There is no one in the room. I do not know why, but I only feel remote fear. Then it feels as if my body is lifting off the bed. I remain wide awake. I resist and my body flicks back onto the mattress, only for a minute, for it happens again. This time I go a greater distance. At some stage I start to circle; the room seems to have grown higher. My circling speeds up and in an instant I am through a solid wall. This is my first journey into what I will later learn is a kind of twilight world, half way to the natural world of my inner spiritual self.

Most of these out of body events that I remember are mainly flying experiences and happen alone. I see much landscape, often in silvery blues. Many times I try to visit people I know, but am either unskilled or disobeying the laws of the Spirit. The only fear I experience is when I attempt to land, often from great heights. It feels as if gravity will smash me into the ground but it never does. I always land on my feet without pain. One memory that is very clear is when I travelled away from the Earth; it seemed to me over vast distances in only seconds. I could see flashes of light which, I presumed, was caused by me flashing past great numbers of stars.

These events occurred in groups during my early years up to about the age of thirty, then virtually ceased. I could perhaps help bring them on, but never had total control of when they would come. However, I could stop them from occurring at any time and I would instantly return to my place of rest, even from my journey into deepest space.

I have read of tachyons. These particles are believed to gain infinite mass when they slow to the speed of light. They behave much like our atomic structure only at beyond the speed of light, and are able to remain in the one body location while having the capacity to move past the speed of light without gaining infinite mass.

I wonder if tachyons are perhaps a glimpse of one of the aspects of the structure of the Spirit, or our tiny part of that Spirit.

158

Now I am a fifty-five year old man living on Earth in 2005. The date is the 22nd July. I have often thought of how much I would write when I reached the time of 'the writing'.

My life has had high points of great interest and low points of great hardship. In other words I have, so far, lived the life of the majority of people, taking my journey as it comes while never losing the ability to strive for greater opportunity. I could write much of the journey of my life and the eventual reasons for writing my story that I think of as being written in co-operation with the spirit of the human journey.

I, Malcolm, present 'REDO ME again and again' as spiritual fiction. I believe that there is much that is special about this book that comes from a conscious existence outside the existence that is my physical awareness. Perhaps this is my subconscious soul.

I started writing 'REDO ME again and again' to give awareness to people I love very much. I had first thought to call it 'When the Time is Right'. I wanted to express three aspects of my knowledge:

- *Present great logic and discoveries are at a level, when compared to future knowledge, of the cave man looking at the flames of his first fire.*
- *I believe a great number of the future discoveries of the sciences will take them into the realm of spiritual knowledge.*
- *I believe that it is a good thing, for the stability of all, to find a belief and base your life on this.*

So I say, be of your faith but as the wonders of discovery emerge, open your heart, mind and soul in order that all may, some day, have a chance to abide in harmony, supported by humanity's discoveries.

I believe that the spirit many call Mother Earth is awakening to bring an opportunity of balance between humankind and the planet we dwell on. The order that has developed, mostly over the last two millennia and long before as well, has blown the long-term future of all quality of life to a rapidly approaching extreme.

Once again I have returned to the spirit world. The spirit, at this time, has finished its journey with Malcolm.

After Malcolm

159

I am born again in many forms over vast distances and hundreds of thousands of years until the following life unfolds.

They came for me when I was by the river. They were four men and three women. They told me I was needed to answer or explore questions that they think only I can help them with. An arrangement was made with the local community that my parents, siblings and I are part of, for me to be spared from my work to help these strangers. They obviously have influence, as all their requests are obliged.

In the following days I learn they are members of a Society of people connected to a continual Knowledge going back a greater distance into the past than I would be able to understand. They have in their care the writings of millions of individuals that have been preserved in various forms, over countless thousands of years. I am to help them in a journey of quest concerning a simple text called 'REDO ME again and again'. As far as they can estimate, it was written about 457,000 years ago. Somehow they have tracked this ancient writer to me, as the form that is now the rebirth of the one of the continual existence of this entity. Although I am just a simple worker in the gardens of a rural community, spiritual rebirth is now and has been, I thought, forever a part of Knowledge, so this is easy for me to comprehend. However, what they want of me is not so easy for me to understand.

I am released from duties and I am to go to them after my morning meal and ablutions. I say a tearful goodbye to Horake, the partner who most pleases the woman that I am. They have told me the journey I will help them with may take weeks or months of preparation. I am curious, even though curiosity has not been noted as a personality trait of mine.

So the days pass. I eat, drink, and increasingly learn to enter a deeper and deeper form of meditation. My mind seems to be changing with a growing clarity of a kind of conscious awareness, of what I know is spiritual presence. Also there is a growing awareness that two of the women, and one of the men, are increasingly becoming a part of my journey into the subconscious realm.

I am learning that these two women and the man are experienced guides, there to meet me in this world, and guide me in the direction they have apparently designed for me. I know not how, but I am aware of the difference between the other world powers of these people and me. I become aware that, as the weeks pass, an increase of a substance is steadily being introduced into my body, with the effect that I am less and less aware of my physical surroundings. Then I begin to travel great distances, at first with little cultural change.

One day, surrounded by my guides, who I can see are becoming a part of my conscious mind, I know I am moving past lifetime after lifetime into my own past, at a pace increasing to a blur that becomes a radiant light of colours beyond description and beauty. At last, as if at the end of a great tunnel, one clear light is seen and I am aware that it is the time and location we are flashing towards. We are emerging into a silvery blue twilight world that I recognize as being close to the world I know, and I hear the guide thoughts telling me I have arrived in the life of the one at the time of the writing.

We are high above a seaside resort. Cliffs and buildings nestle on the headlands, and there is evidence of a harbour being built in the bay. Then I can see the blurred image of a family in a tiny house. We enter on one prominent headland above the new harbour. Then I am aware that I am looking at me from another dimension; me from a lifetime over four hundred thousand years ago, on a continent called Australia, in a town called Portland.

I see my ancient self. I am looking through the eyes of a woman of the far future at a five year old boy who once held my spirit. I realize he cannot see us but he is sensitive to presence. The guides make me aware that it is not possible for both of me to exist in the same dimension. By using me, they have been able to reach the writer from ancient times.

We progress through his lifetime. As my guides draw him in a semi-conscious state into our dimension, my entity is pushed to an earlier time. They are now exploring his journey. I open my eyes exhausted, back in my own body, a little shaken but exhilarated too, and willing to do it again.

As the weeks pass we leave the lifetime of the one called Malcolm, and move back through a past of huge populations and joint communities to a far more primitive time. We come to a barbaric world, and I see him in many undignified brutal lives and some good lives, both male and female. I become aware that my guides are frustrated to find Malcolm's descriptions in 'REDO ME again and again' are not accurate. There are strange similarities and sometimes uncanny accuracies, but sometimes my ancient spirit is not at said location or is in entirely different roles.

Now, as I return to my body each time, much I have seen sends my mind into shock, and I am dimly aware of someone saying: "These will soothe you." They are controlling my reactions to the horror of worlds that break every rule of our gentle times.

By the position of the moon, I guess that two moons have passed by the time these journeys stop. Then one morning I am released back to my family, wiser but still not sure what they were after. However, I am aware they found much of what they sought, with an ancient me clouding old reality and important human development with his over-ripe ego and imagination.

My part in these events fades as the strange Society people, who none seem to know the origins of, disappear from amongst us.

160

Much excitement is in our community, as people from far places are coming this year to share with us the celebrations at the annual gathering. From ancient times at the beginning of spring, when leaves come back to the naked trees and new life emerges from the ground, people have travelled to express a joy for life and to share the gifts from learning.

It is also a time when a person gets to explore the joy of sex and find partners, sometimes for life. Our life can be for a long time, as we have the capacity to replace the aging process and can reach ages of hundreds of years. However, I am twenty-two years old, and this year I hope to have time with a man from the river country of people of great music.

Our elders select participants in co-operation with those from around the Earth, often to learn of environmental and cultural developments and also to help with new partners for genetic diversity. I am from the land of Europea, north of the warm regions of the planet.

For longer than 350,000 years we have known the laws of the Spirit, and across all of this time and this world we have obeyed them. For 350,000 years we have been aware that our home, this Earth, is a conscious entity aware of all creatures and their effects upon the health of the living planet. So we give reverence to the spirit of Mother Earth, and can only dwell in such fashion that is harmonious to her wellbeing. This is, in return, harmonious to our wellbeing.

We endeavour to live a life that uses only those resources that we can replace, or at a rate that we can replace them. We live in harmony with all nature. Our people retain the population at a rate suitable to the environment, and teach their children to use nature at a sustainable rate. We sometimes control animal species if they, in turn, use more than nature can provide. Thus they provide us, in turn, with protein as the Earth designs.

We spread out across the Earth in family groups with community centres that are globally connected. We have long ago learnt that construction of huge cities is not sustainable. We have, for thousands of years, used the processes of the living planet to comfort our lives: the sun, tides, wind, waves and running water, even going so far as to harness and preserve such ocean currents as circle the oceans, that have in times gone by ceased to function, bringing dramatic climate change. We recognize the health of the Earth relies upon these climate changes, so treat such as necessary and adjust with Mother Earth.

Ours is, we think, the most spiritual, knowledgeable, and physically responsible development of humankind to happen on this our living planet. These are the teachings that are brought to each gathering.

I see perhaps five hundred people arrive in flyers about an hour before dusk. They raise their simple tents not far from the facilities we provide. I see they are an attractive people, firm in body and strong in muscle.

Tomorrow will begin the music, dancing, sharing of spiritual stories, and past knowledge of legend and history. We will also learn of the skills of our guests. Many areas specialize in one or two fields of science. They then pass the gifts of science to all other areas of the living Earth, to combine and return with the gifts of other knowledge. I sleep soundly this night and dream of the excitement to come.

The new day begins and the events at the amphitheatre proceed. My mind turns to the young men from the newcomers. As I look to the crowd a face is staring at me, with no attempt at discretion at all. Before I can turn away I am awe struck. I do not know this person but every nerve in my body, and every hormone, feels as if it is on fire. Without knowing him I know I have always known him, and have waited for the spirit of this person to find me, or me him, through countless lifetimes.

We are both breaking protocol for we have risen and are leaving the gathering. We come together and I hear our voices exchange names. He is Gorokean and I am Arrosea, called Goroke and Arrose.

He is running before me now. The trees part to show a stretch of sand and water beyond. The cloth wrapper, like some ancient Roman toga, falls from his slim muscular body and I wonder at his beauty before it plunges into the sparkling water. I follow him in like fashion and, before I can reach the surface, I see his face and feel the touch of his lips. We gasp for air as we surface and his arms enfold me, and the contours of my breasts and the valley of my femininity come up against the hard masculinity of his body. For this I am happy to live ten thousand lifetimes.

A new day breaks and we are happy in the gift of each other. As we leave the privacy of the dwelling, I am stunned to see a woman and man step forward who were my guides. The one with the blue circle smiles gently and shows me a copy of 'REDO ME again and again', then opens it to a page near the end. There to my amazement I see the words that describe all that has occurred in this recent journey. I look up and they are gone.

Epilogue

715,000 years after the time of writing.

I feel the gentle hand of my ten year old granddaughter who stands between her mother, my beloved daughter, and me. The soft line of the light of the coming sunrise is glowing from mauve to pink along the horizon. It is three centuries since the Gulf Stream started to flow again, bringing the warmth that gives life to this island home, and removing the ice that is the endless cycle of a healthy planet; the immune system of this our living Earth.

As the light clears, the thousands of people across the plains become evident. Only twice in my eighty-six years have I been granted the opportunity to be here for the winter solstice.

The sun's rays stretch towards the ancient circles of stones, long ago restored to what is hoped is its original condition. This morning, with numerous other people, we are about two thousand steps from the 'ancient temple', if that is an accurate term for that which they once, we believe, called Stonehenge.

I hear the soft sound of my granddaughter's voice and answer her as well as a simple man can who, after all this time, still stands at the edge of the beginning of knowledge.

Grandfather, what is it?

It is like the one two days walk north of here. It is one of the highest of human achievements, and one of the few remaining symbols from a time when humans saw that they were a part of, and not separate from, life that was, and is, our world.

Grandfather, what did it represent?

It recognized what others failed to see. These people derived spiritual knowledge over immense time and learnt the Earth had a spiritual intelligence. They knew that the Earth was, by design, given an immune system that evolved.

Grandfather, when was it built?

They say it was built over 720,000 years ago, before the time humankind became god over Earth, and thought that the Earth was there to serve them. They used technology and resources to grow in numbers, to such an extent that it became humans that triggered the ancient immunity of the Earth to reform, in order to enable life to carry on.

Grandfather, why was it built?

This monument was built to express to an entity many called Mother Earth, their recognition that they must live in harmony with all life. Even at the dawning of man's worship of himself or his image as god over all, the remnants of these temple builders called the Druids were recorded, by a Roman called Tacitus, as those who worshipped the spirit of life in all nature. For nearly two thousand years, a campaign was waged to wipe off the face of the Earth the priestesses who clung to ancient knowledge. They were depicted as the witches of evil covens. Mostly the opposite was true.

Grandfather and mother, it is beautiful.

In the morning light, the smaller blue stones form a blue circle between the clean large stone circle and the large crescent shape in the middle, with these two shimmering with a golden light reflected from their surface.

Grandfather, how do you see it?

To you Woodlands, and you Wildflower, I say. These builders were asking Mother Earth to hear their hearts and witness their respect for her health. So the great ice that had come so close to these temples in times of adjustments would remain in far places, so flowers can bloom and monsoon rains fall to deliver the cycle of life.

Grandfather, is this certain?

There is no certainty, but I am happy to choose a faith and abide by it.

In this case it offers the best, I know, of a place for happiness for all who now live, and gives hope to the unborn to live their own future. There is happiness within our own resurrection and this heaven on Earth.

PO Box 919
BULIMBA QLD
AUSTRALIA 4171

Dear Reader

The galaxy is full of life.

For an emerging species such as humanity to become a part of the consciously participating, communicating, and perhaps travelling member of the galaxy/universe/universes... do our scientists have to learn what our inner alien spirit has perhaps implanted upon our subconscious?

It may be that, if a species survives to the level of scientific understanding of what's called 'spiritual belief', we are able to take our part in the profoundly fulfilling universal completeness. Then the door will open to a vast panorama of consciousness.

The means are within human capacity.
The obstacles are immense.
The rewards are beyond imagination.

The Author

Printed in Great Britain
by Amazon

29263060R00235